Where men are men and the women are glad of it!

Scotch on the Rocks

by

Lizzie Lamb

'I recommend Lizzie Lamb's books to anyone who likes romance with a light, comedic touch'

For Maggie,

who accompanied Bongo Man, Jasper and me on our road trip to

the Highlands of Scotland.

She had to sleep in a cupboard for a week and never complained.

Well, hardly ever!

To
Sue,
good luck in your
writing career 😊

Lizzie

Table of Contents

Glossary of Gaelic Terms

Readers have told me that they would like to know how the Scottish Gaelic words in my novels are pronounced. I have been helped greatly in this by Mrs Edna Walton who lives on South Uist, a Gaelic speaking community off the North West coast of Scotland.

Eilean na Sgairbh – Cormorant Island – Aylan na Skirriv

Ailleag – the jewel – ah-llyak

Bidh gaol agam ort fad bheatha, thusa's gun duine eile – I will love you to the end of my life and no other – Bee geul akam ort fat moh vay-ya, oo-sa's gun dooinya ayla

An Dà Allt – Twa (two) Burns – an dah owl-t

Sguaban Arbhair – sheaves of corn – sqwawban arbayr

Teuchter – a derogatory name for a highlander – chew-ch-ter

Tràigh Allt Chailgeag – the beach of the burn of bereavement and death – try ahlt - chal-yach-ag

Tapadh leibh – thank you – tappa lave

Slainte mhath – your good health (a toast) – slancha vah

I have also used many words, phrases and sayings from the central belt of Scotland, more particularly the west coast. These words are used by my family and Scottish friends.

messages – shopping, items you would buy from a supermarket/ general store/errands *hen* – a term of endearment you would use for a female friend or relative

weans – children – pronounced way-ns

sleekit – a sly person

laldy – do something with vigour or enthusiasm

bawbees – coins of low value

But and Ben – a two-roomed cottage; a humble home

palpatooral – a mild (!) heart attack - palpitations

Teenie frae Troon – an oddly dressed woman

wee bauchle – a shabby-looking person, especially a small one

purvey – the food supplied for a gathering such as a wedding or a funeral

You may find this website of interest – www.dsl.ac.uk (Dictionary of the Scots Language)

Chapter One
A Wing and a Prayer

Ishabel Stuart raced her car against the combined forces of time and tide, a thunderstorm snapping at her heels. The wind gave her car a rough shake and she glanced in her rear view mirror at bruise coloured clouds rushing to overtake her. With an involuntary cry of alarm, she squared her shoulders, focused full attention on the road and prepared to tough it out. By her calculations she had just minutes to reach the causeway linking the mainland to *Eilean na Sgairbh,* Cormorant Island. Any later, the land bridge would be submerged by the incoming tide and she would be unable to make the crossing.

If that happened, home, the loving arms of her Aunt Esme, the comfort of a shower and hot meal would have to wait until the tide ebbed the following morning.

Worse still, she'd have to spend the night in her car or – God help her, at Mrs MacKay's Highland Guest House, where she'd be forced to sleep beneath a candlewick bedspread, shower with a sliver of grimy soap and a scratchy towel no bigger than a face flannel. Then, over a meagre breakfast of watery porridge and burned bannocks, she'd be bombarded with a thousand personal questions no one had any right to ask. Least of all Mrs MacKay - the biggest gossip this side of Fort William.

'Okay, Stuart - man up. You know this road like the back of your hand. If anyone can beat the tide, it's you. You've done it hundreds of times.' Glancing at her father, who was fastened securely into the back seat, she added grimly: 'Hold on, it's going to be a bumpy ride.' But, for once, James Stuart had no criticism to level at his daughter's driving skills, or her foolhardiness. Biting her lip, Ishabel slipped into a lower gear and started the descent down the sloping jetty and onto The Narrows, a causeway packed hard by over eight hundred years of continuous use by *Eilean na Sgairbh's* highland community.

At this time of year the tide came in faster than a man could walk, and so her tyres squished in the shallow water which splashed up the sides of her Mini. Holding her nerve, she gripped the steering wheel, switched the headlights onto full beam and peered into the descending dusk. If she got stuck half way across and was forced to abandon her new car or – worse still, call out the coastguard to rescue her from an ill-timed attempt to cross to *Eilean na Sgairbh*, she'd never live it down.

If that happened, the inhabitants of Cormorant Island would give a collective shrug and say such recklessness was no more than expected of Miss Ishabel Stuart. She was James Stuart's flesh and blood, after all, and - like her aunt Esme, was bad news as far as they were concerned. However, Ishabel wasn't about to give them the chance to shake a collective finger at her, or the satisfaction of sending her censorious looks next time she went in the General Store. She'd make it across, and damn anyone who harboured a less than flattering opinion of her – or her family.

Pushing her driving glasses further up onto her nose with her forefinger, she made for the lights on the farther shore. It'd take more than a summer squall, a neap tide, and recent events to keep her from the island where she'd grown up. And, if she'd lately grown apart from it, she was coming home to make amends and to reacquaint herself with *Eilean na Sgairbh*, a place she'd once held dear.

Ten minutes later, and with the water now almost reaching the door sill, Issy cleared the jetty on the far side of The Narrows and let out a long, slow whistle. She stopped by the harbour wall and looked back at the distance she'd travelled (now submerged beneath the waves) and acknowledged she'd made it by the skin of her teeth.

She wasn't a natural risk taker, if anything she liked to think things through before deciding on the best course of action. But recent events had shown her that, when push came to shove, she'd inherited the determination, stubbornness and sheer bloody-mindedness which marked her out as a Stuart. Qualities which she considered demonstrated a kind of foolhardy courage, but which the islanders regarded as arrogance and mule-headedness.

She glanced one last time at the submerged Narrows and then at her father on the back seat.

'No need to say it, Daddy, I know I'm reckless. How could I not know it? You've told me enough times, haven't you? So like my mother, so . . .'

At that, her breath snagged – but with the same determination which had made her race against the tide, she put the thought behind her and drove forward, pausing only to test the brakes after their dip in the harbour. They worked just fine and she felt confident enough to journey the few remaining miles along the coast road to her aunt's house without any mishaps. There was so much she wanted to discuss with her aunt in the warm fug of her kitchen, hopefully over a glass of Stuart's Twa Burns single malt whisky.

Which, neatly, brought her back to her father, buckled into the back seat for safety.

His opinions on women drinking whisky, having careers and driving souped-up cars in dangerous weather conditions, were on record. He didn't consider any of it proper – which, conversely, would make Ishabel savour every drop of the peaty whisky when she reached her aunt's house.

Reflecting on the life-changing decisions she'd made on her journey from Edinburgh to *Eilean na Sgairbh* and her race against the elements, Ishabel considered that whisky, given the role it had played in the Stuart's fortunes over the last century and a half, was aptly named:

Uisge Beatha.
The Water of Life.

Chapter Two
Cool in a Kaftan

Ishabel parked outside *Ailleag*, her Aunt Esme's house, dropped her head onto the steering wheel and groaned. Just when she longed for her aunt's sensible counsel, she could see the back yard filled with a collection of decrepit looking old bangers which looked as if they'd never live to see another MOT, let alone pass it.

Her aunt had guests – damn.

Guests? Issy pulled a face. Well, that was one word for them – she could think of other, less complimentary ones.

Scroungers.

Freeloaders.

Lame Ducks.

Spongers, who were not averse to feeding off her aunt's generosity and open house policy. Esme Stuart was famous on the island for never turning anyone away from her Bed and Breakfast, the polar opposite of Mrs MacKay's Highland Guest House. Whereas guests couldn't get away from Mrs MacKay's fast enough, they were always reluctant to leave Esme's house. Another black mark chalked up against Esme; some of the stuffier islanders considering she took the concept of highland hospitality just that little bit too far.

Now, thoroughly grumpy, Ishabel got out of the car and into the rain, running the last few metres towards the former fisherman's cottage as a flash of lightning lit up the cobbled yard. She didn't bother to ring the bell. Her aunt never locked the door and, besides, *Ailleag* was as much her house as Esme Stuart's.

Oh, how she longed to crash in her bedroom after a hot shower and . . .

'Issy!' Her aunt, obviously having heard the car pull up and seen its headlights sweep across the hall ceiling, opened the door wider and ushered Ishabel out of the rain. 'Och, lassie, you're soaking wet. Ye've never raced the tide, have you? Come away in, darling; come away in.'

Issy hugged her aunt, holding onto her for several long, comforting seconds. She breathed in Esme's personal fragrance – a mixture of Chanel No 5, clean, pressed linen and . . . something else.

Something only too familiar.

'I see you have guests,' Issy said as pleasantly as she could, following her aunt through into the sitting room where a group of ancient hippies were seated cross-legged on the floor, passing round a bong. Like Esme, they were in their mid-seventies, but unlike her, they didn't seem to have weathered the passage of time half as well. Esme caught Issy's disapproving look and pulled an apologetic face.

'Don't start, Ishabel – they . . . *we'll* be gone tomorrow and –'

'Oh, but Esme, I hoped . . .'

'What is it darling? Trouble?'

Hiding her dismay at the thought of Esme's imminent departure, Issy affected a careless shrug. 'Oh, it's nothing; nothing that won't keep.' She knew her aunt would change plans if she thought for one moment Issy needed her. But Issy couldn't be that selfish.

'Really?' Plainly, her aunt was taken in by her throwaway remark.

'Really,' Issy affirmed, knowing the longed for heart-to-heart would have to wait.

'*You silly tart!*' a voice cut in from the corner of the room, dragging Issy's attention away from her aunt and her problems. '*Feck off, all of youse.*'

Issy walked over and greeted a large blue and yellow macaw in its cage in the corner of the room. 'Hello, Pershing,' she said. 'Still as rude as ever, I see?' Reaching out, she scratched the parrot's poll with her forefinger while it regarded Esme's house guests with a baleful eye. 'How's tricks? Still banning the bomb?'

'*Ban the Bomb. Ban the Bomb.*' The peacenik parrot shuffled sideways along its perch, glancing towards the senior citizens smoking dope as though it would give it the greatest pleasure to bite each one of them in turn. '*Gei'us a wee kiss, dahrr-ling,*' it said in a broad Glaswegian accent, turning its head sideways, beguilingly. In spite of the hellish week she'd had, Issy laughed.

'Pershing's always pleased to see you. As am I,' her aunt said, stepping over two of her friends in the lotus position on the floor, looking as if their arthritic bones had locked in place. Evidently, they considered it a matter of honour to pretend they were still in the first flush of youth and not on the NHS waiting list for new hip joints. Esme chucked the parrot under his chin and avoided Ishabel's gaze.

'Except?' Issy prompted, picking up the vibe and sensing bad news.

'Except, we're travelling down to Manchester to take part in an anti-fracking demo at Barton Moss. Pershing's booked into The Pickled Herring for a little holiday while I'm away. I wasn't expecting you for another week, at least.'

On cue, one of the relics creaked to his feet and proudly displayed a t-shirt which bore the legend: FRACK OFF. Oh, if only they would, and leave her and Esme in peace.

She had so much to tell Esme, so much to explain. Now it looked as if she'd have to wait for her return, whenever that might be – Esme had never been one to stick to a timetable. She glanced fondly at her aunt; she really was a card-carrying activist – whether it be against nuclear weapons, proposed bypasses through chalk downland or, as it now appeared, fracking to find untapped gas deposits in the north of England. Esme looked pale and tired and Issy's heart squeezed with love and concern. It dawned on her that her aunt, like her pensioner guests, really was growing older. A shiver of premonition travelled the length of her spine.

'I'd put it off, of course, *except* . . .' That word again.

'I know,' Issy sighed, 'people are depending on you.' They always were. Just as *she* depended on Esme to listen to her tale of woe, provide good counsel and a shoulder to cry on, others looked towards her for help with planning their latest protest. It was ever thus. Esme gave Issy a keen look and then a light went on, as though she'd suddenly remembered something. 'Your father! Ishabel, I'd quite forgotten. Where is he?'

'Securely fastened into the back seat of my car,' Issy answered, bracing herself for Esme's reaction.

'I won't have him in the house. You know that, don't you?' The years slipped away and Esme Stuart was once again the firebrand who'd been arrested in the early sixties for climbing the anchor chain of the USS tender, *Proteus,* anchored in Holy Loch. The activist who'd taken part in the Grosvenor Square riots, frozen to death at Greenham Common and, more recently, tied herself to a tree, protesting against the Newbury Bypass and destruction of the chalk downs.

Where Issy stood at five foot eight, her aunt was bird-boned and fragile – but indomitable; her bright blue eyes holding a steeliness Issy ignored at her peril.

'Well, I guess he won't come to any harm for just one night. But he'll have to be dealt with. He's left instructions.'

'He would have,' Esme sniffed. 'Such as?'

'Very specific instructions for his Memorial Service at the wee kirk. A teetotal wake. Then taken up a Munro, the only one he didn't 'bag', and his ashes scattered on the westerly wind,' Issy explained.

'He was a pain in the arse when he was alive, and death hasn't altered *that.*' Esme tossed her head with a distinct lack of sisterly feeling. 'Very well, leave him outside for tonight, and tomorrow you can put him in one of the sheds at the back of the house. It overlooks The Narrows – which is more than he deserves.'

'Bit harsh, isn't it, Esme,' one of her friends ventured. 'Karma, and all that . . .'

'You know nothing about it,' she rounded on him, her strawberry-blond hair falling into her eyes. 'So keep the hell out of it.'

'Okay, chill.' He held up his hands to ward off her anger.

Issy didn't know the reason for the bad blood between her father and his sister, either, come to that. Maybe now he'd been rendered into ashes at Edinburgh's finest crematorium in his eco-friendly, banana leaf coffin, her aunt would finally level with her and lay that ghost to rest, too.

But not tonight.

'Now,' Esme suddenly became brisk. 'We have a problem, Issy. I've taken in a paying guest and put him in your old room. I wasn't expecting your arrival, my darling. Tomorrow, after we leave, Lindy will change all the beds and he can move into the guest room which overlooks The Narrows. He'll be leaving soon after that. However, just for tonight . . .' she bit her lip, then spread her hands. 'You have my bed and I'll sleep on the futon.'

'Indeed you will *not*,' Ishabel reposted. 'I'll have the futon and Lindy and I can sort things out in the morning. No arguing, Esme – it's time we were *all* in bed.' She sent her aunt's friends such a stern look that they creaked to their feet and shuffled off to their rooms. Rooms which, as usual, they wouldn't be asked to pay for. Rooms which could have been occupied by paying guests who, doubtless, Esme had turned away.

Unaware of her niece's uncharitable thoughts, Esme waited until they'd all disappeared and then spoke softly.

'This has been a rotten homecoming, Ishabel. Something's upset you; above and beyond James' death.' She didn't quite spit on the floor, gypsy fashion, at the mention of his name, but looked as if she wanted to. 'I'll be gone for a couple of weeks. When I return, we can have the heart-to-heart you look in dire need of.'

'Okay,' Issy was too tired to argue.

On the map, the journey from her flat in Leith, Edinburgh to *Eilean na Sgairbh* looked like a stroll in the park. But in reality it'd taken the best part of a day. Thanks to twisting roads and beautiful but distracting scenery, no one travelled anywhere quickly in the highlands of Scotland. The futon might be lumpy but, given the length of the journey and the amount of cannabis in the air, she suspected she'd fall into a drugged, if not dreamless sleep. Small wonder her aunt kept the window open, and Pershing, with his delicate respiratory system, well out of the way of the smokers.

Esme left the room, returning with clean bed linen under her arm, and they made up the futon.

'Sure you'll be okay, *hen*?' Esme asked, using the familiar pet name.

'Sure.' As Issy put the finishing touches to her bed, Esme abstractedly stroked the parrot under his wing, before covering him up for the night.

'Issy . . . One thing –'

'Mm?' Was it her imagination, or was Esme finding it hard to meet her eye?

'Our paying guest. The one who'll be staying on for the next few days. . .'

'Yes?'

'You should know that he's . . .'

'Martian? A serial killer? Not a *Presbyterian*?' Issy joked.

The Free Church of Scotland dominated the lives of those living on Cormorant Island and took a very dim view of Esme Stuart's unconventional lifestyle. The fact that, as a lone, unmarried female – albeit in her seventies, she took in guests to supplement her pension and – horror of horrors – refused to attend the kirk of a Sunday.

Issy had encountered most of the guests who'd stayed with Esme; the good, the bad and the downright weird. Nothing could surprise her. Esme turned back from covering the parrot's cage with a large black cloth and gave Issy a weak smile.

'Worse than that . . .'

'What could possibly be worse than *that*?' Issy teased.

'He's American.'

There being nothing more to add, Esme closed the sitting room door behind her, leaving Issy standing on the old rag rug in front of the dying embers of the fire, trying to fathom the implications of Esme's killer exit line.

And the expression on her face as she'd said it.

Chapter Three
Dressed to Thrill

Next morning Issy woke to the sound of Pershing throwing toys around in his cage. Her aunt had removed the cover, and the parrot, sensing a playmate was awake, sidled along its perch and gave Issy a considering look. '*Breakfast read-eee?*' it asked.

'No, it isn't,' Issy said in a no nonsense voice, drinking the cup of tea Esme had left on the floor next to her elbow. Pershing watched as she raised the cup to her lips and then made accompanying gulping noises - finishing with a loud, satisfied belch.

'*Manners,*' it said, before turning its back on Issy and proceeding to forage on the cage floor for a tasty morsel of leftover supper.

In spite of herself, Issy smiled. The parrot was a beast, it really was – but an amusing one. As a child she'd been frightened of its large claws, flapping wings and hooked beak. However, she and the parrot had bonded over the years. Or, should she say, the parrot had deigned to admit her to the charmed circle of people it never bit.

But she had weightier matters on her mind this morning than a refusenik parrot. As she drank the now tepid tea, she ticked them off.

One – Her aunt's imminent departure.

Two – Her father's Memorial Service, wake and the disposal of his ashes. How many Munros were there? And, how did one set about climbing them? Would she need permission before she scattered his ashes? She rather thought that she would.

Three – The letter she'd left for the Director of Ecosse Designs, outlining her reasons for resigning from her position as Head of Overseas Projects.

And, at **number four** the most intractable of her problems. The one she wouldn't give voice to. Not yet. The one which refused to go away, no matter how hard she pushed it to the back of her mind.

Pershing dropped a large Brazil nut onto the floor of his cage, breaking her reverie and bringing her full circle to her aunt's impending departure for the fracking demo. All Issy wanted – longed for, was the chance to off-load some of her anxiety. But she knew that would have to wait. Nothing and no one got in the way of Esme's causes. Not her beloved niece, her problems – or, for that matter, her brother's funeral, cremation and the disposal of his ashes.

The tea cup rattled in its saucer as Issy rolled off the low-slung futon and landed inelegantly on the floor on her hands and knees. 'And if you call me a *silly tart*, just once this morning,' she warned the parrot with more humour than she felt, 'you're going in a pie. Under a flaky pastry crust. With a side order of vegetables.' It was an old threat and one the parrot knew she'd never carry out. Giving her a contemptuous look, he ruffled his feathers, hunched up his shoulders and spat another Brazil nut onto the cage floor.

'*Dirty bird*,' he cackled.

Flipping onto her back, Issy took a deep breath and psyched herself up for everything she'd have to sort out this morning, mentally lining things up in order of difficulty. At that moment, the sitting room opened and a shadow fell across her, making her aware that her limbs were splayed out at an unbecoming angle. Like a starfish, stranded by the turning tide.

'Hi there,' a deep, well-modulated voice drew her attention away from the bird, her problems and her inelegant pose. 'I hope I'm not interrupting – I heard voices . . . and I thought – Actually, I'm looking for Mizz Stoo-art and the kitchen?' His voice went up at the end of the sentence in a manner Issy found both annoying *and* affected.

'Well, you've found her,' she snapped, pulling down the grungy t-shirt she'd slept in last night to spare her blushes. 'Well, one of them at least.'

Upside down, she gave the stranger a thorough examination. He looked vastly amused and not in the least put out by her unfriendly greeting. Issy gave thanks that she'd slipped on a clean pair of knickers before clambering onto the futon last night. Some of Esme's desiccated hippie friends were not above corridor creeping in the dead of the night, searching for the Free Love so much a feature of their now distant youth.

TUNE IN. TURN ON. DROP OUT.

Sadly, for them, those days had long gone.

However, even when viewed upside down, it was plain that the man standing in the doorway belonged to a different generation. He gave her long legs and makeshift nightie a swift inspection - as any red-blooded male would, then his smile was back in place; bland and unthreatening. Nowadays, if any man ogled a scantily dressed female as though it was his right, he was asking for trouble. Which brought Issy back to **number four** on her list - the reason she'd come racing back to Cormorant Island in the middle of a violent thunderstorm - as though she couldn't bear to spend another second in Edinburgh.

Freeing her mind of the perplexing thought, she glared at the stranger in the hope he'd get the message and leave the room. She had no intention of giving him another look at her legs as she scrambled to her feet. Or, more shaming, what lay beneath the grungy t-shirt. As if reading her mind, the stranger reached out for the candlewick dressing gown Esme had draped over the back of a chair.

'Allow me,' he said, inclining his head, as if he were Walter Raleigh laying his cloak over a puddle so Good Queen Bess could trample it into the mud.

Issy's thunderous expression made it plain that she was in no mood for pleasantries or chivalrous gestures. She was perfectly capable of getting to her feet and slipping on the dressing gown without *his* – without *any man's* – help. But either he was thick-skinned, or determined to act the gentleman, because he stood there smiling, hand extended – waiting for her to take the dressing gown from him.

Sensing a test of wills, even if the stranger was smiling without a trace of guile, Issy felt at a distinct disadvantage, lying scrunched up at his feet. As the seconds stretched out between them, a betraying stain of colour crept across her cheeks, alerting him that his continued presence unsettled her.

'Put it down over there.' She indicated the top of the futon. There was no way she could get to her feet without showing him more of her than was strictly necessary. Scowling to hide her discomfiture, she went on, 'The kitchen's across the hall. Just follow the smell of bacon frying. You'll doubtless find my aunt in there serving breakfast.'

He turned his head in the direction of her pointing finger and she used the moment to scramble to her feet and drag the shapeless dressing gown over her t-shirt and lacy knickers. Tying the belt, she knew she looked as alluring as a sack of potatoes. Not that it mattered. Yesterday, on the drive over from Edinburgh, she'd sworn off men for good and had made up her mind to die an old maid, surrounded by cats, and buried beneath back copies of Vogue and Harpers, until discovered by her cleaning lady.

Yet - here she was, wearing an oversized dressing gown like an escapee from some institution or other, and not looking her best. Whereas *he* looked as if he'd stepped out of the pages of a GQ special - *How to Dress While on Holiday in Scotland*. Expensive cotton shorts, dark blue polo shirt with an upturned collar and some swanky logo over the left breast, and brown leather deck shoes. He was lightly tanned and thick auburn hair sprang back from his forehead, full of life and vigour. She'd lay even money on the fact that he used skin products and smelled as good as he looked. He looked like he should be sailing a yacht off the coast of Nantucket with the Atlantic breeze ruffling his hair.

Instead, here he was – under her feet and getting in the way . . .

She was annoyed to find that it was possible to harbour antagonistic feelings towards him, yet at the same time find him sexually attractive. Get a grip woman, she advised herself. **Number four** - remember?

Hold on to that.

The stranger paused on the threshold as if waiting for something or – less likely, as if unable to tear himself away from the alluring vision before him. 'The elder Mizz Stoo-art mentioned something about *the full Scottish*?'

Issy felt unreasonably irritated by another of his sentences ending in an upward inflection, but was glad of its gadfly sting. It reminded her that he was in the wrong place at the wrong time and she'd be glad to see the back of him. He looked like trouble with a capital 'T' and instinct told her it would be best to avoid him at all costs – good looks notwithstanding.

'Go into the kitchen and you'll find out. My aunt's breakfasts are legendary. You'll need to stock up before you *leave*.' There - that was about as polite as she could be without actually telling him to pack his bags and go. She'd come home to lick her wounds, not to find an unwanted guest in situ who'd doubtless come to search for his Scottish roots and probably considered himself a direct descendant of Bonnie Prince Charlie.

'Got it. Kitchen.' He smiled, nodded in the direction of the hall and clicked his fingers together. 'I'd better . . .'

'Yes, you had.'

Wheeling round, he left her standing in a pool of sunlight, feeling overheated and thoroughly out of sorts. She put both down to recent events and the fact that she was wearing a thick dressing gown which smelled of patchouli and felt slightly damp. Catching her reflection in the age-spotted mirror over the fireplace, she grimaced. Oh, gr-eat. She looked like she'd just emerged from bed after a bout of flu – pale- faced, eyes dark-circled with fatigue. Her one asset, long, thick dark hair was sticking up at odd angles as if she'd spent the night wired into the national grid, and was a stranger to conditioner.

So alluring.

Not.

She was surprised that he'd managed to keep a straight face. Another deep sigh escaped as she tried to smooth her hair into a semblance of style, pinch colour into her cheeks and look less like an extra from *Zombie Apocalypse*. Not that she cared a jot what the stranger thought of her, or any of her aunt's friends come to that. But self-respect demanded that she at least *looked* like she was the (former) Head of Overseas Projects at *Ecosse Designs*, used to handling multi-million pound contracts and much in demand across the globe. But the moment had passed and she was left with the uncomfortable feeling that she'd behaved churlishly towards one of her aunt's paying guests, and broken every unwritten rule governing Highland hospitality.

Worse than that, she'd made herself look spoilt and petulant into the bargain.

'*Silly tart*,' the parrot informed, wiping his beak along his sandpaper perch to clean off fragments of Brazil nut.

This time, she was forced to admit that the feathered fiend was bang on the money.

Chapter Four
Her Name was Lola – she was a cleaner

I shabel followed the American into the hall.

At least, she assumed he *was* the American her aunt had referred to last night. Their brief exchange hadn't given her enough time to get a handle on his accent. And to be truthful, a kind of mid-Atlantic *lingua franca* was spoken by most of her generation, weaned as they were on MTV, American Blockbusters, TV Box sets and cult US sitcoms. Nowadays, it was almost impossible to pinpoint accurately where anyone came from.

Take herself, she had an Edinburgh accent - refined, educated, clipped. Whereas her aunt's voice held a sing-song highland inflection, the result of having spent most of her life on *Eilean na Sgairbh.* That is, when she wasn't driving off in her converted library van – known affectionately as *THE COW* – righting wrongs and speaking up for those who had no voice. A true card-carrying activist from the moment she'd joined the Campaign for Nuclear Disarmament in the early sixties, whilst studying art at Glasgow University. Issy wished she was more like her, having something she believed in, a cause to fight for. Instead, lately, she'd been beset by a mass of contradictions, her head full of *what-if* and *what-could-be;*

anxieties resulting in sleepless nights and restless days.

Her stomach gave a hungry growl, putting angst, accents, six foot three Americans blown in on a storm wind, and Esme Stuart's lost causes from her mind. She paused briefly at the kitchen door and listened with her ear pressed up against it. *Voices!* She was in no mood for company, but owed it to her aunt to be polite to her guests.

'Och, Brodie, get away with you!' A female voice, full of laughter, greeted Issy as she pushed open the green baize door and entered the kitchen. The scene which welcomed her, did nothing to improve her bad mood or the impending headache building behind her eyes.

The Stranger – whom she assumed she must now address as *Brodie*, was sitting at the head of the table as if he belonged there. His seat commanded the best view of The Narrows which linked *Eilean na Sgairbh* to Jamestoun on the mainland. It was the chair reserved for her father when he paid Esme one of his rare visits, or stayed over when he came back to the island to preach hellfire in the *wee kirk* up the road.

Now, she felt sorry that she'd left him out in the Mini all night, trussed up on the back seat like – like an unwanted parcel, despite what Esme had said. She gave an almost inaudible whimper of despair which encompassed her relationship with her late father, the American visitor, Esme's crusty friends, and her state of mind. A couple of the old hippies were finishing their breakfast at the scrubbed pine table, and chatting amiably to Brodie. However, when they saw Issy in the doorway, they mopped up the last of their egg and bacon with Esme's homemade bread and exited the kitchen, stage left.

The only other person in the kitchen was Lindy Tennant, Esme's nubile cleaning lady and sometime breakfast chef. Leaning across the table, she was topping up *Brodie's* coffee from an ancient electric percolator. Issy harboured the uncharitable thought that Lindy was more concerned with giving Brodie an unhindered view of her jacked up bosom than refreshing his cup with finest High Andes coffee.

Not that Issy was surprised . . .

From the moment Lindy Tennant had arrived in the world, red-faced and demanding attention, Issy had been appointed to look after her, curb her worst excesses and keep her out of trouble. They weren't related by blood or marriage, Lindy being the only daughter of Mary and Tam Tennant who managed the General Store/Post Office in Killantrae, and had done since Issy could remember. Yet, over the years, Issy had taken on the role of Lindy's elder, more sensible, sister. But today it looked as if she was late to the party. Miss Tennant was working the *Vamp of Cormorant Island* look for all she was worth. Telling her to back off from the American would have the opposite effect. And, in her present mood, Issy couldn't summon up the necessary energy to save Lindy from herself.

She had weightier matters on her mind.

'Save some of that coffee for me, Lindy, if you don't mind.'

Issy's tone was sharper than intended and her request sounded more like an order. Obligingly, Lindy sashayed over and splashed coffee into an empty cup.

'By the way,' she hissed in Issy's ear, making sure that Brodie couldn't hear. 'I've changed my name to *Lola,* I'll explain later . . . Lindy has left the building, ta dah.' Giving a little twirl, she put the percolator back onto the kitchen counter and then returned to give Issy a big hug, holding her at arm's length and wrinkling her nose. 'Great to see you, darlin', no one knew you were coming. But, just so as you know, you smell just a wee bit –' she struggled for the adjective.

'Damp?' Issy volunteered.

'And look –'

'Like an extra from *One Flew Over the Cuckoo's Nest*? Yes, I am well aware of both of those facts, thank you, Lindy. I left Edinburgh in a bit of a hurry and . . .' Issy glanced over at Brodie and then paused, intimating to Lindy that there was a tale to tell.

But not right now.

Not in front of a stranger.

'Yes. Esme said. And you've got your puir Da in a wee sweetie jar on the back seat of your car and she won't have him in the house.'

This time, Issy felt that Brodie was owed a bit of an explanation, otherwise he might think them heartless beasts. Or worse, there was some weird Scottish tradition which dictated one kept the urn containing one's father's ashes on the back seat of one's car.

'There was no love lost between my aunt and my father. Ancient history, really.'

'We don't usually leave a man's earthly remains on the back seat of a car,' Lindy added. 'You see . . .' Lindy looked as if she was about to give Brodie chapter and verse of the feud between Esme and James Stuart, and why Issy and her father hadn't got on, so Issy forestalled her.

'Well, enough of *that*,' she said with finality. 'Good morning, *Lola*; or should that be *caramba?*' She gave Lindy's outfit of chopped off denim shorts, white off-the-shoulder blouse cinched in at the waist with a red leather belt, and strappy cork-soled mules a pained look. It looked as if Lindy was in full hunting mode with Brodie as her quarry. She'd even tucked a silk gerbera behind her ear, just in case Brodie didn't 'get' it. A fine contrast they made, Issy reflected, tying the belt of her dressing gown tighter in case any flesh was on display. Old Mother Hubbard and her feistier, sexier daughter.

'*Caramaba?*' Lindy looked puzzled for a moment and then laughed. 'I've dressed Tex-Mex in Brodie's honour. He's from –'

'Mexico?' Issy questioned, a sarcastic little barb spiking her voice. With his dark auburn hair and green eyes, the last thing their guest looked was Hispanic. He had, she noted, a fine jaw line and a chin which suggested that beneath the amiable smile there lay a stubbornness and determination to match her own.

'America,' he explained unnecessarily, getting to his feet and extending his hand towards Ishabel. 'Hi, I'm Brodie . . .'

Unsettled by the thought of his hidden steeliness, Issy used the pretext of feeding bread into the ancient Dualit toaster to turn her back and ignore his outstretched hand. She was not in the mood for small talk, unexpected guests or watching Lindy (make that *Lola*) playing to the gallery. When she turned back, Brodie had returned to his breakfast, a fixed smile on his face. It was plain that he considered her rude and standoffish, but was doing his best to keep those feelings hidden.

For now -

For now? What had made *that* particular thought pop into her head? His opinion of her didn't matter, one way or another. He'd be gone by tomorrow, or the day after, and she'd have the cottage all to herself. She'd come home to lick her wounds, reassess her life, and no one was going to prevent her from doing that.

'Och, sit down Issy – I'm in charge this morning.'

Using both hands, Lindy pushed Issy onto a chair with more force than was necessary. Just to make her point, Issy suspected. Then she grabbed the toast which had popped out of the toaster and Frisbee'd it onto Issy's plate. Next, walking over to the fridge, she bent down - all the better to show off her cute derriere and bare, tanned legs, and brought out more eggs and bacon.

'So, Brodie,' Lindy continued, as she rustled up Issy's breakfast on the old stove. 'Is there a Mrs Brodie and lots of *wee* Brodies back in the states, pining for you over their granola, forby?' She spoke with an exaggerated Edinburgh accent, all the more to mock *her*, Issy suspected. But if Brodie was fazed by her directness, he didn't show it. Rather, he looked amused by her interrogation and entered into the spirit of teasing banter.

'I thought you Brits were supposed to be all buttoned-up and reserved?' He grinned at Lindy and then sent Issy a challenging look from beneath, straight dark brows. A look which appeared to say: *lady – you fit the bill, for sure.*

'I'm no British,' Lindy pretended affront. 'Ah'm Scottish. Through and through.'

'Like Cormorant Island rock,' Issy observed, buttering her toast. Lindy shot her a - *you're cramping my style,* look from over by the cooker. Brodie looked a little bemused by the reference to 'rock' and Issy didn't feel like explaining.

'Well?' Lindy waited for him to answer her original question, one hand on her hip while she flipped the egg over with a spatula. 'Wee Brodies?' she prompted.

'No to the first, and as for the second,' he half-turned in his chair to face her, 'there may be some paternity suits outstanding. I'll have to check with my brother.'

'Paternity suits? Brother?' Lindy sputtered, almost as fiercely as the bacon frying in the pan.

'My brother Alistair is an attorney,' Brodie explained, poker-faced. 'He usually handles that kind of thing . . .'

'That kind of thing?' Lindy gulped and her smile slipped. Now she was wondering if the Mexican Torch Singer rigout had all been for nothing. How many illegitimate *wee* Brodies were there out there?

Ishabel glanced at Brodie and caught his mischievous look. Obviously, he found Lindy highly diverting and was enjoying teasing her. Catching Issy's quelling glance, he held it with one of his own – dark, and so not amused. Then he turned his attention to Lindy, laughed and the mask was back in place. As soon as his raking glance swivelled away from her, an involuntary shiver travelled the length of Issy's body - as if someone had poured a jug of iced water down her neck.

She frowned and pulled the dressing gown away from her skin. It must be damper than she thought.

'Just fooling,' he told Lindy. 'About the kids, I mean. My brother's an attorney in our family law practice.' Judging by her expression, Lindy's brain was in overdrive. Attorney? Family law practice? Kerching! Issy could almost see the dollar signs flash in her eyes, like a cartoon character. Practically throwing Issy's breakfast plate onto the table, she perched on its edge and continued to give Brodie the third degree.

'So you're not married, then?'

Again, the smile, as if he found Lindy's less-than-subtle probing amusing. He ran his hand over his chin, which was covered in a fine, auburn stubble, and pretended to consider her question.

'Not last time I looked. But I'm open to offers.'

'Offers?' Lindy looked ready to take notes.

'You know. If the right woman came along . . .'

'The right woman?' Lindy was practically purring and lying across the table, like Michelle Pfeiffer on top of the piano in *The Fabulous Baker Boys*. But Issy had had enough. There was only so much vamping she could take on an empty stomach. Besides which, this nonsensical conversation did not suit her present mood or her current situation.

'Li-Lola,' she cut Lindy off in mid-vamp, 'let Mr Brodie eat his breakfast in peace.'

'No Mr - just *Brodie*.' Brodie's easy smile slipped and the warmth left his eyes, replaced by something harder, more calculating. He sent Issy a cool look and Lindy glared at her, too.

'Haven't you heard, Ishabel, we Brits have a *special relationship* with our American cousins.' Lindy ran her hands down the sides of her shorts as if she wanted to turn the *special relationship* into something more personal. 'Special,' she repeated, pushing herself off the table and bringing more coffee over to Brodie.

'Brits? I thought you were Scottish, through and through,' Issy reminded her, biting into her toast. 'You said so, just now.'

'Ah *am* Scottish. But my spiritual home is America,' Lindy declared, sending Brodie a look.

'Based on the number of times you've visited there. Obviously.' Issy added the last in a snarky tone and then regretted it. Lindy was the little sister she'd never had. While *she'd* enjoyed all the advantages - money, education, a good job – Lindy had spent most of her life serving behind the counter at Cormorant Island's General Store/Post Office. All she had to help her cope with the ordinariness of her every day existence was a barrowload of unfulfilled dreams. Who was Issy to deny her that escape? Issy felt mean-spirited and for a few brief moments didn't like herself or her behaviour this morning.

However, she couldn't help it. She was tense, on edge, out of sorts with the world and - checking against the calendar on the kitchen wall, she couldn't even use PMT to excuse her conduct.

Other things maybe . . .

Momentarily, Lindy appeared crestfallen, but bounced right back with a toss of her copper curls.

'Oh, but I know all about America from movies and the television. I mean, I don't need to *go* there to establish that it's the place for me. I *feel* it; here.' She tapped her breastbone and then turned bright eyes on Brodie. 'I bet you fell in love with Scotland before you arrived, didn't you, Brodie. The history, scenery, culture.'

'Sure. The stories my family told . . .' He glanced once at Issy and checked himself - as if he'd given too much away. Then, he continued in a perfectly reasonable tone as if the pause hadn't occurred, and Issy wondered if she'd imagined his hesitancy. 'The books I read as a child. Walter Scott, Robert Louis Stevenson, John Buchan. Oh, and that movie: *Local Hero* . . . the one where the guy sees the Northern Lights?'

'Go on,' Lindy encouraged.

However, Brodie wouldn't be drawn and before Issy had time to curb her enthusiasm, she found herself blurting out: 'I *love* that movie.'

Her reaction was so genuine that Brodie smiled at her encouragingly as if believing that the ice was melting. Regretting her outburst, Issy bowed her head over the bacon and eggs. Her stomach knotted as she remembered that she was at war with the world – and the reason for it. Picking up her coffee, she drank the hot liquid and clamped her lips together to prevent further outbursts.

'Och, that's old hat, Issy.' Lindy pulled a *where have you been* face. 'You'll be mentioning Brigadoon next. Brodie, have you seen *Trainspotting, Salmon Fishing in the Yemen* or *Sunshine On Leith*?'

'Nope. Do you recommend them?' He addressed Lindy, but was looking directly at Issy, as if trying to fathom her out.

'Highly. I've got the DVDs. I'll bring them over and we can watch them tonight, or tomorrow night if you're still feeling jet lagged. Or –' she paused meaningfully, 'maybe after Issy goes. Back. To. Edinburgh?' Seemingly, Issy was not only raining on her parade, she was cramping her style, too.

Tomorrow night? Issy's head jerked up. *Did that mean –?* Just how long did Mr Brodie intend staying at her aunt's? So much for her plan to return to *Eilean na Sgairbh*, put distance between herself and the mess she'd left behind in Edinburgh and get on with her life.

Eilean na Sgairbh's self-appointed film buff was about to have her run off the island while she gave the American a crash course on Scottish culture, as portrayed by Danny Boyle, Dexter Fletcher, Lasse Hallström et al – along with slightly less cerebral matters, the nature of which Issy could only guess at.

She felt surplus to requirements, a stranger in her own home and found that it mattered.

'Tomorrow night?' she repeated, faintly. Brodie caught her

downcast look and was quick to elaborate.

'Yes, I'm staying over until the end of the week. There was a mix up with the booking, stateside, and the eco-lodge which I've hired for the summer, won't be ready until then.'

'And *I* will be cooking, cleaning and generally making myself *indispensable* to Brodie for the duration of his stay. Introducing him to the locals down at The Pickled Herring, showing him round the island . . . that kind of thing.' Lindy puffed out her already impressive chest and adjusted the silk flower behind her ear, as if it was her badge of office. She also sent Issy a very unsisterly 'back off,' hard stare.

But it was Lindy's use of *that kind of thing* which worried Issy and made her forget her own problems. Lindy acted all worldly-wise but really she was an innocent abroad, and unused to . . . to men like Brodie. Then, getting the message, Issy pushed her plate to one side and stood up. Lindy was twenty-two years old, for goodness sake; it was time she stopped looking after her and started sorting out her own life.

'You're staying on. Really?' Issy replied, looking between them.

'Yep, I'm going to be around for quite a while. The *other* Mizz Stoo-art,' the one, his tone implied, with better manners and a warm welcome for strangers thousands of miles away from home, 'said it was OK to stay over in the B and B.' He said *B and B* as if the words were alien to him. 'She's leaving for England and will be gone some time.' He made England sound like a foreign country on the far edge of the world. 'Lindy will look after me just fine, so don't you worry about me.'

'I wo -' Just in time, Issy stopped herself from saying: *I won't*, and sent the American a searching look. She had the unsettling feeling that he was stringing them along with his oh-so-affable smile, and winning ways. It felt false; it *was* false, of that she was sure. There was nothing she could actually put her finger on, but she had the nasty suspicion he was playing with her – with them all; that his lips said one thing but his eyes said another.

She picked up her mug, pushed her chair back under the table and took great delight in bursting his bubble.

'Your staying here is quite out of the question, Mr Brodie. This is a small island, its inhabitants thrive on gossip and rumour. You might be happy to be the chief topic at the local Post Office,' at that, Lindy's head jerked up, 'and at the kirk after Sunday Service, but I can assure you I am not. My late father was a lay preacher there and I have to maintain a certain –'

'You'll be leaving, then?' Lindy looked pleased.

'*I'm* going nowhere,' Issy said firmly. 'I'll find Mr Brodie alternative accommodation – perhaps Mrs Mackay's Highland Guest House in Jamestoun?'

'Issy! You wouldna send a *dog* there.'

Issy put aside Lindy's remonstrance - and her own objections to staying there last night. It'd do the American no harm, she thought with grim satisfaction, to experience faulty showers, fat-loaded breakfasts and statically-charged nylon sheets.

Instinct told her it was imperative that she got Brodie and his newly acquired cook/cleaner/tour guide out of the cottage and out of her hair. There would be no peace for her until she'd achieved both objectives. She wanted space, time to herself, so she could properly evaluate her life and what the future held for her. She'd half expected a further wail of protest from Lindy at the thought of Brodie being subjected to Mrs Mackay's tender mercies. Instead, however, Lindy was staring in apparent disbelief at Issy's ring finger where a large solitaire diamond had formerly nestled. Knowing that Lindy wouldn't let the presence of a stranger rein in her curiosity, and sensing that a whole load of impertinent and unnecessary questions were about to descend on her head, Issy did the sensible thing.

She shoved her left hand into her dressing gown pocket amongst ancient tissues and a scrunchie dating back to the nineties when Esme had had long hair. She sent Lindy a warning look which, for once, she had the sense to obey.

'I'll leave you to finish breakfast without me. I need to have a word with Aunt Esme. There are *things,*' she paused meaningfully, 'which have to be sorted out before she leaves for Manchester.'

The look she directed at Brodie made it plain that he was chief amongst them.

Chapter Five
Chapter and Worse

Ishabel bumped into Esme in the long corridor which linked the front and the back of the house, via a square, inner hall. The front door opened directly onto a view of the causeway and the fishing village of Jamestoun on the farther shore. As a child, Issy had loved when the warmer weather arrived and the door was left open to allow the sea breeze to skoosh through the house, blowing away the cobwebs, and the feeling of being sealed in for the winter. The open front doorway framed the scene, turning it into a living, breathing postcard and never failed to beguile.

However, today she didn't notice the sun dancing on the waters of the bay, or how the white painted fishermen's cottages stood out in stark contrast to their red, pantiled roofs. All she saw was the American, sitting in her father's place at the head of the table, as if he belonged there.

For some unfathomable reason, that made her blood soar above regulation 98.2 degrees.

'Issy, sweetheart, lend a hand, will you?' Esme's voice came muffled from behind the pile of bedding she carried. Issy bent down and easily scooped the linen into her arms.

'Where's it going?' she asked.

'Laundry basket, I need to strip the beds before I set off for the fracking camp and . . .'

'Indeed you do *not*.' Issy dropped the dirty linen on the hall floor and kicked it into touch. 'I'll do all that when you've gone. It'll give me something to do - and *Lola*,' she pulled a face, 'can lend a hand. If she can spare the time from making herself indispensable to *Mr* Brodie.'

'Ah yes, she does seem rather struck by him,' Esme laughed. She'd always had the ability to see Lindy's posturing as amusing rather than irritating, and cut her yards of slack. 'I think she regards him as a one way ticket to her latest 'dream job' -working the tables in a Las Vegas casino. Hence the newly acquired 'stage name'.' Laughing afresh, Esme led the way to the small room at the front of the house which she'd converted into a study many years ago.

'I see.' Issy followed Esme into the room which commanded another fine view of the mainland and the blue hills in the distance. '*Her name was Lola - she was a cleaner -* that it?' She tried to sing it but it defeated her. 'Sorry, it doesn't scan. Besides which, it's hard to take Lindy seriously. Last year she was saving up enough money to travel to Switzerland with the intention of becoming a chalet girl. I suppose we're just lucky that she didn't take to growing plaits, calling herself Heidi, and keeping goats. Before that, she was hell bent on sweeping the floors in an ashram in India in order to banish the bad karma she's convinced keeps her trapped on *Eilean na*

Sgairbh.' This time, Issy smiled – until she remembered *her* recent run of bad luck. Was bad karma contagious, she wondered?

'I love, *Eilean na Sgairbh,* it's my home. But there's nothing here for Lindy, or youngsters like her. I wish she'd settle for going to university and pursuing a career, as you have. But she hankers after the bright lights. However, let's forget about the Lovely Lola for a moment. I'm more interested in what's driven you back to Cormorant Island, at the height of an electric storm, racing the tide as though the devil was on your heels. Something other than bringing your father's ashes home, I'm guessing?'

Esme sat in her favourite place – a patched up typist's chair next to an old pine desk which held laptop, books and pots of pens. Issy took up her usual position on the cushioned window seat opposite, knees up to her chin and arms clasped around her legs. This moment of peace was what her soul longed for, craved for; she knew she had to make the most of it, Esme's departure was imminent. How many times had they sat like this over the years, she wondered? Esme listening, and her off-loading whatever angst was bothering her, and then Esme offering sage counsel and – more often than not, a solution.

Issy took a deep breath, about to tell Esme everything, but then stopped. Her aunt was recovering from a bout of pneumonia she'd succumbed to in the New Year. She looked tired, she'd lost weight, her strawberry-blond hair hung limply and her skin felt paper thin when Issy had kissed her last night. She was about to drive hundreds of miles in convoy to a fracking protest in Manchester, while her dippy-hippy mates drove her to distraction chattering in the back of The Cow. She needed a clear mind for the task and to enjoy the 'experience', if it could be called that. Issy pulled a face as she looked out to sea – she was hardworking and, like her late father, had a slightly driven personality. She simply didn't get her aunt's predilection for lost causes, however worthy.

Esme had been her surrogate mother for years, now it was time for Issy to look after *her*. It would be selfish to draw Esme's attention to her lack of engagement ring, unemployed status and shattered dreams. Time enough to tell Esme that *Eilean na Sgairbh* was to be her home for the foreseeable future, when she returned from her fracking demo.

'I needed a break from jet setting round the world overseeing the completion of design projects.' Issy dragged her eyes away from the sparkling waters beyond the window and told a little white lie. 'I've had enough of *Auld Reekie*. I want to spend the summer on Cormorant Island, kicking back and doing all the things I did as a child. Simple pleasures.' She sucked in a breath, but when she let it out on a long sigh, it sounded like a sob.

'Hm, why am I *not* buying this? You – giving up your dream job and social life in Edinburgh, to get wet and dirty down on the shoreline, as if you were ten years old. Has your father's death made you examine your own life and reset the coordinates? Not a bad thing in itself, Issy, but you've worked hard to get where you are. Don't throw it all away because your father's death has rocked your boat.'

'I won't, Esme – and it's more than that.'

'And what does Mr Jack Innes-Kerr think to you taking a sabbatical, hmm?' Esme gave Issy a searching look and raised an eyebrow, quizzically. 'Ishabel Stuart, you always were a rotten liar. Don't take up poker, my darling, your face betrays your inner thoughts. And, right at this moment, I'm trying to guess what those are. However, we'll let it rest there. I'm more concerned about the fallout from my American guest and you sharing the house.'

'Fallout? Think my virtue is in danger?' Issy laughed. That tingle of awareness she'd experienced in the kitchen, earlier, the one which started at her hairline, coursed all the way down to her toes and then back up, made her shiver anew. It was as if her brain was giving her psyche a once-over, like a hand-held scanner in the airport, and she'd been through enough of those to know exactly how *that* felt.

She frowned - what was her brain searching for? Second thoughts - regrets?

'No. Not for a moment. You are engaged to be married this autumn and that should guard you from the wagging tongues at the Post Office. And Lindy's mum would be quick to scotch any rumours on that score.' It was a standing joke that the women who frequented the General Store/Post Office had inbuilt radar for scandal, disaster and trouble. They knew what was going down on Cormorant Island before it even happened. Did they possess *da shealladh*, the gift of second sight which most highlanders believed in? Or were their second guesses merely lucky ones?

Issy didn't know; but if their talents could be channelled by the Ministry of Defence, the United Kingdom would never be in danger. Shaking her head free of the preposterous thought, she asked: 'So?'

'So . . . I wondered if Lindy should move in, too. Just until I get back in a week's time?' Esme began, tentatively.

Issy laughed. 'I'm not sure what the Gaelic might be for *mènage a trois,* but I imagine that the thought of *three* of us shacked up here, unchaperoned,' she pulled a wry face, 'would get them clucking even louder.'

'You're right,' Esme said thoughtfully. 'It's just . . .'

'Yes?'

'Having an *American* staying at my house might be . . . well, it might be just enough to dredge up the past – a past I'd rather stay buried.'

'Such as?'

'All that business back in the sixties with the Polaris fleet, my arrest at Holy Loch for climbing up the anchor chains of the USS Proteus when I was a student. They have long memories in these parts, for many highlanders Bannockburn and Culloden happened only yesterday. They haven't forgotten - or forgiven – me for joining CND and protesting about the presence of the US Fleet in the Holy Loch. I wanted them gone and *they* wanted to welcome the servicemen with open arms and get them to spend their Yankee dollars on *Eilean na Sgairbh* when they were on shore leave.'

'But Esme, it happened such a long time ago; you were nineteen, for God's sake. Do you really think . . . ?'

But her aunt appeared to have zoned out after uttering 'open arms', leaving Issy with the impression that there was more to the story than she was prepared to tell. All Issy did know was that her aunt shied away from all things *American*, regarding anything and everything that came from the Land of the Free, a harbinger of bad luck. All the more surprising, then, that she'd offered board and lodgings to Brodie until such time as he could move into the eco-lodge on the far side of the island. What was she not telling her, Issy wondered?

'Esme?' Issy prompted, pulling her out of her dream.

Getting to her feet, Esme took down a yellowing newspaper cutting in a simple black frame from her study wall. It showed her being dragged by the hood of her duffle coat into a Black Maria along with other protesters. She was soaking wet from being hosed down with sea water in an attempt to dislodge her and her fellow CND members off the Proteus' anchor chain.

LOCAL GIRL ARRESTED DURING PROTEST AT HOLY LOCH

It had been Esme's defining moment and, as far as the islanders were concerned, had sealed her fate in their eyes.

She polished the dust off the old frame with her sleeve. 'I really thought James was about to burst a blood vessel when he came to collect me when bail was granted. To me, it was the best day of my life. I'd made my point, stood up for something I believed in. I like to think we made a difference. But to your father, who'd just been accepted as a lay preacher at the local kirk, I'd left a bloody great big blot on the family escutcheon. Mind you, it did give him something to beat me over the head with, figuratively speaking, over the years. Maybe now he's gone, I'll have peace; closure.'

Sighing on the last word, she replaced the picture frame over the bright rectangle of unfaded wallpaper its temporary removal had revealed. It had pride of place amongst other things on the wall - CND posters, mementos of her time at Greenham Common and, looking out of place, a photograph of Issy on a trip to Italy to visit her mother.

'Peace,' Issy echoed, drawn back to the reason for her homecoming. Now that all looked in jeopardy with the arrival of *Brodie*. He seemed very much at home in the kitchen, with his new best friend Lola dancing attendance. Issy doubted that he'd leave her aunt's comfortable lodgings for Mrs MacKay's guest house on the mainland, unless . . . unless she made his stay here so uncomfortable that he'd be begging to leave by the end of the week.

It was a problem, but not an unsurmountable one. She could be very determined when she put her mind to it. And, obviously, this cottage wasn't big enough for the both of them. Once her aunt had left, she'd make it her business to ensure that Brodie wasn't far behind.

'Penny for them,' Esme said. 'You look very . . . determined, all of a sudden.'

Issy laughed and waved away her aunt's perceptive comment. 'Just planning my week. I'll have to organise Daddy's memorial service, as per the specific instructions in his will. The wake.

Climbing a Munro,' she grimaced at the last. How like her father to make her do the one thing she hated – mountain climbing in all its forms.

'Aye, you'll be kept busy. What's been settled about the penthouse in Leith you shared with James?'

'You know how father felt about inherited wealth. He'd seen too many of his friends' children waste their lives spending their inheritance on drugs, fast cars and ill-considered business projects. He's left me nothing except a few shares in *Stuart's Solutions*. His lawyers are to dispose of the flat, and the money raised will be invested in an apprentice scheme at his factory outside Edinburgh. His executors are taking care of the details, I'm not involved in any part of it.'

Now it was Esme's turn to look fierce. Her blue eyes blazed in her, otherwise, pale face, and she spat out: 'I doubt he's left me a penny. But if he has, it can go to charity. I don't want a farthing of his rotten money. Your grandfather left the cottage to me and I, in turn, will leave it to you. I have a small pension and that's enough for me. Taking in paying guests –'

Like Brodie . . .

'Artists, birdwatchers and the like, during the summer months, keeps me afloat. There's nothing to spend your money on Cormorant Island. Anyhow, you don't need his money, Issy. You have brains, determination and a head for business that's quite passed me by. You have the ability to spin straw into gold, once you set your mind to it.' She placed her hands on her knees and levered herself out of the chair. 'I'd better finish loading The Cow. We're meeting up with a convoy at Gretna Services before travelling south. I wouldn't want to keep them waiting.'

Coming over, she ruffled Issy's tangled dark hair and then planted a light kiss on her crown, before leaving the room. Issy rested her head against the panelled shutters and turned her face to the causeway. Compared to her feisty aunt, she'd led a life of privilege provided by the money her entrepreneurial father had generated through his IT business: *Stuart's Solutions*. Her thirtieth birthday was fast approaching, it was time she mapped out her future – a future without her former fiancé, her well paid job in Edinburgh, the penthouse flat in Leith she'd shared with her father, and the fringe benefits which came with being a rich man's daughter.

In short, it was time she stood on her own two feet and found out if she had what it took to make something of her life.

Chapter Six
Bear With Me, Caller

Issy walked back down the corridor, into the square hall, bent down and scooped up the dirty laundry left there earlier. Then, pushing open the kitchen door with her bottom, she reversed into the room. The scene was exactly as she'd left it; Brodie, handmaiden Lindy in attendance, appeared to be on his third, if not fourth cup of coffee, and looking very much at his ease. He must have a bladder the size of a rugby ball, Issy thought uncharitably; served him right if he was twitchy for the rest of the day on a caffeine high. She gave them both a severe look and, unbidden, the line from the Tempest sprang into mind – the bit where Miranda sees Ferdinand for the first time and declares, *Oh brave new world that has such creatures in it.*

Lindy was regarding Brodie with the same Miranda-like, adoration. As if he was the first man she'd ever clapped eyes on. Having dealt with the fallout from some of Lindy's previous 'crushes', Issy was filled with foreboding. Now in a thoroughly bad mood, she threw sheets and pillowcases in the general direction of the overflowing linen basket in the utility room and let out a huff of annoyance. *This* was Lindy's job – when she wasn't helping her mother out at the Post Office. Esme didn't pay her to dress up as a carrot-haired Carmen Miranda and spend all day mooning over one of her guests.

Then, remembering she had volunteered to help Lindy strip the beds, some of Issy's anger – which wasn't directed at Lindy in any case, dissipated. None of Esme's guests had ever looked like Brodie, nor many of the men on the island, come to that. If Lindy had stars in her eyes, who could blame her? Brodie was the real deal, with that air of entitlement, education and privilege which only money, serious money, could provide.

The same could be said of her, she realised, feeling thoroughly narked by the very idea she and Brodie had anything in common.

'If you have no objection, Mr Brodie, Lindy and I will move you into the guest bedroom. You can stay there until you *leave*.' Issy spoke without looking at him, concentrating instead on pushing the linen into its wicker basket. 'I'm sure my bed is too short for you, and you'll be nearer the bathroom, too.' Unbidden, the thought of his long limbs stretched out along the short frame of her girlish bed, made her feel suddenly warm. Damn that dressing gown! Turning, she caught Lindy's expression which was bordering on the mutinous. 'Am I missing something, Lindy?'

Lindy tossed her head, almost dislodging the silk gerbera tucked into her bright, copper curls.

'Well –' she glanced over at Brodie, openly enlisting him as an ally. 'We – that is, Brodie and me, wondered if we - I - could borrow your Mini to drive over to the mainland while the tide's out. Brodie arrived two days ago in one of Big Annie's taxis and has arranged for a hire car to be dropped off this morning. I promised I'd take him over there to pick it up . . . in case he gets lost,' she finished, lamely, unable to meet Issy's eye.

They both knew that Jamestoun across the water only had three streets: Main Street, Upper Street and Lower Street. The chances of Brodie getting lost were quite remote.

'Sure . . . why not? Seems perfectly reasonable. You take Brodie over onto the mainland and I strip all the beds.' Issy smiled with deceptive calmness. 'Then, *Lola,*' she put heavy emphasis on Lindy's stage name, 'you and I need a little talk. Yes?' Again, her tone was so equitable that anyone other than Lindy would have been completely taken in by it. 'Here.' She unhooked her car keys from behind the kitchen door and tossed them over to Lindy. 'Have fun, children.'

She walked out of the kitchen, heading in the general direction of the sitting room where she'd left all her belongings last night. A shower, a change of clothing and some make-up would, hopefully, restore her good humour.

Her mood wasn't improved when she tripped over a collection of rucksacks and camping equipment abandoned in the hall by Esme's fellow protesters. Esme, standing by the open front door supervising their haphazard attempts at packing The Cow, was becoming less patient by the minute. She turned, saw Issy trip over another carelessly placed tent pole, and pulled a face.

'Issy, I'm sorry to leave you and Lindy with all the clearing up.' Issy was about to make a sarcastic remark about her co-worker having added chauffeuse to her list of talents, but restrained herself. Her aunt seemed guilty about dumping the bed-changing on her as it was. Instead, she pulled the cord of her dressing gown tighter, rolled up the over-long sleeves and started to ferry stuff out to The Cow. Hadn't Esme done as much, if not more, for her over the years? She returned for a second load, struggling with a rolled up tent bristling with escaping poles and guy ropes, looking for all the world like a trussed up porcupine.

Suddenly, the weight was taken out of her arms and she almost fell over.

'Allow me, Ma'am,' Brodie said, standing so close that his breath ruffled her tangled hair.

Issy looked up into his face and a tussle of wills took place, the camping equipment moving backwards and forwards between them. She was not his *'Ma'am'* – God, that made her sound like The Queen! Neither did she need his help. She was just about to say as much, when she caught sight of Esme hovering in the doorway chewing her bottom lip somewhat distractedly, and held her peace. Hadn't she shown enough hostility towards their guest for one morning? He got the picture. For goodness sake, it wasn't his fault that he was in the wrong place at the wrong time, and that that place happened to be *Ailleag*, the Jewel of Cormorant Island.

Glancing up at him, Issy was caught off-guard by the determined look in his eyes. But, this time, instead of exhaling in annoyance, she drew air into her lungs and held it there longer than was strictly necessary. A different set of emotions overtook her, as if she was walking across shifting sands and her world was tilting on its axis. Overcome by a light-headedness which she put down to sheer bad temper at being forced to give ground and hand over the tent to Brodie, Issy took a step back from him and exhaled.

Did she imagine the look of triumph which flashed across his face, fleetingly, before being hidden behind one of his megawatt smiles? Dropping her arms by her side, she shrugged as though the matter was of no importance to her, and to indicate he'd won a hollow victory.

Soon, Brodie had The Cow loaded and ready for departure. He walked across to Esme and politely shook her hand, inclined his head slightly and uttered another: 'Ma'am'. Esme smiled, climbed on board The Cow and, with a few shouted instructions about how the boiler had been playing up recently, waved her hand and took her leave. Issy and Brodie watched from the doorway as the former library bus, newly painted in the black and white livery of a Belted Galloway – hence the name, The Cow – disappeared round the bend and out of sight.

It was strange, the two of them standing there and waving Esme's convoy on its way. It was as if they were a bonafide couple who, in the normal run of things, would walk into the cottage with their arms round each other's waist and get on with their day. Searching for words with which to destroy the unintentional moment of intimacy, Issy could only summon up a terse - *Thanks.*

Esme's departure left her feeling unexpectedly overwhelmed by loneliness and dislocation. Even if *Ailleag* had been her home for as far back as she could remember, she felt displaced; out of step with everything and everybody. Maybe her recent bereavement had taken a greater toll on her sensibilities than she was prepared to admit. She glanced over at her Mini convertible parked in front of the cottage. The urn containing her father's ashes was hidden from sight, strapped into the back seat – and that wasn't right or respectful. Now The Cow was lumbering its way across The Narrows, she could put him somewhere more . . . appropriate. Tears misted her eyes and her throat became constricted as she thought back to his funeral and cremation which she'd attended alone, apart from some of his business associates.

The issues which had divided them in life – her determination to pursue an artistic career when her father would have preferred her to consider something more academic; her engagement to Jack Innes-Kerr whom her father regarded as a 'loafer'; and her entreaties that he rebuild Twa Burns distillery with the money he'd made from his IT business, would forever remain unresolved, due to his sudden passing.

She coughed to clear her throat and blinked away her tears.

Now was not the time to show weakness. Not in front of this man.

'I – I'd better . . .' Issy broke away from Brodie who was regarding her intently and with a fair degree of empathy in his green eyes, as if he guessed what she was going through. However, that was extremely unlikely, unless he, too, had the gift of the Sight.

'Sure. No problem.' He stepped aside to allow her to precede him down the corridor. A few seconds later there was a sickening thud, followed by a muttered: 'Jesus . . .'

Issy turned to see Brodie rubbing the top of his head where it'd come into contact with one of the black crossbeams supporting the low ceiling.

'Are you okay? These cottages weren't designed for six foot three Americans,' she threw over her shoulder, making it sound very matter of fact but at the same time, subtly insulting. It was his fault that he was too tall for her aunt's cottage and taking up too much space for one man. She just hoped that Esme kept her public liability insurance up to date, Brodie looked like the kind of man who would sue the arse off them if it suited him. 'A diet of smoked herring, porridge and few vegetables has restricted the growth of the locals. Five foot ten is considered a good height on Cormorant Island.'

With that, she left him rubbing his crown and headed for the kitchen. So much for that moment of intimacy, she'd chased it away with its tail firmly between its legs.

'Guess I'll live, don't you give it another thought,' he remarked, when it became plain she wasn't about to rush for the first aid kit or dab his crown with teatree oil. She'd leave such tender ministrations to Lindy. Brodie, seemingly picking up the vibe, spoke again, 'Mizz Stuart,' he pronounced it Stoo-rt. So familiar, yet subtly different . . . 'If my being here inconveniences you –'

That should have been Issy's get out clause. Didn't she long to be on her own, to have the time to mourn her father, and to figure out where life would take her now she'd resigned from her job? Instead, she remembered that little surge of loneliness on the front doorstep and tried to make light of his offer. Company – even *his* company, was better than none.

'I am not inconvenienced in the slightest by your being here, Mr Brodie,' she said formally, waving away his concerns. 'Once Lindy returns from the mainland with my car and you have your hire car, we should be able to rub along nicely until your other accommodation is ready.'

'Rub along nicely?' Brodie questioned, as if the phrase was unknown to him.

'Oh, yes,' she replied without enlightening him further. If he didn't understand the expression he could look it up on Google. 'We will meet at breakfast and at dinner but other than that . . .' She left him to draw his own conclusions. 'I have matters to attend to and I'm sure that, through a combination of Lindy and a sat nav, you'll soon find your way round *Eilean na Sgairbh*. It's hardly the Gobi Desert.'

Although, she reflected, by the end of his stay she would probably wish it were.

Although she'd made light of it to her aunt, she could well imagine what the wagging tongues at the Post Office would make of Brodie staying in her aunt's cottage as a paying guest. Doubtless, over the Mother's Pride and bags of homemade tablet on the counter, they'd quiz Lindy about sleeping arrangements. When she went to fetch the *messages*, the shop would fall silent – and the honky-tonk piano in the corner would stop playing when the shop door swung open to admit her. No doubt they would also add – after she'd left the shop, naturally – how she was *just* like her aunt and no better than her mother. The Stuarts were a bad lot and all the lessons James Stuart had read in the kirk as lay preacher, and the money he'd spent improving the island's infra-structure, wouldn't change that.

Blood will out, they'd declare - and Issy, in her present angsty frame of mind was prepared to give them a run for their money. In fact, she'd derive a certain unholy amount of pleasure at the thought of the gossip which Brodie staying with her, an unmarried female, would generate.

But unlike her aunt, she didn't give a fig for their – or anyone else's opinion.

That thought banished the bad case of the blues which had dogged her since waking and accounted for her less than sunny mood. Maybe company, in the form of Esme's American and an overexcited *Lola*, might be just what the therapist ordered. She'd be so busy sorting them out that she wouldn't have time to think about the mess her life was in.

'You sure?' Brodie pursued the point. 'Because I'd like to stay here until the eco-lodge is ready and . . . and my family join me.' Issy raised her eyebrow at *family*. Had he been lying in the kitchen when he said there was no Mrs Brodie or Wee Brodies? She'd be keeping an eye on him, for *Lola's* sake.

'I'm sure,' she said with finality.

The kitchen door burst open and Lindy rushed out, ending the discussion. When she saw the cut on Brodie's forehead, she acted as if he'd been borne in on a stretcher from the Heights of Balaclava with his life in the balance. Happy to play Florence Nightingale to his wounded soldier, she gasped out: 'Brodie. Brodie. What have you done, man?'

'Just banged my head on the low beam . . .' He grinned, seemingly shamefaced at being the cause of such a fuss.

'Och, come away into the kitchen and I'll patch you up before we leave for the mainland.'

'You'll find the triangular bandages and splints in the first aid kit under the kitchen sink, Florence,' Issy said, with the no nonsense briskness of a hospital matron. Brodie's look conveyed that Lindy's reaction was more to his liking and that Issy was no more than a heartless beast. Receiving a black look from Lindy, Issy walked towards her bedroom, leaving them to it. Then she remembered it was no longer her bedroom until she and Lindy had stripped the beds and set Brodie up in one of the guest bedrooms.

Making her way back to the sitting room, she stood on the threshold and surveyed the collection of dirty pots, empty wine glasses and the unmade futon. The sweet scent of hashish hung in the air and she pushed upon the window to disperse it. As she walked past the parrot, Pershing greeted her with an annoyed squawk but looked pleased to see her. She blew him a kiss.

'Issy will let you out later, if you're a good boy,' she promised.

'*I'm a good boy,*' he repeated dutifully, but the glint in his eye gave lie to it. '*Want walkies.*' His request wasn't as crazy as it seemed. Pershing had a harness which was slipped over his head when Issy or Esme took him outside for a breath of fresh air. It was attached to the end of a long strap which Issy wound round her wrist to stop him flying off. He loved his 'walks' in the fresh air which amounted to no more than Issy sitting on the bench outside the cottage, with Pershing on her shoulder calling out (mostly rude things) to anyone who walked past.

'Okay, let me get settled and we'll see about you going outside.'

Issy's phone on the table rang and she answered it automatically.

Her fiancé, Jack Innes-Kerr's photo flashed up briefly on the screen. It was a photo Issy had taken on their last holiday in Mauritius. He looked blond, tanned and very sure of himself – his default mode.

'Thank God, I've got through to you. The phone kept going straight through to voice mail.'

'Oh really?' Issy said, ice dripping from those two words. 'Anyone would think I didn't want to talk to you.'

Detecting her less than enthusiastic welcome, Jack continued in an upbeat manner.

'Yes. Really. Look, darling - about the other night . . .'

'What about it?' Issy wasn't going to make this easy for him. If this was an apology, she wanted it good and grovelling.

'Let me explain -'

'No explanation necessary, Jack.' She held up her hand in a

traffic-stopping gesture even though he couldn't see her. 'A picture, as they say, paints a thousand words. And I have an indelible picture of you and Suzy the intern imprinted on my mind. Her bum's probably left an indentation on my desk pad, too, for all I know. As object lessons go, it made its point.'

'Ishabel. Sweetheart . . .'

'I'm not your sweetheart, Jack.' With a sigh, Issy acknowledged that she'd been in denial over their relationship which had been straining at the seams for the last six months. Her father's death had been her wake-up call, and sitting alone during his funeral service – which Jack hadn't deigned to attend – she'd known it was time for a clean break, a fresh sweep and a hundred other clichés which had sprung to mind. 'Not any longer. Now, if you don't mind, I'm rather busy . . .'

Funny how attending to Esme's unwelcome guest had assumed greater importance in her mind than patching things up with her errant fiancé.

'*Gei'us a wee kiss, dahrlin,*' the parrot added, blowing loud, smacking kisses at Issy.

'Who's there? Who have you got in the room with you? A man? God, but you're a fast worker – who is he? Some foul-mouthed Glaswegian by the sound of it. Don't tell me that the ice maiden has fallen for a bit of rough trade? If that's what you wanted, you had only to say . . .'

'Jack,' Issy tried to cut him off.

'Oh, wait; I get it. This has been your plan all along, hasn't it?

Break off the engagement, cancel the wedding, leave me at the altar, and make a fool of me. I always suspected that underneath the prim exterior, you were a ball breaker. Just like your mother.' Issy ignored the last remark, suspecting that Jack was trying to push the blame for their failing relationship firmly on her shoulders.

'I'd say that you've managed to make a fool of yourself pretty much without my help, Jack. Know what? I'm not in the mood for playing games. Let's be honest and admit the truth – it wasn't working out between us. Our relationship had run its course, it simply took my father's death with its attendant fall-out to bring that fact into sharper relief.'

'How can you *say* that, so – so coldly?'

'How could *you* miss his funeral? How could *you* not be there when I needed your support?'

'I did try to make it,' Jack began, lamely. 'I cut my meeting short.'

Issy gave an annoyed tut. 'More lies, Jack. What you really mean is that you played nine holes instead of eighteen that day, but still left it too late to get to the crematorium.'

'Give me another chance,' he begged.

'Jack – read the signs. I was never in the UK. You were never in the office. You play off a golf handicap of eight whereas I can't remember the last time I did anything that wasn't work-related. I saved up the money for my share of the deposit on the apartment in Herrick Road in the New Town. You blew your end-of-year bonus on a new Porsche. And – before you say another word, I know you borrowed the money off your father to cover the deficit, but that's not the point, is it?'

'We have the deposit, Issy, we can put it down on the flat on Monday. All I need from you is a show of forgiveness and some commitment towards our future together.'

'Listen to yourself, Jack, do you have no sense of irony. Commitment? That's a bit rich coming from you, isn't it? It's over between us,' Issy added, feeling no sorrow at ending their relationship. Just a burning desire to get him off the phone so she could tidy up the sitting room and attend to the 'Brodie problem'.

'Don't say that, sweetie. We were – *are* – good together.'

'Actually, Jack, I don't think we were; not really. Our relationship was a bit unbalanced, wouldn't you say?' Unconsciously, Issy slipped into using the past tense.

'Unbalanced? You're a workaholic and I'm,' he paused, perhaps realising that he wasn't portraying himself in a good light, 'a bit more laid back about things. But don't blame me for that. Blame your father for passing his Protestant work ethic on to you. No one was surprised when he died at his desk . . .' There was a silence. 'He was eighty-two for God's sake. Who carries on working at his age?'

'A dedicated man?' Issy suggested, but Jack wasn't listening.

'Driven, more like! You'd do better to tap into your mother's genes, Issy. La Bella Scozzese knows how to live! All work and no play, makes Issy a dull girl.' Issy could imagine him tapping the toes of his handmade Italian shoes impatiently.

'I suppose you're right,' Issy went on in a deceptively

reasonable tone, 'I *have* been a disappointment, in many respects.'

'Well, that's a little harsh, darling.' Eagerly, Jack picked up on her heartfelt sigh and took her words at face value. 'Let's settle for - you work too hard, you're a wee bit *too* focused and . . .' He paused, at last realising that, as conciliatory speeches went, this was missing its mark.

'You were saying?'

'Now, don't take on that tone, Issy. We both know that you've never paid me enough attention,' he said, aggrieved. 'You only have yourself to blame if I – wandered.'

'I see – wandered – is that what they're calling it these days? Wandered,' she paused as if to give the term some thought. 'Does Suzy know that's what it was? Or is she hoping for a more . . . permanent arrangement?'

'Suzy's a clever girl, she knows exactly how it works.'

'And I don't, is that it?'

'Exactly. No, wait – *not* like Suzy. She was a mistake, a one off. But – well, you are away a great deal –'

'On company business,' she reminded him.

'A man gets lonely,' he whined.

'I see. So your fucking the intern over *my* desk is all *my* fault. Actually, now I think about it, I can see how that would be the case. And, to be honest, you *are* still in shock after learning that father left all his money to good causes and none of it to me. I understand that. One minute you're marrying a billionaire's daughter, the next you're marrying one of your father's employees. I'm guessing Suzy was a little treat you awarded yourself, to cheer you up?'

Even Jack couldn't remain totally unaware of her sarcastic tone much longer.

'You know, Issy, you don't sound so much upset as pissed off.' Issy nodded, inclined to agree with him. If she loved him, truly loved him – shouldn't her heart be in pieces? Shouldn't her overwhelming emotion be relief, that he was giving her a second chance?

'That's true,' she paused. 'I *am* more annoyed than broken-hearted.'

'Annoyed? Thanks for that,' he snapped.

The gibe about her inheriting her father's Protestant work ethic stung. Knowing that the only fragile thing about Jack Innes-Kerr was his ego, Issy set about exacting revenge.

'I mean, Jack - come on. Boss' son screws intern while fiancée is overseas on business? It's about as original as the ideas *your* design team come up with.'

Now the gloves were off.

'Oh yes, we all know you're Geordie's blue-eyed girl.' His bitterness poured out and his breathing became agitated. 'He's going to be furious when he finds your resignation on his desk on Monday morning. Yes, I've seen it there. All neatly typed. My God, you can't even claim to have dashed it off in the heat of the moment, can you – all misspelled and covered in tear stains? That's my Issy – cool, calm, collected and in control – to the bitter end.'

'Of course, I'm sorry to upset your father . . .'

But Jack wasn't listening. 'When he finds your letter, he'll doubtless blame it on *me*. Like it's all *my* fault. You do realise,' he said by way of a clincher, 'he was going to make you a junior partner. As a wedding present?'

'Like I said, I'm sorry to upset Geordie, he's a good man. But I have my own life to lead, ambitions to fulfil - and catching you with your trousers round your ankles was just the push I needed, if you'll pardon the pun.'

'A bit late for coming over Miss Potty Mouth, isn't it? I might have found that attractive in you, once. However . . .' Then, as realisation dawned, 'Ambitions – what ambitions?'

'You no longer have the right to ask me that.'

'You do realise that I'll be the laughing stock of the golf club.'

'That did give me pause for thought,' Issy said snarkily. 'But I'm sure you'll come up with an excuse, Jack. One which'll make it appear that you dumped me, not the other way round. Look, this discussion is getting us nowhere. We're over - and after I hang up, I'm blocking your calls. Goodbye.'

'*Feck off, ya wee bauchle,*' Pershing added for good measure, picking up on the vibe. His timing spot on as usual, he added, '*Yer head's up yer arse, Man.*' This was followed by piratical laughter and much dancing up and down on his perch.

'You *do* have a man there. What's his name?'

Jack had never deigned to visit Cormorant Island, to meet her Aunt Esme or Pershing, so Issy felt the parrot's aside was poetic justice. The parrot often stayed at The Pickled Herring during Esme's longer trips away, and over the years its customers had taught it one or two choice phrases. Issy neatly parodied one of her father's favourite ear-bashing sermons: *out of the beaks of parrots . . . hast thou ordained strength.*

She smiled at the parrot and blew him a kiss; he'd given her a get out clause.

'To answer your original question, his name's Brodie and he's American, not Glaswegian. Well over six feet tall and broad of shoulder.' There was a silence as Jack Innes-Kerr digested this information. Slightly built, Jack's lack of height was an issue with him and accounted for some of his hang-ups. 'I take it that you found my engagement ring?'

'Yes, nice touch,' he said, dropping all pretence at rapprochement. 'Sellotaping it to the photograph of me winning the amateur golfing trophy at Carnoustie last summer. You know how to kick a man where it hurts, don't you?'

'If you say so.' Issy was impatient to end the call, to cut him out of her life.

'You could have kept the ring, you know. After all –'

'I earned it? Thanks for that. Okay, Jack I'm going to hang up now. Don't bother to ring back as I won't be answering your calls after today.' She hung up and Pershing echoed the sound of the bleep, turned upside down and regarded Issy with his considering stare.

'*You silly tart,*' he informed her.

'I was, Pershing, but no longer; I've seen the light.' She grimaced, she sounded like her father preaching in the local kirk.

Maybe she should add hallelujah, or tap the floor with her walking stick like the older members of the congregation did when the sermon made a point they approved of? 'No man is going to put *this* baby in the corner; not if I can help it. Now, if you'll excuse me – to paraphrase the song, I'm about to wash Jack Innes-Kerr right out of my hair.' Tossing her mobile onto the futon, Issy left the sitting room to collect her suitcases from her Mini, parked outside in the yard.

'*Walkies?*' the parrot called after her, forlornly.

Chapter Seven
Ground Rules

Later, after she'd spent most of the day cleaning, changing beds and washing dirty linen, Issy heard the throb of a powerful engine in the backyard. This was accompanied by the softer, but none the less powerful roar of her Mini Cooper being driven at reckless speed before it drew to a screeching halt on the cobbles, still greasy from last night's thunderstorm. Issy grimaced, imagining the tread being burned off her tyres, and then shrugged. If she'd learned one thing over the past few weeks, it was that material possessions counted for nothing – and that life had a tendency to bite you on the bum when you least expected. Making her way over to the worktop, she switched the kettle on, guessing that Lewis Hamilton and Jensen Button would be demanding tea with menaces the moment they entered the house.

And she was right.

Lindy exploded through the back door with her silk gerbera looking slightly the worse for wear, her expression that of an angry wasp.

'Issy. I didn't realise that I had your Da strapped into the back seat of the Mini until we were half way across the causeway . . .' She carried the urn containing James Stuart's ashes at arm's length as if it was radioactive and deposited it on the kitchen table with alacrity. Issy looked at the urn as if seeing it for the first time, rubbed at a throbbing spot on her right temple - and remembered . . .

'I've had so much to deal with . . . I actually forgot he was still there. Sorry.' Although just who she was apologising to wasn't clear. Her father for showing lack of respect towards his mortal remains, or Lindy for spooking her. Despite the influence of the kirk, the islanders were notoriously superstitious and Lindy was no exception. Doubtless she'd be having nightmares and seeing signs and portents in cloud shapes for weeks to come.

Best to stop her histrionics in their tracks.

'Well, it just wasn't very . . . nice. I don't know what Brodie thought.'

Issy sent her a dark look. She hoped Brodie wasn't about to become the barometer of what was good, bad or indifferent on Cormorant Island. Time to redress the balance and remind them that she, Ishabel Stuart, called the shots here.

'Considering Father's opinion of your driving – of any female in charge of a car, come to that, I'd say it was poetic justice. Take him off the table and put him in one of the outbuildings will you, Lindy?' There. That reminded Lola of her place in the scheme of things. 'He'll have to stay there until the memorial service next week, Aunt Esme was most insistent. After that - '

'I'd love to know what he did to make your aunt take against him so,' Lindy speculated, looking at the ugly brown plastic urn which had been across The Narrows twice in twenty-four hours. 'Is it something to do with the fact that your grandfather, Young Johnny, left the cottage to her and cut your father out of his will? I've often wondered.'

'I don't really know, myself,' Issy managed to get a word in, finally.

'Normally,' Lindy went on, 'Esme's all Buddhist and Zen; she wouldnae hurt a fly in case it was one of her ancestors reincarnated. God, I hope I don't come back as a blue bottle,' she added, going off piste. 'Knowing my luck, I'd be reborn on a muck heap, make it onto someone's dinner plate and then, just as I'm tucking into their steak pie, be dispatched by a copy of The Sunday Post.'

'I'm sure, if you do come back, Lindy, it'll be as a bird of paradise,' Issy soothed. Over the years she'd assumed the role of person-in-charge of bolstering Lindy's confidence. Despite all outward appearances, Lindy suffered from low self-esteem, hence her tendency to overcompensate – massively!

'Thanks, hen,' Lindy brightened up considerably.

'But don't talk about such things in front of my father or the urn will start rocking on the table. Reincarnation is not one of the precepts of the Wee Frees.' Jokingly, Issy referred to the strict, Calvinistic branch of the Church of Scotland which held sway on Cormorant Island and to which her father had been a fully paid up member. 'Father stipulated in his will that his ashes were to be put into a seventeenth century bible box which he'd sourced especially for the purpose. I searched high and low for it at the penthouse in Leith but never found it. So - until his memorial service and the eventual scattering on a Munro . . .'

'He'll be living in a sweetie jar?'

'That's about it. Take the jar over to the outhouse will you?'

'To be honest, I'd rather not. It's creeping me out to think that your father has fitted into that wee jar. He was so tall . . .' She pushed it towards Issy with scant regard for *her* feelings. Issy picked up the surprisingly weighty urn and headed for the back door which opened onto a cobbled yard, surrounded on two sides by large granite outbuildings.

'By the way,' she called over her shoulder, 'Mary rang to ask if you could go straight home, she has some messages for you to deliver on the other side of the island by Crag's Rock.' *Messages*, referred to those items of shopping which some of the good ladies of Cormorant Island had ordered from the General Store over the phone.

Lindy pulled a face. 'Oh, but, Brodie and I have plans.'

'Not today you haven't; not according to your Mah-mmy.' Issy drew out and exaggerated the syllables, to further tease and exasperate Lindy. 'Anyway, you'd better skedaddle, Lola. I'll sort Brodie out.'

'That's what's worrying me,' Lindy said, narrowing her eyes. 'Just remember, I saw him first, Ishabel Stuart, so hands off. I noticed this morning that you aren't wearing your engagement ring. Does that mean you and Jackie-Boy are no longer an item?' When it became plain that Issy wasn't about to share *that* with her, Lindy dismissed the possibility of Issy nursing a broken heart with a casual shrug of her shoulders.

'Oh, don't worry, *Lola.* I won't be fighting you for Captain America,' Issy said as she reversed out of the kitchen via the back door, her father's ashes in her arms. Honestly, Lindy made her head spin. One minute she was disclaiming about incarnation and the next she was all *git your hands of ma man.* Issy's thumping headache got worse, as it often did when Lindy was in the vicinity. They were good friends – really, they were, but somehow everything always ended up as a competition between them. Who could run the fastest, drink the most whisky without falling face down in a puddle, sing the sweetest (in Gaelic, naturally) at the ceilidh, or make the best steak pie on New Year's Day. Given the present set of circumstances – her father's ashes being kept in the outhouses on Esme's orders, her absent engagement ring and an unwanted visitor foisted on her for the foreseeable future, Issy thought that Lindy might have shown a bit of sisterly feeling towards her.

Finding Lindy's posturing suddenly tiresome, Issy continued more sharply than intended.

'You're welcome to Brodie, I have no interest in him – he's simply not my type. And, having a casual affair with a summer visitor is not on my to-do list. Besides, in case you hadn't noticed, I have weightier matters on my mind.' Taking a backward step down into the yard, Issy backed straight into Brodie's arms. She nearly dropped the urn at his feet as she realised he'd overheard every word, and an unbecoming nettle rash spread over her face and neck. His strong brown hands steadied her, encircling her waist before he released her and took the urn out of her shaking hands.

'Mr B-Brodie,' Issy stammered, aware of the brick she'd just dropped. 'I am *so* sorry. What I meant to say was . . .' She caught his frown as he looked down at the ashes, *and* Lindy's smirk as she enjoyed every excruciating moment of Issy's embarrassment. At that point the kettle whistled and they all turned to stare at it as if it was the most fascinating sight in the world. No one spoke as the whistling reached its crescendo, and then Brodie broke the spell.

'Why don't you deal with your father's ashes and I'll make us some coffee?'

'That sounds . . . I'll just . . . Great.' Taking the urn from him, feeling that this morning was beginning to resemble a game of *pass the parcel,* Issy ducked under his arm and almost ran for the sanctuary of the granite outhouses. Cheeks burning, she placed her father's urn in one of the deep window embrasures where it could face out to sea. Which, considering his soul was now elsewhere, was probably rather pointless. Feeling guilty and deciding that her father's ashes demanded more respect, she bowed her head and whispered a little prayer over them. Her piety was short-lived, however, when she caught a glimpse of herself in the broken mirror over by the door.

She looked like a car crash . . . pale skin scarlet-red with mortification, black hair resembling a bird's nest, deep violet eyes underlined by smeared mascara. Cursing the Stuart genes which were responsible for her highlander complexion, Issy waited for her high colour to disappear and her composure to return before she considered rejoining Brodie and Lindy in the kitchen. Minutes passed, during which she went over her phone conversation with Innes-Kerr. Another epic fail to add to the list which was getting longer by the hour.

Just as she was wondering how long she could skulk in the outhouse without looking a complete idiot, she saw Brodie advancing across the yard, mug of coffee in his hand. Apparently, if Ishabel wouldn't come to the coffee, the coffee was about to come to Ishabel.

She schooled her features into what she hoped was a welcoming smile.

'Hi.' Brodie entered the gloom of the old stone building, wisely ducking his head under the low door lintel. A quick learner, Issy noted. 'Need to coffee up?'

'You could say that.' She took the mug from him, clasped it in both hands, gulped down a great mouthful and then started coughing until her eyes streamed. 'What the f – what's in there?'

'You looked like you could do with a bit of a boost so I laced it with brandy I found in your aunt's cupboard. Hope that's okay? Lindy was about to tip half a bottle of single malt in there but I stopped her.'

'You did?'

'Sure. I know a little bit about whisky and I'm guessing there aren't many bottles of Stuart's Twa Burns left.'

'You guess correctly. Not counting the one in the kitchen, there are only five bottles in existence. All that's left from the dozen or so my grandfather and Lindy's great-grandfather managed to salvage the night the distillery was bombed in September 1942.' He looked interested, but puzzled, so Issy went on to explain. 'At the start of the war, Stuart's Twa Burns distillery was requisitioned by the government and turned over to making industrial alcohol, as were many distilleries on the west coast of Scotland. One night, two Junkers followed the coast, found the distillery, dropped their bomb load and Twa Burns was no more. I'm told that when it went up, the whole island shook and the flames were seen as far away as Oban.'

'It must have been frightening,' he said, watching closely as she drank the brandy-laced coffee. He leaned back on an old work bench very much at ease, evidently not bothered that it was filthy from years of disuse. 'And the distillery was never rebuilt?' Issy, glad of the chance to move on from her earlier faux pas, was only too happy to give him a potted history lesson.

'No. It had suffered earlier damage during the First World War when it was requisitioned to build landmines for the battlefields of Flanders. The chemicals were volatile . . . there a massive explosion which blew out one side of the distillery. After the war, my family received compensation from the government. However, one of the partner's sons didn't return from France and the heart went out of the business. After that, Twa Burns limped along producing only a fraction of its pre-war capacity until it was bombed for a second time in 1942. But this must be boring you to tears.' She pulled herself up short, realising that her tongue was running away with her. 'Here endeth the lesson. School dismissed.'

'No, I'm interested.' He looked at her long and hard, obviously wanting her to say more. 'Maybe some other time?'

'Maybe, before . . .'

'Before I leave?' he laughed.

'I'm sorry, I didn't mean –'

'Sure you did. You British are so damned polite it's hard to know exactly what you're thinking. But hey,' he spread his hands wide, 'I get it, okay? Your father has passed over, you've brought his ashes home for the wake and you thought it'd be just you and your aunt. Right?'

'Right.' For some reason, she was pleased that he understood it was nothing personal.

The reason she was glad he knew nothing about what had happened between her and Jack Innes-Kerr was more difficult to explain. Seemingly, unaware of the follow-on thought, he continued in the same amiable, amused tone.

'Instead, you get me. An interloper, and an American one at that.' Issy felt she had to put the record straight, well, as straight as she could.

'It's not you *per se*, it's just that there's history between my aunt and some of the islanders which dates back to her protesting about American subs in the Holy Loch about . . . oh, about a million years ago.' She attempted a feeble joke and he smiled back at her to show there were no hard feelings.

'No need to explain. Lindy has given me the low-down on how it works on Cormorant Island. How the folks hereabouts have long memories.'

'Lindy,' she sighed, and then remembered the embarrassing incident at the kitchen door. 'Look, I didn't mean anything back there, you know?' She gestured towards the house with her mug. 'Lindy and me, we're like sisters – and sisters squabble and fall out. It doesn't mean a thing. Although to a casual observer it might look . . . anyhow, when I said you weren't my type, I wasn't implying there was something wrong with you. I mean, God - I'm sure most women would be more than grateful to – to – go out with you.' She squirmed, suddenly transported back to a sixth form dance at the posh boarding school she'd attended when boys from a neighbouring school were shipped in to make up numbers. She recalled cringing every time one of them glanced in her direction. 'You're very . . .' She glanced at him, critically, in the shadowy building. Tall, athletic and outdoorsy looking, he had well-cut auburn hair, a good bone structure, straight white American teeth and green eyes you could lose yourself in. Most women's dream date. 'It's just – well, right now I'm not in the market for complications. *Not*,' she returned to her earlier flustered state, 'that I'm suggesting for one moment, that you . . .'

'I get it. Okay? Me neither.' He smiled, showing he hadn't taken offence. 'I've had my fair share of *complications* and I'm happy to leave them behind in Kentucky.'

'Kentucky?'

Brodie checked himself, as if his coming from Kentucky was classified information. Information he hadn't meant to share with her. What was so special about Kentucky, Issy pondered? As far as she knew, it was famous for three things: thoroughbred racehorses, blue grass music and bourbon. Having regained her poise, she gave a tight little smile to signal that this interview was over, and squeezed past him. If he had secrets, it was best he kept them to himself.

Dismissing the uncomfortable notion that there was more to Mr Brodie than met the eye, Issy stopped short of the kitchen door and turned on her heel. 'One more thing Mr Brodie,' she drew in a breath before continuing.

'Just Brodie, please.'

'Okay, then – *Brodie*. Don't mess with Lindy's head, or get her hopes up. Come the end of summer you'll be going home and Lindy will be left behind on *Eilean na Sgairbh*. I don't want to be the one spending all winter helping her get over a broken heart.'

She sent him a fierce look and thought for several long moments that he would stalk off in high dudgeon. Instead, he returned her forbidding gaze look for look, nodding as he digested her words. Then he stood up and brushed down his cobweb-draped clothing.

'Know what? I think I preferred you all British, polite and distant. Okay, thanks for being open with me. Don't worry, I've got Lindy's number – she's cute and fun to be around, but that's it. She reminds me of my kid sister . . .' Again, the shutters came down and Issy hid her interested look. Her instincts were right, there *was* more to Brodie than met the eye. Exactly what that was she couldn't say –

not yet, at any rate. 'Any more rules I should be aware of?' He gave Issy a comprehensive once-over, much as she had done to him earlier in the outhouse.

'Regarding?' She waited for him to clarify, but sensed that he'd had enough of their head-to-head.

'Nothing I can think of,' he said lightly, but she knew he was referring to *her.*

'Guess that's us done here, then.' Issy walked over to check her precious Mini for chips and scratches. Although she couldn't see him, she felt Brodie's eyes on her as she crossed the yard. Holding her breath, she waited until she heard the kitchen door close and it was safe to turn round. Releasing pent-up breath, she leaned against the Mini, and looking back at the granite outhouse, wondered just what had passed between them in there.

Chapter Eight
You've Got Mail

Sitting at Esme's desk two days later, Issy swivelled the typist's chair round to face the causeway.

The sun was behind *Ailleag*, casting its shadow onto the road and the wide concrete edge which separated the houses in Killantrae from the newly built sea wall – their only defence against the seas which battered the island from December to May. Over on the mainland, Jamestoun was bathed in sunlight so warm and bright that the beam from the lighthouse at the end of the harbour was barely visible. Issy loved that lighthouse, its beam a welcoming beacon every time she crossed The Narrows. Stay a while, give island life a chance, it seemed to say to her. Turn your back on Edinburgh and the world of business, contracts and the constant unpacking/repacking – there's more to life than that.

It had a point.

Despite recent events, now she was back on *Eilean na Sgairbh* Issy felt more relaxed than she had in years. In tendering her resignation she'd not only jettisoned an unworthy fiancé, she'd also granted herself permission to jump off the mad roundabout that was her life, and given herself time. Time to mourn her father, breathe freely and decide where her life was headed. She was at the crossroads, but there were no friendly signs to point the way forward. She'd have to figure out the route for herself.

She flexed her shoulders, rolled her head to release the tension and freed her hair from its pony tail. The Narrows were calm, reflecting the harbour cottages of Jamestoun on their glassy surface and making the fishing port seem twice as big as in reality. Issy loved the red tiled roofs, the whitewashed walls and the three-storey granite building which had formerly housed the local Customs and Excise. Although they weren't visible from this distance, she could picture the old railway lines which dissected the cobbled road. Back in the day, when Jamestoun had been a thriving fishing port, langoustines were landed first thing in the morning, packed onto ice and sent down to London, via Oban, to grace the dinner plates in swanky hotels.

Now the harbour was mostly filled with private yachts and the occasional fishing boat which took tourists out to the bird colonies in high summer. The brown hills beyond the harbour could look bleak in the winter, but today the sun warmed them, picking out the old fort (now almost covered in vegetation), built after the '45 Rebellion to quell the unruly Scots. It reminded them that the town might be named after a Stuart king, but they were the subjects of the Hanoverian usurper, whether they liked it or not.

Talking of usurpers . . . Issy wondered what Brodie's plans were for the day.

Since their tête-à-tête in the outhouse, he'd pretty much stayed out of her way. Which suited her just fine. Tonight, over dinner, she'd broach the subject of his leaving *Ailleag*, or at least get a definite date when the house would be hers – and hers alone. This was what her soul craved more than anything, apart from a break from Lindy!

Lindy had left the cottage after serving breakfast. Her departure had been accompanied by much slamming of doors, stomping of feet and protests to Mary Tennant, via her mobile, that '*Issy and Brodie need me more than the Post Office*'. Mary Tennant evidently thought otherwise and had ordered Lindy home, guessing, correctly, that Lindy was sticking to Brodie like a new species of limpet.

Issy smiled as she watched Lindy marching up the hill in high dudgeon towards her end of the village. Well, she could vent her spleen stamping pension books and being rude to the senior citizens of *Eilean na Sgairbh* - or whatever helping her mother at the Post Office and General Store entailed these days. When Lindy finally disappeared round the bend in the road, even the house seemed to breathe a sigh of relief. Three days of Lindy in 'helpful mode' tested the most robust of constitutions and the patience of any saint the Vatican cared to nominate. Now the only sound disturbing the silence was the faint scraping of wood against wood as drawers were opened and closed in the guest bedroom where Brodie was sorting through his clothes - washed and pressed by Lindy, naturally.

In a few days he, too, would be gone, Issy reflected - and then it'd just be her and the parrot. Lindy's visits would cease, too, as she'd inveigled Brodie into hiring her as cook/cleaner and general all-round Girl Friday once he was settled in at the eco-lodge. Oh how she relished the thought! Although, to be fair to Brodie, he'd pretty much left her alone since he'd brought the hire car over from the mainland. He appeared to spend most of his time driving round the island photographing its flora and fauna with a very expensive looking camera. His evenings, as far as Issy could make out, were spent down at The Pickled Herring where, by all accounts, he was a welcome visitor – and had been declared an all-round good bloke by the clannish islanders who frequented *Eilean na Sgairbh's* only pub.

Pushing herself out of the chair, Issy padded around the room checking what had been added or changed since her last visit. Esme was an inveterate reader, and books - political tracts, biographies of great revolutionaries and volumes of poetry - were crammed into several bookcases around the room. Issy loved to touch Esme's first edition Penguin novels in their green, blue and orange jackets. Their covers were marked and stained, their yellowing pages marking the passage of time, but they told their own story. These were flanked by modern thrillers: Dan Brown, Jeffrey Archer. Lee Childs et al, romances, crime novels by favourite female writers and a whole set of well-thumbed Virago classics. Issy's fingertips trailed along the spines of her particular favourites: *Enchanted April*, *All Passion Spent* and *Precious Bane*.

It was quite a library. Esme had eclectic tastes and insisted on having something for everyone when her visitors were forced indoors by unexpected summer squalls. Which was quite often on this westerly facing island.

Now thoroughly relaxed, Issy reached into her bag for the books she'd brought with her from Edinburgh. Staggering under their weight, she dropped them on the window seat along with her portfolio of room treatments. They were old friends and, if she couldn't have her aunt's undivided attention, they'd keep her company until Esme returned. It was all so familiar that, as she unpacked, Issy felt as if she'd come home from her alma mater, Edinburgh University School of Design, for the long summer vacation.

In reality, she'd come home for good.

However, for the moment she'd keep that nugget to herself, along with the fact she would no longer be marrying Jack Innes-Kerr in a showy wedding at St Giles Cathedral, Edinburgh, this Christmas as planned. The only thing missing from the familiar scene was her father. But, in a way, even that didn't feel so different. Issy'd spent so much of her childhood trying to catch him between flights as he jetted around the globe, expanding his IT empire that it felt more normal for him *not* to be there.

As for her mother . . . best not go there.

There was a tap on the door and Brodie came in with a laptop under his arm.

'Hope I'm not disturbing you, Mizz Stoo-art,' he began, uncertainly.

'Of course not,' Issy lied, politely. 'How can I help?' Damn, did she have to sound like a hotel receptionist or a stiff schoolmarm every time she spoke to him?

'My laptop isn't picking up a 4G signal.'

Issy burst out laughing at his optimism. '4G? Dream on. This is the Dead Zone – we're so close to sea level here that 3G wi-fi is only a pipe dream. You might do better with a bonfire and a blanket.'

'A what?' He looked at her, puzzled.

'For smoke signals? I would have thought that every red-blooded American would know how to use that means of communication. Don't cub scouts learn that at camp?'

'Only if they're re-enacting a James Fenimore Cooper novel,' he responded in a similar dry tone. 'Seriously, though, I have to make a couple of Skype calls.' He looked at his laptop and frowned, as if it had let him down. Issy knew that look – boys and their toys; hi-tech this and that - the answer to all their problems.

She was used to working from the cottage during her holidays, keeping in touch with her design team and holding conference calls with clients who wanted the particular brand of Scottish Baronial/Country House chic which was her forte. Her latest client – the last one for Ecosse Designs now she'd tendered her resignation, lived in Dubai and wanted it all. Tartan carpets and wallpaper, stags' heads, inglenook fireplaces, including the panelling, and mahogany staircase dismantled from a country house about to go under the hammer – all shipped over at eye-watering expense.

Issy called it the *Salmon Fishing in the Yemen* factor. The sheik had seen the movie and wanted some of that for himself. Hell, he'd even commissioned his own tartan and had the women's quarters decorated like Queen Victoria's sitting room at Balmoral. Not that Issy ever complained, the more difficult the commission, the greater the satisfaction when it was accomplished.

Unaware of this, Brodie, looked so downcast that Issy was tempted to prolong the moment. Hadn't he put *her* out of her bedroom two nights ago? Judging from the way he held himself, his confidence had slipped somewhat; it was obvious that he wasn't used to things not going according to plan. Then she relented, he was a long way from home and she knew the feelings of displacement and loneliness that being away from friends and family could produce. A skype call could make all the difference.

'Despite all evidence to the contrary,' she said matter-of-factly, 'you have entered a high-tech area. The cottage has a great wi-fi signal, courtesy of the signal booster my late father installed. Not to mention the newest laptops, tablets, and all kinds of technological gizmos which he deemed necessary for survival on Cormorant Island. Take this PC, for example, it's still at the prototype stage – he was working on it, right up until . . . until he died.'

It saddened her to think that her father would never see his latest baby become a technical reality. She looked over at the mainland, the houses brilliant white in the sunshine, the white crests on the waves out by the headland. How could the world keep turning and her father not be at its hub? Unutterably sad that she and her father had never understood each other, she zoned out and was lost in her thoughts for a few moments.

'Your late father . . .' Judging by his tone, Brodie appeared to be searching for words to make her feel better. That surprised her. 'Lindy explained that he was *the* James Stuart - of Stuart's (IT) Solutions? His work is his monument,' he said simply.

'Thanks.' Trying hard not to think about the urn in the window embrasure, Issy turned away from the scenery and back to Brodie. He took a step towards her and she thought for a moment he was going to lay his hand on her arm, consolingly. But he appeared to think better of it and nodded towards Esme's laptop instead. The laptop was light and ultra slim and belied the power of the processor behind the dull, battleship grey housing.

'Impressive,' was all he said. Then he added as though he was reading from a technical magazine: 'Your father was a giant in his field, his integrated processors revolutionised laptop and tablet construction.' Issy hid her smile. Like most men, Brodie shied away from the emotional towards the practical, the down to earth.

'Yes, my father hates – hated,' she corrected herself, coughing to hide the catch in her voice, 'out of date technology. Not to mention the whole shortbread and tartan tea towel image of Scotland peddled by the gift shops. And to a certain extent, me.'

'How's that?' he asked, puzzled.

'Oh, you know, going to unlikely corners of the globe and decking them out in Royal Stuart hunting tartan or the like. My last – latest commission,' she corrected herself, 'was for a sheik in the Emirates who wanted a full scale Scottish castle with all the trimmings erected in his backyard. Father would so not have approved.'

'Really. I would have thought bringing such a commission to life would require talent and vision.'

Issy looked at Brodie just to check he wasn't making fun of her. Satisfied, she continued, 'He wanted Scotland to go forward into the twenty-first century aware of its heritage but not held back by it. Scotland punches above its weight when it comes to scientific discoveries and inventions,' she added, having heard the argument since childhood.

'Penicillin, Body Scanners, television, the telephone . . .'

'More to us than deep fried Mars bars and faux highland bonnets complete with orange wigs, laddie.' She laughed to dispel the notion that she was preaching to him from the pulpit of Scottish Nationalism. Glancing in the direction Lindy had recently taken, she added, 'Although, hair doesn't come redder than *Lola's*. If she starts to bug you – and she will – tell her that her hair's the colour of Irn Bru.'

'Irn Bru?'

'A soft drink,' she explained.

'Soda. I get it.'

Issy glanced up, noting how the sunlight slanting in through the windows picked out the auburn threads in his hair and burnished them to copper. She blinked to make the after-image of Brodie framed against the light disappear. The air between them thickened and shimmered as they exchanged a smile, one weighed down by what wasn't being said.

'Do you have Scottish ancestry Mr – I mean, Brodie? Your

name and your colouring suggest that you do.' Then she faltered, *that* made it seem as if she'd been studying him and taking notes. If he noticed her gaffe, he was gentleman enough not to show it.

'Scottish? Nah. My family roots are more Cajun – Louisiana French, than Caledonian.' He steered the conversation away from himself, something he seemed quite adept at. 'As for *Brodie,* I think my mother got it from a novel she was reading while pregnant.'

'Yet, here you are. In Scotland. Do you mind if I ask *why*?'

At last – the thousand-dollar question.

He put his laptop down on the window seat, pushed her books and portfolio to one side and sat next to them. He turned his head away and looked out towards Jamestoun. Issy wondered if that was a deliberate move on his part, a ploy to hide his expression when he gave his answer.

All the better to lie to her, perhaps?

'Sure, you can ask why. But first, you gotta tell me what a deep fried Mars Bar is.'

Issy laughed. 'It's a thick chocolate bar, coated in batter and then cooked in a deep fat fryer. Sounds revolting but is strangely delicious, about once every – oh, five years or so. Don't worry, it's not on the menu tonight but I think you should try one next time you're passing the chippy.'

'Chippy? Oh, I get it – the chip shop, right? The Mars Bar thing sounds a whole lot like deep fried banana sandwiches.'

'Who could have guessed that our two great nations were also united through a common desire for artery-blocking desserts? Elvis and Rab C Nesbit, soul brothers; who knew?' Apparently, that was a cultural reference too far, and she waved her whimsical sentence away with a flick of her wrist.

'Yeah, who knew?' This time he turned and grinned, an amused light dancing in his eyes.

'So,' Issy drew him back to their earlier conversation. 'What brings you to a windswept island where cormorants outnumber the inhabitants ten to one?'

There it was again, that slight hesitation before he answered, leaving Issy with the impression that he was weighing his words carefully. She suspected that whatever he revealed in his next breath would only be half of the story. Where that feeling had sprung from, she couldn't say, but she couldn't dismiss it. Even if Brodie's reply came back smooth as silk and carried with it a thousand kilowatt smile.

'I work in the bio-chemistry industry, researching new ways of treating polluted marine environments – especially coral reefs, without destroying the delicate macro system those reefs depend upon for survival. You could say that I'm kinda the *King of Plankton*.' He laughed as if this was a tried and tested joke and waited for her response.

'All very laudable,' Issy murmured, wondering how her chosen career as an interior designer could compete with that! Not that she was about to apologise to *him* for her talent in sourcing rare/vintage fabrics and early versions of plaid, instead of saving coral reefs. She had plans aplenty for her future life on *Eilean na Sgairbh* – and plankton played no part in them. 'And?' she prompted.

'It's been on my bucket list to swim in Scottish coastal waters warmed by the Gulf Stream, down a dram of single malt produced in a local distillery and to eat freshly caught langoustines in a harbour restaurant where the nearest landfall, to the west, is America.'

'You've come to the right place. Thanks to my father's ingenuity, you can keep in touch with your team back in the lab – and with your family.' She raised a questioning eyebrow at 'family', encouraging him to enlighten her further on the subject.

Instead, he skirted round the issue.

'You mean I *can* get a signal?' he asked, as if she'd fast forwarded several centuries and brought him into the here and now.

'Of course. Maybe not 4G – and taking into account the time difference between here and . . .' She paused slightly, allowing him to fill in the gap. 'Kentucky? Wasn't that where you said you hailed from?'

He came back with, 'More East Coast, actually,' just a little too quickly for her liking.

'Ah . . .' Well, that explained why his accent was more Upper Class American than Kentucky Fried Chicken.

'I figure they'll be waking up, round about now'. They glanced at their watches and then at each other. The silence lengthened between them before Brodie broke it. 'Wi-fi code?'

'Of course.'

Issy rooted in the desk drawer and brought out the small ring-bound notebook containing all Esme's passwords for Twitter,

Facebook, Instagram and so on. She wrote down the code on a Post-it and handed it to him.

'I'll do it later when I've had a chance to go through the photographs I've taken of the island,' he said, looking down at the piece of paper thoughtfully.

'Whatever.' Issy felt dismissed by him. As if he'd got what he came for and had no further need to prolong their conversation, or be sociable. The need to be alone overwhelmed her – God, was she developing a Greta Garbo complex?

'Thanks.' Another one of his kilowatt smiles.

'No problem. Dinner will be at seven thirty, if that suits?'

Too bad if it doesn't, her tight smile implied, and the brief moment of rapport was gone.

'Suits me fine.' With that he left Issy to contemplate the view and to wonder why a small worm of unease was eating away at her innards.

And why - if he was a marine biologist who probably spent most of his time looking at plankton and bleached-out bits of coral reef under microscopes - did he have the arms and upper body muscles of someone who could wrestle a giant squid into submission?

'Curioser and curioser,' she said under her breath as he closed the study door behind him.

Chapter Nine
Bambino Mio Caro

Issy decided to eat dinner in the sitting room the following evening, leaving Lindy and Brodie alone in the kitchen. When Esme had paying guests, Lindy was hired as chief cook and bottle washer. The deal relieved Esme of the tedium of domestic duties and Lindy received cash-in-hand which went straight into her 'running away fund.' Running away from Cormorant Island, that is – and in the general direction of Las Vegas, if her latest madcap scheme was to be believed.

Issy tutted and shook her head as she ate her pasta. Lindy had turned up for evening duties in skinny jeans and a t-shirt. So far, so respectable. However, the t-shirt was two sizes too small and bore the legend: *don't knock it 'til you've tried it.* No prizes for guessing what 'it' was. When Lindy tied on a 1950's style frilled pinafore and started batting lash extensions at Brodie, Issy left the kitchen before she brought up her dinner.

So, here she was on a Tuesday night in high summer, sitting in the bay window of the sitting room, feet up on the window ledge and eating pasta alla carbonara off a lap tray, with a parrot for company.

At her age, she should be livin' the Vida Loca. Not that the Vida Loca was easy to find on *Eilean na Sgairbh*. Even the eponymous cormorants were fewer in number as the years passed, voting with their wings if not their feet, moving on to rocky outcrops and feeding grounds anew. Just like any islanders with get up and go and an ambition to make something of themselves.

'*Want some. Want some,*' Pershing said from behind Issy, sliding sideways along his perch with all the panache of a heavy-footed ballerina. Evoking no response, he gave Issy a winsome over-the-shoulder look, before adding: '*Eat up big man.*'

Issy grimaced. She had a vision of Lindy saying the same thing to Brodie as she spooned food into his mouth, whilst making a noise like an airplane coming into land.

Argh!

'She's going to drive me crazy, Pershing. Know that? The sooner our resident Yank moves into the eco-lodge, the happier I'll be.' She threw a piece of pasta onto the floor of Pershing's cage and the parrot slid off its perch to forage for it. In search of peace of mind, Issy turned back to the view and watched the setting sun leave a burning path from the horizon to the shore. The ribbon of beaten gold across the causeway looked so real, she could almost believe it was possible to walk along it. She stared until her eyes ached and the image was left behind her eyelids when she closed them.

She wanted peace, closure - but peace eluded her. The acrimonious phone conversation with Jack Innes-Kerr had upset her more than she cared to admit, even to herself. Finishing her pasta, she reached over for the glass of red wine perched precariously on the window ledge. Maybe she'd find the answer to her dilemmas at the bottom of the glass. She frowned – *that* would be easier to achieve if she knew what she was seeking. At times, it felt as if she was searching for herself, the *real* Ishabel Stuart – whoever she might be.

But – how would she recognise this changeling when she found her? She'd been sober, hardworking – and, yes, *boring* - Issy Stuart for so long, it was hard to change.

Her mobile rang and she reached down to the floor for it, heart beating at the thought of it being Jack Innes-Kerr. Perhaps simply thinking about him had conjured up his presence. After their last conversation, she'd blocked him on her phone - but it would be just like him to use a different phone in order to get through. She really wasn't in the mood for more of his lies . . .

A quick glance at caller ID revealed a problem of a different nature.

'Hello, Mother,' she said warily.

'Carissima,' her mother crooned and then launched into Italian. 'How are you? Why don't you phone me, Ishabel? What have I – your Mother – ever done to offend you?'

It would have given Issy immense satisfaction to ask, *how long have you got*? Instead she answered with commendable calm: 'I've been busy, Mother. Organising Father's funeral, remember?'

'Of course I remember, Issy. How could I forget that my husband had died?'

Again, Issy resisted the urge to say: *pretty easily, actually, considering that you've lived apart for the last twenty-odd years; didn't attend his cremation or ring to ask how I was coping with his death.*

Oblivious to her daughter's less than enthusiastic greeting, Isabella rattled on: 'You are so harsh with me, your own mother,' Issy heard her sniff prettily. No doubt into a lace-edged handkerchief embroidered with her initials and drenched in Acqua di Parma *Amalfi Fig*. She assumed that her mother had an audience because she was definitely playing to the gallery. Doubtless, surrounded by her entourage who fawned over her and hung on her every word. Or, possibly a new admirer besotted with Isabella Tartaruga, the opera singer.

Or, as her legion of fans the world over knew her - La Bella Scozzese - The Beautiful Scottish One.

'To be honest, Mother, I've been too busy to ring you. I've had to organize Father's memorial service, on my own, as Esme is away from home. Mungo, the minister of the local kirk, is coming to see me tomorrow morning to finalise arrangements. '

'Pah. A man of your Father's standing, having a memorial service in that awful *wee kirk*.' She swapped her Italian accent for one which identified where she'd been born and bred – Dumbarton, just outside Glasgow. 'It should have been held in St Giles Cathedral in Edinburgh. But, at least, we'll be holding your wedding there at Christmas,' she said, slightly mollified.

'We both know that isn't what he wanted,' Issy said tightly and in passable Italian to get her mother back on track. She thought it best not to mention her broken engagement, La Bella Scozzese had a soft spot for Jack Innes-Kerr. She sighed, knowing what was coming next and pictured her Mother wrinkling her nose.

'Your accent is appalling, darling. You must come to stay at the villa and have some lessons to improve it.'

'Okay, when?' Issy asked, calling Isabella's bluff.

Isabella lived close to Milan where she performed her interpretation of the Bel Canto - Donizetti, Rossini and Bellini at the world-famous opera house, La Scala. She had a habit of issuing invitations to stay at her villa in the Tuscan Hills and then forgetting she'd asked her friends over. Famously, Issy had turned up on her mother's doorstep, only to be informed that la Signora had left that morning for New York, where she was performing Donizetti's *Lucia di Lammermoor* at the Met. And she wouldn't be back for several weeks!

New York, London, Paris – it didn't really matter. Isabella Tartaruga was unreliable and her daughter was in no mood for playing her mind games tonight.

'When? Oh, Cara – if only it were that simple. Let me consult Maddelena and my diary.' It went quiet on the other end of the phone. Issy could hear Maddelena, her mother's PA, rustling through the pages of the giant dairy she carried everywhere – and her mother snapping out: *pronto, pronto.* 'Ah, but I remember why I rang you now,' her mother changed the subject before a date could be fixed. 'My schedule allows me to attend your father's memorial service on my way to New York. So, could you make a room ready for me and inform that Mongo person –'

'Mungo,' Issy corrected automatically. 'The Minister of that *awful wee kirk* you mentioned earlier?'

'Whatever he's called,' her mother said dismissively. 'Tell him your father's *bereft* widow will be in attendance and to reserve me a seat on the front row.'

'Mother, it's a church service, not the first night of Tosca.'

Issy pictured her mother tossing back her luxurious black hair; the self-same hair she'd passed on to her daughter. However, whereas La Bella Scozzese had dark brown eyes and a smooth, olive skin reflecting her Italian ancestry, Issy was blessed with the colouring of her Stuart ancestors: bright blue eyes and skin so pale she spent a fortune on Factor 30 sunblock. Good thing she lived in Scotland where the midges caused more problems than the sun, she thought, as her mother rattled on in her usual inconsequential fashion. She'd burn to a crisp in a warmer climate.

In order to survive her mother's phone calls, Issy had learned to zone out and just pick up on crucial words and phrases, as and when they came along. However, Isabella's next sentence made her sit bolt upright and take notice.

'Tell Mungo I'll be performing your Father's favourite aria from *Turandot* at the service. I was singing the lead role at the Edinburgh Festival when I first met your father.' She feigned distress and a telling little sob snagged her voice. Actually, Isabella had been busking in the street with some other music students during the

Edinburgh Festival when James Stuart had seen her and been instantly smitten – but Issy let that pass. Her mother preferred the biography dreamed up by her PR team.

Issy rushed on, 'I don't think your turning up for the memorial service is a good idea. Or singing a Puccini aria. It's very Low Church here – it wouldn't go down well. *The Lord's My Shepherd* to the tune of *Crimond* is what Father requested.'

'I am your father's wife.' Isabella must have felt Issy's pause as well as heard it, because she went on. 'We may not have lived together as man and wife for a number of years . . .'

'Twenty-five to be precise,' Issy supplied helpfully.

'But I have a right to be there,' La Bella Scozzese insisted.

Issy wanted to say that Isabella had *no* rights where she or her father were concerned, but held her peace. Issy was named after her, which was as far as it went – her mother was totally lacking in maternal instinct, or wifely sentiment. The strange thing was, James Stuart had never taken steps to divorce her, and she had kept her marriage vows, in name at least, even if suitors were queuing at her door.

Perhaps it suited them both that way? James too stubborn to let her go; Isabella too Catholic to consider divorce. Like the good Presbyterian he was, James had refused to convert to Catholicism and they'd married in the Edinburgh register office. Isabella was wont to blame their estrangement on the fact it hadn't been a 'proper marriage ceremony', or had the blessing of the church.

Her broken marriage, she insisted, had nothing to do with her disenchantment with marriage, domestic duties, a demanding toddler – and her ambition to be the best soprano the opera world had ever seen. Opera scouts had heard her sing, offered to train her voice in Milan. Fame and fortune had beckoned and Isabella was cute enough to know that she would never get another chance if she turned this opportunity down.

She left England as Isabella Stuart and emerged from a strict training regime a year later as Isabella Tartaruga - and the legend of the Diva from Dumbarton was born.

To Issy, James Stuart's love of opera always seemed at odds with his driven, work-orientated personality. Yet, one night she'd surprised him in his office listening to La Bella Scozzese singing *One Fine Day/Un Bel Di Vedremo* from *Madama Butterfly* - on his state-of-the-art sound system, naturally. She felt sure she'd seen him dash a tear from his eye, unaware that he was being observed from the doorway.

Love; actually, there was no accounting for it.

'Very well,' Issy conceded wearily, returning to the conversation. 'But very low key and dignified. No singing. No three-ring circus and,' she added as an afterthought, '*definitely* no cameras or film crew. It's a funeral, not a promotional opportunity for your next concert.'

'How could a child of mine have such cold blood in her veins? I blame your Presbyterian upbringing, crazy Aunt Esme and that dreadful climate. You have been denied the warm sun of the south and it has turned you into an icicle.' That made Issy laugh. Her mother was such a *diva* – almost comically so. Over the years, Issy had grown up, and outgrown her mother; Isabella's casual indifference no longer had the power to hurt her. In fact, lately, she'd felt their roles were reversed – *she,* exasperated by her mother's behaviour, as one might be with an attention-seeking child.

'Okay. I'll email Maddelena with the times, etc. The wake will be held at the cottage. VERY simple, no fuss. Got it?'

'Si, ciao Cara. I will see you soon and I will do as you have asked.' Somehow, Issy doubted it. 'Now, before you hang up – *e come sta il mio tesoro* Jack? You are so lucky, Ishabel, to have such a handsome and attentive fiancé.'

Issy gave a noncommittal reply and wondered what her mother would think of her wonderful ex-fiancé if she knew what he'd been up to. Knowing her mother, she would probably give an expressive shrug of her slim shoulders – *overweight divas are so last millennium, Cara* – and excuse his playing away from home as something men did. Something, Issy would have to get used to when she married Jack Innes-Kerr. She'd been boxing above her weight to 'land' *il mio tesoro Jack* in the first place, as her mother had been quick to point out.

Issy tried to forget the embarrassing phone calls during which her mother had outlined, in graphic detail, what a woman had to do in order to hold onto her man. As far as her mother was concerned, Scots knew nothing about sex; leave it to the Italians. In her view, Love and a Cold Climate simply didn't mix.

Unusually, however, today Isabella Tartaruga picked up on her daughter's diffidence.

'A lover's tiff? I can sense it.'

'That's one description for it.'

Issy tried to block from her mind the scene she'd walked in on when she'd returned to her office after hours to fetch her iPad. Unfortunately, Jack having noisy and enthusiastic sex with Suzy the intern over *her* desk was an image that simply refused to go away. She looked down at her naked left hand, musing how strange it felt not to have her diamond engagement ring to twist round on her finger when she was agitated.

Like now . . . for example.

'*Una tempest in un bicchier d'acqua,*' her mother laughed. 'Or as you British say – a storm in a teacup. Pre-wedding nerves, nothing more.'

You British!

It really got to Issy that her mother pretended she was more Italian than Botticelli's *Venus.* When it was on record that the Tartarugas had owned a fish and chip café/ice cream parlour in Dumbarton.

'Look, Mum,' she said, feeling like a deflated balloon. Conversations with her mother had that effect. 'I have to go. I'll coordinate everything with Maddelena. Okay?'

'Si.' Then the connection was broken, as if La Bella Scozzese had tired of the conversation. Or had got what she wanted with regard to the memorial service. Issy sighed – when it came to manipulation and emotional blackmail, Isabella made Machiavelli look like a rank amateur. Issy gave thanks for the fact that, over the years, she'd built a defensive wall round her heart. One which her mother no longer had the power to breach.

Added to that, she was grateful that her mother hadn't asked searching questions about her errant fiancé – or, *Darling Jack,* as her mother was wont to call him. *That* would take more explanation than she had time for right now.

Maybe she really did have ice in her veins; or perhaps she'd never found a man capable of bringing her to the heights and depths of passion so beloved by romantics and opera buffs the world over.

'Pershing, bambino bello - we don't think so, do we?'

Pershing responded with another of his favourite phrases. *'Shuddupyerface.'*

Good advice. Getting to her feet, Issy tickled his head through the bars, picked up her empty plate and glass and went through to the kitchen.

She skidded to a halt on the threshold in the manner of a cartoon character.

Her mind had been so preoccupied by her mother that, momentarily, she'd forgotten about their resident American. Seeing him drinking *the blood red wine,* alone, at the kitchen table caused an involuntary 'Oh', to escape. Realising that, once again, she must appear unforgivably rude, Issy covered up her exclamation with a cough.

'No *Lola?*' she asked, glancing round the room.

'Some friends rang to say they were meeting at the local pub.' He let the word roll around his tongue as if it was unfamiliar and quaint to his ears. 'She's gone to join them. She did invite me, *but*,' he put heavy emphasis on the word and gave her a long look. One which made her spine tingle in a quite unexpected fashion.

'But?' she prompted. Surely – surely, he hadn't stayed in on her account? She turned away to hide the colour sweeping across her face. He soon put the record straight.

'I'm still a tad jet lagged. Plus - and, don't get me wrong here, Lola's a great kid . . .'

'I'm guessing, you've had your *Lola* quota for the day?' Issy gained control over her embarrassing tendency to blush whenever she was close to Brodie. She had the strangest feeling that he wanted something from her – but what that 'something' might be, she had no idea. They exchanged a humorous, conspiratorial look which made Issy's internal temperature gauge soar dangerously into the red for a second time.

'Guess so. Anyhow, what's with the whole *Lola* thing?'

Issy was glad of the excuse to clear the table because she could hide her expression, collect her thoughts and regain her poise under the guise of being busy and efficient. Conversations with her mother unnerved and unsettled her. There was a real possibility of La Bella Scozzese turning up at the memorial service and causing a scene, she'd have to factor that into her ever expanding To Do List . . . memorial and wake, scattering of the ashes, and returning to Edinburgh to wind up her life there – avoiding ex-fiancé, if possible.

'Miss Stoo-art? Ma'am . . .' Seemingly, from a distance, she heard Brodie repeat his question. She made a conscious effort to drag her thoughts back into the room. 'Lola?'

'Oh, *Lola*,' she breathed heavily, wondering where to begin. 'Lindy wants to go to Vegas to work as a croupier in one of the big casinos. She figured that she needed a stage name and chose *Lola*. She's started using it so that she can grow into the role. Barry Manilow has a lot to answer for.' That came out more waspishly than she intended, so she tempered it with: 'I dread to think of what she'll get up to once she's off the leash. We will probably never know. How does the saying go? *What Happens in Vegas –*'

'*Stays in Vegas*?' Brodie finished.

'Something like that.'

Brodie looked out over The Narrows, backlit by the brilliant sunset. Esme's shadowy kitchen seemed a long way from the neon lights of the Sunset Strip. Light lazered through the window, touching his hair and deepening its coppery tones. In that moment, Issy forgot her problems, overwhelmed instead by an impulse to stretch out her hand and touch it. Sensibly, she resisted, curling her fingers into her palm to make a fist. She remembered her aunt's warning: *They have long memories on Eilean na Sgairbh.* She didn't doubt it for a second; however, she had plans to make, plans which didn't include an entanglement with a summer visitor.

'It's beautiful here,' Brodie said, unaware of her tumultuous thoughts. He turned away from the sunset and returned to their previous conversation. 'Lindy's a smart kid - needs to spread her wings, wouldn't you say?'

'I agree.' Issy sat down at the table and pushed a dirty plate aside. 'However, she hasn't even been to London and has only visited Edinburgh a couple of times. I wish she'd start spreading her wings somewhere nearer home, then if everything turns pear-shaped we can fetch her back.'

'Maybe she won't need rescuing,' Brodie suggested.

'Maybe she will,' Issy countered. 'In any case, this is all rather academic. Every time Lindy's 'running away fund' has enough in the jar to buy an air ticket to . . . wherever,' she spread her hands wide. 'Some emergency crops up, she has to dip into it – and it's back to square one.'

The look they exchanged demonstrated they'd both reached the same conclusion. Lindy might seem ballsy and full of chutzpah, but beneath all the bluster she was just a scared kid, fearful of the change which moving to Las Vegas - or wherever -would require. Fearful, too, of spending her life on *Eilean na Sgairbh* and looking back one day full of regret for what might have been. Perhaps, the real reason her 'running away' fund never reached the magical one thousand pounds mark was because it gave her a 'get out clause'. Just as she was on the brink of leaving, lack of funds anchored her to the windswept island of *Eilean na Sgairbh* for another year.

'Tell me if I'm talking out of turn here . . .' He pushed his chair back from the table and carried his supper things over to the dishwasher.

'Go on.'

'Lindy says you've got some high-powered job in a posh Interior Design business, right?' He said 'posh' in the same faux Lowland Scottish accent he'd used for 'pub'.

'High-powered when measured against manning the Post Office and helping change Esme's beds – yes.' She wondered where he was going with this. What else had Lindy told this astute American? Things, perhaps, which Issy didn't want him to know?

'Why don't you loan her the money, set her free? Call her bluff if you like? Or would your fiancé object to that?'

Fiancé? Issy's blood ran ice cold at the mention of the word but she maintained a calm exterior. There were no secrets on Cormorant Island and it seemed that *Lola* had been very free with her information. But at least breaking off her engagement was still classified information – and she meant to keep it that way, for as long as she could. 'First of all, I don't have to run everything past my – my fiancé; and second of all - I don't think Lindy's pride would allow her to accept my help.' She stood up and made her way over to the pantry with those items which weren't destined for the dishwasher. 'Get out clause number two.'

'Okay.' He held up his hands in surrender. 'I crossed a boundary there. I get it. Just to say . . .' He forestalled her as she made her way towards the back door and her car which Lindy had left badly parked earlier that day.

'Yes?'

'That if Lindy did make it over there to Las Vegas and things didn't work out, I'd make it my business to bring *Lola* home.' That was so unexpected that Issy stood on the threshold of the door, hand glued to the handle, tears pricking her eyes. She'd been rude to this man, made it clear he was unwanted. Yet, here he was, prepared to play the part of the Seventh Cavalry should Lindy need rescuing, thousands of miles away from home. Her expression must have said it all, because he added, 'I'm a nice guy. We just got off to a bad start, is all.' He crossed the room in three easy strides and stood in front of her. 'And in case you are wondering if I have any ulterior motives where Lindy's concerned . . .'

'Of course I don't,' she blustered, blushing afresh at his ability to read minds. She felt like an ancient maiden aunt trying to keep the feisty heroine from a Regency pot boiler – *The Yankee Duke and the English Virgin* - under control and away from the dashing rake.

'Sure you do. You don't know me from Adam. She's a smart kid and reminds me of my sister - that's what attracts me to her. Nothing more.'

Silence lengthened between them. Issy felt sure he was about to say: Whereas you, Mizz Stoo-art, intrigue me in an entirely different way. However, he kept his counsel and gave one of his charming smiles instead. The one which made her stomach lurch unexpectedly and adrenaline shoot through her in a quite unwelcome and unasked-for manner.

'Fine.' Issy rubbed at a spot between her eyebrows with two fingers. Her mind was a jumble – first her mother and now *this*. She could feel the onset of one of the tension headaches she suffered from, soon electric blue zig-zag lines would appear in her line of vision, and she'd be forced to take to her bed. The last thing she wanted. Time to make a swift exit, drive to the far end of the island where she could watch the sunset in peace, away from Brodie; away from everyone. Have space to breathe freely and sort out the turmoil in her mind.

When she next glanced at Brodie he had extended his hand. 'Friends?' he asked.

Her muddled brain took a few seconds to realise what was required of her. 'If you like,' she shrugged. Clearly this wasn't quite the answer Brodie was looking for as he kept his hand extended between them. 'Very well,' she sighed and put her hand in his. It fitted perfectly, his large and warm and hers small-boned and cold as ice. Within seconds, some of his warmth transferred to her cold fingers and as he shifted his hand to grasp hers more tightly, his fingernail grazed across her palm. Sexual awareness scudded through Issy's veins, making her start, momentarily. Brodie must have felt the rush, experienced the same jolt of awareness because he released her hand as thought the touch of her flesh against his was too much to bear.

Moving away, he pulled his t-shirt down over his jeans, raked his hand through his hair and let out a long breath. When he turned to face her, he had possession of himself once more.

'Okay. Go do whatever it is that's burning away at you. I'll clear up here, then I'm gonna Skype my family.'

Issy didn't stop to wonder if a paying guest should be clearing away supper. Running out of the kitchen, she climbed into her Mini and gunned it out of the yard, leaving purse, mobile phone, house keys, confusion, and spinning gravel in her wake.

Chapter Ten
Mungo Park, I Presume?

Issy was hard at work in one of the outhouses and covered in dust and cobwebs when Mungo Park, the Presbyterian Minister who would conduct her father's memorial service, came calling. He walked over to where she was dragging an old whisky still from the back of the outhouse into the light.

'I'm guessing this is pretty old,' the minister said, giving Issy a hand.

'I found it at the back of the outhouse covered in sacking and a tarpaulin, with a load of other junk. God knows how long it's been there. Oops, sorry,' she said, referring to her casual use of 'God'.'

'Dinnae fash yourself lassie,' the minister laughed. 'He is everywhere and knows everything. Well, what a find,' he added, walking round the still. 'It looks very collectible - and I would imagine, very valuable.'

Issy rubbed at the copper cylinder's coils and tubes with an old rag, revealing bright metal and a temperature gauge whose calibrations were still readable.

'Straight out of *Antiques Roadshow!* My father must have

hidden it at the back out of the way, years ago. I never noticed it before today. As I'm sure you know, he was very much against alcohol – the *demon drink* and all that . . .' She brought a duster out of her jeans pocket and wiped her hands. 'It was the main reason he refused to rebuild Twa Burns distillery, although he could easily have afforded to. Back in the day the islanders drank more whisky than tea and alcoholism was rife. Your church tried to limit their consumption but thanks to Twa Burns Distillery, whisky was cheap and plentiful.'

'It took a German bomb to achieve what the church could not?'

'Quite. Father saw it as an act of God - although it destroyed the family business and killed many islanders, including his mother. Shall we?' She led the way back across the yard and into the kitchen.

'We had many a discussion about it,' the minister went on. 'I felt that rebuilding the distillery would bring much needed employment to the island and maybe stop another generation from leaving. I reminded James that Jesus turned water into wine at the wedding in Canaan and that whisky has been a vital part of highland life as far back as anyone can remember. But he wouldn't change his mind.'

'That was my father,' she said. 'Everything black and white and with no shades of grey in between.'

'Yet,' the minister continued thoughtfully, 'he was one of the first to welcome me to *Eilean na Sgairbh* when the congregation was – caught on the back foot, shall we say, at finding themselves being preached to by a minister whose family had emigrated from Nigeria a generation earlier.'

'A very lucky congregation in my opinion,' Issy countered, giving the minister a straight look. Mungo Park, his wife Gillian and their children had assimilated into island life over the last ten years and worked wonders with the local community. They'd built up their congregation, encouraged summer visitors to attend the lively family service and campaigned to keep the village school open. Then she went on, 'I've always wondered - how did you come by your name? I'm assuming that you *aren't* a direct descendant of the Scottish explorer who navigated the river Niger back in –'

'Seventeen ninety-six? No way. Although, it is quite a story,' he said as Issy poured out two coffees. 'When my parents emigrated to the UK in the seventies, they ended up in Glasgow as many émigrés before them had done.'

'Like my Italian grandparents . . .'

'They had Christian forenames – Rebecca and James, but a Nigerian surname *Anikulapo-Kutis* - which no one could pronounce, let alone spell. When my brother and I came along, they decided to give us Anglicised names. Or should that be Scottish-ised names? I was christened Mungo Park Anikulapo-Kutis after Saint Mungo, the patron saint of Glasgow and in honour of the man who discovered the river Niger.'

'I always wonder about that, you know. People 'finding' something that was already there,' Issy grinned at him over the rim of her coffee cup.

'I suppose you could say, he drew it to the attention of

Europeans? My brother, David Livingstone Anikulapo-Kutis, is named after the great Scottish explorer and Christian missionary. I only use my Nigerian surname on official documents nowadays - *Mungo Park* rolls off the tongue more easily. And most people, although they don't realise it, already know the name – an echo of their school days.'

'Ah …' Issy pushed the biscuit tin over to him. 'That explains it. But, I've always wondered how you came to be minister at our wee kirk.' Her direct look suggested to Mungo that she thought him destined for greater things.

'Gillian, the weans and I, all like it here and I'd love nothing more than to see the island thriving as it once did. I've been offered different parishes over the years – but we've made *Eilean na Sgairbh* our home. And unless the Church deems otherwise, here we shall stay.'

It was on the tip of Issy's tongue to tell him about her plans for converting the outhouses into workshops where artists could hire space to make and then sell their work to tourists. A mini version of the Balnakeil Craft Village in Durness she'd visited earlier that year. But, today wasn't about her, it was about finalising the details of her father's memorial service - and warning Mungo about possible 'incoming', in the form of her mother.

'Mungo – a bit of a problem has arisen. My mother wants to attend the memorial service.'

'La Bella Scozzese? Gillian and I are great fans; we heard her sing in Edinburgh years ago, before she was really well known. Her

Tosca is legendary. . . '

'As is her propensity for hogging the limelight and – to put it bluntly, showing off.'

'I'm sure we can accommodate her,' Mungo said evenly. 'In my Father's house there are many mansions,' he quoted. 'Apart from which, she has a right to be there, as your mother and James' widow. Your father left specific instructions on how his memorial service is to be conducted. I'll be keeping to his Order of Service and respecting those wishes – it's not open to interpretation or negotiation. By anyone.'

Issy sent him a fond, wry look. He didn't know her mother. Then Mungo's words hit home – it was typical of her father to have ensured everything was stitched up and decided, without involving or consulting her.

'Thanks, I didn't know,' was all she said.

'Don't take it personally Ishabel; it was just another example of James being – James.'

'Like not telling me he'd been having tests, or how ill he was; and then my having to fly home from Japan on the red eye when he had his heart attack? He died, alone, at his desk. Do you have any idea how that makes me feel?' her voice snagged. The image of her father slumped over his desk, his hand reaching out for the telephone and no one coming to his aid, haunted her.

'Perhaps he kept how ill he was from you, because he wanted to spare you pain and anxiety?' Mungo suggested.

Issy shook her head. 'Just another example of his need to control everyone and everything.' Then she gave herself a shake. Now wasn't the time or the place to rake over her relationship with her father. 'The service?' she prompted.

'Plain, simple and with no fuss.'

Amen to that, Issy thought. She pushed the biscuit tin towards the minister and took another chocolate digestive herself. They'd need to keep their blood sugar levels up if her mother stuck to her promise to attend the memorial service!

Half an hour later, Issy waved the minister off and walked through into the inner hall.

Walking past the study, she noticed the door was ajar. She could've sworn she'd closed it behind her earlier that morning.

Inside the study, directly opposite the door into the hall, a mirror hung on the far wall over the fireplace. In it, she could see Brodie using his mobile phone to photograph old family pictures which were scattered all around the room. He also snapped faded posters from her aunt's glory days in the CND; including one of Esme as a member of the *Glasgow Eskimos* who'd tried to block Dunoon harbour and the Polaris Fleet with their canoes in the early sixties. Next, he took the family bible off the bookcase and photographed its end papers where generations of Stuart births, marriages and deaths were meticulously recorded.

Finally, he picked up a photograph of two young soldiers in the uniform of the Cameron Highlanders, circa 1914, flipped it over and photographed the piece of paper stuck on its reverse. Almost as if he'd known it'd be there. His actions were systematic and purposeful, and Issy backed off into the hall, keen for him to remain unaware that she'd been observing him.

'You can have a bath tomorrow. If you're good, Pershing,' she called over her shoulder to the parrot in the sitting room.

'*Wanta bath. Wanta bath*,' the parrot chorused, gamely joining in with her subterfuge. '*Inaminute.*'

'Yes. Inaminute,' Issy agreed. Then she walked into the study and feigned surprise at finding Brodie there. 'Brodie! You gave me quite a turn.' But not as great as the one she'd given him, if his guilty start was anything to judge by.

'Sorry, Mizz Stoo-art – I was browsing your aunt's library in the hope of finding something to read. Quite a collection.' He slipped his mobile casually into his back pocket. Esme encouraged her guests to help themselves to her library of books during their stay and to leave behind those books they'd read as a fair exchange. These days, most people brought a kindle on holiday. But they were always keen to read a well-thumbed book sitting by Esme's coal fire in the front room when summer squalls battered the windows.

'Yes?' She wasn't going to make this easy for him.

'So, tell me, what's with the charred copy of *Lady Chatterley's Lover* on the book stand?' He picked up the old paperback and fanned its pages. The edges were scorched, as if they'd been in a fire. Issy took it from him, ran her fingertips over the singed orange cover and then replaced it on the small wooden easel which doubled as a book stand.

'It's a first edition. In 1960 Esme and a couple of university friends hitchhiked down to London and queued outside Foyles for hours in order to buy a copy. Esme looked younger than her years and, apparently, the assistant was reluctant to sell a copy to her until she produced her driving licence.' She laughed at the thought of Esme the pocket rocket standing her ground back in the days when Feminism and Women's Lib were but a pipe dream.

'She's quite a girl, huh?' Brodie said, admiration in his voice.

'Esme said that most of the other customers were *men,*' Issy said, as if they were a species not to be trusted, and sent him a look. Taking the book down from its stand, he subjected it to a second, more thorough, scrutiny.

'How come it's burned at the edges?' Brodie asked.

Knowing Esme didn't like the book being manhandled, Issy took a step closer to Brodie to retrieve it. He smelled of newly washed hair, clean clothes and a subtle, lemony aftershave. Holding the book in his palm, he caressed the cover with long, tanned fingers. Issy was taken back to the other night when they'd shaken hands, and remembered the warm touch of skin on skin. Despite being distrustful of his motives, she was mesmerised by the slow circling of his thumb over the phoenix in the centre of the cover. Her eyes travelled upwards, past his lightly freckled knuckles and traced the fine auburn hair on his wrists and arms. When she finally drew her gaze away, Brodie was looking at her with a steady beat, waiting for her answer.

There was something about this man that set warning bells

jangling in her head. It wasn't just his obvious physical attributes, too charming smile and easy, open manner. Nor was it the expensive, casual clothes he wore, as if playing the part of a well-heeled Yank on holiday in Scotland. No. There was more to it – to *him* - she was convinced of it. He wasn't just another tourist blown on to Cormorant Island on the back of a storm wind.

He was – well, what *was* he exactly?

Too cocksure of himself, too calm and unruffled and aware that as far as women were concerned he was catnip. It bothered her that no matter how rude or offhand she acted towards him, he kept coming back for more. It wasn't natural. He had an agenda, she was sure of it, a secret one at that. There was dark purpose to his photographing the pictures and the inside of the family bible, she felt it in her water. She didn't know what, but she'd make it her business to find out.

'What does the forward slash between the three and the six signify?' Brodie asked, bringing her back to his earlier question about the fire-damaged paperback.

'Oh that. It separates the shillings from the pennies, the book cost three shillings and sixpence. That's about thirty-five pence in today's money.' She took the book off him for a second time. Somehow, Brodie holding the former inflammatory and sexually explicit text unnerved her. It brought to mind an image she'd rather forget – Jack Innes-Kerr's pale white buttocks rising and falling as he brought Suzy the intern to orgasm over her desk. Issy's mouth pulled up at one corner as she considered that final affront – could he not, at least, have rogered the ambitious intern over his own desk?

Or was that the point of the exercise?

The image was burned into the synapses of her brain. Remembering it made her feel sick.

'Esme hid the book under her mattress knowing that her brother, my father, would go ape shit if he found it . . .' she faltered, losing her train of thought. *'Is it a book you would wish your wife or servants to read?'* she intoned the original judge's words, focusing on the book until the wave of nausea passed and the ringing in her ears diminished.

'Hey. You okay? You've gone very pale. Here, sit down and I'll fetch you some water.'

Issy waved away his concern but did allow him to guide her over to the window seat. Restored by the warmth of the sun on her back, she carried on with the story.

'Father found the book and tossed it onto the back of the fire in a fit of Episcopalian outrage. Esme rescued it from the flames and ran out of the house with a scorched paperback and badly burned hands – she still has the scars. She hid the book in the outhouses until after grandfather's death.'

'After his death – is that significant in some way?' Unlike Jack Innes-Kerr, Brodie was interested in Stuart family history. Issy suspected that his interest wasn't purely academic, but for once didn't clam up. Talking was good - it took her mind off other things.

'Grandfather willed the cottage to Esme after his death. My father was too proud to contest the will, but it provided the spur he needed to leave *Eilean na Sgairbh*. He stormed out, headed south and worked on the docks at Clydeside until he could afford a one-way ticket to California and Stanford Industrial Park, where he found work in the newly formed semi-conductor industry. He started as a gopher, rose through the ranks and went on to invent a streamlined form of semi-conductor . . .'

'. . . the forerunner of the micro-chip,' he said, finishing the story. 'Wait. Don't tell me it was your father who patented the *Stuart Micro Chip*?'

'Yes, it was. He returned from America in the eighties, set up a small factory in Slough - our version of Silicon Valley, and then moved production to Edinburgh once he'd built up his reputation. His heart belongs in Scotland, it always has . . .' she thought of his ashes resting in the window embrasure and was overcome with sadness. 'The rest, as they say in all the best novels, is history.'

'How come . . .' Brodie hesitated, as if aware he was asking too many questions.

'Go on.'

'How come your grandfather cut your father out of his inheritance?'

'Now *that*,' Issy said, getting to her feet glad that the dizzy spell had passed, 'is something that my father and Esme refused to elaborate on. All I know is that Father did Esme a great injustice, one she never really recovered from. One she will never talk about.' She thought of her aunt's vehement assertion that she wouldn't have the physical remains of James Stuart in her house. 'What he actually *did*, I have no idea. So,' she got to her feet, 'better get on, there are things I have to do this morning.'

'Of course, I shouldn't have bombarded you with questions. It's just that I find . . . family history interesting.'

'You must tell me all about *your family,*' she said, putting the copy of *Lady Chatterley's Lover* back on its stand. 'Before you leave.'

Again the charming smile: 'Sure. It'd be a pleasure.'

Thinking Brodie had done enough snooping for one day, Issy indicated that he should precede her out of the study. With a perfect show of manners and a smile that didn't *quite* reach his eyes, Brodie stood back to allow her to leave the room before him.

Chapter Eleven
Scotch on the Rocks

T he phone rang in Issy's pocket. She pulled it out, checked the caller ID before answering.

'Lindy.' She flicked over to FaceTime on her iPhone.

'I *hate* my mother,' Lindy exploded in full-on, stroppy teenager mode, although she was twenty-two years old. She should have learned to handle her mother by now, Issy thought, preparing to deliver another counselling session over the phone.

As far as Issy was concerned, Mary Tennant was the perfect mother – calm, loving, fair-minded and supportive of Lindy's flights of fancy. Her husband, Tam, was equally forbearing, and if from time to time they demanded that Lindy did a stint in the Post Office, Issy saw nothing wrong in that.

'What's she done this time?' Her calm response appeared to inflame Lindy further.

'Only ruined my life . . . I promised I'd take Brodie round the island, show him the sights and – well, *everything* . . .'

'That won't take long,' Issy cut her off in mid-tirade. Much as she loved *Eilean na Sgairbh*, she was the first to admit that it had its limitations – compared to Vegas, for example.

Lindy steamed ahead as if Issy hadn't spoken. 'But no . . . she *has* to go to Glasgow, to meet up with a load of old biddies in some tearooms – after they've hit The Barras, naturally. Which means I've got to wait in for the delivery man. See me, Issy? When I get to Las Vegas, I ain't never coming back to this fucking island.' Anger deepened her accent, her copper curls bounced in indignation and her blue eyes blazed.

'So, what's your problem? I can give Brodie his breakfast and I'm sure he's quite capable of making his own bed.' What else is he capable of, she wondered, seeing him in her mind's eye systematically working his way round Esme's study taking photographs? 'Besides, you'll see plenty of him when he moves out and you pamper to his every need at the eco-lodge.' Lindy, obviously missing the edge of sarcasm in Issy's voice, carried on regardless of her audience.

'That's true and you won't be –' Lindy pulled herself up short.

'I won't be around – cramping your style. Exactly, you'll have free access to Himself; twenty-four-seven – the equivalent of a backstage pass.' Judging from Lindy's expression she didn't believe that Issy would be able to stay away from Brodie. Issy recalled her conversation with Brodie about Lindy's narrow horizons and lack of opportunity and decided to cut her some slack. She'd been feeling mildly depressed since arriving back on Cormorant Island and had attributed it to coping with her father's sudden death and missing out on the counselling session with Esme.

Perhaps, after the memorial service and wake, once she got stuck into her plans for the outhouses, life would pick up again. She missed being in demand at Ecosse Designs, of being needed, wanted and – she grimaced – feeling important. Determined to cheer up Lindy, and herself into the bargain – and to prove that she had no ulterior motives where Brodie was concerned, Issy set about talking a load of nonsense.

'*Och Brodie,*' Issy began, in a broad Scots accent, '*I can tell it's me ye want, Lindy Tennant. Dinnae bother tae hide it, Big Man. Ah cannae wait for us tae be alone in the eco-lodge – ah'll show ye hoo to dance a highland fling that'll bring the colour tae yer cheeks, mah man. Ye'll never wah-nt tae go home to those skinny-ersed Yankee gurls – that's for sure. Not when there's prime, Aberdeen Angus right on yer doorstep, ken?*' She patted her rump for emphasis and gave a sexy wiggle.

'Shuddup!' Lindy said, spluttering with laughter and forgetting her bad mood. 'Your accent is terrible. I prefer *Miss Jean Brodie* to *Teenie frae Troon,* any day.' Lindy used the time honoured name for an oddly dressed woman from Troon on the west coast.

Issy gurgled with laughter, too. It seemed ages since she and Lindy had laughed together and acted like idiots. It was usually their default mode and she missed those times. Time she lightened up – life was for living, not stressing over love-rat boyfriends, dysfunctional relationships with parents and whether or not La Bella Scozzese would hijack the memorial service.

She found that once she was in role, it was hard to stop.

'*Aye, take me in yer arms, Brodie mah Boy and have yer wicked way with me. Not once, not twice but many times. Cormorant Island is fu' o' shags and it's time I had one mah-self . . .*'

It had gone very quiet on the other end of the phone – and when Issy glanced at Lindy, she was staring fixedly into the space behind Issy's left ear.

'*Och now, lassie, dinnae be after pretending I've shocked ye and ye havnae been thinking impure thoughts aboot Oor Brodie. Ah have; ah cannae sleep at night for dreaming aboot . . . you know what.*'

'Issy . . .' Lindy said in a strangled voice.

'*By the way, lassie, do you know how you can tell which clan a man belongs to?*'

'I don't think I do,' Lindy replied in an accent borrowed straight from The Queen.

Issy was only too happy to explain. '*Ye put yer hand up his kilt - and if it's a quarter pounder you know he's a MacDonald.*'

'Issy!' Lindy choked out. 'Don't –'

'*Aye, dinnae fash yersel' lassie, ah'll no be fighting ye over Big Mac. He's is all yours, hen.*' Puzzled at still getting no response, Issy looked at a now pale-faced Lindy and asked in her normal voice: 'What! What?'

'I think she's trying to tell you that Big Mac is standing right behind you,' a dry voice said.

Issy span round and bounced off Brodie's chest. Her face burned at what he'd overhead, aware that *this* display surpassed that time in the kitchen when she'd asserted he wasn't her type. She ended the phone call and shoved the phone back in her jeans pocket. She didn't want Lindy witnessing the grovelling apology she was about to deliver to a now poker-faced Brodie.

Standing on the threshold of the outhouse - which was a step higher than ground level, Issy rocked on the soles of her flimsy espadrilles. Reaching out, Brodie steadied her – holding her fast by the upper arms in a manner she found altogether too familiar and intimate. The extra inches gained by standing on the outhouse step brought her level with Brodie's lips – which, much to her relief, were now quirked back in a smile. It was hard to say whether the smile was wry amusement or plain irritation. His cool green eyes looked down into her dark violet ones with a speculation that was quite disconcerting. He gave nothing away but his look implied that she'd dug a hole for herself and he was in no hurry to help her out of it.

'MacDonald, huh?' he asked, when she didn't speak.

'I – I,' she gulped. 'I'm very sorry, I was just trying to cheer Lindy up because her mother . . . well, you probably heard all that.'

'Hm – what are The Barras?'

In no apparent hurry to let her go, Brodie pulled her closer – ostensibly to aid her balancing on the threshold. But, there was more to his holding her close than simply stopping her from falling over. This knowledge impacted on Issy and she became aware of the rise and fall of his ribcage against her soft breasts. The way his breath stirred the loose tendrils of her hair where it had escaped the high ponytail she'd fastened it into that morning. His regard alone was enough to liquefy her stomach and make her buckle at the knees . . . Much in the same way as *Twa Burns* whisky slipped seductively over your tongue and then trailed fire down your throat and into your stomach.

How would it feel, she wondered, to lie naked in his arms, ranged against his long, tanned limbs – tangled in the sheets after making love? Drawing a shaky breath, she fought the traitorous reaction of her body to his touch and blocked the mad thoughts whirling round in her head. She had enough on her plate without getting involved with a *guest,* for goodness sake. Added to which, Lindy had expressed an interest in him and, according to their unwritten code, had 'first dibs' on him. But her response to Brodie was undeniable. It wouldn't take much for her to turn her head sideways, lay it on his chest, wrap her arms around his waist and let out a shuddering sigh.

Instead, she coughed, brought her wayward thoughts under control, and the world governed by reason and common sense, righted itself.

'The Barras,' he prompted.

'It's – it's an area of east Glasgow wh - where there are m- market stalls selling all kinds of goods. Some of them very cheaply,' she said in a rush to get the words out. 'When we were kids, if you wanted to tease someone, you said: *Yer Mammy buys yer clothes frae the Barras.*' Then, deciding she'd spoken enough Glaswegian for one day, Issy reverted back to her normal accent which was – as

Lindy had pointed out, more Miss Jean Brodie than Teenie frae Troon.

Time she apologised, beat a hasty retreat and concentrated on cleaning the outhouse – the task she'd been occupied with when Lindy called. She shook herself free of his hands and stepped away. 'Look, I'm sorry if I offended you.'

He tipped his head back and roared with laughter. 'You didn't. I'll have to remember that one for when I return home.' Unexpectedly, Issy's stomach tightened at the thought of him leaving Cormorant Island. She'd only just met the man - and for ninety percent of the time, she'd been vexed by his presence in her aunt's house. So why the sudden pang at the thought of his leaving?

'Big Mac indeed.'

'Well, I'm sorry; what more can I say? So, if you'll just excuse me . . .' She moved further back into the gloom, hoping to hide her expression, and that he'd take the hint and leave. No such luck . . .

'Say . . .' Sighing, she turned round. *What now?* 'How about driving me round the island, pointing out the hot spots? I'll buy you one of those funny little pies they serve at the pub and a dram of *uisge beatha* as a reward.'

'You know Gaelic?' she asked.

'Some,' was the careful response.

The sun lanced through the window and touched her father's urn where it resided in splendid isolation on the ledge. Like a king on his throne. The ray of light touched her hand and brought warmth to her cold fingers. Quite unexpectedly, the idea of driving round *Eilean na*

Sgairbh and showing Brodie the beaches and rocky inlets which she loved, appealed. Life really was too short for playing games, wasn't it?

'I'll show you round the island on one condition –'

'Which is?'

'You promise never to refer to my conversation with Lindy. Ever. To anyone.'

'Ever?' He grinned, suggesting that she was denying him a simple pleasure. 'Okay, deal.' He held out his hand, almost as if he was daring her to touch flesh with him. Issy wiped her grubby hands down the side of her jeans and stepped up to the mark. She spat on her hand for good measure, like she'd seen them do in old cowboy films.

After all, he was from Kentucky, wasn't he?

'Deal.'

'One thing –'

'Yes?'

'Don't get all gussied up. I like it here on the island but I'm feeling a bit stir crazy. I want to be out there, following the coast road, feeling the wind on my face and be shown where Lindy said there were mermaids.'

'I won't get *gussied up*, as you put it. Just wash my hands and run a comb through my hair. As for mermaids - Lindy's been spinning you a tale. There are no mermaids, not any more, if there ever were. Sightings are more likely to have been seals which the sailors spotted as they sailed past Cormorant Island on their way home. After three months at sea I'm guessing that even a seal begins to look attractive to most men?' Again, Jack Innes-Kerr's energetic sex-gymnastics over her desk flashed into her mind, until she blocked it.

'You okay?' he asked, quick to catch her moue of distaste.

'I was just trying to get my head round the idea of you being a romantic and wanting to see a mermaid.'

'And failing?' he suggested. 'I'll have you know I'm a card-carrying romantic.' Pretending offence, he put his hand over his heart. 'And I know the difference between a seal and a woman.'

I bet you do! Issy sent him a sharp look, then continued in a neutral tone. 'Och well, that's because you don't know the legend of the silkie.'

'Silkie?'

'I'll tell you as we drive round the island.'

His face lit up at her caving, and as she walked over to the doorway, he gave a gallant half-bow, moved aside and allowed her to cross the threshold. Then he reached out and touched her hair. Issy flinched - what was his game?

'Cobweb,' he explained, 'complete with spider. Allow me, Ma'am.' He removed the cobweb and the spider scurried away. Issy stood stock still until he'd finished, and attributed her quickening pulse to the thought of the spider dropping down the back of her shirt. 'Not scared of long-legged beasties, Mizz Stoo-art? Most women would run screaming in the opposite direction.'

'And some men, too,' she countered. 'No, I'm not afraid of

spiders.' Or you; or whatever game you're playing, her pause informed. 'Although, one did inspire one of our national heroes to rise from defeat and fight the English one more time.'

'Robert the Bruce? Don't look so surprised, I'm not some dumb-ass Yank who thinks everyone in Scotland wears a kilt, plays the bagpipes and drinks whisky for breakfast. I've done my research.'

She bet he had. He had an air about him which suggested he was prepared for whatever life threw at him. She wished she could work out his real reason for coming to *Eilean na Sgairbh*. But now wasn't the time – or the place. She'd play along with him, take him round the island, hope to get him to drop his guard and then figure out why he was gracing Cormorant Island with his presence.

'For the record, I'm not afraid of spiders, mice, things that go bump in the night – or anything else,' she asserted. Even if, she hadn't been perceptive enough to tell the difference between her ex-fiancé and a louse!

'I don't guess you are,' he laughed softly.

They walked back towards the house in an almost companionable silence, deep in thought and neither saying another word.

Chapter Twelve
These Old Shades

Issy drove out onto the coast road, wisely circumnavigating the island counter-clockwise so they wouldn't pass the General Store where Lindy was trapped behind the counter, breathing fire like a wee dragon over her mother's gallivanting. Instead, she drove with the sea on their right hand side, and hugged the mountain range, netted over last winter to keep landslides to a minimum. To their right, the land slipped away, behind a well-maintained stone wall running the length of the coast road. The wall helped to prop up the thin ribbon of road and prevented motorists from accidentally tumbling into the sea. Every quarter of a mile or so, road signs warned of landslips and erosion, advising motorists to take extra care.

To the unpractised eye, the rented Land Rover seemed too wide for the narrow road. Issy hid her smile as she glanced down and saw Brodie's foot hitting the imaginary brake on his side of the car.

'Relax, Man; I know these roads like the back of my hand. You're safe with me.' Brodie didn't answer. He held onto the roof grab handle and looked down onto the jagged coastline below where waves creamed onto the exposed rocks. Even today, in high summer, the sea - at first glance a deep, denim blue, wrinkled in a manner which suggested deep currents and a vicious undertow beneath its surface.

They drove on in silence, past designated passing places which looked too small for even a hardy sheep, let alone a large four-by-four. Skilfully, Issy wove between granite hills whose craggy face was covered by sparse grass and scrubby russet coloured vegetation, and headed north. In places, it seemed as if the road would peter out, but then they turned a corner and another stunning view unfolded before them. Issy doubted that Kentucky, or anywhere else on the planet, had anything to match the stark beauty of the *Eilean na Sgairbh* coastline.

'Maybe,' Brodie turned and sent her a wry look, 'next time, we'll take the Mini?'

Issy laughed. 'Wimp. Just be grateful that it's me driving you round the island, and not Lindy.'

'I'm glad it's you driving me round the island - and not Lindy.' His reply was ambiguous, deliberately so, and Issy didn't know which way to take it.

'The road widens on the next section of coastline and sweeps down to the sea. Look.' She pointed with her left hand and Brodie paled a little. 'Sorry, both hands on the wheel.' Now the road swung inland where, in Victorian times, it had been blasted through a small mountain – there being no room for it to follow the coastline any further. 'The Faerie Falls,' Issy said, nodding towards it with her head as they drove past a torrent of brown, peaty water cascading over rocks. 'They say that the wee folk live behind its waters, but I've never seen them.'

She loved showing off her island and took Brodie's silence for appreciation rather than continued nervousness at her driving. Saving the best for last, she cleared the mountain pass and descended down to a small bay whose gleaming sand and small promontories curved before them. Pulling off the road, she stopped to allow Brodie to take in waves lapping the shore and to photograph a sea so still and clear, it was possible to see all the way down to the bottom.

'The Whale's Back.' She pointed to a small group of islands sitting serenely in the clear waters. 'I hope you realise you're getting the five star tour of the island - with a native guide, I might add.' Laughing, she slanted him an unconsciously coquettish look.

Brodie dragged his eyes away from the stunning view, half turned in his seat and then spoke. 'You should do that more often.'

'What? Give guided tours of the island?'

'No; smile. It transforms you.' Issy's smile slipped a little at that conversation stopper. Unperturbed, Brodie turned back to the view to where, now they'd cleared the rockiest part of the coast, soft fells stretched towards distant, blue hills. Issy's brain was in overdrive trying to think of some witticism to counter his statement. But nothing came to mind and she let the moment pass. Was he flirting with her? Or, simply being *Brodie* and saying whatever came into his mind? After some time, Brodie gave out a deep sigh. 'I'd like to see the ruins of Stuart's Twa Burns Distillery, if that's okay with you?'

'Certainly Sir.' She tipped him a salute.

'Mm,' he said, this time without looking at her. 'I find your being compliant actually scarier than the white knuckle ride along the coast.'

Issy didn't reply. She steered them back onto the road, and drove round the sweep of the bay before parking in a large lay-by facing the sea. Opening the car door, Brodie got out and stood facing the sea with his hands in his pockets. The summer breeze ruffled his hair as he looked towards the mainland on his left, seemingly overwhelmed by the view.

Issy would have given anything to know what was going through his mind. She recalled their conversation in the study when he'd outlined his reasons for coming to Scotland – and *Eilean na Sgairbh* in particular.

. . . It's been on my bucket list to swim in Scottish coastal waters warmed by the Gulf Stream, down a dram of single malt produced in a local distillery and to eat freshly caught langoustines in a harbour restaurant where the nearest landfall, to the west, is America . . .

Issy loved Cormorant Island, but she would be the first to admit there were better locations in Scotland to achieve those ambitions. And, as far as she knew, the eco-lodges were more designed for birdwatchers and nature lovers than well-heeled Americans, no doubt used to vitamin enriched rainforest power showers and all the mod cons which wouldn't reach *Eilean na Sgairbh* within the next decade – if ever!

Brodie, however, seemed in another place. While she was thinking about the downside of living on an island it was plain from his expression that he was deeply moved by simply *being* here. Although he hadn't said as much, Issy believed he had come to search for his roots. She frowned, there were very few families on the island with the surname Brodie. As far as she was aware, there were more Brodies on the north-east coast in Morayshire. Perhaps she should say he was looking in the wrong place and suggest he might do better to investigate whether any Brodies had been sent as indentured servants to work on the plantations of the West Indies as a punishment for taking part in the Jacobite Rebellion of 1745.

Reaching down, Brodie selected a flat pebble on the shoreline and skimmed it across the surface of the water. 'Seven,' he said, dusting down his hands and turning to face Issy.

'Look out for the poor mermaids, they don't handle concussion very well,' she joked, glad that his moment of introspection was over.

'I'll bear it in mind. Now – how about showing me the distillery?'

'Look around you. This is where it stood.'

He turned his back on the shoreline and looked across the tarmacadam road to a level patch of land overgrown with weeds and seashore plants. Huge blocks of masonry, some still bearing the white paint which had once adorned the exterior of the distillery were embedded in the earth. They looked as if they'd been tossed around by some petulant baby giant tired of playing with his building blocks.

One of the blocks was marked with a letter 'T' and rooted deep in the turf.

'That's all that remains of *Stuart's Twa Burns Distillery*,' Issy said, leading the way across the road. 'Once, the site was littered with broken masonry, but over the years the islanders have helped themselves to the stones – turning them into hard core for building foundations, using them to rebuild garden walls, create rockeries and so on. Come and see the cairn next to the memorial stone which my grandfather had erected in the fifties.'

Brodie walked right up to the tarnished plaque and read the inscription out loud, apparently forgetful of Issy's presence.

'*On the night of September 6th 1942 Stuart's Twa Burns Distillery was strafed by a Focke-Wulf Fw 190, just as the shift was ending for the day. Many of the workforce were killed. On September 8th two Junker Ju-88 bombers returned with a full bomb load and completely destroyed the distillery which had been turned over to manufacturing industrial alcohol for the Ministry of War.*'

Underneath the inscription was a roll call of those killed and at the foot of the memorial stone someone had left a few flowers in remembrance. The plaque was tarnished by the salt spray blown onto it by the winds and looked as forlorn and forgotten as the distillery which had once employed nearly every adult on *Eilean na Sgairbh*.

Issy traced each name reverentially with her fingertips, pausing over the name of her paternal grandmother, Caitlin Stuart who'd been killed during the bombing raid. Underneath the roll of honour were the chilling words: *NEVER FORGET.*

'Most of those killed were women working for the war effort, the men having left the island to fight in Europe. It ripped the heart out of the community and scarred my aunt Esme, although she was but a toddler at the time. My father was convinced that the raid was God's vengeance on the Stuarts for having built a distillery in the first place.' She flopped down on the nearest of the largest stones, wrapped her arms around her knees and looked out to sea. 'Hard to imagine it on a day like this, isn't it? They say the explosion could be heard as far away as Oban. As a result, Esme became a pacifist when she grew up and my father remained a teetotaller for all of his life. In his eyes, if the Stuarts hadn't built the distillery in the first place, all those people wouldn't have lost their lives. Mother told me that he wouldn't even drink champagne at their wedding breakfast.'

Brodie sat down on the grass at her feet and picked through the stones within arm's reach. 'Were no steps taken to rebuild it?' he asked.

'Grandfather Stuart did receive compensation from the government after the war, but not enough to rebuild the distillery and get it on its feet again. Not properly. The bombing raid was the double whammy after the explosion thirty years earlier when the distillery was turned over to making landmines. The bombing raid explosion was responsible for blocking up and diverting one of the two burns which gave the distillery its name: Twa Burns.'

'Why two burns?'

'One burn to turn the wheel which mashed the barley and one to make the whisky. The warehouses faced out to sea with the doors open which, they say, gave Twa Burns its distinctive flavour. We have half a dozen bottles left and I believe they're quite valuable . . . though, not my tipple.' She got to her feet and began to poke among the long grass with her foot.

'Guess you're more a champagne kinda girl, huh?' He joined her, searching through the grass for debris from the old buildings and warehouses. 'Your father showed no signs of changing his mind, of rebuilding the distillery with the money he made from his microprocessor business?'

'God, no. Quite the reverse, in fact. His will stipulated that a large part of the profits from his processors be ploughed into the *James Stuart Apprenticeship for disadvantaged Scottish Youths.*' Issy gave a 'huff' of remembrance, recalling Innes-Kerr's expression when he realised he was no longer engaged to an heiress, and his anger when she made it plain she wouldn't contest the will. The money was her father's and had been earned through his hard graft. It wasn't her place to overturn his last bequests.

'Hey, get a load of this.' Brodie fell to his knees and began digging in the turf with a pocket knife. After some tugging, he unearthed a piece of shrapnel which he rubbed on the sides of his jeans and then held out for Issy to inspect. Refusing to touch it, she put her hand over his and stopped his excavations.

'Don't dig any deeper. I think of this place as an unquiet grave because not all the bodies were found after that bombing raid. They deserve to be left in peace.' She looked down and realised that she was holding his hand and quickly withdrew her fingers. Standing, she picked a few of the rough wild flowers growing among the salt-blasted grass, kissed them, and then murmured her grandmother's name before laying them at the foot of the monument. 'This beach was originally known as The Laird's Folly but, after the bombing raid, the islanders renamed it *Traigh Allt Chailgeag*.' She went quiet, shading her eyes against the glare of the sun as she looked out across the beach.

'Gonna tell me what that means?' he asked after a long pause.

'*The beach of the burn of bereavement and death*,' she said solemnly. Then she laughed at the expression on his face. 'Killed the mood, haven't I? Well, you did ask . . .'

Brodie glanced at the piece of shrapnel in his hand and then turned the twisted metal over before slipping it into his pocket. 'The distillery deserves to be rebuilt, don't you think? Something to bring the young people back to the island and to give *Eilean na Sgairbh* back its heritage.'

'That would take money. Money I simply haven't got. Father didn't –' She had been about to reveal that, like a latter day Andrew Carnegie, her father didn't believe in inherited wealth. It was to be revealed at his memorial service that he'd left a large bequest to Mungo Park's wee kirk, funds to oversee the building of a new village hall complete with a suite of computers, and the endowment of a sea tractor to ferry foot passengers backwards and forwards across The Narrows at high tide. There was nothing for her mother or Esme, not that they had expected it. As for herself, she had her own plans; plans she intended to implement with money she'd saved for the deposit on the Edinburgh flat she'd hoped to share with Innes-Kerr once they were married.

The way things had turned out, she was grateful she hadn't handed her half of the deposit over to Jack, as he'd requested. She had the feeling she would never have seen the money again.

'I'm sorry if being here has made you feel down,' Brodie said, not knowing the real reason behind her thoughtful sadness.

'Oh no.' She waved away his concern. 'It's just that I have a lot to organise and –'

'And here you are showing me round the island when you should be emptying the contents of your barns –'

'Outhouses,' she corrected.

'Outhouses - into a dumpster.'

'A skip,' she laughed, quite enjoying putting him straight. 'We call them skips in these parts.'

'Sorry Ma'am.' He tipped an imaginary hat, cowboy fashion - and they both laughed. 'One more thing.'

'Go ahead.'

'How did your family come by the piece of land in the first place?'

'That's quite a story.'

'I'm listening.' He sat back down on the grass and patted the ground next to him, indicating that she should join him.

Ignoring the way her stomach flipped over at simply being so near to him, Issy stared out to sea and concentrated on her story.

'Apparently, my ancestor came over from Whitburn, a mining village near Edinburgh, and set up an illicit still with his equally disreputable mate. They got friendly with the laird who owned the island and supplied him with the forerunner of *Twa Burns* whisky. By all accounts it would strip the enamel off your teeth and make you temporarily blind if you drank too much. But then they refined the blend and turned it into a winner.'

'Kentucky bourbon was something like that back in the days of prohibition, when everyone owned an illicit still,' he grinned. 'This is fascinating, tell me more.' He lay back on the grass, propping himself up on his elbows – all long, lean and athletic. Although his amiable smile never faltered, Issy gained the impression that Brodie's quick-fire mind was processing the information and filing it away. To add, no doubt, to the photographs he'd taken in the study, earlier.

Unsure of his motives, Issy kept it light; only divulging the bare bones of the story.

'The laird was wont to play golf at this spot, firing golf balls into the bay. My ancestor, Johnny Stuart, bet the laird that he could drive a golf ball further out to sea. If he succeeded, the laird would grant him a slice of land.'

'And if he failed?'

'Johnny and his partner would supply the laird with as much whisky as he could drink for five years . . .'

'. . . figuring that the whisky would kill him before the bet was played out?'

'Exactly!'

'So what happened?'

'They shook hands on it. The laird, who was an excellent golfer, stood on the shore and drove his golf balls as far out to sea as he could.'

'End of story?'

'Not quite. It started to rain and Johnny and his partner said they would return the following day to honour the bet. And here's the clever part – they returned at low tide when the shoreline was hundreds of yards further out to sea from where the laird had teed off. They drove off, their ball landed half way across The Narrows and they won the bet. The piece of land was renamed The Laird's Folly . . . '

'And the rest is history,' he finished off. 'I guess no one beats a Stuart?' he asked casually. However, his expression was serious as he waited for her to confirm his assessment of her – and her family.

'You'd better believe it, Buster,' she said in a fine American drawl. 'However, all I've done is talk about *me*, how about telling me little more about yourself?'

'Nah. It'd bore you rigid. School, more school, a first degree, then a Masters and, finally, a place in a research lab. *The King of Plankton*, remember?'

'Yeah, I remember.' Her tone was cool, making it apparent she knew she was being fobbed off by him. Brodie, quick to pick up on the drop in temperature, got to his feet and offered his hand. Taking it, and remembering the old adage that one caught more flies with honey than vinegar, Issy smiled and allowed him to hoist her to her feet. She suspected that she'd get nothing more from him without applying thumbscrews or several glasses of single malt whisky, but she was determined to work out his motives for coming to Cormorant Island.

'Has it made you sad, showing me this forlorn place?'

'Not at all. I love it here, in spite of the memories it evokes, it's my heritage; I'm just sad that I can't afford to restore it to its former glory. To rebuild the water course and re-route the two burns alone would cost a fortune.' She raised her face to look up at him. The warmth of the sun and the breeze playing with her long black hair lifted her spirits and made her feel light-hearted. Maybe she was reading too much into his reticence? 'Didn't you mention something about payment? A mutton pie and a glass of uisge beatha down at The Pickled Herring?'

'I sure did,' he replied, seemingly in no hurry to release her.

Issy took care that the uneven ground didn't catapult her into his arms as had happened on the outhouse steps. Crazy as it seemed, part of her longed to feel his arms around her; to be held close and secure, to bury her face in his neck, inhale musky male scent undercut by expensive aftershave, and …

Stop right there!

Evidently, she was missing Jack Innes-Kerr and the bed they'd shared, albeit it intermittently – given the nature of her job, more than she cared to admit. She wasn't about to fall for Brodie, a man with many secrets - or indeed any man, on the rebound.

She deserved better than that.

'Mermaids,' she said, pulling free of him. 'You wanted to see mermaids and Loreleis, didn't you?'

'Did I?' Brodie's look implied that he, too, was aware of the charge of sexual attraction fizzing between them. That it'd been enough to drive all thoughts of mythical creatures out of his head. But, whereas her response was to turn tail and run, his was to embrace life and all it had to offer. He had a light in his eyes that said – *bring it on.*

Something Issy had no intention of doing.

'You – you did,' Issy asserted, making her way back to the car. 'Come on, I'll show you where they sit on the rocks, combing their hair.'

'Really?'

'Really. I know for a fact that they have hair which is either electric blue or puce pink.'

'And how do you know that?'

'Well, if I revealed that, you'd know all my secrets and I'd know none of yours. That hardly seems fair, does it?' Plainly, acting all stiff and frosty didn't work, so she'd pay him in his own coin. Flirting with him, if that's what it took.

'Shucks, Ma'am,' he joked, 'ah'm just a simple hick from the sticks. I don't know nothing 'bout mermaids and such like.' He grinned, looking anything but a country bumpkin. The look he sent Issy was confident, assured and full of sassiness. 'Maybe I shoulda brought along some wax?' He cocked his head to one side and waited, green eyes full of humour, to see if she got the allusion.

'To stop up your ears so that the mermaids don't lure you onto the rocks with their siren song? Of course.' She skipped away from him. 'But don't worry, I carry a pair of *Ulysses' Patented Ear Plugs* in the First Aid Kit for such occasions.'

'No chance of your luring me, I take it?'

'None whatsoever.' She stated it so emphatically that he laughed, not in the least put out by her rejection of him.

'That's too ba-ad.' The way he drew out the last word made Issy forget her early assertion. Her stomach turned flick-flacks and she wondered how serious he was about being lured by her; and what she'd be passing up by holding out against him. He gave her no time to reconsider. 'In that case Miss Stoo-art, lead on.'

Issy led the way back to the Land Rover. Making it plain he was not to be hurried, Brodie took several shots of the scene with his phone before climbing into the car beside her. But the image of luring him onto rocks and into dangerous waters stayed with Issy all the way back to Killantrae.

Chapter Thirteen
Touch Not the Cat

'The house is fine, Esme - our resident American is fine. More than fine, actually, and appears in no hurry to move out. He's been here over a week and now says that the eco-lodge won't be available until the middle of *next* week. Something about a mix up when his travel company made the online booking? I hope he's demanding some sort of restitution from them.'

'Are you okay with that, Issy?'

'Well, I can hardly throw him out, can I?'

'But - are you getting on alright with him? He seems a nice young man.'

For a moment, Issy zoned out, remembering how they'd flirted on the seashore yesterday. She'd steered clear of him after that, his being in the house was beginning to affect her mental and physical well-being.

Dramatically.

'Issy? You still there? You're breaking up.' Her aunt's words were a timely reminder that she'd recently broken off her engagement with Jack Innes-Kerr. She wasn't looking for a replacement, certainly not in the shape of a six foot three American with dark auburn hair, green eyes and – *STOP IT*!

'He has a handmaiden to pamper to his every need. What's not to like? No, not me, Esme – the Lovely Lola. I've been too busy clearing out the large outhouse and measuring up workbenches for my project to worry about Mr Brodie. Not to mention organising the memorial service, with Mungo's help – and the Wake afterwards. In any case he's leaving soon - Brodie that is, not Mungo. Yes, I'll be glad to have the house to myself,' she answered with a half-truth.

The reality of her situation had struck her that morning as she'd laid the table for breakfast.

Once Brodie left there would be no need for Lindy to visit twice a day. It'd be just her and Pershing until Esme returned after the memorial service. A familiar wave of loneliness and mourning washed over her, making her shiver. She suddenly felt overcome by giddiness and . . . well, under the weather. As if she was recovering from a particularly nasty virus or a bout of flu. She disguised a heartfelt sigh as a yawn, so as not to alarm Esme, and dismissed the feeling of malaise as being tired and emotional at the thought of what lay ahead.

It would be selfish of her to worry Esme, or have her come home early just because *her* life was in turmoil.

She was a big girl, used to travelling the world on her own – it was who she was; what she did. So, why did this feel different? And why – of all things, did she dread Brodie leaving?

'No, I haven't forgotten Pershing's bath,' she tuned into Esme's rambling conversation. 'He's been demanding one all morning. How on earth he knows it's Sunday and bath day, I'll never know. That bird is too clever for his own good,' she added with mock-asperity. 'In the olden days you would have been drowned for a witch in The Narrows at high tide and he'd have been roasted over a fire as your familiar. . .'

'Issy, do you have no feeling?' her aunt laughed. 'Pershing's my baby.'

'I love the beast, you know I do, Okay; gotta go - laters; have fun and don't get arrested, Auntie.' She pronounced her last word: an(t)-ie, Glaswegian style, without the glottal stop. It was their little joke and how they usually signed off, on the phone or when Skyping each other.

Nevertheless, Issy was only half-joking. She never knew what Esme would get up to next and was aware that compared to the sprightly sexagenarian she must seem the most boring person on the planet.

University. Design School. Plum job at Ecosse Designs. Engaged to the boss' son.

Dull – with a capital D.

And now?

Unemployed. Back on the market. Biological clock ticking away like a time bomb.

To sum up: she was home for good and, on the face of it, good for nothing.

Maybe she was being too hard on herself. A fault of hers. By clearing the outhouses she'd taken the first, tentative step towards achieving her ambition of creating workshops which some of her fellow graduates could rent to follow their dreams. Talented contemporaries from Edinburgh University who, due to lack of money or suitable premises, were unable to pursue their calling as artists across a range of media – sculpture, painting, pottery, jewellery-making, interior design.

Two years ago, when she'd gone through the first of many rough patches with Jack, and had thought of calling off their engagement and leaving Edinburgh for good, she'd been granted outline planning permission for the outbuildings. At the time, it was simply her back up plan; insurance against things not working out between them. Now fate had thrown her a curve ball in the shape of Suzy the intern, she was glad she'd had the foresight to see her plans through.

Given that the outhouses had previously been commercial buildings – used for storing whisky barrels and other distillery paraphernalia, her application had ticked all the boxes regarding appearance, means of access, landscaping, layout and scale. Now all that remained was to get the final go-ahead from the local authority – and she'd been practically promised it would be passed through 'on the nod'. New ideas which attracted people to the island and reversed the trend of people leaving *Eilean na Sgairbh* were always looked upon favourably by the planning authorities.

Okay – so, she couldn't afford to rebuild the distillery - this was her way of giving something back to the island. And something back to herself. It had taken the last few years travelling the world to convince her that her heart belonged on *Eilean na Sgairbh*. Jack's infidelity had saved her the trouble of breaking that news to him and facing his wrath.

This time she gave full vent to the sigh, resting back against the wall of the window seat overlooking The Narrows, knees drawn up to her chin. She held the phone in her right hand and tapped it against her upper lip, reflecting on the past week. She'd heard nothing from Jack Innes-Kerr, and had interpreted that to mean he'd given up on the idea of a reconciliation. She'd heard nothing from her mother, either – and that she found more disturbing. La Bella Scozzese was at her most dangerous when she appeared most docile.

She put both of them from her mind . . .

Her father's ashes were still on the window ledge waiting to be 'dealt' with. Maybe she should ask Mungo if they could 'lie in state' in the kirk until his memorial service? Being stuck on the window ledge was so undignified; perhaps that had been her aunt's intention? Mungo's number was on speed dial and she was just about to ring him when she remembered it was Sunday. Although the islanders were more open-minded about Sabbath Observation these days, especially as they couldn't afford to turn tourists away by closing craft shops, the pub and bed and breakfast establishments during the summer months. But old traditions still held fast on the island.

A commotion in the bathroom stopped her mid-dial.

'Fucking bird, get off of my foot! Jeezus.'

'Oh no. Pershing –' she gasped. She'd forgotten to warn Brodie about the parrot!

Jolted out of all thoughts about Sabbath Observation and the Wee Frees, Issy dropped the phone, rushed out of the study and headed for the bathroom. Without stopping to consider whether Brodie was decent, she threw open the door to find Brodie hopping around the bathroom like a Dervish – and with a bad-tempered, bedraggled parrot hanging onto his big toe.

'Get it off, can't you?'

'Oh, for goodness sake!' Issy was unimpressed by his yelling, the parrot's squawking and frantic wing flapping as it struggled to cling to Brodie's foot. 'Be still. You'll hurt Pershing -'

'It's doing a pretty good job of hurting me,' Brodie protested, as Issy wrapped the parrot in a bath towel and detached it from his foot.

'Puir wee man,' she crooned, stroking the wet parrot and ignoring Brodie.

Glancing down, Issy saw that the floor of the wet room was smeared with blood. Brodie's blood. Worse still, when she looked up, a naked and fully erect Brodie filled her line of vision. Must be the excitement, she thought, dragging her eyes away and concentrating on the parrot instead, to cover her blushes.

Pershing, meanwhile, was giving Brodie one of his baleful stares.

'Thanks for nothing,' Brodie seethed. 'Jeezus, will you look at the blood . . .'

'Oh, don't be such a big wean,' she laughed. Although, standing in front of her it was obvious that he'd left childhood behind many moons ago.

'A big *what*?' he demanded, hands on hips – forgetting for the moment that he was stark naked.

'A wean – a child. Here, you might want this . . .' Averting her eyes, she threw a towel at him, trying hard not to laugh at his discomfiture.

'Jeezus,' he said for the third time, and wrapped the towel around his narrow hips, sarong style.

Issy got to her feet and held the parrot, now wrapped in the towel and unable to struggle, under one arm. 'It *is* Sunday,' Issy reminded him. 'Such blasphemy.' She tutted and then caught Brodie's far from amused glare. 'I'd better dry Pershing.'

'Dry him? He's a bird, in case you've forgotten. Don't they get wet all the time in the tropics? You'll be putting conditioner on him next.' He was reserving all his sympathy for himself and his mauled big toe.

'As a matter of fact his feathers do get sprayed with aloe vera. And, in case you hadn't noticed, this is Scotland, not the rainforest and . . . and if Pershing gets cold . . .'

'Okay. I get it. What was he doing in here, in any case?' Brodie demanded, refusing to be mollified or to show any sympathy for his feathered attacker.

'He has a bath every Sunday, as befits a gentleman. I normally leave him in the shower cubicle with the water trickling, he sits on the plastic perch - and when he's all done, shouts: 'Ready', and we fetch him out.'

'*Ready*,' Pershing said. '*Ban the Bomb. Ban the Bomb.*'

'A parrot with left-wing sentiments. I wonder how he came by those!'

'He flew into my aunt's tent one cold, dark October night in the mid-eighties. She was camped outside the perimeter fence at Greenham Common Airbase with other women, protesting against the deployment of cruise missiles by the USAF on British soil.'

'Polaris. Greenham Common. Just what does your aunt have against America?' he asked.

Issy ignored his outburst. 'Pershing was just a baby then and still had a soft beak.'

'Unlike now, you mean?' Brodie asked testily, looking down at the blood-smeared floor tiles.

Issy bent down, kissed Pershing's horny bill and continued with the story. 'Esme placed adverts in the post office but no one came to claim him.'

'Guess they were glad to get rid of him,' Brodie said, unfeelingly.

'*Gei'us a kiss, dahrr –lin*',' the parrot responded in a broad Scots accent. '*Ah, nice kiss . . . no bite - Pershing.*' It gave Issy a smacking kiss and even Brodie couldn't help but laugh.

'*Pershing?*' Brodie questioned. 'Go on, enlighten me.'

'After the missiles the USAF deployed at Greenham Common. Isn't that right, mah wee peacenik?'

'*Aye, see you Jimmy*,' he replied, starting to struggle free.

'I'll leave you alone,' Issy said to Brodie. 'If you need any help

_'

'I think I can manage, if you give me a Band-Aid. A what d'you call it - a sticking plaster? My shots are all up to date, so don't worry on my account.' The last was said sarcastically, as it was clear she wasn't in the least bit concerned for his welfare. Or if he contracted lockjaw, or whatever tetanus guarded against these days.

Seemingly put out by her lack of sympathy, Brodie turned away and limped over to the sink where he'd set out his shaving equipment. Issy watched the play of muscles across his shoulders as he reached out for shaving foam and squirted some into his cupped hand. Despite the wriggling parrot in her arms, she was loathe to leave the steamy bathroom or drag her eyes away from Brodie's lower back and slim waist. Her eyes travelled his length, admiring his tan, which, judging by its depth and colour, hadn't been acquired in the northern hemisphere. Maybe he'd been diving down to some coral reef looking for – plankton?

As always, thinking about Brodie left her with more questions than answers. Time was running out - he was leaving, and soon there would be nothing left for her to puzzle over.

'Was there something else?' he asked, half turning, obviously aware that she was still standing there.

'No – no,' she stammered, embarrassed at being caught checking him out.

As she turned to leave, Issy noticed a tattoo on his left shoulder - a looped belt, with its tongue coiled through the middle and with the buckle on the left hand side. Inside the circle formed by the belt, was a large orange cat with fierce, red claws - more tiger than ginger tom. The motto round the crest read: *Na bean don chat gun lamhainn.*

TOUCH NOT THE CAT BOT A GLOVE.

Issy frowned.

As far as she was aware, that was the badge of Clan McIntosh. Yet - wasn't he a Brodie? And Brodie was not a sept of the McIntoshes. Maybe her joke about Big Mac wasn't so wide of the mark, after all? Her brain switched up a gear, and despite her earlier resolution to stop speculating about him and his motives, she was back to trying to figure him out. Had he, she wondered, been playing with her - with all of them, since the moment he'd been blown in on the storm wind?

Was there any truth behind the statement that his eco-lodge was double booked? Or had he used that as a ruse to stay longer in her aunt's house? But for what reason? Issy remembered his furtive photographing session in the study, his questions about the distillery, her aunt's political affiliations. Once again, she concluded there was more to Brodie than met the eye. More than he was willing to share.

'Is there something else?' Brodie asked, catching her eye in the mirror – and, did she imagine it? – turning his shoulder away from her too-perceptive gaze.

'No. I'm outta here,' Issy said in an exaggerated American accent, to annoy him and to throw him off the scent. 'Got me a parrot to dry. Laters.'

'See you later, *hen*,' Brodie parried in broad Scots, using the term of endearment he'd earlier confessed to finding quaint. Taking the hint, Issy left the bathroom carrying the parrot under her arm, and headed for the sitting room. As she crossed the inner hall she heard Brodie close the door behind her, no doubt with a deft, backward flick of his bloodied foot.

Chapter Fourteen
More Questions than Answers

After drying Pershing with a hairdryer – held at arm's length and set on a very low heat, Issy topped up his feeding dishes and left him to preen. She returned to the study to send some emails to her friends from university telling them, briefly, of her break-up with Jack Innes-Kerr - and her plans for renting the outhouses as workspace, for a peppercorn rent. A few minutes later, Brodie limped into the study wearing Superdry flip flops and a plaster on his big toe.

'Thanks for leaving the first aid kit on my bed. As you can see, I've survived the savage mauling.' He pointed at his toe.

'You'll laugh about this with your family when you return to the States, telling them how you were set upon by a wild beast in the Highlands. I'd leave out the bit about the shower, if I were you. But, at least you have one thing to be thankful for.'

'I do?'

'Lindy isn't here. Otherwise your foot would be swathed in bandages and she'd be insisting that she push you around in one of those bath chairs you only see in comics. You know, where crusty old colonels with gout are wheeled around with their bandaged foot propped up.' She took in his puzzled expression. 'Okay, that *might* have lost something in translation.'

'You think?' he frowned.

'Don't you?' she countered.

'At least Lindy would show some fellow feeling,' he said, sounding aggrieved. Issy laughed and then Brodie, catching her amused expression, laughed too. 'You think I oughta man up. Is that it?'

'Aye, these are the highlands, laddie, where men sport beards, kilts and no underwear. Where the men are men and the women are glad of it.'

Wow, that was a bit too close to home, considering she'd got a pretty good look earlier at what would be concealed by the thick folds of a kilt. She'd bet even money on him going commando, if it came to it. Getting wayward thoughts under control, Issy strove to change the subject.

'What are your plans for today?' Watching his expression lighten, she quickly put him straight. 'I've got to tackle a mound of paperwork but Lindy will be in later to make dinner. So,' she stuck her pencil behind her ear and paused, hinting that he should leave. But, as she was discovering, getting rid of Brodie was easier said than done. With a huff of annoyance she fired up the laptop and logged onto the internet, keeping half an eye on him as he limped around picking things up, putting them down.

Issy sensed purpose beneath his measured circuit of the room, and when he picked up an old family photograph and examined it, she felt it was a step too far. He wanted something from her, from her aunt – she was sure of it. But for the life of her she couldn't figure out what. Raising her head and flicking her dark hair out of her eyes, she sent him a cool, measuring look.

'Was there something else, Mr Brodie?'

He gave one of his charming, lopsided grins. 'Just getting a feel for the old country,' he said. 'You carry on. Don't let me disturb you.'

It was on the tip of her tongue to say: *but you are disturbing me.* Instead, she put the laptop into sleep mode and gave him her full attention. She'd guessed earlier that Brodie had Scottish blood in his veins – his name, dark auburn hair, height and build and freckled skin were evidence of it, no detective work necessary. But that was as close as she'd got to figuring him out. Rising, she took the photograph out of his hand and put it back on Esme's desk, making plain that she wanted him to leave.

'So, who're the guys in the photograph?' He indicated two young soldiers in the uniform of the Queen's Own Cameron Highlanders. It was one of those studio photos taken at the start of the Great War before regiments sailed for France. The young men, with their highland caps set at a jaunty angle, looked excited at the prospect of the adventure they believed lay ahead of them. The horrors of trench warfare, the Zeppelin raids on London and dogfights over Belgian cornfields all lay in the future. As far as they and everyone were concerned, the war would be over by Christmas with the Hun defeated.

Piece of cake . . .

'The one on the left is my grandfather, Young Johnny Stuart as he was known. The other one is his friend, and business partner, Archie. As I told you before,' she tried to keep impatience out of her voice, 'our families established Twa Burns Distillery in the early nineteenth century. They turned it from a hotchpotch of illicit stills housed in sheds down by the bay, into a going concern which incurred excise duty.'

She fired back her answers hoping that would satisfy his curiosity.

'They look a fine couple of soldiers,' he observed, giving the cracked photograph another once- over. The dress uniform was probably the first new clothes many in the regiment had ever owned - a natty jacket fastened by a white belt with a brass buckle, thick kilt and sporran, white gaiters over dark socks and boots. There was also a cap with a checked border and two ribbons streaming down the back, worn, jauntily, on the side of the head.

'They were boys, really, only eighteen or nineteen years old. They'd never been further afield than Inverness, or Glasgow. Then, bang – there they are in France, thinking it's all great fun until the first round of artillery fire introduces them to trench warfare. Grim.' She shuddered and tried to take the photo off him a second time. But Brodie was in no rush to hand it back.

'What happened to the boys?'

'Only Johnny returned from France, invalided out after being gassed at the second battle of Ypres.'

'Archie?'

'Buried in an unmarked grave in Flanders,' Issy said quietly. 'His family never recovered from the shock of losing their only son. Soon after, his mother, father, brothers and sisters died in the flu epidemic which swept the country after the war.'

'Is that when *Twa Burns* became *Stuart's Twa Burns* Distillery?' Brodie turned the photo over in his hands to reveal a piece of brown paper, covered in faded writing. 'What's this?' he asked, holding it up to the light and squinting at it.

'Something old and very precious. Precious to the Stuarts, at least.'

'How's that?'

Issy sighed, realising she was getting nowhere until she'd satisfied his curiosity.

'On the eve of sailing for France, the boys made makeshift wills. Each vowing, should only one return, that the survivor would do the right thing by the bereaved family. Look after the aged parents, find work for the boys and husbands for the girls. In those days *Eilean na Sgairbh* was a thriving place, but after the war it was a long time before the distillery was back into production. During that time, young islanders headed south to Glasgow or England, and things were never the same for the island, the Stuarts, or Twa Burns Distillery.'

'Is there any whisky left? I'd like to take a couple of bottles back with me when I leave. A souvenir of my stay and the warm welcome I've received by Lola and your aunt.' Issy noticed that he didn't mention *her* in his list. Stung, but realising it was no more than she deserved because of the off-hand way she'd treated him, Issy got to her feet.

'Six bottles. Five and a half to be precise. Now if that's all . . .' She took the photograph from him a second time.

'Y'know, a good single malt from an extinct distillery could fetch a good price at auction. Do you have provenance for the remaining bottles? Lindy told me that you were trying to raise funds to build some kinda artistic workshops out back.'

'Lindy's got it wrong,' she said stiffly, not wishing to discuss her plan with him, with *anyone,* at this stage. Just in case full planning permission was refused. 'I simply mean to renovate the old outhouses and offer painting, sculpture, metalworking courses and so on - to paying guests who we'll put up at *Ailleag.*'

'Are you going to run the courses yourself?'

Really, the man was *too* much! Why couldn't he model himself on *The Quiet American* in the Graham Greene novel and leave her alone? There being nothing for it, she gave him the barest outline of her plans.

'I have friends who attended Edinburgh School of Design with me and trained in glass-blowing, jewellery-making, silversmithing, animation and so on. Due to the high rent charged for studio space in Edinburgh – and even Glasgow – they've been unable to find anywhere cheap enough to rent to develop their crafts and skills. Let alone make a living from them.' She zoned out for a moment, remembering the exhibition at the end of her post-graduate interior design course and the evening when she'd first met Geordie Innes-Kerr. He was there in the role of benefactor of the Design School and on the lookout for talented twenty-somethings to join his graduate scheme at Ecosse Designs. Accompanying him was son and heir, Jack Innes-Kerr, looking exactly like a golden lion – all sleek and tan after a recent holiday in the West Indies – *and* very full of himself. Issy had been dazzled by him. Now, looking back, she realised that Jack had been on the lookout for talent of an entirely different kind.

First of all he'd seen Issy's designs and then, her ... and had wanted both.

The rest, as they say, is history. A history Issy would rather forget.

'And you want to help by renting them studio space . . .'

'At a peppercorn rent,' she was quick to point out.

'Where -'

'Where they can flourish, attract tourists and paying guests and . . .'

'Bring life back to the island? That'll take time and money,' he said, pausing just long enough to allow her to fill in the gaps by telling him how she planned to fund her grand scheme. But she didn't give anything away – two could play at his game.

'Better sell that bottle of whisky and get down to it then, hadn't I?' was her crisp way of dismissing him.

'Better see if you can find any more lying around. The last

bottle of eighty-year-old single malt went under the hammer for twenty thousand big ones.' Issy looked at him to see if he was joking.

He was deadly serious.

'Pounds or dollars?' she asked, showing sudden interest.

'Pounds sterling,' he laughed, openly amused by her volte face.

'Blimey,' Issy let slip before she could school her features. 'I mean, really?'

'Really.'

'I was saving it to serve to mourners at my father's wake. However,' she paused.

'They can all go hang?'

'I've had second thoughts.' She glanced at her watch and this time he took the hint.

'Catch you later?'

'That depends on what time you get back,' she said. Her tone made it clear that she wouldn't be sitting in the bay window with a shawl round her shoulders, candle in hand and waiting for his return.

'Later, then.' He tipped her a salute and went out via the kitchen to the yard where he'd parked his rented Land Rover. Issy sat stock still until the four-by-four roared off down the road towards the harbour and quay where the tide was on the turn. He was heading over to the mainland, but for what purpose she could only guess.

She retrieved her pencil from behind her ear and began to nibble the end, thinking back to the scene in the bathroom and Brodie's tattoo. The motto's meaning: *Touch not the cat (when it is) without a glove*, kept repeating itself in her head like a mantra – or warning. She'd googled the reference and discovered that the 'glove' of the wildcat is the soft, underpart of its paw. When assuming a war-like attitude, the wildcat spreads its paw, ungloved, revealing dangerous claws. The motto is a caveat to those foolish enough to engage the wildcat in battle when its claw is unsheathed.

She'd be wise to be on her guard, and to treat Brodie with circumspection until she found out the real purpose behind his visit to Cormorant Island. As for his trip over to the mainland, she'd wait until *Lola, Queen of Las Vegas* turned up for duties later and question her. Lindy couldn't keep a secret even if she wanted to.

If anyone knew where Brodie was going and what he was up to – it'd be Lindy.

Chapter Fifteen
The Young Widow Twanky

Later that same day, Lindy turned up to make Sunday Lunch and deliver Brodie's laundry. To give him his due, Brodie had made it plain that he had no need of a laundry maid and was more than capable of using a washing machine. However, Lindy, intent on making herself indispensable had proved difficult to dissuade and his laundry maid she had become.

'Pouf!' Lindy exhaled, depositing Brodie's well-pressed linen on the bed by the side of his open suitcase. 'All done. Where's Himself?' She seemed disappointed to find he had gone AWOL.

'Taken himself over to the mainland. He'll be back before the tide turns and cuts us off for the night, I imagine.' Standing in the doorway, Issy watched Lindy smooth out non-existent creases in Brodie's jeans, his ever devoted acolyte. Then her eyes were drawn to the open suitcase and, against all expectations, she experienced a pang at the thought of Brodie moving on. Once he left it would be just her and Pershing until her aunt's return. For some reason she found the thought depressing.

'Pass me those shirts, will you?' Issy did as she was asked, lingering just a little too long over the task, if the truth be told.

'You're going to miss him when he returns to the USA,' she observed, transferring her thoughts onto Lindy.

'Yes - and no,' Lindy replied, giving Issy a hooded look.

'Meaning?' Issy could almost hear the cogs in Lindy's brain whirring around.

'Meaning - what if I asked Brodie to take me back to America with him?'

'Lindy. Are you *mad*? People usually take home kiltie dolls and swatches of tartan - not fully grown Scotswomen, who - incidentally, don't even possess a passport.'

'Och, that's easily remedied, Issy.' Lindy waved objections aside with an airy gesture. 'He's here for a wee while longer, I could easily nip over to Glasgow and get a passport. Although, I suppose *you'll* be glad to see the back of him. I don't get why you dislike him so much; why you're down on him all the time. Snippy; sarcastic - referring to him as *Mr* Brodie . . .'

'Actually, I'm not down on him all the time. I'm simply being cautious - we know nothing about him, or his life back in the States. But you go ahead with this crazy plan if you want to,' said Issy, more harshly than intended. Lindy bristled at 'crazy plan' and drew herself up to her full five feet two inches.

'Thanks, I will.' She paused. 'You know your trouble, don't you Ishabel Stuart?'

'No. But I have the feeling I'm about to find out.' Issy leaned against the door jamb and folded her arms across her bosom.

'You've let Jack-the-Lad slip through your fingers and you're on your way to becoming a bitter and twisted old maid, not to mention man-hater.' Having delivered her verdict on the present state of Issy's love life, Lindy continued. 'So - you going to tell Auntie Lindy what happened between you and ol' Jackie boy? Or ahm I to guess? I'd lay even money on him playing away from home and you finding out.' Something in Issy's expression must have given her away because Lindy clicked her fingers several times and sketched an imaginary 'S' in the air. 'Sistah, you weren't never gonna hang onto a man like Jack. But at least I hope you've had the sense to keep the ring. Oh. My. God, you gave it back, didn't you?'

'I –'

Lindy brushed Issy's protest aside and looked at her as if she was stupid. 'Everyone knows that you *never* give the ring back. You earned it and it's yours to keep.'

'*Earned* it! You certainly don't believe in letting romance get in the way of business, do you?'

'The way I look at it is this – chances are a girl might have to get engaged two or three times before she finds THE ONE. If she gives the ring back at the end of each disastrous relationship, she's left with a broken heart and not much else.'

'See – I *knew* I should have to come to you for advice first. Or Mother,' Issy said with heavy sarcasm.

Lindy rounded on her.

'It's all very well for you to act like you're *Lady Muck fae Stoorie Castle*. You've got this house coming to you one day, an honours degree and, knowing you, a good wee bit put aside for a rainy day. You should have sold the ring and spent the money on a couple of fabulous holidays. You could have taken me with you; sometimes, Issy, I despair of you. You just don't get it.' Her look suggested that Issy was a simple-minded child. Not only that, by her actions she had selfishly denied Lindy the chance of a holiday somewhere exotic.

Issy tutted. 'You're right. I am self-centred. It just hadn't occurred to me that I'd *earned* the right to keep the ring.'

'Okay - no need to give me that look. You're an intelligent woman, Issy, but sometimes . . .'

'Don't hold back . . .'

'To be honest, Ishabel Stuart, you've been so fixated on this daft idea of an artistic community on Cormorant Island in yer auntie's wee sheds that you obviously forgot the first rule of keeping a man happy.'

'Which is?' Issy asked, ice dripping from every word.

'Feed him carbs and shag him witless. That way he'll come home to you every night, not some other woman. I mean, take last winter for example.'

'Yes?' Issy said in a deceptively calm voice.

'Jack wanted to go somewhere hot, like Maldives, didn't he? But where did you take him – all the way up to Balnakeil on the frozen north coast to look at some *craft village* or other. For God's sake, Issy!'

'It was research if you must know. The former Cold War

bunkers, the remains of early warning posts, were bought out by the community and turned into a craft village. I thought I might get some ideas for workshops -' Her voice trailed off, put that way it did sound rather selfish. 'Jack was able to get in a few rounds of golf while I made notes and spoke to some of the artists-in-residence there. And we did visit the caves at Smoo.'

'Big woopee-do,' Lindy said, with a slow handclap.

'This from the self-appointed Agony Aunt of Shag Rock? You'd know all about holding onto *yer mahn*, would you, hen?' She pronounced the latter sentence in an exaggerated Glasgow accent, all the more to annoy Lindy.

Suitable men were few and far between on the island and Lindy's dates had been confined to the few boys she'd gone to school with, who hadn't moved south to find employment. Or, the fishermen across The Narrows who got drunk on a Friday night and were on the lookout for an easy lay. Not to forget the couple of times she and Issy had stayed with her cousin in Glasgow and Lindy had got so hammered that she had to be carried home, prone, in a taxi. However, Lindy wasn't one to let lack of life experience stop her from voicing an opinion.

'I do know all about hanging onto *mah mahn*, actually, hen.' Lindy brushed past Issy and headed for the kitchen. 'Any time you want some advice, just ask me – sistah. Anyhoo, I didn't come here to fall out with you over Brodie.' Issy followed her into the kitchen where Pershing was sitting on his perch looking out of the window, like a feathered coastguard.

'I'm glad to hear it. Look, Lindy – things are hard for me right now. My father's ashes are on the window ledge of the outhouse, I've broken off my engagement with the man I was supposed to be marrying at Christmas in an extravagant wedding at St Giles in Edinburgh - *and* I've resigned from Ecosse Designs. I don't need us arguing like a couple of teenagers over a guest who's leaving the day after tomorrow.'

'You didn't?' Lindy stopped dead in her tracks, turned and looked at Issy open-mouthed, and for the first time with a degree of admiration. 'Gave up your swanky job as well as Jack-the-Lad?'

'I have – I mean, I did. How long could I go on working for his father when -'

'Och - c'mere, hen . . .' Lindy held out her arms and Issy walked into them, allowing herself to be hugged. Lindy was as mad as a box of frogs and her relationship advice was decidedly shaky, but she had a heart of gold. After a few moments, Lindy pushed Issy away and held her at arm's length. 'What you need is some R and R.'

'Meaning?'

'It's Open Mic Night at The Pickled Herring tomorrow and Jimmy wants to know if you're up for singing some of the *auld* songs.' She rolled her eyes. 'There's a group of birdwatchers booked into the B&B, and they want the *Full Scoddish Experience*: haggis, whisky, clootie dumpling, craic round the fireside and bonnie lassies singing Heilan' Lullabies.' She draped a tea towel over her corkscrew curls, tied it under her chin like a headscarf and adopted a simpering pose. 'That's where you come in.' She started to hum the opening bars of *Annie Laurie*.

'Me?' Issy asked, glad that Lindy had tired of dispensing relationship counselling and they were on amiable terms once more. She didn't want to fall out with Lindy; but sometimes, she was just *too* much.

'Och aye, The Full Monty as far as singing goes. It won't be a ceilidh with the dancing and such, mind, just some regulation stuff – old Jacobite songs, a toast to the King over the Water.' More eye-rolling. 'A bit of The Proclaimers or Runrig. That sorta thing.'

'I haven't sung at The Pickled Herring since last Christmas. I'm a bit rusty. I don't know if –'

'Och, away with ye, Issy. You know very well you've got the voice of an angel. It's the one thing yer mad Mammy passed onto you.' Lindy walked into the pantry and began assembling everything she needed to make the evening meal. 'That, and hair most women would die for.'

'Two compliments in a row. I guess I'd better say yes,' Issy replied, adopting an ironic expression.

'Oh and slip in a few tunes I might know. Adele or Rihanna will do; then we can segue into karaoke. All that Hoots Mon stuff is strictly for the tourists.' She wrinkled up her nose and removed the tea towel from her Irn Bru curls.

'Your love of your Scottish ancestry is touching, it really is. And maybe, just for you - *Lola*, we can add a few Barry *McManilow* songs – '

'*Now* who's being sarcastic?'

'Well, if there's to be a mini-ceilidh tomorrow evening I'd better sort myself out . . .'

'Did someone mention a ceilidh?' Brodie walked in from the hall, jangling car keys in his hand. 'I've been hoping to experience one before I return home.'

Again the pang – identical to the one she'd experienced watching Lindy packing his case.

'Well don't go overboard,' Issy said sarcastically, hiding her feelings behind a cutting remark. 'This isn't Briga-bloody-doon, you know. We don't want you turning up in full highland rigout – kilt, lace jabot, leather brogues and sporting a humongous badger head sporran. In fact,' she paused long enough to let him fill in the gap.

'You hope I won't turn up at all?' he asked, his smile never faltering. But his eyes sent her a different message and his mouth quirked at the corner in anger. She didn't answer, simply stood there returning his inimical look with a frosty one of her own.

'Oh, dinnae mind Ishabel, Brodie. She's pissed off because her fiancé's . . .'

'That's enough, Lindy,' Issy cut her off in mid-sentence. For once Lindy had the sense to keep her opinions to herself and settled instead for an insulted sniff and a diva-like toss of the head.

'Am I missing something?' Brodie asked. When neither of them answered he looked as if he was trying to guess what had passed between them. From his puzzled look, it was clear he was thinking back to how well he and Issy had got on when she'd driven him round the island the other day.

Something had changed and his expression showed he was at a loss to know what it was.

Apparently anxious to make amends, Lindy explained, 'You ought to hear Issy singing *Sguaban Arbhair*, Brodie. There's rarely a dry eye in the house when she's finished.'

'*Sguaban Arbhair*,' Brodie tried to get his tongue round the syllables but failed, miserably.

'It's a lament decrying the passing of the old ways,' Issy explained, now feeling that she'd been unnecessarily hard on him. She put it down to a combination of Lindy riling her – nothing new there – and the realisation that, one day soon, Brodie would be leaving. And his leaving mattered more to her than she was prepared to admit.

'Issy knows all this old stuff,' Lindy put in helpfully.

'As for it being a ceilidh . . . it's more Open Mic Night at The Pickled Herring, very amateurish, Something to draw the punters in on a Monday evening; I'm sure you won't enjoy it,' Issy said, attempting to put him off one last time.

Some part of her didn't want Brodie to hear her sing. She didn't want to share anything – intimate, or otherwise, with him. Which was a bit crazy considering she didn't mind performing in front of locals and summer visitors. In spite of her rocky relationship with La Bella Scozzese, she had – as Lindy had pointed out, inherited her mother's ear for music and sang in a sweet alto. However, there was something personal about singing; you always ended up giving something of yourself away.

And Issy wanted to give nothing of herself to this handsome, enigmatic stranger.

'Oh, very well, come if you must.' Issy shrugged, as though bored with the topic.

'So gracious. Thanks, Ma'am, I will.' There was frost in Brodie's voice and coolness in his olive green eyes. Issy sighed and turned away. She'd managed to annoy Lindy *and* Brodie in the space of ten minutes, maybe she'd take her supper sitting at her aunt's desk and avoid both of them.

'*Ship Ahoy*,' the parrot exclaimed, walking from side to side on his perch, head down and with an evil glint in his eye as he focused on Brodie.

'Looks like he's after your blood,' Lindy laughed, returning to the pantry to fetch the ingredients for a light, pasta supper.

'Not the only one,' Brodie said as Issy left the kitchen, closing the door behind her.

Chapter Sixteen
Skeletons in the Loft Conversion

Issy decided to give Esme's bedroom a thorough spring clean while she was at the fracking protest, in the vain hope that physical activity would keep the voices in her head at bay. Voices which kept her awake at night, haunted her days and left her muzzy-headed and below par.

The memorial service and wake . . . her mother . . . Jack Innes-Kerr . . . plans for the outhouses . . . waiting for Probate to be granted . . . scattering her father's ashes . . .

The list was endless and she seemed to be making little progress with any of it.

Now, standing in her aunt's bedroom with a roll of black bin liners tucked into her belt, she rolled up her sleeves and set about her task with a will. She hoped that clearing the room would prove cathartic. Esme was pathologically untidy – holding onto anything and everything, gathering her possessions around her as if they were a buffer against the world. Ancient CND magazines, yellowing copies of The Guardian, junk mail, pizza offers, plastic charity collection bags and discount vouchers for *Cowboys and McIndians* - the Balti house on the far side of The Narrows.

Issy, on the other hand, was obsessively tidy.

She'd attended boarding school in St Andrews and until the sixth form, had shared a cramped room with three other girls. Nothing was sacred in their eyes; everything of hers was theirs; to be borrowed, shared and returned - broken. As a result, Issy liked order in her life and everything around her *just so*. Hadn't Jack mocked her obsession with order by giving her a plaque for her desk?

A TIDY DESK IS A SIGN OF A SICK MIND?

It had been one of his so-not-funny jokes, one of the many made at her expense. Maybe, Issy reflected as she pushed up the sleeves of her thin t-shirt and applied herself to the task in hand, he had a point. Like her late father, she liked to be in control, calling the shots. Perhaps she needed to relax, to let go once in a while. In her heart-of-hearts she'd known for months she and Jack were badly matched, their disastrous trip to Balnakeil had made that perfectly clear. But Issy was no quitter. It had taken catching him with his trousers round his ankles to give her the final push to break off their engagement.

She expelled a breath - back to Esme.

She, at any rate, had life sussed and was comfortable in her over-stuffed mouse nest of a home. Its interior reflected the years she'd spent abroad supporting various causes, collecting artefacts from every corner of the globe along the way. As a result, *Ailleag* was furnished with an eclectic mix of shabby chic and family heirlooms which Issy treasured, knowing one day they would be hers.

She loved the patchwork bedspread made from squares of

wedding saris, the comfortable William IV armchair near a glass-topped table piled high with books and CDs, and the family portraits on the wall. Her favourite was one of herself, executed in pastels by Esme the summer before she'd taken up her place at Edinburgh University. In it, she looked dreamy, her violet eyes holding a far-away look. In reality, she was in turmoil – recovering from a bruising holiday with her mother in Tuscany, where she'd found herself in the way of La Bella Scozzese and her latest man – Edoardo something-or-other.

Unsurprisingly – he'd made a pass at her. That had resulted in her mother putting her on the first plane back to Edinburgh, accusing her of flirting with the ghastly euro trash loafer. Neither of them had been in a hurry to repeat the disastrous holiday and Issy had immersed herself in her studies instead. But it rankled that her mother had chosen the latest boyfriend over *her*.

Sighing, Issy pulled a black bin liner off the roll, tucked it into her belt and waded in.

Junk mail first, then a good shakedown of Esme's bed – she doubted it had been aired properly through the long, harsh winter which settled round *Eilean na Sgairbh* from October to May in the form of a cold, damp cloak of mist. Esme had suffered a bout of pneumonia after Christmas, so, maybe it was time for the central heating to be upgraded? Surely, there were grants available when Esme's age was taken into account? Failing that, Issy would pay for it herself.

First jobs first, though, she'd move some of her aunt's stuff up into the boarded loft extension for Esme to go through on her return. Then, a phone call to a DIY shop in Jamestoun to hire a carpet cleaner and tackle the valuable Persian rug which was covered in coffee and red wine stains.

Housework and Esme Stuart were strangers.

It was all so different from Issy's penthouse in Leith, Edinburgh. Or, to be more accurate, the penthouse her father had bought as an investment and leased back to her at a peppercorn rent, to remind her there was no such thing as a free lunch. That was her father all over, never showing favour or preference simply because she was his daughter. It made for an uneasy relationship. The penthouse was on the fifteenth floor and had 360 degree views of the Firth of Forth - with its famous coat hanger bridge, the Bass Rock and Berwick to the south and *Auld Reekie's* dramatic skyline at its feet. It was all chrome, black leather, animal hide rugs, blonde wood floors and state of the art bathrooms. Hurt that her father hadn't commissioned her to decorate it, Issy nevertheless regarded the flat as 'home' and had added defiant flashes of Royal Stewart tartan to break up the monochrome monotony. Her father was proud to be Scottish but was more Braveheart than Brigadoon, arguing that the whole *Scotland in a tin* industry was holding his country back.

Technology - yes. Tartan – no, was his watch cry!

Never mind that other people loved Scotland and everything Scottish.

Neither, for that matter, did he approve of family photographs littering up the place. Maybe, memories of a failed marriage, the distance between himself and his daughter and the acrimonious relationship with his sister made for uncomfortable viewing – even when framed in solid silver.

Issy pulled down the ladder which gave access to the loft space; being tall, she managed it with ease. Hot, stale air rushed down to meet her and she turned her head to one side, coughing as dust motes danced in a beam of sunlight. Pausing for a moment, she considered afresh her plans for the outhouses once her father's last bequests were taken care of. She needed the feeling of closure which scattering his ashes would bring, before she could get on with the rest of her life.

'Mizz Stoo-art?' Brodie's American twang broke through Issy's dream. She took a deep breath. The last thing she wanted was more questions about the history of *Eilean na Sgairbh* and Twa Burns Distillery.

'Mr Brodie?' Her bright smile hid her annoyance at his interruption. 'How can I help you?'

'I just wanted to say that I won't be in for dinner tonight. Will you tell Lola? She said something about making - Cullen Skink?'

'Fish soup,' she put in, reading his puzzled expression. 'Smoked haddock chowder, one of Lola's specialties.'

'I recognise *chowder*.' He lingered in the doorway, too uncertain of her mood to venture further without permission. 'That kid can cook, she could make a fortune with the right backing. And it'd be a whole lot safer than working the tables in Vegas.' He frowned as though the idea of Lindy Tenant on the loose in Sin City troubled him. For the first time, Issy felt in sync with him.

'That's just what I've told her!' she said, before she could stop herself. 'But, you know Lindy.' She shrugged and lugged a bin liner of old paperbacks up the ladder and into her aunt's loft. The bag split and the books came tumbling out. 'Bugger,' she said.

'I love how you British say *bugger*. I'm guessing it's a swear word, right?'

'Not to be used in polite society,' Issy agreed, sounding exactly like a Jane Austen heroine – albeit it with a Scottish accent.

'Guess that makes me *im*-polite society, then?'

'Something like that.' This time, Issy smiled, relaxing a little.

'Here, let me.' Appearing to sense a slight thaw in her manner, Brodie crossed the threshold, knelt at her feet and gathered up the scattered books.

The same shaft of dust-filled sunlight which had greeted Issy when she'd pulled down the loft ladder, now touched the top of his dark russet hair, burnishing it. She looked on, entranced, as Brodie applied strong wrists and supple fingers to the task of stacking the books. She admired the way his wrist bones swivelled and turned, how the muscles on his lower arm expanded and contracted as he reached out for the faded paperbacks.

For reasons she could not explain, the sight was most affecting.

'New bag? Maybe double this time?' He held his hand out without turning to face her.

'Of – of course,' she stammered. 'I was miles away . . .'

Miles away imagining those long fingers working their magic as they trailed a line from her breasts and downwards; lower, ever lower. Issy shivered despite the heat and was glad his back was turned towards her and he didn't see her frisson of reaction to the erotic images in her head.

'You often are,' he said. This time he turned round, hunkered down on his heels and gave her a considering, and not unsympathetic look. 'Guess you've got stuff to sort out? Your father's estate and – and so on.'

And so on? Just what had Lindy-blabbermouth-Tennant been saying?

'You could say that.' Issy tore two bags off the roll and put one inside the other. When it was full, Brodie straightened and, with a nod of his head, indicated that she should stand aside. He hefted the sack over his shoulder and climbed into the loft, leaving Issy to bring up the rear, trying very hard not to stare at *his* rear - which was tightly muscled and *very* pinch-able in his long cargo shorts. Luckily, he was too occupied with depositing the bag safely in the loft to notice her interested stare.

'Oh, cool,' he said. The bag of books was forgotten as he walked over to the Velux windows set into the sloping roof. 'Boy – that's some view.'

Through the windows he was able to look out over The Narrows and towards Jamestoun. With the added advantage of height, it was possible to see beyond the white painted fishermen's cottages to the hills beyond. To the left there was a small loch, round and glassy in the sunshine. It reminded Issy of the powder compact mirror she'd used to create a miniature garden in a seed tray when she was younger. It had won first prize in the Under 10's section at the Jamestoun agricultural show. She smiled to herself, she'd forgotten all about it, until now.

'Yes, it's beautiful. When I was younger I used to come up here and pretend I was the princess in the tower awaiting rescue.' She pulled up short, realising she was giving too much of herself away.

'And who was riding to your rescue?' Smiling, he leaned back against the thick window embrasure, seemingly enjoying this rare moment of rapport. He appeared eager to recapture the spirit of the afternoon when she'd shown him round the island and they'd gone down to The Pickled Herring afterwards for a dram and a pie, afterwards.

'Young Lochinvar, of course.' She widened her eyes and grinned, without stopping to consider what he might make of this melting of the ice. 'I mean –' she continued, flustered. Now he probably thought she was flirting with him, when all she'd meant to imply was that she could be good company when the occasion – and the companion - warranted it.

'Hey, I know that guy - Young Lochinvar. The one who comes out of the West riding a horse the modern day equivalent of a Ferrari 458. Right?' He placed his palms on the window ledge and adopted a relaxed pose, long, tanned legs crossed at the ankles.

Knowing she couldn't maintain her frostiness in the face of his attempt to befriend her, Issy answered, 'The very one. We cut our teeth on that poem in *these here parts*.' She slipped into a western drawl for the last three words, stuck her thumbs in her belt, cowboy fashion, and rolled on her heels as if she'd just dismounted from her horse.

He laughed, and the light reflected in his eyes turning them to soft, malachite green. Issy caught her breath and turned away, not quite knowing how she'd found herself at the top of the scariest ride in a water park. One false step would take her over the edge and send her skittering downwards on a trajectory over which she had no control. Feminine intuition told her the ride would be exhilarating, but common sense advised against it.

Who knew where friendship with this man would lead?

Brodie was dangerous, and all the more so because he was charming and had a way of slipping past her guard before she realised it. She wasn't in the market for *dangerous;* there was too much going on in her life to hazard it all on a summer fling with a six foot three, sex-on-legs American with russet hair. No matter how appealing the idea.

Resolutely, she took a step back from the brink.

'I never realised Lochinvar *was* a brave knight until I was about eleven,' Brodie went on, oblivious to her inner turmoil. 'I thought he was cowboy. All that riding out of the West, I guess.' Before she'd had time to apply the brakes, Issy laughed. This time their gazes locked and he held her with a look until she moved away, over to the other window.

Damn. Was *he* flirting with *her*?

'My aunt used to sing a song about a 'cock-eyed optimist', when

I was small. I thought she was singing about a cock-eyed octopus.' She traced a path down the dusty window with her forefinger and looked over to the mainland, unsure why she'd shared that particular memory with him.

'Kids, huh?'

Moving closer, he stood behind her, ostensibly looking over her shoulder at the engaging scenery. But more subtle forces were at play . . . a heady cocktail of sight, sense and touch. Issy smelled his aftershave, felt the heat rising from his sun-warmed skin and pulsing towards her in the airless loft. Reaching up, she slid open the locks on the Velux window and pushed it as far as it would go - however, the air which rushed in did nothing to cool her flushed cheeks. Little realising how close he was, she turned round and almost bumped noses. It would have been the easiest thing in the world to lean in and touch lips; and more than anything at that moment, Issy wanted to know how that would feel.

Shaken by the wanton thought, she took a deep breath, pressed against the window frame to avoid her breasts brushing against his chest and pulled back from the brink - again. Maybe she missed having a man in her bed more than she realised. Even if that man had been Mr 'three minutes and – oh, my God!' Jack Innes-Kerr; including foreplay. The disturbing image of her pushing Kerr out of her bed, holding back the sheet and inviting Brodie in, made heat spiral through her body. A pulse throbbed between her legs and her womb tightened, in response to hormones zizzing through her veins.

All at once, her breasts felt too heavy for her light t-shirt bra.

She wanted Brodie to cup them in his hands, kiss away their bruised tenderness and heal the pain. Dazed, she blinked several times to centre herself and get a grip on reality. *Was she mad?*

'Kids, indeed,' she managed to croak, breaking the stillness which had settled on them like a thick, hot cloak. Turning sideways, before he noticed that her nipples were pushing against the flimsy material of her t-shirt, she ducked under his arm and walked over to the far side of the loft where her aunt's canvasses were stacked against the wall. 'Thanks for helping. I can take it from here.'

'Those canvasses,' he said, swiftly changing the subject. 'Your aunt's I'm guessing?'

'Yes . . .'

'She had a talent.'

'*Has* a talent,' Issy corrected before she could stop herself. 'However, her various causes leave her with little time for painting watercolours.'

'Where did she go to school – Art School, I mean?'

'Glasgow School of Art. In the early Sixties, then –' again, she stopped in her tracks. More questions? Putting space between them had given her a breathing space, the chance to cool down. Now her guard was up and she was back to giving terse, but polite answers to his questions.

'Then?'

'Then she dropped out of university, became involved in the Peace Movement and never finished her degree.'

Issy looked at the paintings covered in thick polythene, the portfolios full of sketches stacked against one wall and the old-fashioned easel holding a canvass covered in wayward, angry brush strokes. Even she hadn't been aware of how many paintings her aunt had executed. She chewed her bottom lip, reflectively. Her aunt had declared the subject of her time at Glasgow Art School off-limits and Issy had respected that.

Nevertheless, she would love to know the reason behind her aunt turning her back on a promising career.

'So – your aunt . . . After the business with the Polaris Fleet. What then?'

Issy hesitated. There were gaps in Esme's history, gaps that her aunt did not care to elaborate upon. Speaking more to herself than directly to Brodie, she mumbled, 'Esme left Cormorant Island and followed the Hippy Trail from London to Kathmandu.'

'That took some guts,' he observed, bending over the canvasses to have a closer look.

'Esme's never been short of courage,' Issy put in, proudly. 'Then, there were no Lonely Planet guides or 24/7 internet connection to show backpackers where to go; where to stay. Esme worked her passage to India by guiding travellers along the route trodden by Marco Polo hundreds of years earlier. And every winter she stayed on Goa, cooking and cleaning for rich hippies who rented houses there, but always making her way back to *Eilean na Sgairbh* come the spring, like a bird of passage.'

'What drew her back home?' Brodie asked.

Issy frowned. 'I have no idea. Something. Someone.'

'She's a fine-looking woman, I'm guessing she had offers . . .'

'She had lovers, if that's what you mean,' Issy interjected. 'Her years of travelling the hippie trail came to an abrupt end, when the Islamic revolution in Iran and the Russian invasion of Afghanistan closed the overland route to western travellers.'

'After that?'

'She left Cormorant island and joined the Women's Peace Camp at Greenham Common, chaining herself to the base fence in protest against the Am –' She pulled up short.

'American Airbase?' he supplied, and Issy nodded.

It felt like ancient history, and one day, there would only be newsreel footage to tell about the protest at the Greenham Camp, all the women having passed on, like soldiers from the First World War. The thought made her feel unutterably sad and reminded her of Esme's mortality.

'After my parents' marriage foundered, Esme dedicated herself to looking after me. When I was old enough to attend boarding school in St Andrews, she went back on her travels. But, there were no worlds left to conquer. In a final irony,' she added softly, twirling one long strand of dark hair round her finger, 'they broke up the runway at Greenham Airbase and used it as hard core to build the Newbury Bypass. Another one of Esme's lost causes . . .'

Brodie got to his feet and brushed the dust off his shorts. 'I'm full of admiration for your aunt. Next to her, I'm just another rich kid who hasn't had to try too hard.'

Which brought her neatly back to the question that dogged her waking hours: *what did he want from Cormorant Island; from her?* Time to call a halt. She clattered down the rickety steps of the loft ladder and was back in Esme's bedroom before Brodie was aware of her intentions. He followed behind her, jumping off the last few rungs and landing expertly on his feet. Like the King of Cats.

Cats!

Touch Not the Cat Bot a Glove

Remembering the Mackintosh tattoo on his shoulder, Issy withdrew to her default position: suspicious, watchful, on her guard. Now was not the time to let her hormones do the thinking.

'So, you'll contact Lindy for me?' he asked.

'Lindy?'

'Cullen Skink.'

'Cullen - ? Oh, of course. I'll tell her not to bother with supper tonight. Have fun,' she added, heading towards another pile of books, 'whatever you have planned.'

Taking the hint, he left her to it.

Chapter Seventeen
Her Mother's Daughter

The punters were packed into The Pickled Herring for Open Mic Night, full of good cheer and cheap whisky. Issy leaned on the bar, asking Irene the barmaid how many had put themselves down to sing that evening. It turned out there were just three – herself and two of the bird- watching fraternity.

Irene leaned in confidentially, polishing imaginary fingerprints off the whisky glasses, and speaking out of the corner of her mouth as if this was a bar in Moscow and spies were everywhere.

'We're putting you on first and last, Issy. That way if the birdwatchers are complete shite we'll finish on a high note before the karaoke takes over.'

'Whatever.' Issy laughed at Irene's forthright manner.

Escaping an abusive husband in Paisley years earlier, Irene had stayed with Esme as a paying guest until her money ran out – and as a friend, after that. She'd been taken on at The Pickled Herring and had remained on the island ever since. She took no shit from anyone and was forthright in her manner. A man had made a fool of her once, and she wouldn't be putting herself through that again, she declared.

Maybe that would become *her* mantra, Issy speculated, as punters filled the pub to overflowing.

Fluffing up her hair and checking her reflection in the mirror which ran the length of the mahogany bar, Issy made ready for her first song. Her sprigged tea dress had cost almost a month's salary from Burberry, London; but was worth every penny. Deceptively simple, it looked demure but clung in all the right places, emphasising her slim waist, womanly curves and full breasts. Thanks to her Italian ancestry, she had the kind of figure which had been out of fashion for years, but which – allied to her height, drew admiring glances. Jack Innes-Kerr had been keen for her to join his gym, to tone up; but seeing as she spent most of her time jetting round the world, paying for an exclusive gym membership made no sense. Her good Scottish blood and Presbyterian upbringing wouldn't allow it, either!

Now, for exercise, she'd settle for walking across The Narrows when the tide was out, or over the hills to the other side of the island. That would be enough, she had other calls on her time and energy. Shrugging, she turned away from the mirror and leaned back against the bar, comfortable in her skin.

'Ach, ye look fine, Issy. Then - you always do, pet.' Irene smiled at her.

Issy's pale skin, violet eyes and cloud of dark hair, gave her the look of a young Elizabeth Taylor - or so people said. She didn't know about *that,* she simply made the most of what God, her genes, and good cosmetics could achieve. Tonight - to give herself a more contemporary look, she'd teamed the tea dress with a pair of biker boots and sheer black stockings which showed off her long legs. As a final touch, she'd accented wide-spaced eyes with smoky eye make-up and teased her hair into a 'just got out of bed' look.

As for being a latter day Elizabeth Taylor – she'd fallen at the first hurdle. Unable to make it to the altar with Husband Number One, let alone Number Eight.

'Aye, yer no so bad yersel', Irene.' Taking a sip from her wine glass, Issy smiled at the barmaid. Irene (pronounced Irene-ee) was the personification of a saucy seaside postcard, a buxom blonde with piled up hair and more curves than Nessie, herself.

Putting down her tea towel, Irene contravened every health and safety rule governing hygiene and the serving of food. She put her hand inside her bra, re-arranged her embonpoint and pushed her breasts until they wobbled like jelly on a plate. It appeared to be a 'look' much appreciated by the punters – if the transfixed expression on the birdwatchers' faces was anything to go by.

'Aye, have a good look boys – ye'll no see tits like these through yer binoculars,' she shouted over the din of the bar. The rest of the pub roared in appreciation and Issy gave Irene a mock-stern look. 'Och away with ye lassie, they love the banter – it's what they come in here for. Besides, they're big tippers and I have a holiday to pay for – and we're talking Cuba, mind, not Portobello or the Isle of Man. The tills have been ringing these last couple of weeks as they drink their fill of cheap whisky. Angus, the stingy old bastard,' she said, referring to the proprietor of The Pickled Herring with whom she had a love/hate relationship, 'has promised the staff a big bonus at the end of the season.'

The mention of *cheap whisky* drew Issy back to the ruined Twa Burns distillery and the afternoon she'd spent driving Brodie round the island. Her smile faltered. She'd enjoyed their tour in the summer sunshine, the shared banter, and – okay, the mild flirting, and the pie and dram afterwards at The Pickled Herring. Why, then, did she have to spoil it all this afternoon by pushing him away?

She *could* put it down to her frustration with Lindy's hare-brained scheme for stowing away in Brodie's suitcase, at the end of his stay. She *could* explain it away by playing the recently-bereaved-daughter/wounded-fiancée card – but none of it would be true.

No, the simple truth was that she was attracted to Brodie and the thought scared her. She'd recently walked away from one ill-fated relationship and couldn't afford to get involved with a stranger whose motives for staying on *Eilean na Sgairbh* were far from clear. Although, God knows, a summer fling might be the very thing she needed; something to mark an end of one phase in her life and herald in another. At the end of the season, Brodie would return to Kentucky – or wherever - and she'd settle down and establish her artists' workshops.

Why shouldn't they enjoy the moment?

Why?

Because she didn't operate like that. Leaping from one man's bed to another before the sheets were cold. Rumours about her and

Brodie would spread round the island like wild-fire and her name would be sludge. God knows, the Stuarts' standing was low enough, thanks to La Bella Scozzese's louche lifestyle and operatic career, James Stuart's refusal to rebuild the distillery - and the fact that he'd left Issy's upbringing to his sister, who the islanders held responsible for single-handedly driving the Polaris Fleet from Holy Loch and ruining their living.

As for herself, the jury was still out. She knew how it worked on the island and couldn't risk gaining a reputation which would take *years* to live down. She could see it now, she'd become *Ishabel Stuart, the woman who'd been dumped by her fiancé, slept with the American and been left high and dry when he returned home.* A byword for reckless behaviour – just like the rest of her family.

As if reading her mind, Irene broke into her thoughts. 'Issy. Is yon gorgeous Big Yank of yours coming doon tae hear ye sing?'

Issy blushed, anxious to deny that he was gorgeous, or *her* American. But she knew that would cause further comment, so she settled for, 'I – I'm not sure. I think Lindy might bring him.'

'Aye, wee Lindy seems mighty struck by him. The punters like him, too. He often buys a round a' drinks and isnae too posh to stand at the bar and chat wi' whoever's in.'

'Oh, so that's where he goes to in the evenings,' Issy said almost to herself. 'And what does he talk to the locals about?' As if she didn't know!

'The auld, bombed-out distillery, your aunt, *you.* Mostly, you.' Irene grinned as she put the last whisky glass back in its place. 'He's awful taken with you, Issy. Probably just what you need now yer mahn's had second thoughts and called off the weddin' - if ye get mah drift . . .' She improvised a couple of pelvic thrusts behind the bar.

Second thoughts? Called off the wedding?

Issy could just imagine where *that* particular rumour had sprung from.

Lindy!

'Och and here he is. Brodie! Away over here, Big Man,' Irene boomed in the voice she reserved for calling time at The Pickled Herring. Issy cringed as Brodie fought his way through the crowded bar towards them, receiving many encouraging slaps on the back and words of welcome from his newfound friends en route. Living up to his newly acquired nickname, Brodie stood head and shoulders above most of the islanders.

Big Man, indeed . . .

'Issy,' Brodie nodded to her when he arrived at the bar.

'Brodie,' she replied, her throat unexpectedly dry. Now he'd cleared the throng at the bar, it became plain that he was wearing a kilt. The very sight of which made all Issy's earlier resolutions fly out of the window and over The Narrows, leaving her feeling light-headed.

'Och, will ye look at him in that kilt, Issy. Is he no braw?' Now openly matchmaking, Irene nodded towards Brodie with a twinkle in her eye. 'Say, Brodie - is there anything worn under yer kilt?'

'Nah, it's all in good working orr-derr,' he said, adopting a convincing Scottish accent. They laughed and then high-fived each other, making Issy suspect it wasn't the first time they'd shared that particular joke.

Issy felt excluded, left out – and was dismayed to find that it mattered.

'Braw, indeed.' She gave Brodie's kilt, t-shirt and biker jacket combo a critical appraisal, hoping to find some anachronism, something out of place she could use as an excuse to make a cutting remark.

But she could find no fault with his outfit – or him.

He wore plaid as if born to it.

His kilt was almost identical to the Black Watch tartan, except for four threads of yellow/black/sky blue – black/yellow and dark green running across it in the form of an 'overcheck'. Brodie had obviously heeded her warning about *badger head sporrans* and was sporting a simple leather sporran with silver chasing. Issy glanced down to make sure that his kilt ended just below the knee, many a wannabe Scot had fallen foul of that simple rule. The kilt was fastened in traditional fashion just above the right knee by a simple pin – not an eagle's claw or anything like that. The pin was more of a badge, really, and showed two dolphins facing each other across 'something' which she couldn't make out. Issy had never seen a kilt pin quite like it – and it belonged to no clan she knew of.

Certainly not the Brodies or the McIntoshes.

'Irene, we're dying o' thirst here. Can ye gei'us a drop o' swally, lassie?' someone shouted from the far end of the bar.

'Och, hold yer wheesht and hang on tae yer simmet, ahm on mah way.' Irene, apparently more concerned with observing the interaction between Brodie and Issy than serving her customers, sashayed over to the other end of the mahogany bar at a leisurely pace.

'A simmet?' Brodie questioned, perplexed by another example of Scottish patois.

'A vest. It's like saying: keep your shirt on. Don't get your knickers in a knot. Comprendez?'

'Kinda.' He smiled, then coughed a little self-consciously. 'Am I allowed to say that you look – beautiful tonight, Issy. Not a cobweb in sight.' Issy blushed under his regard and took a deep, shaky, breath.

'Only if I'm allowed to say that you look *nothing* like Bonnie Prince Charlie's love child. That was crass of me. I'm sorry . . .'

'Yeah. Guess we're both tense at the moment. You've got the memorial service comin' up, whereas I –' Again, he reined himself in.

Issy wanted to scream with frustration, he'd nearly dropped his guard. Instead, she smiled and indicated his kilt. 'That's not a tartan I recognise. What is it, a sept of the Brodies? McIntosh?' *There*, she'd let him know she'd seen his tattoo in the shower and had recognised it, too. He gave no indication that her 'outing' of his McIntosh connection fazed him in any way. 'And, what's that unusual kilt pin?'

'It's my grandfather's kilt and pin. I don't possess one of my own.' He looked down at his kilt, hiding his expressions and evading her question with his usual deftness. 'I kinda like the freedom of it, though.' He smoothed down the front of it and Issy went hot, then cold, as she wondered if he'd followed the tradition and gone commando.

'Not much call for kilts in Kentucky, then?' she managed to say, after taking a large gulp of her vodka and tonic.

'Issy – yer on, sweetheart,' the landlord called over from the bar.

'*Not much call for kilts in Kentucky*. Sounds like a good title for a Country and Western song,' Brodie laughed, as Issy walked away from him.

Over by the 'stage' the band had set up. It consisted of a piano accordionist, a drummer and a young man with an electric guitar. Issy walked over, whispered the title of the first song and they nodded.

'Tonight I'm singing two songs,' she addressed the audience. 'The first, *The Silkie of Sule Skerry* is a lament which tells of a woman who does not know her son's father . . .'

There was some ribald commentary over at the bar, followed by much digging in the ribs by the younger drinkers until Irene called them to order. Issy grinned, catcalling and barracking were part and parcel of Open Mic Night at The Pickled Herring. Part of the fun.

'A man arrives at a woman's bed foot and tells her he is the father of her child - and that he is a silkie . . . a man only when he's on dry land, but a seal in the water. He takes his son, gives her a purse of gold, and predicts that she will marry a gunner, who will shoot both him and their son. You all know the chorus, so please join in. Thanks, Paul . . .' she nodded to the guitarist who played the first mournful chords of the ancient folk song. The whole pub quietened as she sang the opening verses and then those familiar with the ballad joined in with the chorus:

'*I am a man upon the land, I am a silkie in the sea/and when I'm far frae every strand/my home it is in Sule Skerry.*'

After the last chord died away, the pub fell silent – as if no one wanted to break the spell cast by the song. Then the customers broke into spontaneous applause and Issy glanced over at Brodie to gauge *his* reaction, the only one which mattered. Perched high on a bar stool and nursing a glass of whisky, he appeared unaffected by her singing. Then, just as she was about to look away, his eyes narrowed and he sent her a look of such passion that the hairs on the back of her neck stood on end and her insides liquefied. It was as if he was seeing her for the first time; really seeing her. And Issy knew that if she countered his scorching look with one of her own, there would be no going back. For either of them.

With slow deliberation – measure for measure, beat for beat, she returned the look. Brodie took a deep breath, as if to steady himself and during those fleeting seconds – for it was no more than that, the world of ex-fiancés, dysfunctional parents and heavy responsibility counted for nothing. Brodie raised his whisky glass and executed a half bow, acknowledging that this was *her* land, *her* people and she queen of it.

Which made him what, exactly?

An impostor in a kilt?

She didn't have time to give the idea further thought as two of the birdwatchers stepped up to the mike and gave a rendition of the *Skye Boat Song* which was so excruciating, The Young Pretender must have been spinning in his grave. This was followed by a version of The Proclaimers' *Five Hundred Miles* which was so awful, it was good - and everyone joined in, stamping their feet and clapping, laughing at every flat note. When Issy next glanced at Brodie, Lindy was leaning on him, her arm ever-so-casually draped across his thigh, her fingers tapping on his bare knee in time to the singing.

Tonight, Lindy was working the look in skimpy cut-off shorts and a denim halter neck which showed off her fake-tanned, midriff. Issy sighed; she knew that next to Lindy Tennant, with her bouncing copper curls and pertness, she looked as alluring as someone's favourite auntie. Not even biker boots, a designer frock and rock chick make-up could change that, she thought, depressed.

After a few minutes, she regained her poise and confidence and made her way over to the bar. Surrounded by his new friends, Brodie, was engaged in a lively discussion about the phrase *the whole nine yards,* and whether it referred to the amount of cloth required to make a kilt; or the ammo belt designed for the guns in the Spitfire which were 27 feet (nine yards) long.

'If a pilot used all his ammo during an attack,' one man at the bar opined, 'he would say, *I gave them the whole 9 yards.*'

'Naw, sounds too American for me,' another argued. 'What d'ye say Brodie?'

'I think,' he paused and they hung on his words, 'I think Irene should serve another round – on me – and we should drink to Braw Scotsmen, Brave Spitfire Pilots, Yanks with Scottish heritage – and the waggle o' the kilt.' No doubt about it, he had the common touch and they were eating out of the palm of his hand. It wasn't simply his generosity, or the fact that, in the islanders' eyes, he came from the land of milk and honey – it was the way he bore himself; his air of quiet authority allied with affability had won them over. If it hadn't have been for his drawl, he could have doubled up as the laird of Cormorant Island, had the position been vacant.

Not that she'd ever tell him that!

The snare drums played the backbeat to *Sguaban Arbhair* and the electric guitar picked out the tune as Issy made her way back onto the stage. The soft touch of the brushes across the snare drum and the muffled guitar chords brought everyone in the pub to order. They stood with their pints of Heavy or drams of whisky as Issy sang in Gaelic, knowing this was her signature song. The beat was slow and hypnotic and, unconsciously, everyone started swaying in time to the lullaby-like refrain. Issy broke her own rule and closed her eyes as she sang – more to shut out the sight of Brodie looking at her in that calm, measuring way of his, than to get deeper into the song.

When she finished and the last chord died away, it became obvious that the rhythmic breathing of the patrons had fallen into step with the scrape of the brushes across the drum skin. Something about the beat of a drum had the power to enter a man's soul, Issy reflected; small wonder they used to recruit men at the drum head in the olden days. The silence lasted for several seconds and then the punters applauded before turning away from Issy, almost embarrassed. As if her singing had worked some kind of Highland Magic on them and she could see into their hearts.

'Thanks, lads.' She turned to the boys in the band. 'Three pints of Heavy, is it?'

'Aye, thanks Issy – with a whisky chaser, but we'll pay for that.'

She waved away their money and walked over to the bar to place her order.

'Put it on the tab, Irene,' Brodie shouted over to Irene who was pulling the pints of Heavy ale. 'Hi,' he said to Issy, 'that was . . . out of this world. The rhythm, and your singing were quite mesmerising. I had no idea what you were singing about, but that didn't seem to matter.'

'*Sguaban Arbhair,*' she stammered at last. 'It means *sheaves of corn.*'

'Corn?'

'Wheat.' She took a deep breath and rushed on. 'The singer tells of finding a photograph in a drawer which shows him as a young boy gathering sheaves of corn with his grandparents. He laments their death and the way of life which died with them. Now, he sings, he lives in a wooden world with people who do not understand his language – Gaelic.' She stopped talking and thought of the

207

photograph albums in Esme's study which showed the distillery in full production and her own grandparents working in it. She never knew them because her father hadn't married until he was well into his **fifties**, preferring to build his IT Empire and removing himself from the island and a way of life he considered dead and outmoded. 'I wish –'

'Go on –'

She was about to say: *If I had the money, I'd rebuild the distillery and restore my family's reputation. It would mean so much to the island – to me. Instead, she said:* 'Oh, it's nothing, ignore me. Singing the old songs makes me melancholy, all part of my Celtic make-up, I suppose. We're never happier than when we're miserable,' she laughed. 'Luckily, you're Yankee through-and-through,' she couldn't resist adding, and waited for him to contradict her.

'With Scottish roots,' he amended. 'Hey - I can be miserable, too, you know? I listened to a lot of Leonard Cohen when I was in school. And Nirvana.' He shuddered at the memory.

They laughed, and when Issy glanced down, her hand was resting lightly on his thigh, as Lindy's had been. She snatched it back as though the touch scorched her, even though there were several layers of heavy kilt between her fingers and his skin. Blushing, she muttered something indistinct and then stepped away from him.

For a moment, Brodie looked as if he wanted to reach out for her hand and put it back on his thigh. But there was a bit of a commotion as people began moving tables and chairs to the edges of the room and Issy made the most of the opportunity to put space between them. Some of the younger men came over and dragooned Brodie into helping move furniture around. Issy looked over at Irene who shrugged – looked like the karaoke had been abandoned in favour of dancing. A mercy, probably!

The accordion played the opening chords of *Scotland the Brave* and everyone grabbed a partner for the Gay Gordons, lacing their arms over their partners shoulders in time honoured fashion. Brodie made a beeline for Issy but Lindy forestalled him, dragging him into position as the accordion belted out the tune amidst 'hooch-yas' and wild, rebel yells.

Even Irene was persuaded to come from behind the bar and join in the fun.

'Ahm no wearing mah sports bra, lads. Just saying,' she issued the caveat as she took up position.

Issy took the opportunity to slip away from The Pickled Herring and begin the short stroll home in the summer twilight. She hoped that a walk, combined with the smell of the shore at low-tide and the suck of the waves against the sea wall, would restore her equilibrium. Put an end to the turmoil making the pit of her stomach churn like a cement mixer loaded with bricks, and her breath come in snatches.

As the lights of Killantrae hove into view, Issy acknowledged that she was asking the wrong question. It wasn't so much a question of *what* was making her feel lost and uncertain – as *who*. She looked over the harbour wall to a rocky outcrop where the cormorants were feeding their newly-fledged chicks. Across The Narrows, the lightship winked in the *simmer dim*, the name the islanders gave to the long summer twilights. Letting her eyes go out of focus, the light in the harbour appeared to be surrounded by a halo of colour and the cormorants called out to her; was it her imagination – or did it really sound as if they were calling: Brodie, Brodie, *Brodie*?

She didn't need the cormorants to tell her there would be no peace for her until she admitted her feelings to Brodie. But that required courage, a courage she didn't possess at the moment. Tomorrow was her father's memorial service, followed by a wake at her aunt's cottage. After breakfast, Brodie would leave for his eco-lodge and, unless she found the courage to speak, he would drift out of her life and she'd spend the rest of her days wondering – *what if*?

Chapter Eighteen
A Little Help from My Friends

Issy sat on the bench outside the cottage watching the tide turn. As soon as The Narrows was passable, the caterers would arrive and prepare *Ailleag* for the wake. The whole island had been invited to the memorial service and wake which would go on well into the long summer twilight. There had been no need for formal invitations, Mungo Park had simply announced the arrangements in the kirk two weeks earlier and the island tom-toms had done the rest.

Not everyone had seen eye to eye with James Stuart. However, he was an islander by birth and the community respected that; they'd make it their business to give him a good send off. Besides, a full blown wake was such a rare event on *Eilean na Sgairbh* nowadays, no one in their right mind would turn down Issy's invitation. It was her fervent hope that the wake would present her with the chance to show the islanders how fulsome Stuart hospitality could be, let them know she was home to stay – and maybe, lay a few ghosts to rest.

Perhaps best accomplished with her aunt Esme off the scene?

Originally, Issy had intended to stay in Edinburgh until the day before the memorial and then take her father's ashes straight to the kirk before the service - all neat, tidy and respectful. However, finding Jack Innes-Kerr in her office with the intern, had put paid to *that*. The whole business – her father's death, the cremation in Edinburgh and reading of the will, felt hurried and badly executed. James Stuart would have been displeased by his unscheduled death, Issy's handling of the funeral arrangements – and her playing landlady to . . . to . . . well, what was Brodie exactly?

A stranger. Cuckoo in the nest. Call him what you will – it always came back to Brodie.

He and Lola had staggered in at some unearthly hour last night, knocking over furniture, disturbing the parrot, and shushing each other loudly. Cue drunken laughter and half-hearted attempts at making a hot drink, resulting in the kettle whistling its head off as they – seemingly – tried to locate the teapot. Lying in her bedroom, Issy had felt annoyed and excluded, although she knew she could easily have joined them. A combination of vodka shots, perfect highland twilight, a melancholy song and Brodie wearing his grandfather's kilt had made her usual caution desert her at The Pickled Herring. She'd come over all fey and wistful – most unlike herself; living on Cormorant Island had that effect on the most level-headed person. Now, reviewing last night in the cool light of dawn, she was glad she'd stayed in her room. Slipping away during the Gay Gordons had been a timely move on her part, and saved her from making a bigger fool of herself.

She blew out her cheeks and pushed her fringe from her eyes, glad she hadn't blurted out the little speech she'd rehearsed last night, waiting for Brodie to come home. A speech which would have told him . . . *what* exactly? That she was developing feelings for him, contradictory, confused feelings? That something had flashed between them during *Sguaban Arbhair* which couldn't be called back? Apart from his secretiveness, he'd behaved like the perfect guest and she was going to miss him.

There, she'd said it. She glanced at her watch and put Brodie from her mind.

It was time to honour her father and to implement the very specific instructions he'd left for his memorial service and wake. Of course, he hadn't known he was going to have a cardiac arrest whilst pouring over the end of year figures in his office. However, with typical thoroughness and practicality he'd planned his funeral years before - without consulting her, naturally. According to his lawyers, everything was taken care of. All she had to do was make sure the undertakers in Jamestoun carried out his instructions to the last letter.

Which presented her with a problem.

'Sorry, Father,' she said, as waves receded from the shore and revealed the darker patch of sand; the pathway across The Narrows. 'I've made a few changes. Changes you won't approve of, but there it is.'

Her father would hate the fact that she'd issued an open invitation to the memorial service and wake to all the islanders. However, she was about to make her home on Cormorant Island and she had to get the islanders' on side if she wanted her ambitious ideas for the artists' workshops to flourish. Holding a wake which excluded three quarters of the islanders would be a step in the wrong direction.

Secondly, and more importantly, whisky would flow at James' wake. The islanders regarded uisge beatha as the water of life and their unalienable right. Denying them their dram would bring more retribution down on her head than any curses James Stuart might send from the afterlife. A highlander born and bred, Issy experienced a superstitious shudder at the thought of her father's displeasure reaching from beyond the grave. But, she was also a woman of her times, so pushing the thought to one side she walked into the house to put on her funeral clothes and prepare for the ordeal ahead.

An hour later, she was talking to Pershing in the sitting room when Brodie entered the room.

'Mizz Stoo-art . . . Issy,' he began, rubbing his finger along his nose. A gesture which showed he was unsure of himself. 'I've got something to say.'

'Then say it.' Nerves made her speak more sharply than intended. Making a fist, she held out her hand and Pershing climbed off his perch, sidled up her arm and perched on her shoulder. He nibbled delicately at her ear and then teased out strands of her long, dark hair which she'd just spent half an hour arranging. Brodie gave the bird a wide berth, no doubt remembering Pershing's fondness for toes.

'Are you all packed up and ready to go?' In spite of her

businesslike tone, there was an audible quaver in her voice. Quickly disguising it, she asked if Pershing wanted a monkey nut. 'Good boy,' she crooned as he took the nut from between her lips with finesse.

'That's just it . . .' Brodie sent her another oblique look.

'What is?'

'I – I figure I should hang around a couple more days. Help with the memorial service and the wake. Hell, it's the least I can do to repay your family for taking me in when your lives are all over the place. I thought, with – with your fiancé not being around, and your aunt having gone, you might appreciate a . . .'

'Man about the house?' Issy paused, sending him a considering look. She *had* to get this right. Just what exactly was on offer?

'It's a temporary position, I know. But I want to help you – Issy,' he said her name softly, obviously believing they'd moved beyond Mizz Stoo-art and Mr Brodie. The pleasurable, squirmy feeling she'd experienced thinking about him whilst sitting on the bench earlier, now returned.

'Why would you want to do that?' Her heart thumped as she waited for his answer.

'Why do you think?' He stood in front of her, guarded, hesitant – as if waiting for *her* to make the first move.

'I – I really don't know.' Something had shifted and changed since last night. Being with Brodie affected her in ways she could not, as yet express, not even to herself.

'I think you do. I think we both do. Issy –' he said her name again and took a step forward.

There was an openness in his face, a lack of guile or pretence, and Issy's heart soared with hope and expectation. Her resistance was melting, as surely as the spring snows on Cormorant Island's high peaks vanished in May. It all felt new, exciting and quite terrifying, and reading Brodie's expression, Issy could tell that he felt the same.

She smiled, hesitantly, and opened her mouth to speak. Encouraged, Brodie closed the gap between them, forgetting for the moment that his feathered nemesis was perched on Issy's shoulder, waiting to pounce.

'*Och, away with you, man.*' Pershing, picking up on high emotion flowing between them, had no intention of being left out in the cold.

'Saved by the parrot,' Brodie laughed. Tentatively, he reached out for Issy's face but then drew his hand back as Pershing craned his neck forward, fluffed up his head feathers and cackled his piratical laugh.

'Pershing, no bite,' Issy chided, knowing exactly what the parrot had in mind. 'Nice Brodie. Nice Brodie,' she added, stroking the bird's silky feathers to calm him down.

'*Nice Brodie*, huh? Whatd'ya say, Mr Parrot? Can you put up with me a day or two longer?' Bravely, Brodie picked out a monkey nut from the parrot's dish and held it out towards Pershing. 'Think that'd be a good idea?' he asked in a quiet voice. He was addressing the bird but Issy knew he was speaking to her. The parrot gave

Brodie a considering look and then spat out the nut Issy had just given him and took the one proffered by Brodie instead. 'Hey, look at that . . . you – he likes me,' Brodie said under his breath, openly pleased that the parrot had deigned to accept the nut and Issy hadn't frozen him out.

'Looks like Pershing's answered for both of us,' Issy said, her voice catching.

She'd never known the parrot to behave so docilely with a visitor. Maybe, like her, Pershing felt Brodie was no longer a stranger, or a threat? She had an emotional day ahead of her and was suddenly overwhelmed by the thought of it. Tears blurred her vision and she turned away so Brodie wouldn't see them or detect her moment of weakness.

'That a *yes*?'

'Aye, it is,' she said. Brodie laughed out loud, openly relieved, and the parrot spat the nut onto the floor in disgust.

'*Up your arrr-sse,*' it said in a broad Glaswegian accent, and jumped off Issy's shoulder and onto its perch with a flutter of its clipped wings. Playing to the gallery, it moved along the well-bitten perch and closer to Brodie. '*Bombs away,*' it declared, pooping on the sand tray below.

'Pershing, really!' Issy chided the feathered fiend. 'I must apologise, Brodie. When Aunt Esme goes off on a long trip, Pershing stays at The Pickled Herring and has picked up one or two choice phrases.'

'I think we'd better put him in your aunt's room during the

wake,' Brodie grinned. 'We wouldn't want to offend the church elders.'

Issy nodded in agreement. She coaxed the parrot off his perch, back onto her upturned hand and put him back in his cage. Together she and Brodie carried him through into Esme's bedroom, keeping their fingers clear of the bars and Pershing's beak.

'Issy, I —' Without the parrot to cramp his style, Brodie took Issy's right hand and pulled her close. 'I've wanted to do this since the moment I saw you.' As he lowered his head towards her, the front door was flung back on its hinges and Lindy catapulted into the cottage.

'Broh-die. Iss-yy. Where are you guys?'

'In here,' Issy replied, moving away from Brodie and adopting a wry expression.

'*You silly tart,*' Pershing greeted Lindy as she walked into Esme's bedroom.

Brodie looked at the parrot and then at Lindy, a rueful smile quirking his lips at the missed opportunity. 'Kids, huh?' The look he sent Issy, told her that he'd got a rain check for the kiss and would redeem it at the earliest opportunity. When neither parrots, guests nor overexcited Mexican torch singers would get in the way.

The bell atop the kirk tolled as Issy and Brodie left the cottage and started the long walk up to the church. James Stuart's ashes had been collected the previous afternoon by the local undertakers and had lain in state, as per instructions, overnight in the kirk. Issy was glad of it; the day was emotional enough without having to carry the sandalwood wood box containing her father's earthly remains through Killantrae and up to the wee kirk. The sandalwood box had been brought back from India by Esme on one of her many trips and Issy had asked the local undertaker to transfer James Stuart's ashes into it. There was no way she could allow the congregation to gaze on her father's remains in what resembled a sweetie jar. She'd square using the sandalwood box with Esme on her return, but surely she couldn't raise any objections?

Lost in thought, her step faltered. 'You, okay, Issy?' Brodie asked, reaching out and supporting her by the elbow.

'Thanks. My shoes – the uneven ground,' she explained. She walked on, Brodie on one side of her and Mary Tennant on the other. Issy regarded Lindy's mother Mary as a kind of surrogate aunt, and was glad of her support today. It was to Mary she had turned last winter when Esme had pneumonia and she'd been unable to fly home because of being in the middle of protracted negotiations with a very rich but demanding Russian plutocrat. Mary had been there for her then, just as she was now.

As they progressed towards the kirk, cottage doors opened and islanders joined the procession. The islanders didn't say much, they didn't need to; they simply nodded or greeted Issy with the stock phrase: *aw right, Issy?* Apart from the tolling of the bell and the suck of the waves against the sea wall as the tide receded, it was a silent procession. Issy was glad, it gave her the chance to centre herself for what lay ahead.

'Are your shoes Laboutins?' Lindy asked in a stage whisper, suddenly appearing at Issy's elbow and rudely elbowing her mother out of the way. 'I'd love a pair of those. Maybe, when you've grown tired of them . . . Now what?' Lindy demanded of her mother who caught hold of her sleeve and pulled her back. 'Mum, I'm just asking – okay? Chill.' Lindy shook off her mother's hand and moved round to walk on Brodie's left side, rolling her eyes like the overgrown teenager she was.

'Hold your wheesht, Lindy. Now is not the time to be going on about shoes.' Mary Tennant hooked her hand through Issy's free arm and fell back into step. Not for the first time, Issy wondered how someone as calm and collected as Mary Tenant could have produced a live-wire like *Lola*. 'Is your Mother coming today, Ishabel?' she asked in her soft, lilting highland accent.

'No, thank goodness; but, neither is Aunt Esme . . . I could have done with her here, today. Mary, you've known my aunt all your life, haven't you? Do you have any idea what happened between her and my father which might be responsible for her refusing to have his ashes in the house?' She gave Mary a searching look.

'Och, Issy, that's something you should ask your aunt,' Mary said diplomatically. 'But be sure of one thing, though, Esme never does anything without a good reason.' She gave Issy's arm a squeeze and changed the subject. 'I see Brodie's staying on a few days longer to help out? That is kind of him.' She whispered the last sentence so only she and Issy could hear.

'It is,' Issy agreed, as the procession swelled in numbers and they wound their way up the hill towards the kirk.

Mungo Park was waiting for them in the whitewashed porch of his wee kirk, wearing his best suit and dog collar. James Stuart had often stated he had Covenanters' blood coursing through his veins, and was a great believer in the levelling power of the Free Church of Scotland. In his instructions for his memorial service, he had requested that Mungo left off his black Geneva gown, academic hood and stole, in favour of his every day minster's clothes.

Plain and simple is what he wanted and it was down to Issy to ensure that's exactly what he got. The single bell tolled its knell and Issy shivered, it was such a forlorn sound. A capricious breath of wind touched her cheek, bringing with it the salt tang of the sea. She'd never felt so alone in her life and knew that without the support of Brodie and Mary, her knees would have buckled.

'Look!' Lindy pointed across The Narrows and out to sea. 'We've got incoming. Two UFOs, headed our way; break out the lasers, Captain Picard.'

The procession had reached the kirk's wrought iron gates and was making its way along the path to join the congregation gathered in front of the porch, standing on the grass amongst the headstones. As a man, they turned to where Lindy was pointing at two brilliant lights growing larger and brighter with each passing moment.

'In the name o' God, what is it?' a frightened parishioner asked Mungo.

'Avenging angels, come to punish us for our wicked ways,' one of the wags from The Pickled Herring said, taking a nip from the bottle of Bell's in his pocket, and was elbowed in the ribs by one of his drinking partners.

'Unless avenging angels come equipped with engines,' Lindy said out of the corner of her mouth, 'I do believe those are helicopters. And they're headed this way.'

'It's just like in the old days,' someone else stated, remembering the experimental aircraft which had whizzed across the island during the Cold War. 'It's a pity Esme's no here to witness it,' he added, 'it's be right up her street. She could get some of her old banners out and organise a protest.' They all laughed and Issy looked uncomfortable. That was *exactly* the image of her aunt she wanted the islanders to forget.

'Hold your tongue, Bob, and remember why we're here,' another islander said.

'Maybe it's Elvis, staging a comeback,' the same man added, unrepentantly. 'Or space aliens.' He laughed at the frightened faces of some of the older inhabitants. Pensioners who didn't leave the island from one year's end to another. To a man, they believed in signs and portents as certainly as they believed in a one True God.

'Worse than aliens,' Issy said grimly as two black helicopters came into view and landed in the adjacent field, scattering the frightened sheep and almost blowing the congregation off their feet.

'What's worse than aliens?' Brodie was compelled to ask.

'My mother,' Issy replied.

Shaking off his hand, she walked over to join Mungo, as La Bella Scozzese in funereal black, with a lace mantilla covering her lovely face, was helped out of the first helicopter by Jack Innes-Kerr.

Chapter Nineteen
Il Mio Caro Marito

L a Bella Scozzese's 'people' disembarked from the second helicopter and gathered around her. After a brief discussion, two of the entourage linked hands to form a 'seat' and she was carried across the muddy field. From what Issy could make out, Jack had been delegated to carry her handbag and appeared uncertain whether to loop it over his arm, or carry it like an attaché case. In the end he did the former and made himself look ridiculous.

Lindy gave a whoop of joy at the unexpected turn of events and took it upon herself to give a running commentary.

'Oh. My. God – sorry Mungo - it's yer Mammy, Issy - and wait, no it cannae be – it is! Himself - Jack-the-Lad; that's Issy's ex-fiancé, by the by, everyone. The one who called off the wedding . . . jilted her and left her at the altar. Puir wee lamb,' she added, giving Issy a hug without taking her eyes off Isabella's entourage crossing the field and getting closer with every second.

'He did *not* jilt me,' Issy began, '*I* called off the wedding . . .'

'For reasons she has never revealed,' Lindy told the assembled crowd out of the corner of her mouth. They all nodded in understanding, each person's imagination filling in the gaps. 'Not even to me, her best friend.'

'Former best friend,' Issy muttered under her breath.

At this point, everyone started talking amongst themselves, speculating on why the wedding had been called off. Issy couldn't swear it, but she thought she saw one of the regulars from The Pickled Herring opening a book on it and taking bets, while Mungo was distracted. Judging from looks the crowd sent Brodie, it was clear they thought *he* was responsible for Issy's wedding plans foundering on the rocks. A couple of the men gallantly offered to punch Jack's lights out on Issy's behalf. Tempting though the offer was, Issy nevertheless turned it down.

'Get them inside the kirk, Mungo, I have no idea what Mother's got planned. But take it from me, she'll be up to something.'

'Hell-oh,' Lindy said, screwing up her eyes all the better to focus on Issy's mammy. 'Clock that suit. We're talking Armani here – and I don't mean wee Benny Armani who owns the ice cream parlour in Jamestoun. That, my friends, is the first piece of designer clothing ever to grace Cormorant Island.' She said it with such authority that Mungo was unable to persuade anyone to enter the church, so concerned were they that they might miss something of the unfolding drama.

'Is that good, Oor Lindy?' a paid up member of the Post Office Mafia asked.

'Duh. I should say so. Mind you, at this distance I cannae work out if it's Armani or Versace. If I could just get closer . . .' At that, the congregation took several steps forward, making it appear that La Bella Scozzese was royalty and they were keen to bow in her presence.

'I really think we should remember why we're here,' Mungo began in a valiant attempt to bring order and dignity to the proceedings. But this was *Eilean na Sgairbh* and nothing as exciting as this had happened in years.

Ishabel Stuart's Mammy. La Bella Scozzese. On their island – and with not one, but *two* helicopters . . . and Ishabel's love-rat boyfriend, the one who'd jilted her at the altar - if the rumours were to be believed, carrying her handbag. And Brodie – man of the hour, standing by Ishabel's side with a face like thunder.

Plus – the icing on the cake, a grand *purvey* was planned for after the service. During which, this would all be dissected over a wee dram and salmon sandwiches with the crusts cut off.

Aye, this was indeed a red letter day for *Eilean na Sgairbh*.

'See her shoes? The leopard-print heels and gold embellishment on the black velvet?' Lindy was back to giving a running commentary. 'Louboutins,' she said with a satisfied sniff. They had no trouble seeing La Bella Scozzese's shoes as she was carried towards them in the improvised 'chair', the soles of her shoes facing them.

'Aye, ye widnae wah-nt to get your best spikes ruined crossing a muddy graveyard,' Irene from The Pickled Herring pronounced with some authority.

'Aye, yer right there,' everyone agreed.

'My friends, inside the kirk so we can begin the service. Pl – ease.' But they were deaf to Mungo's entreaties. Issy's mother came ever closer and when Lindy revealed how much the shoes had cost, everyone gasped.

'You'll no find *those* in the Barras, in case yer all wondering.' She sent her mother a telling look and then turned to face her rapt audience.

'How come ye know all this, Lindy?' Mary Tennant asked, baffled.

'Research,' Lindy said with a toss of her copper curls.

At that moment, La Bella Scozzese reached the safety of the gravel path leading up to the whitewashed porch. She managed to stand up under her own steam but appeared in no rush to claim her handbag from Innes-Kerr. Her two bodyguards moved back and stood in typical hard man pose with their hands crossed over their wedding tackle, enigmatic in black suits and Raybans. More of Isabella's people rushed forward, brushing down her widow's weeds, raising her lace mantilla and reapplying her make-up. Mungo looked too overwhelmed to intervene. Issy bet that during his years as a missionary in Africa, he'd never encountered anything as bizarre as La Bella Scozzese's Road Show.

'Issy, sweetheart!' Jack Innes-Kerr, judging it was safe to hand La Bella Scozzese's handbag to an assistant, hurried over to Issy's side. He skidded on the gravel when he saw Brodie standing close to Issy, and glowering at him, and the three-ring circus he was part of. Misjudging Issy's mood, Jack attempted to plant a kiss on her cheek and was left kissing fresh air - lips pursed like a simple-minded fish.

'Stop it. What are you doing?' she called out, appalled that he had the nerve to attend the service, *and* considered a Judas kiss in order. She held out her hands to ward him off.

Next thing she knew, The Pickled Herring's resident band were between them, growling their disapproval like three large guard dogs.

'You heard the lady, back off, pal. Is this the wee bauchle who left you at the altar, Ishabel?' Paul the guitarist asked.

'For the last time,' Issy said with heavy patience. 'He didn't leave me at the altar, okay! I broke off the engagement because,' she took a deep breath, '. . . just because.' Her cheeks burned with mortification, indignation, exasperation – and any other *ation* she could think of.

'Oh, aye,' Paul reached his own conclusion. 'Playing away from home, was it, Jimmy?' He took another threatening step towards Innes-Kerr who wisely moved closer to Issy's mother's bodyguards. 'We dinnae like that sort of thing hereabouts . . .'

None too pleased at being upstaged by her daughter, Isabella drew the attention back to herself. 'Ishabel, cara . . . *Dov'e il mio caro marito*? Where is my dear husband? Your father?' Isabella joined Mungo, raising the black veil to reveal a lone, salt tear trailing down her exquisitely made-up face, and dabbing at it with a lace handkerchief. How *did* she manage that, Issy wondered, - crying to order and squeezing out just one, perfectly formed, tear? She probably did it twice a night and three times on Sunday whilst performing Lucia de Lammermoor, or some other Bel Canto role, and could turn it on and off - like a tap.

'He's in the church, Mrs Stuart, erm, I mean - Signora Tartaruga,' Mungo replied, unmoved. 'And stop that!' He swatted away one of Isabella's people who was filming everything on a small hand-held video camera. 'Now, can we all remember why we're here and show some respect for the memory of James Stuart. Are you ready, Issy?' he asked, clutching his bible in one hand and ushering her into the kirk with the other.

'More than ready,' she replied, fuming at her mother and Innes-Kerr's behaviour. Jack, showing more sense than Issy thought him capable of, did not try to escort her into the wee kirk. He held out his arm to La Bella Scozzese and she took, letting out a shuddering sob and dropping the mantilla over her face once more.

Issy was forced to admit that her mother looked good.

In her late forties, La Bella Scozzese had the figure of a much younger woman and the bearing of the prima donna. Her skin was virtually unwrinkled - thanks to factor 50 SPF, Crème de la Mer, and HRT which was holding the menopause at bay. She had many years of plum roles ahead of her and had no intention of letting her ovaries dictate the length and scope of her career. Nowadays, prima donnas were known to take the part of young heroines when long past their sell-by date – and she had every intention of capitalising on that. Her long dark hair showed no signs of grey and appeared full of life and vigour beneath the ebony and silver comb of her mantilla.

'Ishabel, carissima, vieni. Come.' La Bella Scozzese held out her hand. '*Jack Tesoro* and I 'ave come 'ere to support you, child. And support you, we shall,' she said in heavily-accented English. Issy ground her teeth and refused to take part in this farce. Her mother had been born and bred just outside Glasgow - in Dumbarton, and was as Scottish as neeps and tatties. She'd lived with her parents over their ice cream parlour before she'd met and quickly married James Stuart at the Edinburgh Festival. *Tartaruga's Italian Ice Cream Parlour and Restaurant* was always being photographed by her devoted fans. They were even campaigning to have an official plaque erected to mark the spot where the Diva from Dumbarton had been born, such was their devotion.

'Who ees thees?' she asked, pointing rudely at Brodie. Although her face was hidden by her veil, Issy just *knew* she'd be checking Brodie out with a view to adding him to the collection of young men who hung on her every word. And probably shared her bed – but Issy didn't want to think about *that,* not today.

'Brodie's my – my friend,' was all she said. Brodie's eyes widened and he shot her a wry smile at the thought of being elevated to the position of *friend*, if nothing more. Judging by the set of her mother's shoulders, this had not been the answer she'd been expecting. 'And, if you've brought *Jack Tesoro* here in the hope of engineering a rapprochement for the sake of the cameras, think again. He's a *bastardo* - and I want nothing more to do with him.'

'Hm, managed that Italian word without much help, Issy, darling. Anyway, we'll see about *that,*' Isabella said, sotto voce, in a normal Scottish accent.

Issy turned round to look at Brodie who raised his eyebrows in a *what the hell's going on here,* look of inquiry. Issy shrugged – if only she knew! She followed Mungo up the aisle to the front of the wee kirk, thinking all the while that it was years since she'd last been in there. More to annoy her father than because she had no faith, she acknowledged, somewhat guiltily.

The kirk was plain and austere, just as she remembered, the floor carpeted in blue, and whitewashed walls devoid of decoration. Lancet windows flooded the church with light, unimpeded by stained glass or any other ornamentation. The only flash of colour on the otherwise plain walls, was the banner belonging to the Boys' Brigade. The kirk smelled of polish and dusty hymn books, and at the front of the church, in place of an altar, there was a light oak table upon which rested a bible, wooden cross and spray of flowers, provided by Issy. There was no grand organ to pipe them in, just an electronic keyboard on a stand, upon which Mungo's wife was playing a selection of hymns.

In place of the pulpit, there was a lectern with a carved cross overlaid with the keys of St Peter. There was no font. During the Reformation it'd been thrown through the aforementioned stained glass window and had crashed onto the rocks below. In its place, stood a zinc bowl and ewer on a metal tripod; filled regularly with water from the burn at the side of the kirk, in lieu of Holy Water. Here, Issy and countless other children on the island had been baptised. Here, too, as a lay preacher, James Stuart had preached his version of hellfire and damnation, giving a harrowing description of the Day of Reckoning which lay ahead for them all.

Issy shuddered. Owing no allegiance to either the Happy Clappy or Bells and Smells denomination when it came to Sunday worship, she nevertheless felt that the austere church lacked something. Isabella must have been of the same opinion because she paused at the end of the front pew, crossed herself ostentatiously and then sat down. The congregation whispered as they took their places, the morning's diversion of helicopters and designer shoes forgotten. Now they saw only the black mantilla, rosary and genuflection of the Church of Rome. The atmosphere became charged, electric, as they expressed their hostility and disapproval; making it plain they thought the Pope and all his cardinals had taken over their church – and they wanted none of it.

Issy grabbed her mother's sleeve and dragged her into the pew.

'Stop showing off. I have to live with these people once you've gone.'

Issy's plan to rehabilitate the Stuarts back into the good graces of the folk of *Eilean na Sgairbh* had just taken a massive step backwards. Behind her, Jack made as if to sit alongside Isabella in the front pew, but Brodie barred his way and sent him to the back of the kirk where there was standing room only. Then he walked round and sat on Issy's right hand side – a solid, reassuring presence. As if sensing her disquiet, he leaned sidewards, touched her lightly on the shoulder and whispered in her ear:

'You've done great so far. Hang on in there, it'll soon be over.'

She nodded, somewhat distractedly - her mother had started to rock in the pew, as a distressed child might. Next, Isabella started to make a keening noise as though she was the Banshee, announcing a death. Then, before Issy could stop her, she was out of the pew and standing by the table which doubled as the altar. Pausing for an infinitesimal second, to check that her people at the back of the kirk were filming every moment of the unfolding drama, she segued into Act Two.

'*Mio caro marito,*' she wailed, '*mi hai lasciato vedova, sola, e senza niente, ad andare avanti senza di te.*' For the benefit of the non-Italian speakers in the congregation, she translated into English. 'My dear 'usband; you have left me widowed, alone and bereft to carry on life without you.' Then, much to Issy's embarrassment and the congregations' fascination, she threw herself over the carved wooden box next to the bible and began weeping loudly, almost without drawing breath. 'Oh, *Dio, aiutami in questo momento di bisogno?* James, I loved you . . . why you treat me so cruelly? I am only thirty-nine years of age - too young to be widowed.'

Glued to the pew by her mother's outrageous behaviour and dodgy grasp of arithmetic, Issy could only watch in disbelief as Isabella prostrated herself over the Suggestion Box that Mungo had introduced last year to make his sermons more inclusive. A box which Isabella believed contained James Stuart's earthly remains. At first, there was a collective intake of breath at her temerity in approaching the altar table, uninvited. However, when the congregation realised Isabella's gaffe, they started to laugh, and Irene called out:

'Wrong box, hen! Yer mah-n's ashes are in the wahn tae the left.'

Laughter rippled through the kirk, leaving Mungo with the unenviable task of prising Isabella's fingers off the Suggestion Box and explaining her mistake in a whispered aside. At that, La Bella Scozzese straightened up, dusted herself down and adjusted her mantilla before taking her place, back at Issy's side – clambering over so that she was sitting between her and Brodie. Leaning in, Issy put her arm round her mother's shoulders as if comforting her.

'If you don't stop this, Mother,' she hissed, 'I'll escort you from the church myself. Show some dignity and respect – for Father and me, if not for yourself.'

Mungo's wife struck up the opening chords of the Twenty-third psalm to the tune of Crimond, one of James Stuart's requests, and the congregation got to their feet. When Issy looked up, she became aware that Isabella had her head on Brodie's shoulder and was teetering on her six-inch heels. Brodie did the gentlemanly thing and put an arm round her slim waist to support her.

That should be me, Issy thought. I *want* it to be me.

And in God's House for evermore, my dwelling place shall be.

Issy looked at Brodie over her mother's head and their eyes met. He smiled, reassuringly. Fierce emotions swept over her; grief at her father's death, anger at her mother's behaviour and outrage at Jack Innes-Kerr turning up, unasked and unwanted, at her father's memorial service. And finally, as the hymn drew to a close, the one positive she would take from this, the feeling that the islanders were on her side, as sympathy and compassion pulsed towards her in waves.

Maybe, bygones really *would* become bygones after today?

She wanted to look at Brodie again, to draw strength from his closeness but she knew she couldn't take her eyes off her mother. God alone knew what Isabella would do next. The beginnings of a migraine headache made itself felt and Issy massaged the space between her eyebrows. It was going to be a lo-o-ng day.

Next, as previously arranged, Mungo invited Issy to approach the lectern to say a few words eulogising her father. She shuffled out of the pew, stood in front of the packed church and spoke briefly about his love of the island, this church and the way of life. She revealed the bequests he'd made to enhance the simple kirk, build a new community centre complete with computers, resident technician and a broadband system which would reach even the most sparsely populated side of the island. Furthermore, his estate would pay for a manned sea tractor which would take the islanders to and from *Eilean na Sgairbh*, no matter if the tide was in or not.

There was a spontaneous round of applause for James Stuart's generosity. Momentarily, it was forgotten that he'd refused to rebuild the distillery – the one thing which would restore the island's fortunes and change their lives for the better.

'My father loved this island,' Issy concluded, 'and so do I. It would make me very happy if you would walk back to my aunt's house and help celebrate his life in fitting fashion. I'm sure there are plenty of old stories you could share with me, stories I will always cherish.

Although the wake had already been announced, the congregation nevertheless gave Issy a round of applause. She bowed her head in acknowledgement and then turned and smiled at Mungo who was waiting to lead them into the final prayer. When she returned to her pew, her mother had moved away from Brodie and Issy had to shuffle into place between them. She reached for, and held, her mother's black gloved hand, as if to comfort her – but, in reality to hold onto her, as one might a badly behaved child.

They bowed their heads as Mungo said a few words and then led them into the Lord's Prayer. Isabella Stuart shook off her daughter's hand and linked her fingers together as they prayed, and Issy relaxed. It would soon be over and her mother couldn't get up to any more shenanigans.

Mungo walked over to Issy's pew, signalling for her to follow him down the aisle and out of the church. Isabella stood behind Issy and Brodie in the procession, and Issy was comforted to feel the light touch of Brodie's hand in the small of her back, guiding her forward. When they'd reached half-way down the aisle, she became aware that her mother had vanished from the periphery of her vision. Rather than corkscrew her head round in undignified fashion, Issy crossed her fingers and hoped La Bella Scozzese was following behind, head bowed in sorrow, as befitted a grieving widow.

At that point, taped music filled the church and, as a man, the congregation looked behind Issy and towards the altar table. When she glanced over her shoulder, her mother was standing there with her veil thrown back, looking as if she was about to give a performance at La Scala. The music, supplied by her people at the back of the church, was instantly recognisable.

'Oh, no,' Issy said in horror. *Ave Maria* in Latin? She wasn't having any of *that*.

Turning on her heel, she was about to sprint to the altar to stop this charade, but Brodie was quicker. Sensing that La Bella Scozzese would give massive affront to the Presbyterian islanders by singing *Ave Maria*, he strode up to the altar and blocked the congregations' view of her. Almost simultaneously, Isabella's entourage was hustled out of the church and into the graveyard by two elders, aided and abetted by Irene and the band from The Pickled Herring.

Issy reached her mother and rounded on her. 'How *could* you highjack my father's service and upset the islanders by singing *Ave Maria*?'

'You worry too much what other people think,' Isabella said without a trace of regret. 'This is a PR opportunity for me, and I'm taking it. With judicious splicing the final version will look as if I – James Stuart's grieving widow – poignantly sang *Ave Maria* at his memorial service. Perhaps if you had been a better daughter and if he'd left provision for me in his will . . .' she shrugged and left the sentence unfinished. 'He always was a stingy bastard, parading his meanness as principle – and you have shown nothing towards me but coldness.'

Issy let this pass, arguing with her mother was pointless. As with her 'stage age', Isabella Stuart was wont to put a spin on the past, changing events to suit her constant re-invention of herself until she believed it had happened that way . . . From busking in the street before being 'discovered' and singing at the Edinburgh Festival, to the whirlwind romance to a successful, older, businessman, the baby nine months later and then absconding to Italy to train at a prestigious opera school when the situation presented itself. Isabella didn't care who she trampled in the dust in her struggle to make it to the top - all that counted was getting, and staying there.

'Will you come with me, Ma'am?' Brodie asked in a calm voice, taking Isabella firmly by the arm. Unable to resist a handsome man, she allowed herself to be led into the vestry. Brodie signalled for Issy to greet the mourners alongside Mungo at the entrance to the kirk, indicating that he'd deal with her mother. Shooting him a grateful look, Issy hurried down the aisle to stand by Mungo's side in the graveyard.

'Mungo, I'm so sorry,' she began but he held up his hand.

'I think the kirk will survive a few lines of Latin and your mother's histrionics, don't you? Besides, it'll get the islanders onside which is no bad thing.' He understood her desire to make *Eilean na Sgairbh* her home and to leave the past buried beneath the ruins of the distillery on *Traigh Allt Chailgeag*.

'You aw right, hen?' Irene was the first to join them. Along with Lindy and Mary Tennant, she'd agreed to arrive back at Esme's house ahead of the mourners, and check that everything was in readiness for the wake. She gave Issy a big hug and then indicated towards the helicopters in the next field. 'Will yer Mammy be coming tae the purvey, too?' Her expression demonstrated that she thought the *Brave, Mourning Widow* act hadn't quite run its course and more entertainment was to be had.

'Unfortunately I think she might be,' Issy sighed.

'And yon ex-fiancé of yours?'

'Him, too.'

'There might be a queue forming to break his skinny-arsed legs, with Brodie taking first pop.' Issy ignored Irene's blatant attempt to paint Brodie as her knight in shining armour, her own, private Lochinvar - but she got the picture. 'Get your ex-fiancé alone, and gae him *laldy*, dah-rlin', or ye'll never hae closure. Above all; dinnae hae him back,' Irene added for good measure, and the three women made their way down the hill to her family home.

Squaring her shoulders and putting on a brave face, Issy stood by Mungo's side to receive condolences from the islanders, trying to keep her mind off what further treats the day held in store.

Chapter Twenty
I Didn't Know You Cared

In the end, the islanders' curiosity overcame their Presbyterian sensibilities and Isabella's attempted singing of *Ave Maria* in their wee kirk was soon forgotten as they enjoyed Issy's hospitality. Now, La Bella Scozzese was holding court in the backyard, and had them eating out of the palm of her hand as she regaled them with stories of singing with Pavarotti, Carreras and Domingo. Issy glanced once in her mother's direction, pulling a *par for the course* expression at Mary, and then mingled with the mourners who spluttered out condolences while washing down finger food with a fine blended malt whisky.

Issy cast her mind back to the pile of stones in *Traigh Allt Chailgeag* and wished, not for the first time, that she had it in her power to rebuild the ancient distillery. But it was a pipe dream; she barely had enough money to start the renovations on the outhouses. She walked past her bedroom where Jack Innes-Kerr was chatting disconsolately to Pershing, a bottle of whisky by his side. He was explaining to the parrot how hard his lot was, while Pershing nodded his head sagely, murmuring in sympathy. However, Issy knew by the tilt of Pershing's head and the gleam in his eye that he was just waiting for a chance to get close enough to lunge at Jack.

She felt much the same, herself, knowing she would have to exchange a few words with him before he left for Edinburgh later that night. Otherwise there would be no closure for either of them. She was tired, bone-weary, and her feet hurt. Her mood wasn't improved when she entered the kitchen and found Lindy and Irene had Brodie cornered by the sink and were flirting outrageously with him.

'Go ohwn, Brodie – say it again, Big Man,' Irene urged.

'P – poh-lis,' he said, pronouncing *police* in a broad Scots accent.

'Aye, many a visitor has fallen foul of that one,' Irene laughed. 'Is that no right, Issy? Mind you, if you lived in one of the bigger cities where the crack heids hang oot, you'd learn to pronounce it soon enough.'

'Yer life might depend on it,' Lindy added with all the authority of someone who rarely left Cormorant Island.

'You'll be getting him to say: *The Leith police dismisseth us*, next,' Issy commented dryly. 'Here you go, ladies.' She picked up a tray of sandwiches from the table to give to Lindy, and then opened a fresh bottle of whisky and handed it to Irene. 'Keep my guests happy.'

'Aye, of course, Issy. Great purvey, by the way, hen.' Irene winked and stepped aside so that Brodie could squeeze past them and out of the kitchen. Both gave his fit arse a professional once-over, and then sashayed into the backyard where trestle tables and benches had been erected for the guests.Deep in thought, Issy gazed unseeingly across The Narrows for several minutes and then gave herself a little shake and went in search of Brodie. She found him standing on the threshold of the bedroom assessing Jack Innes-Kerr who was trying to feed a crust of bread to a very unimpressed Pershing.

'*Feck off,*' the bird said. It spat the crust onto the bottom of its cage and then pooped. '*Bomb's away!*' it said, gleefully. But Brodie didn't laugh, his brow furrowed as he watched Jack trying to make friends with Pershing.

Brodie was due to leave first thing tomorrow morning and Issy wondered what was going through his mind. Hers was fixated on the thought that they would never meet again, unless she engineered it. Or if they both turned up – oh, ever so casually, at The Pickled Herring on Open Mic Night.

'Brodie, do you have a moment?' she asked, keeping her tone neutral.

'Sure.' He loosened the black tie he'd been loaned by one of the villagers, coiled it round his hand and then put it carefully into his trouser pocket. 'What is it? You okay?' He sent a dark look in Jack's direction, letting her know that her neutral tone hadn't fooled him for an instant. Issy dismissed his concern with a wave of her hand. She had things to say to him, but none of them concerned her father's wake or Jack Innes-Kerr.

Leaving her ex-fiancé occupied trying to win Pershing over, Issy walked into Esme's bedroom and beckoned for Brodie to follow. Then she closed the door, leaned back against it and gestured towards the chair by the window.

'Is there something I can help you with?' he asked, sitting down.

'Yes. Well, no, not really. I just needed a breathing space, that's all. And the chance to say,' she bit the top of her thumb- nail in concentration. 'Brodie . . .' Taking a deep breath, she pressed her palms together, unconsciously making the *Namaste* gesture over her heart chakra as she composed her next sentence. 'I don't know how to thank you. You stopped my mother from creating a scene and making a complete fool of herself - and me, this morning,' she drew in another calming breath. 'Luckily the islanders seem amused rather than offended by her antics.'

'Don't underestimate the power of good food and liberal amounts of uisge beatha. Anyway, you have nothing to thank me for. I sensed today was going to be difficult and wanted to help.' He paused as if he, too, was weighing his words. 'My paternal grandmother passed over recently, so I know how it feels to be bereaved. Your heart's in shreds, your mind's a mush, yet you're expected to be organised, practical - because that's how everyone perceives you. You have to deal with every minor detail the funeral arrangements throw at you, when your heart's broken and you're barely functioning. We knew my grandmother didn't have long to live and were kinda prepared for her passing. You, on the other hand, have had the trauma of your father's sudden death and your fiancé's infidelity to deal with.' Ah – thought Issy, so he knew about that? They glanced instinctively towards the closed bedroom door but Issy didn't care if Jack Innes-Kerr burst in at that very moment and heard every word of what she was about to say.

'I didn't know about your grandmother,' she said to fill the silence stretching between them. 'I'm sorry for your loss, too.'

'Can I level with you? I came here to get away from family mourning, squabbles over her will and what my grandfather . . .' He hesitated, as was his way when he got close to revealing more about himself or his family than he felt was necessary. 'I'm glad to help. I'd do the same for any . . . friend.'

'You would?' Issy shivered at the quiet emphasis he put on the word *friend.*

'Sure I would,' he replied a touch warily. As if he, too, wasn't sure where this *friendship* would take them.

Friends. Is that what they were, now? Had she imagined his slight hesitation on *friend* - as though she meant more to him than that, but he wasn't ready to move their relationship forward just yet? Or was it simply wishful thinking on her part? Her feminine radar was way off beam and needed recalibrating before she was ready to deal with whatever Brodie had in mind. Finding Jack with the intern had dented her confidence even if it hadn't exactly broken her heart. Perhaps she'd misread that sudden blaze of recognition which had passed between her and Brodie at The Pickled Herring.

She'd thought she'd known Jack Innes-Kerr inside out and upside down. And, look where that had taken her. She didn't want to make the same mistake again, with Brodie. But - what if she was reading him wrong? What if his show of concern was nothing more than him being friendly, or worse – a cynical ruse to get into her knickers?

He was a man, after all . . .

Could anything other than trouble result from her revealing conflicting feelings to him?

'I'd say you've gone beyond the call of duty.' Her voice was husky as she thought about Brodie, sex and her underwear in the same beat. She dismissed her heart-searching, pushing herself away from the door and drawing out a stool from beneath a kidney-shaped dressing table. She straddled the stool before realising she'd positioned it so close to Brodie that their knees touched. She could hardly draw back, that'd make her look like a frightened virgin – which was far from the truth, if scenes running through her mind were anything to go by!

To gain breathing space and compose herself, she looked down at Brodie's hands resting on his knees, momentarily entranced by long, artistic fingers covered in freckles, and the turn of his wrist bones. She sucked in a shuddering breath, knowing it would take no effort at all to reach out and cover his hands with hers. But she held back; the right side of her brain reminding her that the last thing she needed right now was more complication in her life.

And Brodie, all six foot three of him, constituted a massive complication. With him in her life how would she achieve any kind of peace - spiritual or otherwise? He'd be a distraction, diverting attention away from her plans for the artists' workshops, and making her less focused. Come the autumn he'd be back to counting plankton – or whatever it was he did, she'd be behind schedule and the graduates she'd been in touch with would be let down. She drew back her hands and in doing so made a conscious decision to pull back from the brink.

From him.

Brodie gave a regretful smile, as if sensing her inner turmoil; as if his thoughts were running on a similar track.

'Your mother's quite a gal. I guess she's caused you and your family problems in the past? ' Deftly, he moved them onto safer ground and Issy was glad of it. Once bitten, twice shy – isn't that how it went?

'You guess right. Mah Mammy's a piece o' work, right a'nough,' she said in a broad Scots accent which made him laugh, further breaking the mood.

'Aye, I got that, ye ken,' he said, almost flawlessly. 'And what's with your ex-fiancé?' He frowned as though Jack Innes-Kerr's continued presence bothered him – *really* bothered him. He leaned forward, his body heat pulsing towards Issy and carrying with it the scent of aftershave and newly washed hair. She tilted back from him – he wasn't making this easy.

'Some misguided notion of my mother's to stage a reconciliation, I'm guessing.'

Brodie looked down at his hands, edging his fingers closer to hers as if he wanted to lace them together. Then he asked the million dollar question. 'Any chance of you getting back with him?'

'None.'

'None?'

'None.'

'Ok-aay,' he drew out the syllables. 'In that case . . .'

At that moment, the door burst open and Innes-Kerr stood in the doorway. Where Brodie's head had almost grazed the lintel, Jack's barely reached three quarters of the way up the door frame. How come she had never noticed how *short* Jack was?

'Aha - I might have known,' he slurred like a badly-rehearsed pantomime villain. 'Typical, Isshy, typical. Heaping the blame on me for a – a tiny, p-p-peccadillo when all the time you've had a man-in-reserve on this godforsaken island whose name I can't pronounce.'

'*Eilean na Sgairbh*,' Issy and Brodie chorused. They smiled at each other, which seemed to rile Jack further. Catching his expression, Issy continued in a more conciliatory tone. 'Brodie's a guest.'

'A guest-with-benefits from what I can see!' Jack fumed, storming into the room to stand in front of them. Commendably, Issy didn't move away from Brodie - she simply turned her head and shot Jack a cold look.

'Yes, that'd really let you off the hook, wouldn't it? Take the blame off you and put it squarely on me. Sorry to disappoint you, Jack, Brodie is a guest in my aunt's house –' Without the support of the door jamb, standing on his feet was beyond Jack's capabilities and he swayed alarmingly. Issy felt more annoyed than angry with him. 'Oh, for goodness sake, sit down Jack, you're making a total arse of yourself, and me, too, into the bargain. And - if you say, *unhand my fiancée*,' I won't know whether to laugh, cry – or, throw up.' Looking as if he was the one about to be sick, Jack crashed down on Esme's bed and it creaked in protest. 'If you vomit over the carpet you'll be the one cleaning it up.'

Getting to her feet, Issy picked up the waste paper basked and plonked it on his lap.

'Man,' Jack said to Brodie in an attempt at male bonding, 'you have no idea what she's like. She's a real ball - I mean, heartbreaker. She's broken my heart and my father's, too . . .'

'Your father's?' Issy questioned. Had she been part of a ménage a trois and not realised it?

'This sounds complicated.' Brodie got to his feet. 'You two have things to discuss so I'll leave you to it. I'll be in the kitchen if you need me, Issy.' He gave Jack a look which suggested it would give him the greatest pleasure to snap him in half, like a twig.

'Wait,' Jack stalled him. 'I get it now – you're the foul-mouthed Glaswegian I heard the other night when I rang.'

Brodie did not deign to dignify the question with an answer. Instead, he laid his hand on Issy's shoulder and looked down into her face; the gesture, coupled with his burning look, confirmed Jack Innes-Kerr's worst fears.

'I'll go and check out how your guests are doing, Issy. Just holler if you need me.'

'I will, Brodie.' She smiled her thanks as he left the bedroom.

Tellingly, he did not close the door behind him.

'*I will, Brodie,*' Jack mimicked, pulling a face like a spiteful child. 'Ho-ho-ho, clearer and clearer, Issy. Clearer and clearer.'

'Cut out the ho-ho-ho's, Jack, you sound like a second rate Father Christmas. It wasn't Brodie's voice you heard the other night, it was the parrot's.'

'That parrot is possessed by the devil. It told me to *feck off,* several times.'

'It could be,' she agreed, thinking how perceptive Pershing was in rejecting Jack's overtures of friendship. 'What do you want, Jack? There's no chance of us ever getting back, you do know that, don't you?'

'Okay, I'll level with you. A complication has arisen,' he began.

'A complication?' Issy went hot and then cold. 'Don't tell me Suzy the intern is pregnant. That would be too shameful for words.'

'Of course not. What do you take me for?' Issy's raised eyebrow suggested that he shouldn't pursue that particular line of questioning. 'Cards on the table?'

'If you please.'

'Father wants you back in the fold, I mean family, and working for Ecosse Designs. Clients are clamouring for you and refusing to countenance any of the other designers we offer them. I want you back, too, darling,' he added, as if realising that his attempt at reconciliation was falling wide of the mark. He tried to stand up for a second time but his legs wouldn't support his weight and he crashed back into the chair. Issy stood over him with her arms crossed;

249

something didn't feel right.

Finally, the penny dropped.

'Oh, I get it. Geordie's told you to get me back at any price. And, should you not be able to persuade me, you'll be sent back out on the road with your salary halved to make up for the commissions Ecosse Designs has lost - thanks to your extra-curricular activities with Little Miss Intern. Feel free to stop me at any time.'

Jack let out a defeated sigh. 'Something like that,' he admitted. 'Okay, okay - you're right. Oh, come on, Issy, we were good together, weren't we? Even if we hardly saw each other due to your being abroad most of the time and my being on . . .'

'The golf course? I will admit, Jack, you do look good in a Pringle sweater but, really, I want more from my life partner than that.'

'Am I permitted to ask how long you've been sleeping with Captain America? Does *he* tick all the boxes?'

'Maybe he does at that,' she said, realising it was true. 'What you need to understand, Jack, is that I'm never coming back.'

Once the words were out, Issy knew that her life in Edinburgh was over. Once probate was granted on her father's will and his lawyers disposed of the lease on the Leith penthouse, she could count her pennies. Hopefully, by then, planning permission for the outhouses would be granted. Recently, a girl she'd attended Edinburgh University with had been in touch, desperate for somewhere to make her silver jewellery. Another former student wanted to move his metal sculptures over to Cormorant Island so he could hammer away, well into the night without neighbours complaining.

'I think you're just playing hard to get, Issy,' Jack said, with unwarranted confidence. 'You're a damn fine- looking woman, but don't overplay your hand. The offer won't be on the table forever.' Giving the impression he considered himself the best thing since sliced bread, Jack smoothed down his thick blond hair. Then, he levered himself out of the chair and for one sickening moment looked as if he was about to reach out and kiss her.

That tipped Issy over the edge.

'Oh, go – go boil your head,' she seethed, 'you smug bastard.' Picking up the waste paper basket, she turned it upside down and rammed it firmly over his head. Cotton buds, tissues and screwed up bits of paper landed on his shoulders. 'To use Pershing's words – feck off, and take my mother and her performing monkeys with you.'

With that, she stormed out of the bedroom, slammed the door behind her and stood in the square inner hall. Then, straightening the neck of her little black dress, she took a deep breath and walked through the kitchen, dusting her hands as she went.

One down and one to go –

Chapter Twenty One
Ae Fond Kiss

L a Bella Scozzese was giving a fine rendition of *Oh Mio Babbino Caro* in the cobbled yard between the house and the outbuildings. Although she drove Issy to distraction with her posturing, histrionics and outrageous behaviour, Issy had to admit her Mother had a voice which could melt a steel heart. She looked so slim and lovely in her Armani (or was it Versace?) two-piece suit and silk camisole, that Issy felt more love than irritation when the aria came to an end. Then she noticed two of Isabella's 'people' surreptitiously filming La Bella Scozzese through the outhouse window, the very window where her father's ashes had resided until last night. She ground her teeth; business as usual - she might have known!

When the last note died away, Isabella looked round her rapt audience and spotted Issy standing by the kitchen door. She launched into full diva mode, arms extended, lambent tears welling up in her beautiful dark eyes.

'Bambina mia. My beloved daughter. Here she is, my friends - darling Ishabel. Come, child, come.' She enveloped Issy in a motherly embrace. Once, Issy had wished for nothing more than her mother's love but now she knew it came at a price. And, on this occasion, was all for the cameras and her next publicity campaign.

'Mum, you're suffocating me – please let go.' She disentangled herself from her mother's arms and walked over to join Brodie who was standing, hands in pockets, lounging against the kitchen wall, watching the pantomime. Deciding that she'd been a bit abrupt, Issy turned and said in a more conciliatory tone, 'You sing beautifully mother. Thank you.'

'Aye, you're a wee *stoater*, right a'nough,' a man called out, and Isabella graciously accepted the compliment. 'And Issy can fair belt out a tune, too. Eh, Issy?' La Bella Scozzese winced, briefly, at the islander comparing her classically trained voice to her daughter's ability to 'belt out a tune'. Then the dark moment passed and she was all charm, smiles and graciousness once more.

'What is a *stoater?*' she asked in halting English. Issy rolled her eyes; it really bugged her when Isabella pretended that she'd been born in Dumenza instead of Dumbarton. Isabella knew full well that a *stoater* was a stunning woman or girl.

'An' here's another,' Irene laughed as Jack Innes-Kerr staggered into the yard. 'Practically *stoating* off the wa's,' she said, using the alternative meaning of the word. Jack careered into a table and muttered something indistinct, adding the F-word at the end of the sentence - none too pleased at being the butt of their jokes, again.

Issy glanced between Jack and Brodie comparing the two men and wondering how she could have fallen for Jack's line of patter and obvious physical appeal. Next to Brodie he appeared . . . diminished, somehow. Brodie was several inches taller, broader in the shoulder and looked as if he ran half-marathons for the hell of it. He was suntanned and his thick, auburn hair had a spring to it which suggested good health and vigour. Jack, despite his drunken state, was his usual well-groomed, urbane self and his suit had probably cost a fortune. He exuded an air of affluence and entitlement, as though everything he had ever wanted had fallen into his hands like a ripe apple. And he'd done nothing worthwhile to deserve it. His skin was weather-beaten from hours spent on Scottish golf links with icy rain whipping into his eyes as he sought the Holy Grail - a golf handicap of four. Compared to Brodie's laid-back insouciance, Jack came across as grouchy and ill-natured, as if someone had stolen the last sweetie from his bag and refused to give it back.

Issy suspected she was that sweetie.

As she glanced between the two men, measuring them against each other, she was struck by the fanciful notion that Jack was like the golden lion rampant on the *Bratach rìoghail na h-Alba* – the Scottish Royal standard, claws raised to strike because he considered he'd been denied the honour and respect due to him. Whereas, in her imagination, Brodie personified not so much *Captain America,* as Jack had snarkily suggested, but a romantic highlander - ready to lay down his life for the ill-fated Jacobite cause. Prepared to follow his Bonnie Prince wherever that might lead; to ruin and exile abroad, if needs be.

Brodie or Jack? The familiar or the unknown? Issy made her choice as Jack's voice, querulous and demanding, brought her down to earth.

'When are we leaving, Isabella? I have an early appointment in Edinburgh tomorrow.' Somehow, Issy doubted that. Jack was rarely in the office before midday, much to his father's displeasure, and usually had to be contacted via his mobile phone. More times than not, the thwack of a well-driven golf ball could be heard close by - when he bothered to answer his phone, that is. Now, thanks to his escapade with Suzy the Intern, it looked as if all that was about to change. No wonder he looked glum! 'Issy, will you walk with me to the helicopter?' His expression suggested he was going to have one last shot at making her change her mind.

'No, I don't think I will. The wake will be going on for hours yet and besides . . .'

'Issy,' her mother cajoled, 'don't be so 'ard on darling Jack. 'E 'as been a silly boy and made a mistake, but 'as apologised. You must − 'ow you say − forgive him. Take him back into your arms, Carissima. Your loving arms.' She held hers out as if to demonstrate the correct stance of the forgiving fiancée. To Issy it looked very much like the pose her mother had struck in many of the roles she'd performed.

'The chances of that happening are extremely unlikely,' Issy said frostily. 'This is Cormorant Island, Mother, not a performance of *Tosca*.'

Looking round, Issy realised that *she* was now the floor show. The islanders, following every twist and turn of the drama, swivelled their heads from right to left between Issy and her mother, as if this was Centre Court at Wimbledon and Venus Williams was playing

255

Anna Kournikova. Today's events would be talked about in the Post Office and over pints of heavy with a whisky chaser at The Pickled Herring for months to come.

Or, until some new drama took its place.

Which would be in about, oh - a hundred years - Issy calculated, disheartened. So much for a new era dawning for the Stuarts on *Eilean na Sgairbh*. She gave a resigned sigh, maybe if she walked to the helicopter with Jack, he'd go quietly. He took another unsteady step forwards, as if he was about to grab her wrist and take her with him – but, Brodie barred his way.

'You heard the lady,' he growled. 'She's given you your answer. Time you left; time you *all* left,' he said, addressing Isabella's people in a voice which brooked no defiance. 'The show's over.' Issy didn't know whether to feel relieved that he'd taken control or annoyed that he considered it was appropriate to do so. The speculative looks on the islanders' faces showed that the same thought was running through their minds.

'And what,' Jack asked with as much dignity as he could muster, given that his blue eyes were crossed, 'gives Captain America the right to stick his nose into *our* business?' Brodie looked down on Jack as if he was no more than a troublesome fly. Then, turning to Issy, he paused as if giving some thought to what he was about to do - then shrugged his shoulders in a helpless gesture.

'This.'

Issy found herself in Brodie's arms being kissed with a thoroughness that showed acquaintance with the practice. And demonstrated that kissing her had been on his mind for some time.

'Brod-ie. Mmph,' she protested against his lips, but didn't pull away.

That was all the encouragement he needed. He deepened and prolonged the kiss, making Issy's blood fizz and sing in her veins. She forgot all about their audience, the fact it was her father's wake and that her erstwhile fiancé was standing two paces away. She discovered that she liked being kissed by Brodie, who clearly knew how to do it properly. Reflexively, she twisted her fingers through his thick hair and pulled him closer. Dimly aware of thinking *Oh, what the hell, the day's in tatters anyhow*, she returned the kiss with interest and twined her foot round his ankle.

Then she whispered his name on a long, drawn out sigh; intimate and breathless: *Och, Br-oh-die.*

Dimly, Issy became aware of Jack Innes-Kerr protesting at Brodie's frontiersman-like tactics, her apparent willingness to be kissed by him, and – adding insult to injury - the islanders' approval of Brodie's gallant gesture. She knew she should call a halt to the kiss, after all, Brodie had made his point. But she'd lain awake in the long watches of the night, wondering how it would feel to be kissed by him and was in no hurry to end the demonstration. A delicious heat spread from her solar plexus to the top of her head and then downwards to her toes in their three-hundred pound shoes. Everything and everybody was forgotten as she focused on the kiss; on Brodie.

In the end, it was Brodie who pulled back.

He looked down at her with the slightly dumbfounded expression of someone who had acted on impulse, only to discover that holding Issy in his arms was what his soul needed. Cried out for, in fact. He gave her one last, hard kiss and then with a show of reluctance, peeled his lips away from Issy's. He then pulled her into his side, and tucked her under his arm, next to his heart. Keeping his arm draped over her shoulders, he turned his attention to a now puce-faced Innes-Kerr.

'You were saying?' Brodie asked.

'Ach Man, can ye no see you've lost her?' the landlord of The Pickled Herring addressed Jack, almost sympathetically. 'Have some dignity. Away into yon helicopter and leave the lassie in peace. Ye had yer chance and blew it; there's no place for you on *Eilean na Sgairbh*.'

The other islanders muttered in agreement. Then, as if it was orchestrated, they all stepped back to let La Bella Scozzese and her entourage escort a crestfallen Jack out of the yard. Issy freed herself from Brodie's arm and tried to think of something suitable to say to her ex-fiancé and show-stopping mother. As Isabella drew level with her daughter, she whispered in perfect English in Issy's ear.

'You win, Issy. No contest; Brodie's the man and Jack's the wee bauchle, no doubt about it. But I don't think you'll be able to keep a man like him satisfied – in or out of bed. So I wouldn't cut Jack adrift just yet, Carissima.'

'Thanks for the couples counselling, Mum, it's always nice to have input from an expert.' But her irony sailed right over Isabella's head.

'Brodie's a fine man, I'll grant you that. But ask yourself this, my girl, what's brought him to this god-forsaken island – and what does he want with *you.*' Then she turned, slipped her hand through Jack's arm in a gesture of solidarity and they walked out of the yard and out of Issy's life. There was an audible sigh of relief from the mourners, who rubbed their hands in glee at their departure.

A piper, one of James Stuart's contemporaries, blew air into the bagpipes, as Mungo Park ceremoniously replaced James' ashes in the outhouse window to the tune of *Flower of Scotland.* The whole yard, including a word- perfect Brodie, joined in with the singing, and Issy's voice broke as she brushed away the tear rolling down her cheek. Her father rarely missed a match at Murrayfield, the home of Scottish rugby, and organised his diary according to the fixture list. He was more likely to forget Issy's birthday than the date of the Calcutta Cup. Some of the rare moments of intimacy and togetherness which Issy had shared with him had involved singing *Flower of Scotland* on a windswept stand, willing the national team to victory.

Mungo paused in the doorway and looked at Issy.

'Shall we away and leave ye in peace, lassie?'

Issy glanced round at the faces turned towards her.

Lindy – openly cast down, realising she was no longer Brodie's number one girl and that her chances of returning to America with him were fading fast.

Mungo – concerned that the memorial service and wake for the island's main benefactor had descended into farce.

The islanders – seeing all the food and drink in the kitchen about to go to waste.

And Irene – sending her a knowing look which said: *I widnae kick Brodie oot o' mah bed, dahrlin'*.

As for Himself - Brodie had released her and was now helping to clear the tables so that dancing could take place. Although Issy wanted nothing more than a chance to get Brodie alone and to demand what the kiss signified, she knew they needed breathing space to put their thoughts and feelings in order. Not only that, honour had to be done to her father's memory.

'No, Mungo. I want you all to stay and help me remember my father and forget today's . . . distractions. Eat and drink my friends, it's what he would have wanted.' She and Mungo exchanged a look. Of course James Stuart would have wanted no such thing, but she wasn't going to mess up a chance of getting the islanders onside because of her late father's attitude towards alcohol and revelry.

'Go oa-hn, Roddy,' Irene cut in, seizing the initiative. 'Gei'us a wee tune.'

This time the piper struck up with *I Love a Lassie* and they all joined in singing and dancing. Issy glanced over at her father's ashes in the sandalwood box, just visible through the grimy windowpane and realised, in a moment of clarity, that James Stuart had loved her to the best of his ability. Suddenly overwhelmed by the need to compose herself, she dashed away another tear and hurried over to the kitchen on the pretext of fetching more sandwiches.

It was much later that evening before Issy had a chance to seek Brodie out and talk things through with him. She found him standing by the open front door of the cottage, the view of the sun setting across The Narrows obscured by the bulk of the Land Rover. At his feet was a holdall with a neatly folded leather jacket threaded through its arms.

All well-ordered, tidy and . . . very final.

'Going somewhere?' Issy asked, heart sinking.

'Issy – hell, what can I say? I overstepped the mark this afternoon...'

'As the injured party,' Issy cut in, 'isn't that for me to decide?'

'Look,' he began, pushing his hair off his forehead. A gesture Issy was beginning to recognise masked confusion and uncertainty. She didn't want him to leave. But how could she put that into words without appearing clinging and needy?

'I *am* looking; and all I can see is a man reading more into a simple kiss than was probably intended.' Her tone was calm, but her face burned.

'A simple kiss. Is that what it was?' He frowned, looking as if he wanted to correct her, to say that the kiss meant more – much more; to both of them. However, Issy realised that he wasn't going to be the one to make the first move. Hadn't he already shown his hand in front of the whole community by kissing her? Now it was her turn – and he was waiting . . .

'A simple kiss,' she repeated, 'a friend, helping a friend. Isn't *that* what it was?' She had to be sure what the kiss meant, what it promised. If he was able to dismiss the earth-shattering kiss so easily, pack his things and take his leave of her – Well, she wasn't about to make a fool of herself by revealing that the *simple kiss* had blown her away. She'd never been kissed like that in the whole of her life. Brodie bent down and picked up his holdall and her heart began to race. Stay. Stay, she wanted to beg; instead, she spoke in a calm, reasonable voice which hid her inner turmoil. 'It got rid of Jack, didn't it? Job done. So, I don't see why you're . . . scuttling off.'

'Is that what I'm doing - scuttling off? I figured that it would be best for you - your reputation if the islanders saw me leaving tonight. That kiss will have the old ladies in the Post Office talking fit to bust. You'll have to live here when I'm back in the States. I don't want to . . . compromise you.' Did she imagine it, or did the tenor of his voice change as he said *back in the states*? Was this his way of hinting that a summer's fling would be the worst thing, for both of them?

'Yes, you're right of course. My reputation . . .' she said in a thoughtful voice. She recalled telling him about her plan to bring the Stuarts back in from the cold. It would be contradictory – not to say out of character, for her to admit that his blistering kiss had turned everything on its head. That being in his arms had, briefly, put the dream of the craft workshops from her mind.

'Issy?' he questioned, sending her another quizzical look.

'Sorry. Daydreaming. A fault of mine – added to which, I'm starting to flag a bit if you must know.'

'It's been quite a day for you. For both of us.'

'I couldn't have got through it without you,' she said, sending him a fierce look which dared him to deny how much he'd helped her. 'Thanks - I mean it.' She held out her hand in a formal gesture.

'Issy . . .' Brodie stepped over his last piece of luggage, took a step towards her and looked as if he wanted to enfold her in his arms. 'I'm glad I could help. I can't believe that we met only ten days ago. I feel like I've known you all my life. Listen, Issy, there are things I need to tell you. Things about me you should know, before . . .'

'Issy, pet, is there any more whisky? This lot have drunk the well dry.' Irene's interruption was both timely, and inopportune. It prevented Issy from making a fool of herself; but it also stopped Brodie from revealing something significant.

The reason why he was on *Eilean na Sgairbh*.

'Yes, I've got a stash in the outhouses, I'll come and get it.' Issy wanted to stamp her foot in frustration but managed a careful smile instead. Irene looked between them, quick to realise that she'd burst in at the wrong moment.

'Are ye off then, Brodie?' she asked, covering her gaff.

'Yes, I've imposed on Issy *and* Mizz Stoo-art too long – and the eco-lodge is ready.' He picked up his holdall and stepped away from Issy. 'See you guys around, huh?'

'You'd better believe it Big Man.' Boldly, Irene came forward and gave him a smacker on the lips. 'If you dinnae come doon tae The Pickled Herring, ah'l come looking for ye. Ye ken?' She turned her back on him, widened her eyes at Issy and jerked her head in his direction, signifying that Issy shouldn't stand there like a lummox, but should kiss him goodbye, too.

But the moment had gone.

'Goodbye, Brodie. See you around,' Issy repeated his phrase and shook his hand. Brodie returned the handshake, holding onto Issy's fingers a moment too long. Then, as if they were exchanging a secret handshake, his middle finger curled into Issy's palm and grazed a path across it. A shock wave of reaction travelled through her, and she knew the kiss wasn't the end. It was the beginning of something new.

'Laters,' he said, releasing her hand and leaving the house.

'Laters,' Issy and Irene chorused, standing together in the doorway and watching him drive off.

Irene must have heard Issy's strangled sob because she put a comforting arm round Issy's shoulders and gave her a squeeze. 'Come on, hen, you've got mourners to entertain. *Stage face*, remember?' It was the piece of advice she'd given Issy years ago at The Pickled Herring the first time she'd sung before an audience.

'Stage face,' Issy agreed, her ears straining until the sound of the Land Rover's engines disappeared from audible range. Then, lacing her arm through Irene's, they walked into the kitchen together.

Chapter Twenty Two
Home Alone

A fter almost a week of endless sunshine the weather decided to break. Lightning, hailstones, anvil-shaped clouds and waves breaking over the harbour wall, gave the days the feel of impending apocalypse.

The weather matched Issy's mood – dark, stormy and unsettled. Since Brodie had moved into his eco-lodge on the far side of the island, she'd seen nothing of him or Lindy. She suspected that Lindy was sulking after witnessing 'the kiss', and was otherwise occupied as Brodie's cleaner/chef/gopher. She'd turn up soon enough when she had something she wanted to share with Issy, she always did. As for the man himself, Issy had no idea what he did with his time. Perhaps she had him all wrong and he really *was* a marine biologist and spent hours exploring the diversity of marine life in the rock pools and shallow inlets of *Eilean na Sgairbh*.

Exploring the island by car wouldn't take longer than a day and if he sought further diversions, that would involve crossing The Narrows at low tide and heading for the mainland. Which, in turn, would entail him driving past her window; or, if he really *was* avoiding her, going the long way round and adding ten miles to his journey. So far, she'd resisted the temptation to pop into The Post Office or The Pickled Herring in the hope of gleaning any nuggets of gossip concerning him. She'd hate to look as if she gave a damn about him or his whereabouts.

However, she had to admit that she was smarting from him not being in touch. Surely they were friends – if nothing more? And, in her book, friends didn't treat each other like that.

Issy sighed and sat back on an old workbench pushed back against the wall of one of the outhouses behind *Ailleag*. Two weeks had passed since Brodie had taken up residence in his eco-lodge. Two weeks during which she'd filled two skips with years of accumulated rubbish: old newspapers, rotting sacking, and whisky barrels whose alcohol-soaked ribs had been eaten away by some very lucky woodworm. The only things worth saving were a couple of illicit stills discovered at the back of one of the outhouses and some empty, unused Twa Burns whisky bottles with peeling labels. Issy wondered if the island museum might find a use for the bottles. As for the stills, she'd rung an auction house in Glasgow and they would be pleased to enter them next time they had a suitable space in their catalogue of industrial antiques. Hopefully, they'd raise some much needed cash for her renovations.

'Here we are again, Dad,' she addressed the sandalwood box on the window.

It saddened her that she was reduced to having one-sided conversations with her father of the sort she could never have had when he was alive. She told him everything, about her plans for the future, her feelings for Brodie, pretending he was the kind of loving father who gave good counsel to his wayward daughter. A daughter he loved very much but didn't really understand. Wiping hands down the sides of her old jeans, she sighed and forgot all about Brodie as a more pressing concern demanded her attention.

'Time I enquired about scattering you on that Munro, isn't it? Will I have to do it in person, do you think? Or, can I hand you over to the Cormorant Island Climbers and hope they'll do the deed for me?'

Until his ashes had been scattered, Issy knew that she would never attain closure. She needed the feeling of having tied up all the loose ends before she could move forward with her new beginning on Cormorant Island with confidence and vigour.

To her shame, she'd been very squeamish about her father's ashes, not daring to raise the lid of the sandalwood box and glance inside. As if he was the genie in the bottle and once released would haunt her days, moaning about the shambles her life was in – and harping on about the fiasco of the memorial service. The only thing he'd approve of was the fact that Jack was now very much an *ex-fiancé*. She'd almost convinced herself that they weren't her father's ashes at all, that the box was empty. She couldn't get her head around the fact that her tall, immaculately dressed father had been reduced to ground up bones, and along with the remains of his eco-friendly, banana leaf coffin, fitted into a cedar wood box which had begun its life in India.

What her aunt Esme would say when she saw her favourite box housing her brother's remains, she'd think about later.

Walking over to the box, she traced the carving with her fingertips.

'What happened between you and Esme, Dad? Why did your father leave the house to her when he died, cutting you out of his will?'

Again, no reply; her father was shutting her out in death - just as he had in life. She sat down on the workbench and waited for the latest squall to pass so that she could dash across the yard and head for the kitchen. Esme's return home had been delayed, too. The fracking demo had ended with most of the protesters, including Esme, deciding to travel over to RAF Waddington, in Lincolnshire, to join members of the End the Drone Wars group picketing the base. She'd sent Issy a selfie of herself in a t-shirt bearing the logo: DRONES ON TRIAL – Every Afghan has a name. WAR is not a video GAME.

Issy hoped Esme wouldn't be charged with criminal damage, as last time she'd protested at an air base, she'd incurred a fine she could little afford. When she returned, Issy vowed to demand answers to all the questions buzzing around in her head like persistent flies, and wouldn't be fobbed off.

In the meantime, she'd got plenty to keep her busy – and her mind off a certain American.

With any luck, final planning permission for the conversion of the outhouses would be granted soon. She glanced over at the sandalwood box nestled on the window ledge. Hopefully, her father's bequests regarding the sea tractor and other legacies he'd left for the betterment of life on Cormorant Island would help swing it for her with the authorities. She was itching to order new made-to-measure workbenches and have them fitted, paint the interior of the outhouses, install heating and update the electricity supply. And, the part she was really looking forward to, convert the loft space above the outhouses into three separate bedsits/studios where the artists could live while they worked. Hopefully, next summer it would all be up and running and she could offer residential courses on different aspects of art, craft and design to like-minded people. There would be additional B&B accommodation available for paying guests in *Ailleag* too, should it prove necessary, bringing Esme in much needed cash.

She let out a satisfied breath. The fulfilment of her dream would use up the money she'd saved from her share of the deposit on the flat in the New Town, Edinburgh, where she'd hoped to start married life with Jack. It'd been love at first sight when they'd stood in the bay window with an estate agent looking over a central garden and an uninterrupted view of Edinburgh castle. Shame they hadn't loved each other quite as much.

'I know you didn't like him, Dad. You were right – he wasn't the man for me.' She picked up a strand of twine and curled it round her wedding ring finger and then held out her hand to admire her handiwork. Not quite the solitaire diamond she'd sellotaped to Jack's treasured photograph of him playing a round at Carnoustie. She pursed her lips and stared, unseeing, at the peeling walls. Should she have kept the ring and sold it to pay for more renovations as Lindy had suggested? She thought not. It would have brought her bad karma.

She hadn't wanted to marry Jack, not really. They'd slipped into the relationship as a result of familiarity, and a lack of time or opportunity to meet new people. In the end, it had been easier to let things slide than to make a conscious effort to break up and start anew. She saw that now.

She imagined Brodie in Jack's place and her heart began to beat faster. If he'd been her fiancé, she would have taken greater care not to let some ambitious intern steal him – quite literally, from under her. She'd relived Brodie's kiss many times, lying restless in bed gazing into the long summer nights, her body demanding release from the need Brodie had awoken in her. It'd been weeks since she'd shared Jack's bed and month's since she'd had satisfying sex with him. Pressure of work in Dubai, Hong Kong or Moscow, had kept her abroad and him in Edinburgh. Now she wondered if that had been engineered by Suzy the intern, who was in charge of contracts and commissions. It was entirely possible.

Well, she had no intention of letting work, even if it was the realisation of her dream, getting in the way of her life a second time. She was a young woman who had not yet reached her sexual prime and Brodie's kiss had reminded her of the fact. She pulled herself out of her dream. The rain had stopped and she walked over to the doorway as rainwater dripped off the broken guttering and down the walls. Something else she'd have to fix; another task to stop her imagining how it would feel to have Brodie in her bed, wrapped in her arms.

A favourite poem came to mind as she waited in the doorway;

Westron wynde, when wilt thou blow,

The small raine down can raine.

Cryst, if my love were in my armes.

And I in my bedde again!

She wondered about the poet who had penned the lines, anonymously, hundreds of years before.

Seemingly, longing for a second chance at love was nothing new.

'Sorry, dad,' she apologised for her erotic thoughts. However, the sandalwood box was exactly where it'd had lain since Mungo had put it there. It hadn't spun on its axis or come crashing to the floor – and for that she was glad.

In the end, Lindy couldn't stay away. She knew things about Brodie – *new things* – which she felt were her duty to report. Issy could tell by the bolshie set to her shoulders, the fact that she was free of make-up, wearing jeans and a simple t-shirt that *Lola* had left the building and Lindy was going through a new incarnation.

Brodie's Girl Friday.

Brisk. Efficient. And – just a tad, too sassy.

'Och, Issy, you should see the eco-lodge. It's braw. I wish I could live there all the time and not above *the shop.*' She spat the last two words out as though she lived in a cellar and was in permanent servitude to her mother and the Post Office's customers.

To wind her up, Issy replied, 'Did you know that Margaret Thatcher lived above her father's grocer shop in Grantham for eighteen years? Didn't do her any harm.'

'Margaret Thatcher?'

'You know, the former Prime Minister,' Issy said, straight-faced. '*The lady's not for turning* and all that?'

'Yeah, whatever.' Lindy shrugged, with all the insouciance of a character out of *EastEnders.* 'As I was saying, it's got satellite television – Brodie and me have watched all the latest American shows on it. Hot tub on the decking overlooking the landscaped gardens and the wee loch.'

'Have you and Himself shared that as well?'

'Not yet. But I keep my swimming costume in my cleaning stuff. Just in case,' Lindy went on, oblivious to the fact that she was being teased. '*And* he went all the way over to the mainland to buy some Pope's Eye steak so that I could cook him – us – his favourite, steak and chips. He calls them French fries, by the by. I told him to have all his food delivered from Sainsbury's on the mainland, we only sell crap stuff in the General Store – tinned tatties, dog meat stew, stretchy white bread and steamed puddings in a *tin.*' Her voice rose at the end of the sentence as though it was an offence to sell such ordinary items to her hero.

'And has he?'

'Nah – the great lummox insists on shopping at mah mammy's shop. Something about supporting the local economy. I don't get it; with all his dosh you'd think he'd have stuff flown up from Harrods, Fortnum and Masons, or whatever.'

'Is that what you came to tell me?' Issy was glad that they were friends once more but in no real mood for an itemised run-through of Brodie's shopping list. Fascinating though the subject was . . .

'Na-a-ah . . .' Lindy really drew out the word this time. 'Brodie's travelling over to Glasgow to pick his grandfather up from the airport. And I thought,' she hesitated. 'I thought you'd like to come over to the eco-lodge and have a good snoop around.'

'Lindy!'

'Keep yer simmet on, I dinnae mean we'd go rooting through his underwear drawer or anything like that. I've seen his boxer shorts, I iron them after all.' Issy stopped what she was doing and her mind went off at a tangent thinking about Brodie wearing nothing apart from well-pressed boxers. 'Anyway, I don't see why you should be so shocked at the suggestion, Lady Muck. The man had his tongue down your throat playing tonsil hockey barely two weeks ago.' She pulled a face as though she'd spent the last two weeks expunging the picture from her mind.

'It was a stage kiss. No tongue action involved,' Issy said in a regal manner. 'It was simply Brodie's way of getting rid of Jack. And it worked.'

'Stage kiss?' Lindy was having none of it. 'Well youse two are pretty good actors then, because you've convinced half the island that I only had to wash *one* set of bed linen during Brodie's stay here. If ye get mah meaning.'

'And the other half of the island?' Issy asked, pausing in the task of getting Esme's bedroom ready for her return.

'They're like me. They think Brodie is way out of your league.'

'Thanks for that. Here,' she threw a pillowcase at Lindy and indicated that she should make herself useful by re-making Esme's bed.

'Don't you want to hear about his grandfather?' Lindy asked, her voice muffled as she tucked a pillow under her chin and slipped it into a clean pillowcase.

'Not as much as you want to tell me, obviously.'

Lindy ignored the put down. 'He's in his mid-eighties, recently widowed and a bit frail. His family are dead set against him making the trip, coming over, but Brodie's told them to back off and let the old man have one last trip to Scotland. And I agree,' she said, throwing the pillow at Issy's head. 'His name's Menzies, although Brodie refers to him as Grandpa Mingus.'

She looked puzzled, so Issy explained.

'Mingus is the old way of pronouncing Menzies,' Issy said, bending over the bed and tucking the sheet under, giving it neat, hospital corners. 'You've heard of Ming Campbell, the former leader of the Lib Dems haven't you?'

'Ah'm no interested in politics,' Lindy said, and rolled her eyes as though Issy was a dusty old school teacher. Margaret Thatcher? Ming Campbell? What did they have to do with anything?

'It's funny,' Issy continued, pushing the duvet into its freshly laundered cover, 'how ex-pats and their descendants are more steeped in Scottish culture and history than we are. Giving their children Scottish names, I mean.' Lindy dismissed the history lesson with an exaggerated yawn and got back to her story.

'They seem pretty close, if their emails are anything to go by . . .'

'Lindy, you haven't!'

'Och, dinnae fash yersel',' Lindy said scornfully. 'I only read the ones which are open on the laptop when I do the dusting. Nothing too personal. Although, sometimes,' she sent Issy a wicked little grin, 'when I'm dusting, I accidently scroll through the emails – and it would be a shame *not* to read them. Wouldn't it? '

'Lindy. Those are Brodie's private emails. Of course they're personal.' Issy was shocked by Lindy's casual admission. Unrepentant, Lindy went over to the window and absent-mindedly drew smiley faces in the condensation, as though she didn't want to face Issy for what she had to say next.

'I haven't given up on the idea of going back to the States with him, you know. Maybe not to Las Vegas straight away. I figured I could make myself indispensable to Auld Mingus and accompany him home, as his nurse. Make Brodie fall in love with me. He'll soon forget all about you once he's back in the States –'

'Thanks for that!'

'Or, if that didnae work, maybe I could win over one of his cousins – any hunky yank would do, as long as they are as delish as

Brodie . . . and I get my Green Card.'

'You wouldn't let a little thing like having no nursing training hold you back, then?'

Lindy turned to face Issy. 'Du-uh. How hard could it be? I'd make the old fellah laugh, take him to the Mall in his wheelchair - hang out with the kids, that sort of thing. It'd buck him up no end, and add *years* to his life.'

'Or shorten his life, significantly.' Issy gave her a severe look.

'He'd learn to love me and Brodie would . . .' She put her hands on her hips, daring Issy to rain on her parade. 'I figure that me and Brodie are back on the cards.'

'Do you, now?'

'Let's face it, hen, he hasn't been near you for almost two weeks. What does that tell you? Maybe that kiss wasn't so much a *stage kiss* to get rid of Jackie Boy as the *kiss of death* to your relationship.' Like a demon sitting on her shoulder, Lindy tapped into all of Issy's insecurities. 'Anyhoo, in my opinion you were a bit reckless dumping good ole Jack, just because he'd played away from home. I mean, Issy, come on! I love you – so, I feel I should be the one to explain the facts of life to you, dahrlin'. You're pushing thirty, your biological clock's ticking away like a demented time bomb. Pretty soon your arse will drop and your looks will fade. Jack was your last chance but you threw him over because you thought you had a chance with Brodie. Mistake. *Big* mistake. Like, major,' she said, acting out her favourite scene from *Pretty Woman.*

Issy curled her hands into fists at her sides. Sometimes, the desire to strangle Lindy almost got the better of her. 'Lindy Murran Tennant – you, you . . .' It wasn't often that words failed Issy but they did on this occasion. Having achieved her intended goal of needling her, Lindy gave a cheeky grin.

'So, are you going to come and have a good old nose round at the eco-lodge?'

'I've already told you. I don't snoop round other people's possessions.'

'Suit yersel, sistah,' Lindy said in an accent which was an excruciating mixture of Scottish and how she obviously imagined they spoke in Kentucky. Based solely on the *Dukes of Hazzard* DVD she'd watched. 'If you change your mind . . .'

'I'll know where to find you – in the back of a police car on the way to a private cell in the island lockup which - as you will discover, doesn't have satellite, hot tub or internet connection. But if you're really lucky they might send you down neeps and tatties and a bowl of dog meat stew from The Pickled Herring.'

Unabashed, Lindy skipped away from the window, crossed the room and entered the inner hall.

'Laters,' she called over her shoulder and ran out laughing.

'Laters indeed,' Issy harrumphed. She put her right hand over her stomach, as if a biological clock was indeed counting down in her womb and her eggs were approaching their sell-by date. Then she dismissed the idea as ridiculous and got on with putting the finishing touches to Esme's bedroom.

Sometime later, Issy was in the study sending emails outlining her plans for the craft workshops to her friends who'd graduated alongside her from Edinburgh University. She mustn't allow herself to get side-tracked into wondering what was going on at the eco-lodge, why Brodie's aged grandparent was flying over three thousand miles against his family's wishes to visit *Eilean na Sgairbh*. Or how serious Lindy was about combining nursing with her declared intention of working the tables in The Golden Nugget Saloon.

'Gah . . .'

Issy laid her head in her hands. Was her life never going to settle down? Her nights were troubled by dreams of Brodie; the nagging doubt that the final stage of the planning application might be turned down was causing her major stress. On top of *that,* she was anxious that the video which her mother's 'people' had made on the day of the memorial service had now been edited and was about to appear on YouTube, promoting La Bella Scozzese's forthcoming tour of *The Merry Widow.*

'Great timing, Mother,' Issy grimaced, pulling a face.

And, to top it all, Lindy was on the fast track to hell - or a night in the cells, because she had no moral boundaries. Issy imagined herself saving Lindy from her worst excesses or springing her from the island lock-up with guarantees for her good behaviour. In that moment she wanted someone to take care of *her;* to smooth *her* troubled brow.

There was only one person in the world who could do that.

No, not Brodie, she chided her foolish heart which had picked up tempo at the thought of him riding to her rescue like Young Lochinvar. Being rescued by him *once* was quite enough, thank you! Raising her head, she looked at the sparkling waters of The Narrows and the path The Cow would take in order to reach *Eilean na Sgairbh*. In her mind's eye she saw the black and white coachwork of the old library bus crossing the causeway, getting bigger and bigger until finally . . .

'Come home, Auntie Esme. Come home, *now*,' she said to the mirage. 'I've never needed you more.'

Chapter Twenty Three
Mermaid Rock

I ssy's iPhone quacked into life signifying a message had arrived. Steeling herself in case the text was from Jack or – worse still, La Bella Scozzese, she was delighted to discover it was from her aunt.

Will be with you late tomorrow evening before the tide turns. I'll pick up a take-away from Cowboys and McIndians and we can wash it down with a bottle of red while you tell me EVERYTHING. No guests or hangers-on. Just Les Girls, like the old days. Love you, E xx

Les Girls. Issy read the text a second time and gave a whoop of joy.

Just the two of them, like the good old days when she'd come home from University and shared all doubts and worries with her indomitable aunt. The thought of Esme's homecoming made the frown lift from between her eyebrows for the first time in weeks. She practically skipped into the sitting room to share the good news with Pershing. He greeted her entrance with a 'pouf' of displeasure and turned his back. Issy laughed and stroked the parrot's rough head where new feathers were poking through, encased in a sheath of skin.

It was strange how stroking Pershing made her feel instantly better. She'd read somewhere that stroking one's pet released oxytocin in owner and pet alike, helped to diminish stress and encouraged bonding. Maybe, she reasoned, as her thumb raked across the spiky feathers of his poll, she should have run her fingers through Brodie's hair. Then he would have felt compelled to call and see how she was doing. Of course, she could go over to the eco-lodge and visit him, but pride and self-respect held her back.

Enjoying her attention, Pershing began to croon in parrot-fashion. '*I'm a good boy, I am,*' he babbled deep in his throat, ventriloquist-like, almost without moving his beak. '*Go oan - gei'us a wee kiss darlin'.*'

'Only if you promise to behave when Esme comes home, Pershing.' Issy bent her head towards him, held his vicious-looking beak between thumb and forefinger and dropped a kiss on it through the bars of his cage.

'*Esme!*' the parrot exclaimed excitedly, sidling back and forth along his perch. '*Esme's boy. Esme's ba-aad boy.*'

'Esme will have missed you, bad boy or not. So, no sulking and definitely no sneaky sideways nips to remind her who's boss. Promise?'

Pershing gave a loud tut and retorted, '*You silly tart.*' If he could have rolled his eyes, he would.

Of *course* he was going to bite Esme - just a wee love bite to demonstrate who the alpha male was around here. And to let her know he disapproved of being left behind in a house whose front porch most recently resembled a revolving door admitting random, uninvited people into *his* house. People he didn't like or approve of. Given that he disapproved of just about anybody who wasn't Issy or her aunt, Issy wasn't surprised by his attitude. Although, the capricious beast had taken a shine to Brodie after the toe-biting incident in the bathroom, probably because Pershing considered he'd won that one.

'Traitor,' Issy said fondly.

The remembrance of Brodie in the bathroom wearing nothing but an angry parrot attached to his big toe, played through Issy's mind like a silent movie. Her dreams were punctuated with images of him, too; how perfect he'd looked in his grandfather's kilt, the tell-tale tattoo vivid on his right shoulder. Sometimes she found herself gazing into space thinking thoughts that might not be considered proper for the daughter of a former lay preacher at the local kirk.

As she'd learned to do over the last couple of weeks, Issy pushed Brodie to the back of her mind. Dismissing him as effectively as he, seemingly, had dismissed her. Their relationship had progressed from loathing to liking in a very short space of time. Perhaps too quickly, given that Brodie would be leaving at the end of the summer. He had a life back in America of which she knew nothing. But one thing she did know - there was little on *Eilean na Sgairbh* to keep him. While she couldn't get over her response to *that* kiss, it seemed that Brodie considered his gallant gesture a big mistake and had decided to back off.

Realistically, there was no future for them. Issy knew from bitter experience that a love affair conducted across thousands of miles of ocean simply didn't work. Brodie was right; best to forget all about the kiss which had simply been a ruse to get her out of a difficult situation.

Best to forget about everything, except her plans for the workshops.

Besides, Issy reproved herself, shouldn't Jack Innes-Kerr be at the forefront of her mind? They'd been together for almost three years and yet she'd hardly given him a second thought since he left in the helicopter. He hadn't been in touch, either, perhaps he'd come to accept it really *was* over between them.

She hoped so.

Glancing at her watch, she found that it was almost noon. Lindy had rung earlier to say she was going over to the mainland to collect emergency supplies and did Issy want anything? With Lindy out of the way, it would be safe to pop into the General Store, buy a bottle of the best Merlot *Eilean na Sgairbh* had to offer, a pack of sandwiches and a drink - without encountering more impertinent remarks about the shelf life of her ovaries! She had a sudden image of Lindy running the barcode gun over her lower abdomen and it coming back with a *void* code.

Feeling the need for fresh air before she went stir crazy, Issy decided to grab her swimming things and drive over to Mermaid Rock. There she could sunbathe on the wide shelf at the foot of the rock and let the tide lap at her feet and wash her worries away.

The climb down to Mermaid Rock was hazardous for those who didn't know where to find hand and footholds. However, within ten minutes of leaving her car, Issy had shimmied down the vertical crack in Mermaid Rock and had spread out her belongings on the wide shelf known as *The Mermaid's Chair*. The shelf wasn't visible from the shore and there were so few children on the island nowadays that Issy was assured of peace and quiet. Apart from the gentle whisper of the west wind and the lapping of the waves at her feet as the tide came in, there was nothing and no one to disturb her.

Pulling off the t-shirt she'd slipped over her bikini, Issy lay down on an old towel, relishing the heat beating up from the rock through the thin bath sheet as if she was a basking lizard. She'd read later, but for now she'd just lie back and remember . . .

. . . remember when Esme had bought two long, nylon wigs – one turquoise blue, one shocking pink from a mail order catalogue - for her and Lindy. Wearing them, they'd come down to the shelf and practised being mermaids, singing at the top of their voices in the hope of attracting merfolk, silkies, or at the very least, seals. But to no avail. Disappointed, they'd tossed the wigs onto the waves and let the outgoing tide carry them out to sea. They'd often speculated in later years, somewhat guiltily, if the Jamestoun Lifeboat had been called out to search for the owner(s) of the wigs, believing they'd drowned. But nothing had appeared in the local papers so, after a few weeks, they figured they'd got away with it.

Issy laughed at how worried they'd been that Esme would chastise them for casting the wigs on the water. She should have known better. Esme had simply shrugged, finding the whole episode amusing and had reminded them that going to university and getting a degree would be of more use to them than luring sailors onto rocks.

Luring sailors onto rocks.

Issy recalled Esme's expression as she'd said the words. Then she'd been too young to pick up on the nuances, but now she realised that beneath Esme's amused smile there was a hint of regret that she'd let life slip through *her* fingers. And that, given the choice, maybe Esme wouldn't have spent her life supporting causes which time and changing attitudes had resolved, almost in spite of her efforts.

Propping herself up on her elbows, Issy looked out to sea, and the sun burned her fair skin. Aware that no one could see her, she untied the strings of her bikini top and let it fall to her waist. Then she covered herself with Factor 30 suntan lotion. The gentle breeze teased her nipples, and the smell of coconut in the sun cream took her back to the last holiday she and Jack had spent in the Bahamas, three years ago.

'All work and no play makes Jack a dull boy,' she said under her breath. 'And Issy the dullest of fiancées.' Is that what had happened between them? Had she *bored* him into another woman's arms? Did she only have herself to blame for what had happened? Strange, how she had always thought and referred to him as Jack Innes-Kerr, never just *Jack*, as if she had to remind herself who he was; fiancé, boss' son and the man she had planned to spend her life with. The man she'd let slip through her overworked fingers.

It had been the exact opposite with Brodie – to her, he'd simply been Brodie from the very beginning.

'Get him out of your head, Ishabel Stuart,' she said more loudly than intended. Her voice bounced back from the shelf, which acted as a sounding board, and was carried out to sea. Remembering her lovely turquoise blue wig, she laughed properly for the first time in months, realising that at last she'd rediscovered *herself*.

She wasn't Innes-Kerr's former fiancé, nor James and Isabella Stuart's errant daughter. More to the point, she wasn't someone who made a fool of herself over a summer visitor and became the talk of the island.

She was Ishabel Stuart. Capable of standing on her own two feet and as much an entrepreneur as her father before her. She needed no man's approbation to succeed in life, her Aunt Esme had taught her that.

All of a sudden she felt infused with a can-do spirit. She got to her feet and sang to the waves.

"*I am a man upon the land, I am a silkie in the sea/and when I'm far frae every strand/my home it is in Sule Skerry.*'

Now she was a fully grown woman, perhaps she'd have better luck with the mermen. She certainly had more to attract them with these days, with or without the wig, she thought, glancing down at her breasts. As she sang, she recalled her performance down at The Pickled Herring the night before her father's wake. The night she'd looked across at Brodie seated at the bar, the scales had fallen from her eyes and she'd seen him properly, for the first time. Getting into the spirit of merman whispering, she sang the chorus again feeling ridiculously carefree and full of joie de vivre.

She shaded her eyes against the shimmering waves and looked out to sea for any signs of life.

Nothing.

Then – a line of bubbles, heading her way. And, were her eyes deceiving her, a raised flipper in the shallows?

Although she knew there was no such thing as a merman or a silkie, Issy was caught up in the moment and sang the song again. As the bubbles came ever closer, she shivered, wondering what sea sprite she had awoken. Not surprisingly, she felt afraid, as if something other-worldly was heading her way. Slowly, Issy backed away from the edge of The Mermaid's Chair until the rock pressed against her back, solid and reassuring. Knowing she'd be unable to climb to the top of the fissure before the bubbles reached her, Issy gathered her wits about her and stood with her legs splayed, the wind playing with her hair - and a large bottle of mineral water in her hand to use as a club to ward off the sea creature.

The bubbles gathered in a mass and broke the surface as, simultaneously, a dark head raised itself from the water. Then came a pair of broad shoulders carrying scuba diving equipment. Not so other-worldly, after all, but a threat to a lone female nonetheless. The vision stood up some feet away in the shallow water - large, male, wearing a wetsuit and with hair slicked back like a seal's. For a few seconds neither of them moved and then the 'silkie' removed the breathing tube from his mouth and pushed his face mask onto the top of his head.

'Brodie!' Issy didn't know whether to laugh or cry and went for indignation instead. 'You scared the life out of me.'

'Did I?' He waded through the sea which came up to his chest. 'I didn't think mermaids were so easily frightened.' He grinned and Issy's stomach performed flick-flacks in response. Her heart was racing like a wild thing and her breath caught in her throat as she drank in every detail of him. So familiar - yet looking so different in a dark navy neoprene wetsuit. He not only *seemed* part of the sea, but almost as if he had been conceived in the waves and belonged there.

When Issy tried to speak, she found that her tongue had cleaved to her palate. She swallowed. 'Neither did I – know mermaids spooked so easily, I mean. Until now.'

'You know I'd never do anything to hurt you, don't you?' Brodie unfastened his air tanks and belt weights. He laid them down on the wide shelf, adding his mask, breathing apparatus and a mesh bag full of shells. 'Is there room for two up there?'

'For the King of Plankton, of course.' Although she made light of being afraid, her teeth were chattering and her stomach lurched with a mixture of excitement and apprehension.

She extended her hand and helped him onto the rock, although she suspected that he was quite capable of levering himself up without her help. Tugging harder than intended, she pulled Brodie upwards and forwards until he was standing on the rock, pressed up against her breasts. Breasts which she now remembered were uncovered after applying suntan lotion earlier. They looked down at her breasts and then up into each other's eyes. The shiver which coursed through Issy had nothing to do with the wind, but everything to do with the look of intent in Brodie's green eyes – and the message he did not bother to hide.

'Issy,' he began.

'I'd better . . .' She moved away from him, all the better to retrieve the minute triangles of cloth flapping in the light breeze, like bunting. There was little room for manoeuvre, allowing Brodie to cover her hands and prevent her from re-tying the bikini strings.

'Don't.' Brodie shook his head.

'Don't?'

'No, don't.' Imprisoning her hands, he drew her closer to him. 'Issy, I've dreamed of you, of this moment. I can't . . . God help me, I've tried to stay away. To give you breathing space. But, I can't bear to spend another day without you . . . '

Wordlessly, neither seeking nor asking for permission, he bent his water-slicked head and took one of her nipples in his mouth. The shock of warm mouth encircling cold nipple and the trickle of seawater onto her heated skin made Issy pull in her stomach. Without raising his head or stopping the teasing grate of teeth against delicate skin, Brodie released her, curling one hand over her buttock and cupping her free breast with the other.

'Brodie.' Issy knew the sensible thing would be to draw back, push him into the water and throw his scuba gear after him. Then he'd get the message and leave. But she wanted him more than she'd ever desired anything in her life. More than that, she'd missed him and needed to touch his skin, all of him to remind herself he was real and not just the product of her fevered dreams. However, the wet suit was proving an effective barrier to her desire. Reaching behind his neck for the strap attached to the long zip running from neck to lower back, she began to tug it downwards. Every inch she uncovered was met with a corresponding pull on her nipple and her knees almost buckled beneath her as Brodie worked his magic. Once, he raised his head to look at her, to check that *this* was what she wanted, and she nodded, mutely. Brodie looked at her dazedly, his eyes cloudy with desire and, after taking in a deep breath, applied his mouth and tongue to her other breast.

When at last she'd released enough of his body from the wetsuit to enable her to touch the cool skin of his back and shoulders, it became apparent *this* wasn't enough – for either of them. Pausing just long enough, Brodie peeled his suit back, freed his arms and rolled the wetsuit down to his waist. Then he knelt down on the flat rock shelf and pulled her down so that they were facing each other. As if they were giving homage to the sea god who'd delivered him to her.

Skilfully, he untied the remaining strings of Issy's bikini so that the top fell onto the bath sheet at their knees, and then he lowered her back onto the towel, supporting her head with his hand as he joined her on the rock. After that, Issy's world contracted to one of sensation and response. The wind playing over her skin, the rough towel against her back and shoulders, the taste of the salt on Brodie's skin, the full weight of him on her body and the guttural, croaking of cormorants on a nearby rock. Issy was engulfed in a delirium of sensation; she didn't want to open her eyes, knowing that if she did so, her brain would engage and remind her of all the reasons why she and Brodie shouldn't become lovers.

She didn't know him - she'd just come out of a messy relationship - she should be concentrating all her energies on establishing her workshops. But, as sensation overruled logic and common sense, the thoughts faded from her mind and she gave herself up to him.

Apparently sensing the change in her, Brodie trailed kisses from her chin to her navel and then over her flat stomach, only stopping when he reached her bikini bottoms. He pulled the strings on either side, raised her up and slid the material from under her. Now she lay naked in his arms. A shuddering sigh, which was almost a sob, escaped her lips and she acknowledged this was what she'd wanted . . . from the first moment she'd set eyes on him. Now there was no need for pretence, artifice.

'Och, Brodie,' she whispered in his ear, her tongue licking the salt out of the hollow there. Then she guided his head around so that she could communicate all her longing to him in a kiss. Their lips met and their kisses grew ever more heated until, soon, kisses were not enough. Brodie's hand slid lower and as his mouth fastened on her breast, his fingers slipped between her legs and touched her, intimately. At first Issy tensed at the intrusion, and then she moaned and instinctively raised her hips to encourage his fingers to explore more deeply - until they found the most delicate, sensitive part of her.

Brodie said her name, once, drawing out the syllables against her lips before kissing her with a fervour which Issy more than matched. Especially as his fingers were skilfully bringing her to a peak of rapture and the point of no return. She tried to wriggle his wetsuit past his hips so that she could feel all of him against her, but it was stuck fast. Brodie stopped her and wrapped her hands round his waist, shaking his head.

'This is for you,' he said, growling deep in his throat and continuing his skilful lovemaking.

Issy sighed and gave herself up to his caresses, hardly noticing that the tide was flooding in and covering the rock, and them, with its salty caress. Nothing mattered except the mounting urgency building within her as the climax Brodie promised came ever closer. She'd never felt so intimately connected to any man, nor given such an untrammelled response. And as Brodie raised his head from her lips, she held it in both hands, curled her fingers through his damp hair and guided it back to her breast.

'Don't stop. For God's sake, don't – don't . . .'

Brodie laughed and pulled her closer into his body, openly revelling in his ability to bring her to fever pitch. Then, almost in synchronicity with the waves lapping at their hips, Issy climaxed and bright suns burst behind her closed eyelids and she shouted something; something wild and primitive. The cormorants on the nearby rock cried as one in response and then flew off across the island, leaving them alone.

Later, as she tied up the strings on her bikini and helped Brodie to fasten on his diver's belt and air tanks, Issy felt at peace with the world. The tide was coming in at a walking pace and she handed Brodie an ancient waterproof swimming bag into which she'd crammed her belongings. She was certain that her legs hadn't the strength to climb back up to the top of the rock, so she'd have to wade ashore with the bag held above her head before the sea reached past her shoulders. She slipped into the water alongside Brodie and he steadied her before handing the bag to her.

'How come you knew I'd be here and . . . oh, everything.'

'Time for that this evening when you come over to dinner at the eco-lodge. Don't worry,' he grinned, apparently reading her expression. 'I've banned Lindy from calling in unannounced. She's a great kid, as I've said before, and I don't want to hurt her feelings - but I need a break from her. Jeez,' he laughed, 'she's missed her vocation. She could get a job interrogating prisoners for the CIA – or MI5, she's relentless and works on the principle that if she goes on long enough, you'll crack.'

Issy laughed and then added, 'Her technique usually works. What if I have a few of my own tonight? Questions I mean.'

'I'll answer them as truthfully and honestly as I can without breaking any confidences I may have made to . . . another party.

Don't worry, it's not what you think. I'd never play you false and there is no other woman in my life.'

'No Mrs Brodie and lots of wee Brodie's, to use Lindy's words?'

'Only you.' He drew her to him and kissed her hard, as if daring her to doubt him. Taking him at his word, Issy turned away and struck out for the shore. Then she looked back at him over her shoulder.

'What time this evening?'

'Eight o'clock?' It all sounded so prosaic after their scorching lovemaking that Issy hid a smile.

'Suits me fine.' She watched him wet the interior of his mask with sea water as the waves buffeted her, almost knocking her off her feet. 'Brodie –'

'Yeah?'

'Leave the wetsuit on its peg.' She sent him an incendiary look, leaving him in no doubt as to her intentions.

'Yes, Ma'am.' He saluted, once and then dived into the waves. Issy watched from the shore until he reached the deepest part of the bay and disappeared.

Then she smiled to herself.

Maybe she was a silkie-whisperer, after all.

Chapter Twenty Four
Come On Over to My Place

Pershing was none too pleased to have his cage covered by the regulation black cloth while it was still twilight.

'*What you doin'?*' he demanded in the querulous voice of a child being put to bed too early on a summer's evening. '*I'm a good boy,*' he added, just in case Issy had got the wrong end of the stick. As far as he was concerned, being covered in the black cloth was synonymous with being punished.

'I know you are, Pershing, but I might not be back this evening.'

Issy wasn't quite sure why she was telling the parrot this, she felt light-hearted as if on her way to a party, the best party in the world. 'I've been a bad girl and intend to repeat the experience,' she said, and stroked the top of his beak, just above his nostrils where the feathers began. 'I just hope I don't have to be covered with a black cloth before this night's out.'

'*Silly tart,*' Pershing pronounced, as the cover went over his cage, and then chuntered a bit more before settling down.

Issy giggled, picked up her car keys and the bottle of red she'd bought earlier for Esme's homecoming. 'Sorry, Esme, I'll buy another one,' she addressed the bottle of Merlot. 'It's all in a good cause.' Then she left the house by the back door, climbed into her Mini and turned left at the end of the short drive. The route she was taking added several miles to her journey but avoided driving past the General Store/Post Office.

She had a vision of Lindy sitting in her bedroom window with submarine glasses mounted on a tripod, trained on the cottage and clocking her movements – with a notebook and pen, flask of coffee and a pile of sandwiches at her elbow. It was a fanciful notion, but her head was full of whimsy this evening and she giggled again. It was a sound she was unused to; she'd worked punishingly long hours for Ecosse Designs and living with Jack, she now realised, had been a dull affair. The two combined had crushed her spirit and turned her into an automaton, unable to feel, to experience life.

However, all that had changed the moment she'd driven up the causeway on the night of the storm.

The night Brodie had entered her life.

The eco-lodges were situated on the far side of the island not far from the ruin of Twa Burns Distillery and *Traigh Allt Chailgeag*. That side of the island caught the chill north wind and was almost deserted apart from a few New-Age crofters. The majority of islanders preferred to live close by The Narrows, with access to the mainland and the gentler kiss of the south-westerly wind. The local authority and tourist development board had been keen to encourage the eco-lodge development because it provided jobs for the islanders without upsetting conservationists. There was little in the way of wildlife on the north-east side of the island, and what there was – mostly flocks of migratory birds – was unaffected by tourists tramping over the moors. And the ramblers who climbed the modest range of hills forming the spine of *Eilean na Sgairbh* disturbed nothing more than a few hardy sheep.

Issy had driven past the lodges many times without really seeing them but for some reason she showed more interest in them tonight! That reason was Brodie. She shivered at the thought of him, so tall, straight and good-looking, with gorgeous green eyes which seemed to see into her very soul. She thought again of his skilful lovemaking on Mermaid Rock and quivered with pleasure at the remembrance.

How would tonight pan out, she wondered?

At last the lodges came into view. They consisted of wooden A-frame buildings constructed to a Scandinavian model, complete with decking and hot tubs which took full advantage of views across the Wee Loch, towards the coast. Each had a huge satellite dish on its solar-panelled roof to ensure visitors could download favourite TV channels, and a signal booster delivering a fair to middling internet connection. Issy was a proud islander, but tonight she was more interested in who resided in lodge Number Six than energy efficiency ratings and the promise of much needed employment for the islanders. In fact, as she drew nearer, her heart began to thump and her palms became sticky. She felt like a teenager on a first date, not a grown woman who had surrendered, without reserve, to a *silkie* on the rocks.

That fanciful thought drove anxiety away and her skin tingled at the thought of what the *silkie* might have planned for this evening. Whatever transpired, tonight would set the tone for their relationship - however long it lasted; wherever it took them.

Ishabel and Brodie.

Coupling their names together felt strange, yet at the same time, totally right. Their names were as old as the island itself and Issy felt a strong connection with the past as she parked her Mini at the foot of the eco-lodge's wooden steps.

Brodie must have been keeping watch. Before she'd even had time to pull on the handbrake, the lodge door opened and he strode onto the decking. Ignoring the steps, he vaulted over the wooden balustrade and was alongside the side of the Mini, impatient for her to join him. Suddenly shy, Issy used the pretence of fiddling with her seat belt, handbag, and the bottle of wine to give herself more time. Brodie, however, was having none of it. Grinning like a schoolboy, he opened the car door and, before Issy had time to draw breath, she was in his arms being kissed with a passion which made the lodges, beautiful scenery and stunning sunset pale into insignificance.

Enjoyable though the sensation was, Issy nevertheless pulled back and glanced round at the other lodges whose windows reflected back the Wee Loch and the glorious sunset.

'Mr Brodie,' she said primly. 'What will the neighbours think?'

'They'll think I'm a lucky bastard. The one who has Ishabel Stuart in his arms and intends to keep her there until daybreak.'

'Is that right?' She played along, exaggerating her Edinburgh accent and making it sound clipped and proper next to his laid-back drawl. Another pleasurable shiver travelled the length of her as she looked up at him and read the unequivocal message in his moss-green eyes. 'And, do I have any say in this, Mr Brodie?'

'Nope,' he said, entering into the spirit of the thing. 'Shall we?'

He held out his arm and Issy took it, inhaling deeply in a futile attempt to slow down her pulse and stop her stomach from turning little somersaults of pleasure. Her body was showing no such reticence, however; it remembered their lovemaking on Mermaid Rock and hormones were scudding through her veins like heat-seeking missiles, wanting to repeat the experience. In spite of that, Issy managed to apply the brake. They had things to settle tonight before they moved onto more pleasurable activities. Her cheeks burned at the thought of how this evening might end and she guessed that her eyes were shining, revealing too many of her inner thoughts.

To hide her expression, she feigned interest in the eco-friendly wooden decking and looked down at the floor. Brodie raised an amused eyebrow as he led her into the lodge and seemed willing to pretend that the interlude at Mermaid Rock hadn't happened.

'My humble abode,' he said, closing the door behind them and spreading his arms wide. He'd gone to a lot of trouble . . . the wood burning stove was lit, the table was set with candles and flowers and delicious smells wafted towards them from the kitchen.

'Not so humble, Mr Brodie.' Issy tried to bank down the happiness bubbling up inside her. She turned towards him, hands on hips and adopted a reproving expression. It was a stance she'd seen some of Mungo's parishioners take when they thought his sermon was light on hellfire, damnation and chastisement of those who'd transgressed the bible.

Issy guessed she was right up there with the worst of the transgressors!

'You like it?' He looked anxious, eager to please and Issy couldn't resist teasing him.

'Aye, its fine right enough, but ah dinnae ken what Mr Parks, the meen-ister would say at such decadence. Satellite television, a sofa big enough for a family to sleep on, wood burning stove, stripped floors and handmade rugs. Not tae mention state-of-the-art *everything.* I could ha' got ye a good price on the rental of a *But and Ben* up the hill, if ye didn't mind having nae running water or toilet. As for this place, it's more than a simple island lassie like me is used to.' She said it in a lilting highland accent, maintaining a censorious look only with the greatest of effort.

'Shucks, Ma'am, I know your daddy was a preacher man, an' all,' he said in a sexy southern drawl. 'But ah wor kinda hopin' you'd put that aside tonight and let me show you a good time. An' don't you worry none, ah'll make sure ah git you home in time for the prayer meeting. But ah figure that you won't want to go anywhere near the church after tonight. Not for a long time, anyways.' The look he sent her should have sent any God-fearing, self-respecting island lassie running in the opposite direction.

Instead, Issy laughed and felt light-headed at the thought of their being alone together - at last.

'Brodie, stop it. I keep hearing *Duelling Banjos* from

Deliverance playing in my head. You'll be selling me moonshine, sassafras and bottles of snake oil, next.'

'And ah'd give ya a right good price, too, Ma'am. Ah know your Scottish blood would expect nothing less.' *That* was too much for Issy, she burst out laughing while he pretended affront. Then, all at once, he was deadly serious and there was a light in his eyes which dazzled Issy and made her fear for her reason. 'C'mere, Ishabel Stuart.' He held out a hand and spun her into his side and then dipped her over one arm, as if this was the opening credits of Strictly Come Dancing. 'You sure are gorgeous, Mizz Stoo-art, know that?' He looked down into her face and Issy's heart stuttered, briefly, before picking up its rhythm once more.

'You make me *feel* gorgeous, Brodie, do you know *tha-at*?' She drew out the vowels and looked at him wide-eyed. Apparently unable to resist, Brodie kissed her again and Issy knew that, like her, he was filled with wonderment at the situation they found themselves in. Neither of them had looked for, or expected, their relationship to take this unforeseen turn.

That unexpectedness of it all, added an extra frisson to the evening.

Righting her, Brodie straightened her shirt where it had rucked up.

'Time out?'

'I think so.' She flapped her hands at her flushed cheeks in an attempt to cool them down.

He led her through to a large, modern kitchen at the rear of the lodge with a utility room leading off it. 'My wetsuit. Hanging up, as per instructions.'

Leave the wetsuit on its peg, she'd said as they'd parted on the beach. The phrase in the old ballad of Sule Skerry came to mind – how the silkie shed his seal skin when he left the water and became human. The thought made her smile and Brodie looked at her questioningly.

'What's that smile for?'

'I was just looking at your wetsuit, remembering the legend of the silkie and . . .' she brushed his interest away. 'Och, never mind.' Under his regard she became unexpectedly shy, which was crazy considering he'd made fireworks explode in her head on Mermaid Rock. Brodie regarded her reflectively, his eyes shining with a luminosity she was beginning to know and love.

She suspected their thoughts were running on the same track.

'No pressure, Issy.'

'No pressure,' she agreed, letting out a relieved breath.

'Will you promise me one thing?' Brodie indicated that she should sit on one of the high stools flanking the workstation in the middle of the kitchen. He then fetched a bottle of champagne out of the fridge, popped the cork and poured out two glasses.

'What's that?'

'Whatever happens tonight, whatever I reveal about my reasons for being on *Eilean na Sgairbh*, you won't turn tail and run out on me.'

'That's a big ask, Brodie.' Her stomach lurched and her skin prickled all over with goose bumps, but with apprehension this time, not lust.

Brodie handed her a flute of champagne into which he'd dropped a raspberry. Showing scant regard for the fragility of the crystal, he clinked their glasses together. 'To the future,' he toasted. Issy fiddled with the long stem but didn't take a sip. Instead, she placed her flute on the granite worktop, to indicate she wanted to get down to business.

'You sound awfully sure there is a future. For us, I mean.' Her face clouded and her forehead puckered in consternation. Brodie's passionate look promised much, if only she could bring herself to trust him fully.

'Issy, I've found you, and I'm never going to let you go. I told you back on Mermaid Rock that I'd never do anything to hurt you. You believe that, don't you?' He put his glass down on the worktop next to hers, sat back on the high bar stool and waited for her answer.

Oddly enough she did believe him. 'Not intentionally, perhaps . . .'

'. . . or any other way,' he finished the sentence. 'You have to believe that.' He looked and sounded sincere, and Issy knew if she wanted to hear his story, she *had* to trust him. God knows, she wanted to believe in him, she really did. But Jack Innes-Kerr had sown so many doubts in her mind concerning her allure as a woman, and the trustworthiness of the male species, that she no longer took anything as a given.

It was this mixture of fear and lack of self-belief which prevented her from falling head over heels for Brodie and trusting him completely. It had nothing to do with the man himself. Issy wasn't an airhead, she didn't take everything a man said at face value, especially if that man had declared that they would be spending the night together. But she was also aware that she'd have to follow her instincts and get back on the horse, if she was ever to get over Jack's infidelity.

Not all men were unreliable bastards. Maybe Brodie would be the exception to the rule; maybe it was time to start believing in love again.

'To the future,' she said, picking up her glass and taking a sip. She replaced the flute on the worktop and set about making her position clear. 'Okay, Brodie, show time. You must have a pretty good reason for being on *Eilean na Sgairbh*. However, before you reveal what it is, I have to tell you how things look from my side of the fence. Okay?'

'I guess.' Brodie's mouth pulled in at the corner, a sign he was eager to get this part of the evening over and done with. Then they could progress onto more pleasurable pastimes. Issy felt the same, but caution made her hold onto one last bit of restraint.

'Since your arrival on Cormorant Island you've been on a charm offensive – and it's worked. You've been virtually declared unofficial laird by the locals at The Pickled Herring, the Post Office Mafia and even dear old Mungo.'

'It's your approval I'm interested in winning, Issy. Not theirs . .

,

Issy held up her hand. 'Please, Brodie, I have to say my piece.'

'I'm listening,' he said.

'I've tried to freeze you out since the moment I laid eyes on you, but it hasn't worked. On the other hand, in true topsy-turvy fashion, Lindy – and others – have smothered you with too much attention.'

'It's you I've wanted from the start, Issy. Surely you know that?'

With an effort Issy ignored his passionate outburst and ardent look which willed her to believe him. She nodded and carried on. 'You've met my crazy, self-obsessed mother – and saved me from shame and disgrace by preventing her from singing *Ave Maria* at my father's memorial service.'

'Good thing Mungo had that - whatd'you call it – vestry, attached to the wee kirk or it coulda gotten ugly.' Issy loved that he played down his role in the *Ave Maria* incident; Jack would have bigged up his part and it would have grown in the telling.

'In three weeks you've probably learned more about my family than you can possibly have wanted. Aunt Esme, by the way, thinks you're the best thing since sliced bread.'

'Sliced bread, huh?'

'She's inquired about you and your welfare in every phone call since she left, and her feelings about Americans are well-documented. Her allowing you into her house, is a bit like Doctor Van Helsing inviting Count Dracula in for a cup of tea.'

He laughed out loud. 'I'm glad I've been able to lay that

particular ghost . . .' The scorching look he sent her way made it plain that ghosts weren't the only thing he wanted to lay. She let out a shaky breath, determined not to be diverted by smiles, charming or otherwise – or the promise of what was to come.

The only way this could work was if they were totally honest with each other.

'You've won Pershing over - apart from a playful nip to your big toe. And, like Young Lochinvar, you've seen off the 'dastardly' bridegroom. I shall be in your debt forever, for that alone.'

'I didn't know I had a Neanderthal gene, until I met that son of a bitch, Jack. I wanted to punch him in the face, good and hard,' Brodie declared and then looked rueful. 'But, I guess we don't do that anymore? In the old days I'd have run him through with mah claymore,' he added in an impeccable Scottish accent. Issy felt like saying, *more's the pity,* but she restrained herself.

The next part of her speech was harder to deliver and she had to stay strong, focused.

'And, finally, when your time comes to leave *Eilean na Sgairbh,* half the island will line The Narrows at low tide to see you off. Everyone, except me, Brodie.'

She kept her tone light but her mouth was dry and she took another sip of wine. Lowering her eyes, she traced the fault line which ran through the polished surface of the granite worktop like a scar. Dismayed to find her bottom lip quivering at the thought of him leaving Cormorant Island, she finished off her champagne and stiffened her resolve. If she looked at him now, she'd be lost.

'Why except you?' His voice was soft and Issy sensed that her answer really mattered to him.

She looked up through a sheen of tears. 'Because I couldn't bear it.'

Her voice cracked and Brodie looked as if he wanted to reach across the worktop and pull her into his arms. Demonstrating commendable restraint, he nodded, then continued. 'That was quite some speech. But you missed out the part where you sang in Gaelic at The Pickled Herring and I fell for you hook, line and sinker.'

'You – you did?'

'Yes, Ma'am. And you didn't mention how you enticed me out of the water with a song and bewitched me. To be honest, you cast a spell on me from the moment I saw your cute ass – sorry – derriere, sticking up in the air the morning after you arrived home. You even looked sexy and gorgeous wearing Esme's old robe. Believe me, Issy, if I coulda gotten that wetsuit off this afternoon – or, more to the point, back on again, all this . . . hesitation and your lack of belief in yourself – in *us* – would be academic.'

'It would?'

'Sure it would.' He walked over to the oven to check dinner wasn't burnt to a cinder and then turned back to face her with the oven cloth draped over his shoulder. It was all so reassuringly domestic that Issy relaxed.

'I see.'

'But you're right, it's time to lay the cards on the table. Time for me to level with you about my reason for being on the island - or you won't believe anything else I tell you this evening.' He turned the oven temperature right down, led her back into the sitting room and sat beside her on the large leather sofa. 'Where to begin?'

'Just start in. I can stop you and ask you to fill in any gaps, or to clear up any misunderstandings. Deal?'

'Deal.'

He walked over to a teak sideboard which took up the whole of one wall and picked up a box file. Crossing one leg over his knee to support it, he sat by Issy's side again, and lifted the lid. He glanced at the contents and then at Issy, seemingly deliberating if he was doing the right thing.

Taking a deep breath, he began.

'Recognise this?' He passed over an old, creased photograph.

'Why, that's identical to the one in Esme's study,' Issy exclaimed, puzzled. 'The one of Johnny and Archie taken before their departure for France.' She glanced down at the photograph of two young men wearing the uniform of the Cameron Highlanders and then back at Brodie for clarification. 'I don't understand, why do you have a copy?'

Without replying, he handed her a piece of faded brown paper upon which was scribbled, 'The Last Will and Testament of Archie Murran McIntosh'. It was a carbon copy of Johnny Stuart's will pasted onto the back of the photo in Esme's study. The room slipped away and Issy was back in *Ailleag's* hall, watching Brodie making his way round Esme's study, photographing everything in sight. The replica of this photograph in her hands, the copy of the will, an old daguerreotype photograph of Twa Burns Distillery circa 1906, and the pages of the family bible which recorded Stuart births, marriages and deaths.

'I don't understand.' Despite her feelings for Brodie, Issy couldn't help feeling he'd overstepped the mark that day.

'Okay, let's backtrack a little, huh? According to your family history, Archie perished at Ypres and was buried in a mass grave along with thousands of others.'

'Correct.'

'His family were wiped out in the flu epidemic which followed the end of the war.'

'Right, again.' She couldn't quite fathom where he was going with this, but an uneasy feeling was growing in the pit of her stomach.

'The distillery was damaged manufacturing landmines and took a long time to recover, by which time many of the skilled workers had left the island, taking their expertise with them?'

'Ye-es,' this time more cautiously.

'Then the distillery was bombed by two Junkers, effectively sealing its fate because no one had the money or inclination to start over? Not to mention your father's aversion to the whisky trade and its attendant evils, as he saw it.'

'This is ancient history and well-documented. I can't see why you have an old photograph and a copy of Johnny and Archie's will in your possession. Or why it has *anything* to do with you. With us.' The excitement and happiness which had travelled alongside her from Killantrae to the eco-lodge evaporated, leaving a sense of foreboding.

The photograph and copy of the will fell from her slack fingers, landing at her feet. Neither bothered to pick them up, the picture and scrap of paper were now redundant. Issy glanced over to where she'd left her handbag on the table next to the bottle of Merlot. Grim-faced, she edged forward to the front of the sofa, making her meaning plain – she wanted out of there.

Brodie closed the gap between them and put his hand on her arm, detaining her.

'How about if I told you Archie hadn't died at Ypres but had been found badly injured and unconscious by a detail on burial duty after the battle. Somehow, he'd wandered away from his regiment, had passed out from his injuries and lain unconscious before being loaded onto a wagon with the rest of the dead. He came round just as our troops were about to lay him in the mass grave.'

'By 'our',' Issy said quietly, 'I assume you mean American troops?' Brodie nodded and she had an inkling where the story was going.

'He ended up in a US field hospital and was shipped back to the States, shell-shocked and unable to speak. His uniform had been removed at the field hospital when his wounds were treated and he was wearing no dog tags – if he'd ever had any. Other than this photograph and copy of the will - which he refused to be parted from, no one knew a thing about him. Who he was, where he came from.'

'Did he die in America?' Issy at last found the voice to ask.

'Hell, no,' Brodie's reply was emphatic and he laughed, dispersing the gloom which had fallen on them. 'He was put on a hospital ship, recovered, found his way to Kentucky and started distilling illegal hooch with the best of 'em. By the time Prohibition ended, he'd made enough money to go legit and set up his own distillery producing the finest bourbon whiskey in the state of Kentucky. Blood will out, huh?'

'I don't understand, why didn't he return to Scotland?'

'The way he told it, he had no family to return to and Twa Burns was only working at a tenth of its pre-war capacity. He was in no mind to start over. He'd turned his back on the past; in his eyes, America was the land of opportunity, the future, he was glad to leave the Old World behind. He had a flourishing bourbon business and was highly regarded as a distiller who could produce alcohol out of almost anything. As my family tell it, he was paranoid about returning to the UK; of being classed as a deserter. He'd seen what'd happened to the poor suckers in his regiment who'd fallen asleep on duty or left their posts to get some respite from the shelling.'

'But he could have written. Let us know he'd survived the war and wasn't coming home. My aunt has often told how Young Johnny – her father – had returned from the Western Front a broken man. He'd been unable to save his friend, locate his body or mark his grave. It was cruel and selfish of him to disappear like that.' She scowled, implying that being cruel and selfish were family characteristics.

'I agree, but cut him some slack. No one returned from the Western Front unscathed - and clearly he'd suffered psychological as well as physical damage; a true casualty of war. His family had been wiped out by the flu epidemic . . . I figure that turning his back on Scotland was his way of dealing with what he'd seen and, more to the point, been forced to do as a soldier. There was no one on hand to counsel him or countless others returning from the Front suffering from post-traumatic stress disorder.'

'Shell shock? Possibly,' she conceded. 'So, you've travelled thousands of miles to let us know that Archie McIntosh survived and founded his own dynasty in Kentucky. A dynasty I'm guessing you're part of. I saw the tattoo on your shoulder the day Pershing bit your toe, remember? *Touch Not the Cat Bot a Glove* – a McIntosh through and through.' The way she said it, it sounded like a curse. 'I also know that the story about the eco-lodge not being ready was a ruse to stay at my aunt's house. To snoop around, photograph documents.'

'Thanks to Lindy, I'm guessing?'

'Never mind that. I – you . . .' Heat burned through her at the thought of how she'd fallen for his line of patter. Had fooled herself into believing that she'd seen something in his eyes that night at The Pickled Herring, something she recognised . . . *Idiot. Idiot. Idiot*, she chastised herself. 'Now *I'm* guessing you're here to find out if the stories Archie McIntosh told are true and if your family has a claim to half of Twa Burns? What am I saying? Of course you are. Isn't that why you asked so many questions, and - fool that I am, I gave you all the answers.'

'Yes and no,' he replied. 'Of course my family is interested to know if the stories passed down through the generations are true. If Archie was the laird's illegitimate son, as he'd hinted at.' He pulled a face at Issy's expression and huff of disbelief. 'Guessing that one's not true, huh? I guess all families embellish the past in order to make a better story, don't they?'

Issy ignored his feeble attempt to lighten the atmosphere.

'So what do you want? There's no money in Twa Burns as you've discovered for yourself. The only inheritance is the site of the distillery, if you want to claim half of a piece of blasted earth, be my guest. My aunt's cottage and the outbuildings belong to her alone. There are the ruins of the McIntosh property which fell into disrepair after Archie's family died during the flu epidemic. I can show you where they are – all part of the five star service,' she said bitterly. 'I'd hate you to go home feeling short-changed.'

'What do I want? I want *you*, Issy, isn't that clear? All this –' he bent down, picked up the photograph and Last Will and Testament at Issy's feet and put them back in the document box, 'means nothing to me. I only want to know the truth for my grandfather's sake.'

'Your grandfather?'

'Yes. After Grandma died last fall and he'd decided he wants to return to *Eilean na Sgairbh* one last time.'

'Return?' She sent him a puzzled look.

'He's in his mid-eighties, but back in the day - like in the song, *he joined the navy to see the world*. After gaining his commission he was posted to the USS Proteus, a tender anchored in Holy Loch servicing nuclear subs. One furlough, he came over to *Eilean na Sgairbh* for some R and R, and stayed a while researching the family tree. Checking out the old stories Archie had shared with him.'

'And?' Her snarky tone suggested the McIntoshes never did anything without a reason, including *him.*

'And – nothing.' He shrugged to indicate how unimportant all this was compared to what they, potentially, could have.

'Nothing?' Blue eyes narrowing, she sent him a sceptical look.

Brodie shook his head. 'Never so much as mentioned his time in Scotland before Grandma passed. Now it's become almost an obsession with him, something he has to do before . . .' His voice snagged as if he couldn't bear to finish the sentence. It was obvious he thought a great deal of his grandfather, and Issy respected that. 'Much against my family's wishes, he's flying over from the States. I'm picking him up at Glasgow airport and bringing him over to Cormorant Island. He's flying in on the red-eye, but once he's over the jet lag, I want you to meet him.'

'I don't understand.' She only half-registered that Brodie wanted her to meet his grandfather, and that in some way he was conferring an honour on her. 'Is that all there is to it? An old man making his last pilgrimage to Scotland? You haven't come to reclaim half of a ruined distillery for the McIntoshes, after all these years?'

Issy looked at Brodie with something approaching regret. Things were much simpler when she thought of him as simply

Brodie. No wonder he had been in no rush to disclose his surname.

'Quite the reverse.' He gave her a long look as if wondering how much more he should tell her. How much more she could take.

Issy pushed herself off the sofa and picked up her handbag. Delicious smells were emanating from the kitchen but the very thought of food turned her stomach. Feelings of loneliness and bereavement which had dogged her since her father's death, returned. However, this time it was the loss of the relationship she *could* have had with Brodie which was at the root of her grief.

She hooked her handbag over her shoulder and made for the door. Brodie got to his feet and caught her by the elbow.

'Don't go. Please, Issy . . .'

'I have to. Oh, don't look at me like that, Brodie, I'm not made of stone. I've got to process everything you've told me, think about it, then –'

'And then, what?'

'I don't know,' she said, simply. Life was moving too fast for her to keep up. She needed breathing space, some time out. Above all, she needed to get away from *him* . . .

'Issy stay, you've only heard half the story. Listen to what I have to say and then, if you still feel the same, you can walk out of my life and I'll respect your decision. Please, Issy . . . give me a chance.'

Where had she heard *that* phrase before?

Shrugging off Brodie's hand, she stumbled down the steps to where her Mini was waiting. She couldn't see properly because her eyes were cloudy with tears, but she gunned the Mini Cooper down the drive and onto the coast road – intent on putting as many miles between herself, Brodie and his double-dealing as was physically possible.

Chapter Twenty Five
Don't Leave Me This Way

Ironically, the place where Issy pulled in to wipe away her tears was the lay-by opposite the ruin of Twa Burns Distillery. Compared to the fate which had befallen the workers twice in a generation, her disagreement with Brodie paled into insignificance. She banged her head on the steering wheel, trying to knock some sense into it. Was she turning into a *bolter*? One of those women who ran away when things weren't going according to plan?

After all that subterfuge – concealing his real identity, staying at Esme's B and B when he should have moved into the eco-lodge, secretly photographing items in the study, and the imminent arrival of his grandfather – it was apparent that Brodie had been working to a plan. One he'd been about to share with her, if only she hadn't acted so hot-headedly.

Taking a deep breath, Issy got out of the car, crossed the road and stood in front of the memorial erected to those who'd been killed during the bombing raid on the distillery. The inscription on the Roll of Honour - *NEVER FORGET* - swam into focus, chastising her for an ill-timed exit, their names a blur through her tears. It was her duty to find out what the McIntoshes had in mind; instead, she'd left the eco-lodge in a strop and let everyone down. Brodie's stricken face superimposed itself over the names on the Roll of Honour, adding to her sense of shame.

Badly done, Ishabel Stuart. Badly done. One diva in the family is quite enough.

Turning her back on the patch of scorched earth formerly known as Stuart's Twa Burns Distillery, Issy looked out across the water towards the mainland and considered her next move.

There really was only one course of action open to her – wasn't there?

Go back; find out the truth; make things right.

Executing a half-turn, she touched the memorial for luck and then walked back to her Mini. The tyres had gouged channels in the gravel where she'd pulled off the road at high speed and applied the brakes. Not only had she acted as if she was Lindy Tennant, she'd started to drive like her, too.

Grimacing at the thought, she climbed into the car, fastened her seat belt and drove off in the direction of the eco-lodges. If Brodie refused to speak to her, or made it plain he thought she was a complete flake, who could blame him? He'd set the scene and she'd exited stage left before the first act had played out. She'd have to take every criticism he levelled at her and suck it up. There was more at stake this evening than wounded pride, saving face, or the Macintoshes' claim to a half share in a bombed-out ruin - and her heart knew it.

The highland gloaming was settling on the hills, and fading to purple as Issy rounded a tight bend in the road, almost colliding with a Land Rover. It was travelling at warp speed on the wrong side of the road and its headlights were blazing.

Brodie!

Simultaneously, both vehicles ground to a halt well beyond the stopping distance recommended in the Highway Code. Car doors opened, engines ticked over as they cooled, and the smell of burning brake pads and scorched rubber hung in the air as they squared up to each other. Seizing the initiative, Issy ended the Mexican Stand-off.

'What do you mean by driving round the island on the wrong side of the road, like an idiot?' Her tone was far from conciliatory, but her heart was racing at the realisation that Brodie had come after her.

'I was trying to avoid the craters. Why doesn't the Queen, or the Scottish Parliament – or whoever's in charge, invest in a decent highway?'

'By *decent,* I assume you mean a four-lane highway which would take up half the island? This isn't Sunset Strip, in case you hadn't noticed.'

'Yeah – strange how I missed that,' he parried. 'Thanks for pointing it out.'

'Bloody Yank,' Issy said, but there was banked-down humour in her eyes.

'*Teuchter*,' Brodie chimed in, proudly using the new Gaelic word he'd learned.

'Brodie!' Issy protested, 'that's a derogatory term for a highlander.'

'Because *Yank* isn't an insult, right?'

'Touché,' she acknowledged. 'I'm sorry, I shouldn't have used it. Not in this context.' She poked at a stone with the toe of her strappy sandal to avoid looking at him.

'No, you shouldn't. And, for the record, my Kentucky ancestors consider themselves Southerners, not Yankees.'

'I've said I'm sorry, haven't I? Anyhow, where were you going in such a tearing rush that you forgot which side of the road to drive on?'

'I guess you know the answer to that, Issy.' He spoke quietly, and when she didn't respond he put his finger under her chin and tilted her face towards him. 'I was coming after *you*. I'm not prepared to let you walk – scratch that – *storm* out of my life without putting up a fight. How about you, Mizz Stoo-art?'

Issy drew her gaze away and regarded the stone at her foot as if it was the most fascinating sight in the world.

'I was on my way back to the eco-lodge, to apologise for acting like an idiot - if you must know. Happy now?' This time she raised her head and sent him a direct look. In the gathering dusk his eyes shone bright as malachite and the corner of his mouth quirked in a half-smile.

'Kinda.'

'Kinda?' She'd worn her heart on her sleeve and *kinda* was the best he could come up with.

Brodie took a step towards her and then checked himself, giving the impression he wanted to be sure about her reason for returning to the lodge before he declared his hand a second time. 'We have unfinished business, Issy, you know that. And I'm not just referring to Twa Burns Distillery and my family's claim to half of it. There's more at stake here,' he said, echoing her earlier thoughts exactly, 'isn't there?'

A slide show of the afternoon they'd spent making love on Mermaid Rock played through Issy's head. Images of how she'd originally thought the evening would end, put in an appearance too – the romantic dinner, champagne, making love in front of the wood burning stove . . . spending the night together.

Whoa. Now she was getting ahead of herself.

'Come back to the lodge and let's talk things through calmly and collectedly,' Brodie pleaded.

Letting out a sigh, Issy dropped her hands by her sides and adopted a more relaxed stance. He didn't need to know that was exactly what she *had* planned to do. It wouldn't do him any harm if she played hard ball a little longer; for one thing, it kept the sensual images swirling around in her head at bay.

'Very well, you lead and I'll follow. We'd better get our cars off the road in case some visitor to the island comes round the corner – on the wrong side of the road? Driving at high speed?' It took all of Issy's powers of concentration to remain expressionless as conflicting emotions flickered across Brodie's face. He was apparently finding it hard to figure out if she was joking or not.

Then, as if detecting that ice was melting, he grinned and the light was back in his eyes – just discernible in the descending highland twilight.

'The Cormorant Island rush hour? How could I have forgotten! Any moment two sheep and a *heilan' coo* could come careering round the corner at three miles an hour. Pretty damned racy by island standards. Not only that, we could be mowed down by a madman - breaking the speed limit to drive after the woman he loves.'

'That we could.'

Had she misheard him - *the woman he loves?* Given the way things had gone, she didn't feel she could ask him to repeat himself. However, there was no mistaking his burning look, or the impatience with which he climbed back into his Land Rover. He was a man on a mission; a man who wouldn't rest until he'd said his piece and straightened things out.

Heightened awareness made it seem as if Issy's feet were floating several inches above the rough highland B-road. Emotions and senses in turmoil, she concentrated on following Brodie back to the eco-lodge, ensuring she didn't end up in a ditch. This time, she noticed, he showed greater respect for the speed limit, the terrain and the imminent appearance of any random sheep or heilan' coos.

Chapter Twenty Six
Act One – Scene Two

'Can we start over?'

Brodie built up the fire, poured two glasses of champagne and led Issy back to the leather sofa. Nodding, she retrieved the photograph of Archie and Johnny from the document box and smoothed out its creases.

``I'm not sure what Aunt Esme will make of all of this. Twa Burns is her inheritance – not mine.'

'It'll be yours one day, I guess?'

'A day *many* years from now.' She didn't want Esme following in her brother's footsteps any time soon. 'Twa Burns should have been my father's, of course, and then pass to me after his death. However, for reasons I don't fully understand, everything was left to Esme - and father didn't contest it. There are secrets and lies in every family, but one day I'd like to know the reason behind that decision.' She saw herself on WHO DO YOU THINK YOU ARE? baffling researchers, heir hunters and genealogists alike.

'From what you've told me about your father's attitude to liquor, I'd say he was glad that Twa Burns wasn't his.' Brodie clinked his glass against hers, ironically, before continuing, 'I totally 'get' your aunt; hell, I even admire her anti-American stance. She's held those views since the early sixties from what you've told me, and she not about to change now. Quite a gal, isn't she - up for anything and frightened of nothing. Surely she'll see the sense in our proposal.'

'By *our*, I'm assuming you mean the McIntoshes? As for *proposal*, you haven't mentioned any proposal . . .'

'Okay. I'm getting ahead of myself, again. It's just that –' He gave her another one of *those* looks. The one which suggested his securing a deal for half the distillery land was nothing compared to the relationship they, potentially, could have. He pulled himself together, 'Okay – backstory; let's start with Archie McIntosh and the distillery he founded in Kentucky.'

'I've never heard of McIntosh's Bourbon.' Issy frowned over the rim of her champagne flute.

'That's because it's called *Mac's Kentucky Moonshine*. The name isn't important – what you need to know is that my family has made its fortune distilling bourbon whiskey according to his unique formula. We're up there with Jim Beam and Jack Daniels,' he said proudly. 'Archie was smart, he hid his illicit stills from the Prohibitionists in the woods on the border between Tennessee and Kentucky. When things got too hot, he jumped across the state line to avoid prosecution, waited until the heat died down, then hopped back and started over.'

'I assume he wasn't the only one doing that?'

'Right. But, don't forget he had the knowledge of several

generations of whisky distillers behind him. That gave him the edge over the other moonshiners and meant his hooch was sought after. It didn't make you go blind and it had a smoky, fuller flavour which other moonshiners couldn't match.'

'I'm guessing that hooch which doesn't make you go blind is a good thing,' Issy said with a trace of dry humour, but then her smile died. 'For a marine biologist, you seem to know a great deal about distilling bourbon whiskey. Or is all that stuff about you being the King of Plankton a smokescreen?'

'Issy, I've never lied to you. I might have held back . . . certain bits of information about myself, about the McIntoshes, but everything else I've told you has been the truth. I am a fully qualified marine biologist, however - over the last couple of years, as Grandpa's gotten older and frailer, I've felt drawn to the family business. I've learned it from the bottom up, too - in case you think I'm some spoiled rich boy playing at running the family store. I've learned how to temper barrels, studied the blending process. Hell, I've even taken my turn loading the wagons and giving the twenty-dollar tour on board *Mac's Moonshine Bus*. I'm not afraid of hard work.'

'I don't doubt it, if your muscles are anything to go by. I mean,' she blushed, 'not that I've been looking at them you understand. I wouldn't. I - Oh, stop smiling Mr Smart Arse. Okay, so I've been looking.'

He laughed, rolled up his sleeve, made a fist and invited her to feel his muscle. 'Does that mean you aren't entirely indifferent to me?'

'I think that was established this afternoon on Mermaid Rock, don't you?' Issy blushed and then got to her feet.

'Whoa. Where do you think you're going?'

'I've got a cramp in my foot and –'

Before she'd even finished the sentence, Brodie had raised her legs off the floor and laid them across his lap. Next, he slipped off her shoes, cracked his knuckles and ran his fingers across her toes. 'Left or right?'

'My left, your right.' Issy suspected this wasn't a good idea, but the need to feel his hands cupping her feet and bringing warmth to them was overwhelming, and overruled caution. More urgently, cramp was making her toes cross over, and her wince in pain. As Brodie started his rhythmic massaging, she put some extra cushions behind her back so that she was sitting upright and holding herself away from him. Something told her she needed to keep her wits about her this evening.

'How's that feel? Good?'

'Better. G – go on – with the story, I mean,' she added severely as his smile widened, suggestively.

'Yes, Ma'am.' His eyes crinkled with laughter, the green of the irises devastatingly attractive against his tanned skin. Issy caught her breath - this wasn't going to be easy. Perhaps he'd had the same thought because he stopped smiling and was suddenly very serious. 'You're calling the shots tonight, Issy, so - here's what's on the table. My family would like to invest in Twa Burns.' He massaged her feet as he waited for her reaction, perhaps hoping the massage was the equivalent of smoothing any ruffled feathers the proposal might cause.

'Invest, in what? Acres of scorched earth, some rusting machinery and a few stones? Why would you want to do that? I'll tell you now, to put you out of your misery, that's all the ruins of Twa Burns will ever be - ruins. You'd never get planning permission to erect holiday cottages on the land.'

'Who mentioned holiday cottages? We don't want to build a holiday complex, we want . . .' He paused, realising that what he said next would set the seal on their relationship.

'Go on,' Issy prompted.

'Let's start at the beginning. In the original will, drawn up by Archie and Johnny on the eve of leaving for the Western Front, each bequeathed their share of the distillery to the other. Should either of them die in battle – and providing there were no other descendants to pass it on to? Correct?'

'I believe so.'

'As the McIntoshes see it, Johnny *and* Archie's combined share in the distillery has – wrongly - passed down the line to the Stuarts, ending with Esme.' He waited for her reaction to his statement, and Issy keep him waiting. Wordlessly, she withdrew her feet from his lap and tucked them beneath her.

'My family inherited Archie's half of the distillery in good faith,' she said quietly, looking down at her hands. 'We believed Archie lay in a communal grave in Flanders, and – after his family died in the flu epidemic, Johnny Stuart did the only sensible thing. He tried to rebuild the distillery – for the benefit of everyone concerned. Not just the Stuarts. ' She didn't like the way her family was being portrayed as grasping and opportunist, even by default. 'We waited the requisite number of years to legitimise our claim. We had no way of knowing that Archie was building himself a new life in Kentucky.'

He held up his hands to ward off her righteous anger. 'I'm just telling you how my family see it, Issy. No slight intended.'

She ignored the peace offering. 'What do you intend?' she asked, bluntly.

Brodie sucked in his breath. 'The McIntoshes want to rebuild Twa Burns. For that to happen we need your and Esme's consent.'

'Naturally,' she agreed, giving him a shrewd look. 'And, should we agree to your claim – and I'm not saying that we would, there is no way we could match, pound for pound, any investment your family could bring to the project. Esme has the house, her state pension and the little bit of money she makes from her B and B – that's it. My father left me nothing in his will and all my money is earmarked for the renovation of the outhouses. Once they turn a profit – which could take years - that will be my only source of income until I find another design job. If that's the road I choose to travel.'

'Money wouldn't be a problem.' Issy's raised eyebrows and cool look of disdain implied that he didn't live in the real world where people struggled to put food on the table and meet the bills.

'That didn't come out right, Issy, let me start over. Once the distillery is up and running, your and Esme's share of the profits would be ploughed back into the business until the debt was paid off.' The word *debt* made Issy's blood run cold. She had her father's abhorrence for owing money to anyone, no matter how attractive the proposal appeared on paper. 'Look on it as an interest-free loan.'

'But that could take years. I wouldn't want Esme shouldering a massive debt, or dying with it unpaid. Nor do I want to spend the rest of my life in hock to the McIntoshes.' Judging by his expression, Brodie didn't care for her plain speaking, but Issy wasn't about to hold back. 'Anyway, why the sudden interest? Why hasn't your family come forward sooner?'

'As Archie's son, and heir to Mac's Moonshine, the decision to proceed has been down to my grandfather. As I told you earlier, he'd come over to the island on furlough during the sixties in search of his roots. To discover if Archie's stories were true and if his claim could possibly be legit. He decided it was – but something happened during his posting in Scotland which led him to abandon the quest.'

'Such as?'

'That's the thing, he never speaks of his tour of duty on the Proteus, or the time he spent on the Holy Loch servicing the subs. But last year, he finally caved under family pressure to pursue the claim and demand what is rightfully his. Ours.'

'Why now, after all these years?'

'Last Fall, Grandma died, and everything changed. Gramps was bereaved, of course he was, but at the same time he was more energised than I'd seen him in years. It was as if he'd woken up from a long dream and remembered that he was a McIntosh of *Eilean na Sgairbh*, proud of his Scottish roots. He wants the McIntoshes to return to Cormorant Island, where they belong. It's his intention to leave behind a lasting legacy, one which he believes the McIntoshes *and* the Stuarts will be proud of.'

'Let me get this straight. You want to rebuild Twa Burns, with Aunt Esme and your grandfather as equal partners, albeit with one of the partners having a massive debt to repay?'

'That's about the size of it. Come on, Issy, think about it – rebuilding the distillery is what you've always wanted, dreamed about. The McIntoshes have the same dream. We want to become part of *Eilean na Sgairbh*, give something back to the community, much as your father has done. It goes without saying that funds would also be available for you to renovate the outhouses, should you choose to. Whad'd'ya say?'

Issy sent him a considering look. He certainly knew how to sugar the pill, trading on her feelings for the derelict brewery and her dream of the artists' studios. She shifted along the sofa and away further from him, so she could think straight.

'It isn't up to me,' she said, picking up a large mohair cushion and hugging it across her breasts, defensively.

'Of course it is. Without you on board, the renaissance of Twa Burns would be nothing more than a pipe dream. My family won't invest unless you *and* Esme are one hundred and ten percent behind the project.'

'One hundred and ten percent? Let's hope that your whisky distilling skills are better than your maths.' Brodie made as if to add something but she forestalled him. 'Don't say another word. I need to think this through.' He was bombarding her with too many ideas, expecting her to think on her feet when he'd had months, years even, to talk this over with his Grandfather. Issy rubbed at the tightness puckering her forehead and building into a fine headache. 'Your grandfather, how old is he?'

'Early eighties.'

She pursed her lips in thought; that meant Menzies McIntosh was of an age with her father. She pictured the sandalwood box nestling forlornly on the window ledge of the outhouses, waiting to be carried up that final Munro, and her heart squeezed. 'Had my father lived, there is no way he would have countenanced the rebuilding of the distillery. Even if it was Esme's inheritance, he would have done his best to block her – and the McIntoshes - every step of the way. Maybe,' she said, with a touch of Highland other-worldliness, 'he passed over when he did so that the distillery *could* be rebuilt?'

To his credit, Brodie didn't jump in and capitalise on her half-formed thought.

'Maybe,' he repeated, cautiously, his eyes never leaving her face.

'When Esme passes,' Issy went on, as if he wasn't there, 'half of Twa Burns will be mine.' She snapped out of her dream, raised her head and sent him a look of dawning comprehension.

'Don't even go there,' Brodie warned. 'Imagining that what's between us, what I feel for you is nothing more than a ruse to get you into my bed. And then, when you're delirious from lovemaking, I'll produce some papers – prepared in advance by my attorney brother – and persuade you to sign away your inheritance? Boy - you have a pretty low opinion of me.' Brodie shot her a blistering look.

'I don't have a low opinion of you, Brodie,' Issy said softly, aware that she'd angered him. 'Quite the reverse - but you have been rather economical with the truth.'

'Of necessity,' he responded. 'The truth wasn't mine to share, until now. I was sent over here on a fact-finding mission – Grandpa's orders. He didn't know if he'd have a fight on his hands or if Esme would see sense and accept his offer. I'll rephrase that – if Esme would give our proposal her full consideration.'

'You never know with Esme.' Issy was thoughtful. 'She's always been very loving and protective towards me, but she *is* secretive by nature; she never gives much away. She's always hated the distillery as much as my father, but for different reasons. It took her mother from her when she was only eighteen months old. That's not something you get over lightly, even after many years have passed.'

'So where does that leave us?' Brodie asked. 'Friends? Enemies Frenemies, as Lindy would say? Lovers . . .' His voice was full of hope and he didn't bother to conceal how *he* wanted the evening to end.

'No contracts to sign? No affidavits to be witnessed, first?' She gave him an arch look which suggested that it'd take more than a night in his arms to make her sign away her life.

Brodie was quick to pick up the vibe. 'None. And, if you're wondering, Issy – yes; I *am* that good.'

'Get over yourself.' She threw a cushion at his head as a feather of desire unfurled within her, drawing her back to this afternoon on Mermaid Rock. She could hardly blame him if he thought her easy; a pushover. Time she made it very plain to him that he'd got her all wrong. She prised herself out of the sofa and made as if to leave. Apparently having no intention of letting her bail twice in one evening, Brodie leapt forward, caught her hands and pulled her down onto his lap. Off balance, Issy's face ended up in his neck and she breathed in his delicious scent – a combination of sharp, man muskiness and clean linen.

'You're staying put until I've finished what I have to say, Issy.'

'Seems like you have a lot *to* say . . . and I have no choice but to listen.' She wanted to stay in his arms forever but she had no intention of letting him know that. Or making this easy for him.

'That's about the size of it.' He settled her more comfortably in his lap and started to stroke her dark hair, pushing a long strand aside to reveal her delicate ear lobe. 'You're smart, and I know how that over-tuned brain of yours operates, so – for the record, I do want to get you into my bed.' He whispered the last sentence in her ear and when he felt her shiver of reaction, manoeuvred them along the sofa until he was lying on top of her. That left Issy in doubt as to how *much* he wanted her in his bed. 'Not because of contracts, distilleries, Grandfather's last wishes, claiming what's rightfully ours, or - '

'Then what?'

'Because of this . . .' He bent his head and touched her lips. Then he raised his head, propped himself up on his elbow and looked down on her. 'And, because . . .' He kissed her more deeply this time, freeing his hand to cradle the back of her head. 'Because,' he whispered against her lips, 'you mean more to me than the combined forces of the McIntoshes and Stuarts, ancient wills, bloody uisge beatha and Mac's Moonshine all rolled into one.'

'I do?' She looked up into his face, starting to believe him.

'Sure.' He grinned, happy to confirm his feelings for her. 'Issy, I've fallen for you – hard. You're smart, sassy, determined and beautiful; how could I fail to love you? I came into your life at the wrong moment – your father has just died, you'd broken up with Innes-Kerr and your mother was intent on making a scene at his funeral. If I'd levelled with you then and told you about my fact-finding mission, you would have stormed out of my life – for good.'

'That's true,' Issy agreed.

'I knew I should leave Esme's house. My grandfather's instructions were to stay there for a couple of days, have a snoop around – okay, I want you to know, I'm not proud of that. But I had to find the evidence we needed; the evidence which matched - *our* photo and copy of the will. Don't ask me how, Grandpa knew it was there, but he did. Your aunt was so kind to me that I felt a heel, a fraud. I was about to leave and let Gramps know it was mission accomplished – but you were blown in on the storm wind and – click – I had to stay. So, I made up the story of the eco-lodge being double-booked as my cover. That's the only lie I've ever told.'

'But I was so *horrid* to you,' Issy protested. 'Why did you stay?'

'I could see you needed help and support and I decided, with Esme on the fracking demo, I would be the one to provide it.'

'You did - and more.' She laughed and Brodie looked at her, perplexed.

'What?'

'Jack's face - when you kissed me at the wake and threatened to run him off the island.'

He let out a sigh of relief. 'I thought I'd seriously mismanaged that one. But I had to kiss you, because you looked so . . . alone that day. Not to mention sexy in that black suit and those high heels. Boy, you blew me away - I knew I would only have one chance to make it plain to Innes-Kerr that he'd had his chance with you. There was a new kid in town . . .'

'Young Lochinvar, eh?' Issy's lips twitched at the image those words conjured. Emboldened by the fact that she hadn't pushed him away, Brodie settled more comfortably on the wide sofa. He brushed her dark hair off her face again, and rained little kisses wherever his fingers touched her skin.

'I needed to make it clear to you that I was *interested.*'

'You made it plain to the whole island that you were *interested.*' This time, she gave a relaxed giggle.

'So, are we good?' he asked, worriedly. 'My mission is

accomplished, everything is down to Esme and Gramps, now. We need to get them together as soon as she's home and he's gotten over the jet lag. But, whatever the outcome, Issy, I don't want it to spoil what . . . mmph.'

His words were lost as Issy, deciding to take him at his word, twined her fingers in his hair, pulled him towards her and kissed him – hard. Next she released him as though the blistering kiss had had no effect on her.

'Och, Brodie,' Issy teased in a highland accent, 'ye talk too much, Man. Will you no shut up and repeat what you said on the roadside? Or I may be forced to kiss you again.'

'What did I say? I can't quite remember.'

He grinned at her, daring her to carry out her threat, his eyes shining a pure unsullied green, full of love and humour. He pretended to give the idea careful thought as his hand moved teasingly up from her waist and found the curve of her breast. He lightly circled his thumb over the fine material of her shirt, grazing her nipple through the fabric and causing a frisson of desire to surge through her.

'Brodie!' she gasped. 'Answer the question.'

'Yes, Mizz Stoo-art, as you command. I'll tell it tae ye in all the languages I know, until you believe it's true,' he said, with a convincing highland inflection. 'French, *je t'aime,* Italian *ti amo,* German *ich leibe dich* and lastly, Gaelic - *Tha gaol agam orst.*' With each 'I love you', he undid one of the pearl buttons fastening her shirt. As the last button was dealt with and the thin silk parted to reveal the lacy cups of her bra, words really did fail him. He bent his head and kissed each breast in turn and then looked up at her, as if seeking her approval.

'Why have you stopped?' Issy squirmed, moving beneath him into a more comfortable position. 'Let's get rid of this.' Fumbling, she undid his belt buckle, then slid the belt out of its loops and tossed it onto the floor. Eager hands untucked his shirt from the waistband of his trousers and then she splayed her fingers across his lower back, pressing him closer. 'How do you like this?'

There was a muffled moan of pleasure as he lowered his head and nuzzled where her lightly-boned bra separated her breasts. His head stayed there for what seemed like a long time and Issy could feel the strong rhythm of his heart against her ribs. Then he moved his head to the right, sought for and found her nipple through the fine material of the bra and sucked, hard. It was Issy's turn to let out a moan, and she threw her head back - her eyes closed. Taking this as encouragement, Brodie's mouth moved onto her other breast and repeated the action. Deftly, Issy levered herself up from under him, unfastened the clasps at the back of her bra and dragged it down her shirt sleeves.

Then she tossed it onto the floor.

Brodie, unaware that the underwear she was wearing tonight was part of her honeymoon trousseau, didn't realise the symbolism of her discarding her lingerie as though it didn't matter. Instead he laughed and asked, 'How did you do that?'

Issy, light-hearted and full of love and confidence managed a teasing reply, 'Have you ever been in the circus?'

'No,' he said, puzzled.

'Then I can't tell you. But I can tell you this . . .' She raised herself a little higher and removed her blouse, tossing that onto the floor, too. 'I love you, Brodie McIntosh. At first you angered me, because you were an unwanted visitor when I wanted to be alone. Then you looked at me at the end of my song and it was as if we shared the same dream – and I was lost. If I was frosty towards you, it was because I was in denial – right up to the day of the wake when you moved out. Then . . .'

'Then . . .' Brodie looked at her naked breasts but held himself in check, waiting for her answer. This was important; he, *they,* couldn't afford to get it wrong.

'I missed you so much that it was almost like a physical pain. If you hadn't happened upon me on Mermaid Rock this afternoon, I don't know what I would have done.' There she'd said it. For a moment his eyes held a look of triumph, but it was the look of a man who knew he'd only achieved victory by a hair's breadth. And that he owed everything to Issy's wish to put the past behind her and move on with her life.

Issy pushed him off her and panic flashed across his face.

'Where are you going?'

'Nowhere,' she replied. Taking him by the hand, she pulled him to his feet and helped him to remove his trousers and shirt. She wasn't happy until they were only wearing one item of clothing each - her lacy, Brazilian cut knickers, and his Calvin Klein boxers. She pushed him back onto the sofa, pulling the cashmere throw off the arm and wrapping it round her as she stood before him. With one fluent movement she removed her knickers, kicked them into the air and then laughed exuberantly as they landed in the log basket. Naked apart from the cashmere throw, she edged forward until their knees were touching, and then she reached out and stroked his dark auburn hair. She delighted in the way the setting sun streamed through the window and burnished it, like a flame.

She trailed a finger down his long, straight nose, past his lips and down to his chin. Pausing, she looked him in the eye, hoping he understood her inner turmoil.

'*Bidh gaol agam ort fad mo bheatha, thusa's gun duine eile.*'

These were the words she'd learned for the exchange of vows on her wedding day at the wee kirk. Brodie didn't need to know that, neither would the thought of the life she could have shared with Jack Innes-Kerr be allowed to ruin this perfect moment.

'What does that mean?' He looked at her as if she was indeed a silkie whisperer and belonged to another world, far removed from the here and now. A mythical, mystical creature from a time when people were more in tune with their feelings and the cycle of the seasons. A time when commerce, spreadsheets, profit and loss counted for nothing.

'*I will love you my whole life, you and no other.*' She whispered against his lips, their skin seemingly licked with fire wherever they touched.

'Do you mean it, Issy?'

Issy's heart contracted at the uncertainty she saw in his eyes, and part of her revelled in the knowledge that she'd put it there. And, in that moment, she knew that he'd never play her false. As the words struck home, she drew the cashmere throw more tightly around her and lowered herself onto his lap. There was a sublime moment when she felt his erection pressing against her inner thigh and the world stopped spinning. She threw back her head, closed her eyes and tried to steady her breathing. 'God help me, Issy,' Brodie managed brokenly, when at last he could speak, 'you've made me feel – God, I don't know *how* you've made me feel. There are no words . . . I thought this day would never come.'

'As intended,' she laughed softly. 'But, *mo chridhe*, you're a wee bit overdressed.' She eased his boxer shorts over his hips and Brodie took in another shuddering breath. Taking their combined weight on the palms of his hands, careful not to dislodge Issy from his lap and bring this delightful torment to an end, Brodie raised them off the sofa. Issy peeled off his boxer shorts and then dropped them over the back and out of sight. She sighed as the last barrier was removed and she felt his skin against hers - warm, intimate, enticing.

Bending her head, she kissed him. Words became superfluous and the world blurred at the edges as their kisses grew more passionate; tongues touched, skin felt scorched and they tasted blood on their lips. Grasping the cashmere in both hands, Brodie pulled Issy so close that she pressed against every last inch of him. Then, as though dragging himself out of a dream, he raised his head and

340

looked at her, his eyes cloudy with desire.

'What about . . .' he began. 'I don't want to break the mood . . . but, shouldn't we. . .'

He left the sentence hanging, but Issy understood. Kissing him, she raised herself onto her knees and clambered off his lap. Unaware of her intentions, he leaned forward to keep her close but Issy pushed him back, and the cashmere throw slithered off the leather sofa and onto the floor. Buoyed by the thought that he was concerned enough for her welfare to pause their lovemaking and think about taking precautions, she smiled at him over her shoulder.

'I must keep my promise to the *silkie.*' She turned away, crossed the wooden floor and retrieved her handbag. She rooted through it for the pack of condoms she'd dropped in there earlier. Quickly, she unpeeled the foil, removed the contraceptive and returned to the sofa, holding it in the palm of her hand. If this didn't convince him that she was serious enough about their relationship to plan for this moment, nothing would.

'I think the *silkie* can manage this part on his own.' Brodie took it from her and, to give him some privacy, Issy retrieved the throw off the floor where it had fallen. She swirled it theatrically over her head before settling it on her shoulders. After that, she returned to her previous position on Brodie's lap, tucking her legs under her, hands gripping the back of the sofa to keep her balance. Fleetingly, it crossed her mind to wonder if the hiatus in their lovemaking might have killed the mood, stone dead. However, Brodie's ardent look as he drew her closer and bent his head to kiss her just above her navel, soon put that thought to flight.

Remembering what had brought her pleasure on Mermaid Rock, Brodie repeated the lesson. After some delirious seconds during which she felt her grip on reality slipping, Issy released her hold on the sofa and cradled Brodie's head closer to her breasts.

'B – B – Brodie,' she stammered, arching her back and closing her eyes as his warm mouth suckled her. 'For God's sake, don't stop.'

'Now, why would I do that, Mizz Stoo-art?' Laughing, he raised his head, adding, 'as a matter of fact . . .' His hand slipped between her legs and she gasped as long, cool fingers touched her tenderest spot. Shock and surprise gave way to pleasure as Brodie began stroking, rhythmically. Issy slipped into a state of near delirium and everything inside her tightened in anticipation of what was to come. Skilfully, to give them both maximum pleasure, Brodie manoeuvred Issy into a different position on his lap – and then he slid inside her with one effortless thrust. He paused and raised his head, as if he wanted to remember this moment for the rest of his life.

The moment when the world counted for nothing and all that mattered was the two of them and the realisation that they'd each found the person they would spend the rest of their life loving.

Issy clung to his shoulders as he trailed kisses along her neck and moved deeper inside her. Now it was his turn to twist in pleasurable torment as instinct drove Issy to rise and fall rhythmically against him. He placed his hands under her buttocks and matched her rhythm, thrust for thrust until she moved faster, ever faster and then cried out in release. Seconds later, he rolled her onto her back and climaxed after one last, powerful thrust of his hips. For long seconds they stayed on that higher plane between heaven and earth until their heartbeats slowed, holding on to each other as if they would never let go.

Chapter Twenty Seven
Stay With Me Till Dawn

It never really got dark during high summer on Cormorant Island, so when Issy woke the following morning to bright daylight, she had no idea of the time. All she knew for certain was, after they'd made love on the sofa, Brodie, had carried her into the bedroom. Then - after making love a second time and third time, they had showered together before falling asleep.

Now, her right cheek was pressed against Brodie's chest so that he felt her smile, even if he couldn't see it.

'What?' he asked, drowsy with sleep.

'You. Me. Us.' She snuggled in under his arm and traced a line from his knee to his groin. 'This.'

'Are you gonna be talking in monosyllables all day, Mizz Stoo-art?'

'Possibly. I seemed to have lost the power of coherent thought, not to mention speech. No, there – it's back.' She trailed her fingers higher and Brodie's response suggested that words were superfluous. 'We don't have to talk, of course.'

'I agree, words are very overrated. Unless . . .'

'Unless?'

'Unless you're saying that Gaelic phrase –'

'*Bidh gaol agam ort fad mo bheatha, thusa's gun duine eile,'* she repeated obligingly.

'And I, not having the tongue for it, can only say, '*I will love you my whole life, you and no other.'* Kissing the top of her head, he drew her closer until it was impossible to say where - in the tangle of limbs and sheets, she began, and he ended. 'It loses nothing in translation, does it?'

'Not a thing,' Issy agreed. 'Oh My Good God!' She sat up, startled, having glanced at the clock on the wall opposite the foot of the bed. 'It's half past seven. What time does Lindy arrive to make a thorough nuisance of herself?' In her rush to get out of bed she knocked a silver quaich – a small, two-handled cup used for drinking whisky, onto the floor.

'Leave that, I'll pick it up later and – relax . . . I gave Lindy the morning off. I thought we might end up – that is, I figured . . . scrub that – I hoped . . .' He hesitated, obviously not wanting to give the impression that their becoming lovers had been a foregone conclusion.

'That's okay, I get it.' Issy's voice was muffled as she leaned out of the bed, picked up the silver quaich and put it back on the bedside table. 'You *hoped* we might end up in bed together, but took nothing for granted? Same here.' She tapped her breastbone and then snuggled back into Brodie's side, wrapping her leg around his. 'That's why I drove over to the mainland a couple of days ago to pay a visit to the chemist.' She wondered if Brodie could feel the tell-tale warmth of the blush staining her right cheek.

'Chemist?' he queried.

'The pharmacy, on the mainland.'

'Why the mainland?'

'Can you imagine the reaction if I'd bought condoms at the General Store? I'd be denounced as a scarlet woman in the wee kirk this coming Sunday. '

'Great minds think alike.' Reaching across her, he pulled open the drawer on the bedside cabinet to reveal an unopened pack of condoms. 'I bought them from the – chemist – on the mainland, too. I have my reputation to think of,' he said in a very proper, English accent, and Issy giggled. Then he sobered and turned to face her, nose almost touching nose. 'I knew, from the moment I set eyes on you at your aunt's, and after we looked long and hard at each other that evening at The Pickled Herring, that we'd become lovers . . .'

'Did you now?' she asked with some asperity, pretending affront.

'What I mean to say is, I *hoped* that we'd become lovers. But I knew that the business with the wills and Twa Burns might get in the way. Hell, I'm going to buy a thesaurus on my next trip off *Eilean na Sgairbh*, I so want to get the words right, Issy. '

'Who needs words?' Issy asked, returning to their earlier conversation. She stretched languorously at his side, pushed him over onto his back and raised herself up onto one elbow to look down on him. 'I'm naked and in your bed – isn't that answer enough, Brodie?'

'You're right. We're wasting time - I've gotta pick Grandpa up from the airport today.'

'And Esme's returning this evening . . . We'll never have the chance to be alone again.' Sighing, she buried her face in Brodie's chest, exalting in the rise and fall of his ribs, the rough hair that tapered downwards, his strong heartbeat.

'There's always Mermaid Rock.' At that, he untangled himself, and rolled her onto her back. He raised her hands above her head and then spread her limbs wide, until she lay beneath him like a starfish. 'Can you ring ahead and book a reservation? Wait, maybe I'd better add a tide table to my list, huh? So I know when it's safe to meet the silkie whisperer . . . '

'You'd better. Now, no more words.' To ensure that he complied, Issy raised her head off the pillow and kissed him as deeply as she could, given her awkward position. Brodie released her hands, gathered her to him and did as commanded.

Issy stood by *Ailleag*'s kitchen window, wondering when Esme would be home. According to the tide clock on the kitchen wall, it would be low tide for the next few hours. After that, the tide would rush in and The Narrows would be under water. Anyone wishing to cross over to the island after that, would have to wait until tomorrow. Esme was a notoriously bad timekeeper, and Issy was worried that she'd leave it too late to make the crossing. But she also knew that few islanders travelled beyond Cormorant Island without a copy of the tide table in the glove compartment of their car – Esme included.

Mind you, she was one to talk – wasn't she? She cast her mind back to the night of the storm when she'd crossed The Narrows with only moments to spare. Just as well her aunt had been too preoccupied with her guests - and Brodie, to realise what a risk she'd taken.

Preoccupied with her guests - and Brodie.

Issy glanced round the kitchen which, like the rest of the house, was shining like a new pin. Not that Esme would notice. She regarded domestic duties as an unnecessary evil and was on record as stating that childbearing and housework was a patriarchal society's way of ensuring that women were kept barefoot, pregnant and in the kitchen. However, tidying the house had proved to be a good distraction, it'd kept Issy's hands busy and her mind off Brodie.

Unlike her bohemian aunt, Issy craved order in her life and she wondered if that was her way of compensating for being 'abandoned' by her mother and left in her aunt's care while her father built his IT empire. Maybe she'd simply inherited his tendency towards OCD; she'd undoubtedly inherited his driven personality and Protestant work ethic. She hadn't inherited her tidiness gene from her mother - Isabella was laziness personified. Her slovenly housekeeping had been the source of many arguments between her and James during the first years of married life.

Barefoot, pregnant and in the kitchen.

Perhaps that was why she'd jumped at the chance to further her operatic career and bolted to Italy? Now an army of staff ensured that La Bella Scozzese's villa was filled with fresh flowers, the fridge brimming over with Tuscan delicacies and chilled wine, and delicious meals appearing on the table at her command. She had the money to fund her indolence and saw no reason to change. Now that she was a widow, Issy surmised, Isabella would doubtless be looking for husband #2, one who would subsidise her expensive lifestyle – her voice and looks wouldn't last forever.

Issy glanced over at the outhouses whose large double doors were open to the sea breeze. The wind blew through them, banishing years of dust and neglect. She'd been over there earlier, but had been in a dreamlike state, quite unable to summon up enough energy to bring the ladders round to dust the high beams. Nor could she bear to look at the sandalwood box sitting so forlornly on the window ledge. It silently reproached her for sleeping with the enemy, as her father would have seen it.

She raised her fingers to her lips, still bruised from Brodie's farewell kiss when they took a long goodbye on the verandah prior to her leaving.

Sighing at the thought of decisions which would have to be made once Menzies McIntosh arrived, and the attendant fallout, she locked the memory away to be savoured later. Trouble lay ahead, no matter how Esme responded to news of the shared inheritance.

Pershing's indignant squawk at being ignored for so long broke her dream. She walked into the sitting room, held out her arm and he hopped on, making his way onto her shoulder. He pulled at her ear to let her know he wasn't a happy boy and then flapped his wings to exercise them as she walked through to the kitchen and put him on his perch.

The perch gave him a grand view of The Narrows where he would see The Cow lumbering across the hard packed sand well before Issy would even be aware of it. His excited squawks would alert her that Esme was on her way home, just as he had done over the years.

'*Ship ahoy*,' Pershing announced, suggesting he knew what was required of him as he watched the first vehicles making their way across The Narrows.

'That's it, Pershing. Look for Esme. Call her, call her.'

'*Esme's good boy*,' he said, pleased with himself.

He tilted his head sideways and curled a large, scaly claw over his face and beak. That always made Issy laugh, it looked as though he was sucking his thumb, as a child might. She reached out and stroked his poll, rubbing the short, nubbly feathers above his beak with her fingernail. Petting and stroking the parrot brought her a degree of comfort – she was missing Brodie so badly, it was almost a physical pain. She zoned out once more; remembering their lovemaking and how much she wanted to repeat those magical hours. However, she knew they'd have to be patient, they couldn't spring Twa Burns' disputed ownership on Esme after her long drive up from England. Or expect Menzies McIntosh to attend a family pow-wow while jet lagged. The business over the distillery had to be handled with subtlety and discretion, taking Esme's and Menzies' age, health and physical wellbeing into consideration. Nothing could be rushed or pushed through.

Issy let out a huff of frustration. She only hoped that the distillery wouldn't prove to be a flash-point between their families. Between her and Brodie.

'And you *do* like Brodie, don't you, Pershy? Even if you did try to sever his toe from his foot?' Pershing stopped in the middle of cleaning his scaly claw and gave her a despairing look.

'*You silly tart. Silly, silly tart,*' he repeated, just in case she hadn't got the message.

'Let's hope not, Pershing, let's hope not.'

An hour or so later, Pershing sprang into action.

'*I---ts Es-mee.*' He drew out the syllables - just as Issy had taught him when she was a child. Rushing to the open front door, she shaded her eyes against the light. Sure enough, a convoy of vehicles was making its way towards Cormorant Island, and Issy could pick out the black and white coachwork of The Cow.

How on earth the parrot recognised Esme's old library bus, she'd never know. But he did - hopping along his perch in a high state of excitement which reached fever pitch as Esme parked The Cow in the yard.

'*Come on . . . Es-mee, dinner read –ee; dinner read-ee.*'

Dinner! Issy hoped her aunt had remembered to collect the takeaway she'd ordered from Cowboys and McIndians on the mainland. She was starving, and made a great show of straightening the cutlery and checking that the plates in the warming oven hadn't cracked, as Esme parked. Pushing the back door open, she waited for Esme to switch off the engine and climb down from The Cow.

'Esme!' Sounding remarkably like Pershing, she ran into the yard and hugged her diminutive aunt so hard that Esme protested her bones would break. Esme returned to The Cow and brought out a white plastic bag bearing the logo of Cowboys and McIndians, lettering outlined in tartan with the crossed flags of Scotland and Bangladesh on the front. The scent of the food in its foil dishes made Issy's stomach rumble. Unbidden, the image of last night's spoiled pasta dinner lying forlornly on the worktop at the eco-lodge found its way into her consciousness. She pushed it away impatiently. She *had* to get Brodie out of her head – otherwise she'd go mad.

Apart from which, her aunt deserved her full attention.

'How are you, hen?' Esme used the term affectionately, and kissed her on both cheeks.

'Starving! Let's eat and you can tell me all your news over dinner.'

Esme handed over the plastic bag and Issy ushered her into the kitchen. Much to Pershing's delight, Esme came straight over to stroke him while Issy dished up the curry and poured two glasses of wine. Esme and Pershing spoke nonsense to each other and renewed their bond until Issy handed the parrot a poppadum, so it would leave them in peace to eat their dinner. Esme had thoroughly spoiled the beast and he shredded most of the poppadum and spat the rest on the floor. Smiling, albeit it a trifle wearily, Esme took up her customary position overlooking The Narrows. Her strawberry-blond hair hung limply, the pale copper and cinnamon tones that had once been so vibrant, gradually being lost among the white. She looked tired and defeated, and appeared to have aged years during her time away.

Issy's heart squeezed with love and she was fearful of the effect the McIntoshes claim to half of Twa Burns might have on her.

'You look –'

'You look –'

They laughed, then Issy began again. 'You first, Esme.'

'I was about to say you look blooming. Much better than when I left you. Something's brought the colour to your cheeks – or should that be *someone*?' Esme's bright blue eyes missed nothing as Issy busied herself serving up the rice. 'Blushing, Ishabel Stuart? What *have* you been up to?' Although her voice was weary, some of her former sparkle returned. 'I'm guessing young Brodie's responsible for putting the roses in your cheeks?'

'What makes you think that?'

'He was a paying guest for three weeks, yet you barely mentioned him when I phoned every day, unless I prompted you. *That's* what makes me think *that*.'

'Oh well, you know,' Issy shrugged.

'Well, actually, I don't know. That's my point. But if he's taken the place of that wee bauchle Innes-Kerr, then I'm glad of it. Although,' she tore a piece off her Peshwari Naan, 'it wouldn't be sensible to get too deeply involved, sweetheart. He'll be leaving at the end of the summer and –' Issy wasn't quick enough to hide her woebegone expression and Esme picked up on it. 'Och, will ye listen to me? Not home five minutes and I'm telling you what to do.'

'Nothing new there, then,' Issy teased.

'You always were a cheeky wee besom, Issy, you never took much heed of what anyone said to you.' Esme sliced up a banana and spooned out natural yoghurt to cool down fiery Prawn Balanchaung – a speciality of the house.

'Not always with the best result.' Issy sent her aunt a rueful look. Esme ate her curry, tossing morsels of food to Pershing, which missed the mark and landed on Issy's clean floor next to the shards of poppadum. Pershing danced along his perch and gave one of his piratical cackles.

'Missed me, Baby?' Esme addressed the parrot. The colour returning to her cheeks, she exhaled a pent-up breath and appeared to relax.

'I see the household fairies have been busy,' Esme observed as, some time later, Issy cleared away the plates, swept the floor and switched on the coffee machine. 'And can I smell fresh paint?'

'I've given your bedroom a makeover, Esme. I hope you don't mind.'

'Not at all. I was going for shabby chic and a bohemian vibe but, recently, it was starting to look more like 'when's the skip arriving?' She got to her feet and pushed her chair away from the table. 'Come on, show me what you've done?'

'Aren't you tired?'

'The sight of my bed and familiar surroundings will revive me. I take it there aren't any guests booked in over the next week or so? I need to kick back – maybe driving over to RAF Waddington was a protest meeting too far?' It was the first time Issy had ever heard her aunt admit to feeling tired or having overstretched herself. A little flutter of anxiety made itself felt as Esme preceded her down the corridor, into the square inner hall and to her bedroom. She pushed the door open, stood on the threshold and looked in. 'Oh, Issy . . .' She clasped her hands together as if in prayer, taking in freshly painted walls and woodwork, the rag rug and new bed linen Issy had ordered online. There was even a new bedside lamp and couple of reed diffusers to give the bedroom a welcoming ambiance.

'You like it?'

'I do, darling, I do. But where's all my –'

'I've put everything in the loft in see-through, plastic boxes with lids. Labelled, appropriately, of course.'

'Naturally,' Esme teased, rubbing Issy's upper arm affectionately. 'I wouldn't expect anything less from my darling Issy.'

'You can sort through them in your own time, and put them all back if you wish.' Issy hoped that she wouldn't, but knew Esme was like a little mouse who prefers a nest lined with paper and bits of wool.

'Well, maybe after a few days I might bring *some* things back. And – oh, goodness me - where did you find that photograph?' Apparently forgetting her tiredness, Esme practically ran over to a Minton-tiled, Victorian fireplace. In lieu of wood and coal, Issy had filled the grate with pine cones, interwoven pieces of ribbon and seashells. Esme, however, oblivious to the finer points of interior design snatched a silver framed photograph off the mantelpiece.

'It's been on Father's dressing table for years. I always meant you to have it,' Issy explained, 'but he wouldn't part with it. Now . . .' she shrugged, 'it's yours, by default.' Esme held the photo frame to her breast, then she polished it with her sleeve, although there wasn't a speck of dust on it.

'It's my – my family,' her voice faltered. The way she said *my family*, almost broke Issy's heart. 'James looks about eight years old … and there I am, plump as a gooseberry, swaddled in a shawl and sitting on Mammy's knee. It's the only photograph of all of us I've ever seen. Oh, Issy – he must have taken it with him when he left home for good. Me and Mammy,' her voice wavered as she ran her fingers over the photograph. 'Mammy and me.'

The photograph showed 'Young' Johnny Stuart, his wife Caitlin, and their children James and Esme all dressed in their Sunday best. Caitlin was sitting at a table in the yard with the sun streaming down on her, making her squint. It must have been some kind of party because the table was covered in a white table cloth and loaded down with food and bottles of Twa Burns. Esme was sitting on her mother's knee and James leaning into his father's side. A happy family photo; yet, six months later, Caitlin would be dead and Twa Burns a smoking ruin. Esme kissed the picture, then turned to Issy, her eyes brimming with tears.

'You don't know how much this means to me, Issy. I was barely two when my mother was killed during the bombing raid on the distillery. James was almost ten; at least he has – had – some memories of her. It's a good thing the future is hidden from us, otherwise it would be too much to bear.' She sank down on the bed, rooted up her sleeve for a handkerchief and then blew her nose, noisily. Issy was concerned, it wasn't like Esme to come over all tearful and emotional. If this was how she reacted to an old family photo, God alone knew what she'd do when Brodie and his grandfather dropped their bombshell. Issy would have to stage-manage that one very carefully.

'Let me see, Esme.' Gently, Issy prised the heavy silver frame out of her aunt's hands. She looked at the faces, they were her family, too. Yes – in the scowling-faced school boy, she could see the man her father would become. She'd never known her grandfather, he'd died twenty years before she was born. Round about the time Esme had dropped out of Art School and James left home for good. It was all connected, somehow, but only Esme could tell the story, now – if she chose. Issy studied the family group, again; judging by their clothes, the food, the bottles of whisky and the silver quaich to drink it from, the Stuarts had a good life, before war changed everything.

Esme took the photo out of her hands and replaced it on the mantelpiece. Walking back, she kissed Issy on the cheek. 'I love my room, sweetheart, you've worked so hard. I think I'll have a shower and then we can sit on the bench overlooking The Narrows, finish our wine and you can bring me up to date with events on Cormorant

Island.'

Chapter Twenty Eight
Consider Yourself Dumped!

The next morning, as Issy and Esme were finishing their breakfast in the kitchen, Lindy breezed in through the back door. Judging by her clothes - blue and white striped shirt/skirt combo, cinched in by elasticated belt with a silver clasp, sensible shoes and little make-up – Lola *had* left the building, and in her place was a latter day Florence Nightingale. Bemused, Esme and Issy took in Lindy's copper curls which were hidden underneath a fifties-style turban affair, and exchanged a look.

'Morning, y'all,' she drawled in a Texan accent, walking over to the percolator and pouring herself a coffee. She leaned against the kitchen unit as she drank it, all the better for them to see her. Aunt and niece held their peace; it was best not to comment before Lindy revealed *who* she was. *And,* what she was up to on this fine July morning.

'Good morning, Lindy, and how are you?' Esme carried on eating her toast, as though Lindy dressed as a nurse was nothing out of the ordinary. Her tone was the usual mix of amusement, exasperation and wonderment with which she greeted Lindy's transformations. For reasons Issy never quite understood, Esme had always excused Lindy's wilder excesses as high spirits. Furthermore, she'd hinted on several occasions that Issy should acknowledge Lindy's many talents and view her antics with less obvious exasperation.

However, having spent the night tossing and turning, worrying about the future of Twa Burns and dreaming of Brodie, Issy was in no mood for Lindy's play-acting.

'Morning, Lindy,' Issy greeted with false brightness. 'You okay?'

'I'm good,' Lindy replied, reaching across the table and removing a slice of toast off Issy's plate. Her use of the American *I'm good* as opposed to the Scottish *I'm fine/awright,* further grated on Issy's nerves. This dressing up game was all part of Lindy's plan to return to America with Brodie and his grandfather, no doubt about that. 'How are you guys?'

'Absolutely fine and tickety boo,' Issy replied, sounding deliberately like a character out of a Noel Coward play, to make her point. 'However, I see no *guys* in this kitchen, only ladies.'

'Women,' Esme ever-the-feminist corrected.

'Well, you know, *guys* is a pretty general term these days, Issy,' Lindy declared, waving her toast in an airy fashion. 'Time you got down with the kids. If you want my opinion.'

'Well, I don't.' Issy pushed her chair back from the table and tipped the rest of her coffee down the sink, having had her plans for a long, leisurely catch up over breakfast with her aunt ruined by Lindy's sudden appearance. She gave an impatient tut, which

Pershing promptly mimicked – sending Lindy a calculating look as if he, too, was trying to work out what her game was.

'Don't go,' Lindy beseeched. 'I have something to say.'

'Well, make it quick, I have a long list of jobs to work through this morning, starting with the outhouses. I have the cross-beams to clean before I paint them. Esme's volunteered to hold the ladder steady – any chance of you lending a hand?'

Lindy rolled her eyes in disbelief. 'Wot? Get my unif- clothes dirty? No thanks.' It was plain that she'd meant to say *uniform,* but had changed her mind at the last minute. Issy sent Lindy a stern look and her blood pressure rose a few more notches as Lindy wiped butter off each of her fingers and onto a clean tea towel. 'I've come to tell you *ladies* that I'm dumping you in favour of spending more time at Brodie's. His grandfather arrived yesterday and he needs the care and attention of a nurse . . .' She glanced down at her clothes, straightened her belt with an air of self-importance and then paused, leaving Issy and Esme to fill in the gaps.

'Meaning you?' Esme's stiff tone suggested that Lindy had gone too far this time.

'Well, maybe not for serious stuff, just general looking after,' Lindy amended, wilting under Esme's look of disapproval. 'Making him laugh, dishing out his pills - that kinda thing.'

'Did you attend the course Doctor Brown organised last winter for the three defibrillators my father had installed at strategic points around the island?' Issy inquired severely, knowing the answer.

'Well, now you mention it. . .'

'Just how frail is Brodie's grandfather?' Esme asked.

'I haven't actually met him yet,' Lindy admitted, looking less certain of herself. 'Brodie told me to stand down until his *Grah-mps*,' she pronounced the word with an exaggerated American twang, 'got over his jet lag. I'm cool with that, because Brodie wants me to take over all cooking and cleaning duties – plus helping him to look after his grandfather and showing him a good time.' She made it sound as if Brodie would be taking Menzies McIntosh clubbing at the earliest opportunity.

'What will that entail?' Esme queried.

'Taking him round *Eilean na Sgairbh*, down to The Pickled Herring for a wee dram, showing him the hermit's cave on the far side of the island.'

'That's the first day taken care of,' Issy observed, snarkily. 'And after that?'

Plainly, Lindy didn't care for Issy's tone and came back with, 'Maybe touring as far as Oban and Fort William, if he's up to it. I'll probably be going with them. I've ordered a wheelchair from the Red Cross over in Jamestoun and Brodie has asked me to help push his grandfather around in it. Keep an eye on his health, and so on?' Her gaze slid away again, making it plain that Brodie had asked no such thing. 'Anyhoo,' she spread her hands to demonstrate it was all beyond her control, 'I'll have to let you go.'

She said it so seriously that Esme and Issy had to look away and bite their lips to stop themselves from laughing.

'Of course, you must do as you see fit.' Issy adopted a solemn

362

expression. 'I think we can cope. Esme?'

'Just about,' Esme agreed, poker-faced.

'Everything will be back to normal when they leave,' Lindy said.

'And you'll pick up where you left off?'

'Duh – of course. How else will I earn money in the winter?' She looked at Issy as if she was simple-minded. 'Unless . . .'

'Unless they take you back to America with them?' Issy's bright smile never faltered. Primly, Lindy folded her hands over the silver belt buckle, bowed her head and said no more. She deduced, correctly, that Issy would rain on her parade if she revealed the finer details of her master plan. Then, in true nurse's fashion, she read the time on the fob watch pinned to her breast. Issy had long suspected that Lindy had a dressing-up box full of clothes she ordered off the internet to go with the multiple personas she adopted.

The vintage fob watch confirmed it.

'Okay, gotta go.' Dismissing them without a qualm, Lindy headed for the back door. 'And if my mother rings up, asking if you've seen me - you haven't. Right? It's delivery day and I need to lay low - over at Brodie's.' The thought that her mother might need her help, patently never crossed her one-track mind. She paused, hand on the door knob. 'Are you *guys* coming down to The Pickled Herring on Friday night? I think they're hoping you'll sing again, Issy. I could introduce you to Brodie's grandfather, if you like.' She gave a nonchalant shrug, casually bestowing the favour and reinforcing her position as Brodie's go-to Girl Friday.

Issy did not like! The last thing she wanted was Esme and Menzies McIntosh making each other's acquaintance for the first time down at The Pickled Herring. If there was a deal to be brokered, The Pickled Herring was the last venue she'd choose.

'Maybe. I'll let Irene know in good time.' The thought of how much she missed Brodie hit her, like a physical pain. She acknowledged that much of her fevered tossing and turning in bed could as easily be ascribed to sexual frustration as worrying about Twa Burns. She longed to feel his hands on her, working their magic, breath in his unique male scent and . . . She pulled herself up as Esme said something to her and she didn't take it in. As the old song had it, love was a drug and she needed a fix, urgently. She glanced surreptitiously at the tide clock, already planning a rendezvous at Mermaid Rock in her head.

'I'm outta here,' Lindy said, jolting her further out of her dream.

Once she was gone, Esme regarded Issy with a curious expression, giving the impression she was wondering what was on her niece's mind. 'Outhouses?' she suggested.

'Please . . . It'll help us to get over the shock and disappointment of being dumped by Florence.' Esme snorted in unladylike fashion as she cleared the table and Issy was happy to hear her laugh. She'd been worried about Esme since she'd stepped down from The Cow last night, but this morning she looked much brighter, more like her old self. 'Are you sure you're up for this?'

'Of course,' Esme reassured her.

Issy's shoulders relaxed. 'Cool. I'll fetch the ladder.'

'Sorry Esme,' Issy said as another load of grit and grime descended on them.

'Just get the job done, Issy.' Esme's voice was muffled by an old tea towel she'd tied over the bottom half of her face, highwayman fashion. 'I'm dying for a cuppa, aren't you?' Standing at the foot of the ladder, she held onto it with both hands and braced one foot on the bottom rung to steady it. Although they wore headscarves and old clothes to keep them clean, years of accumulated debris still fell around them, filling their nostrils with dust and making them gasp.

'One last push should do it,' Issy said, dislodging an abandoned swallow's nest with a hand brush. Reaching into the darkest corner of the cross-beams, she dragged more debris towards her. There was a loud 'whoosh' as an old tartan shopping bag fell to earth, striking Esme a glancing blow on her shoulder as it went.

'What the . . .' Esme coughed.

'Hold the ladder still, Esme, I'm coming down.' Once on firm ground, Issy used a clean yellow duster to brush cobwebs and assorted rubble off her aunt's shoulders and checked that Esme hadn't been injured by the falling bag. Esme kept her eyes closed as the dust settled, but when she opened them and looked down at the collection of pale blue envelopes which had spilled out of the bag, a gasp escaped her.

'Oh, My God.' Eyes widening in disbelief, she removed the tea towel and picked one up one of the blue envelopes, edged in dark blue and red stripes. Following suit, Issy bent down and picked up the rest. Each was addressed to *Miss Esme Stuart, Ailleag, Killantrae, Eilean na Sgairbh, Argyllshire.*

'Esme, are these yours?' she asked, unnecessarily. 'Had you forgotten you'd put them there?' Her aunt didn't reply, she continued to stare, transfixed, at the small blue envelope in her hands. 'They're all unopened. What the - Esme?'

But Esme wasn't listening. She carried the envelope over to the door and examined it in daylight. Hands shaking, she turned it over and extracted a sheet of paper, so thin that the light shone through it. Sensing that something important was unfolding, Issy gave Esme space to read the letter through.

After reading it for a third time, Esme doubled over as if in pain, clutching the letter to her heart. Issy rushed to comfort her, removed the envelope from Esme's shaking fingers and then guided her over to sit down on a workbench.

'Esme. What is it? Bad news?' Stupid question. But it helped to break the dusty stillness which had settled on them. Then the silence was broken by another sound, no more than a faint moaning at first. But then it increased in volume, becoming an unearthly, blood-curdling expression of grief which made the hairs on the back of Issy's neck rise, as if the Banshee herself had cried out.

It was several seconds before Issy realised that the sound was emanating from her aunt.

At last the keening stopped and Esme raised her hand to her

throat, as if to massage away the pain. Worried, Issy took a step a forward, but Esme held up a hand to keep her at bay. That gesture scared Issy more than the mourning sound and she was suddenly fearful of what secrets the letter might contain.

Her aunt whispered something garbled and indistinct. Shaking her head as if speech was beyond her.

'What, Esme, what?'

'G - Give me a moment.'

Obeying, Issy took a few steps back and concentrated instead on picking the envelopes up off the workbench. A cursory glance showed that the date on the majority of them was 1961. Surely, whatever had transpired back then would be ancient history by now? She handed the envelopes to Esme who checked each one for its postmark and place of origin. Still moaning, but more softly now, she arranged the letters in date order, in an agitated, yet businesslike fashion.

'Wasted. Wasted. My life; wasted - ruined . . .'

'Esme, you're frightening me.' Moving closer, Issy put a protective arm around her aunt's shoulders. Esme shrugged her off, in a manner so unlike herself that Issy believed the contents of the letter had tipped her over the edge. If she was to help her aunt, she *had* to find out what those letters contained. 'Let's go into the kitchen, Esme and . . .'

'No!'

'No?'

'No. Leave me alone, Issy. I – I – I've had a shock. I want to be left . . . to work it out.' With that, she walked across the yard and into the house, slamming the kitchen door behind her; making it plain that she didn't want Issy to follow her or interfere, however well-intentioned.

Abandoned on the threshold of the outhouse, Issy chewed her bottom lip and frowned. Without knowing *who* had sent those letters, what they contained - and why they'd been stuffed in an old shopping bag and hidden behind a beam for over fifty years, she was in no position to help her beloved aunt. She'd never known Esme be anything other than gentle and kind; unswerving when it came to her 'causes', sure, but never - in all her twenty-seven years, had Issy been *dismissed* by her.

Hurt and bewildered, she remained in the doorway unsure what to do next.

The sun burst from behind the clouds and touched the brass edges of the sandalwood box nestled on the window ledge. Frowning, Issy glanced over at her father's remains and wondered what secrets he'd taken to the grave. There was a connection between him, Esme and those airmail letters – she was sure of it. Turning, she picked up the old tartan shopping bag and looked inside for clues, but there were none.

What was she to do?

In that moment, she realised she had no real friends on Cormorant Island, no one she could turn to in a crisis. Boarding school, university, and globe-trotting to far flung destinations for Ecosse Designs had left little time to sustain any friendships she'd formed at Killantrae Primary School. Lindy? She'd get no sense out of her; she spent most of her time in *Lindy World*, planning her escape from Cormorant Island. As for Esme's contemporaries, she'd left most of them behind when she'd attended Art School. Her involvement with the Campaign for Nuclear Disarmament had set her further apart from everyone and everything on *Eilean na Sgairbh* and the breach had never been healed.

Issy needed help; and the only person on the island she felt she could call upon was a relative stranger – Brodie McIntosh. Extracting her mobile from her dungarees, Issy found his number on speed dial. She listened as the number rang out and the voicemail kicked in.

'Hi, you've reached Brodie McIntosh. Leave a message and I'll get back to you.'

Ignoring the robotic voice which followed, asking her to speak after the tone, Issy ended the call. Where was he? Had the journey proved too much for his grandfather and he'd taken a turn for the worse? She shook her head. She couldn't start worrying about an elderly gentleman she'd never met and who, if her instincts were right, would be bringing further trouble to Esme Stuart's door. It looked as if she'd be handling this crisis on her own, or at least until she found out exactly what she was dealing with. After that, perhaps, she could ask Mary Tennant to come over. Apart from Issy and Lindy, she was the only person on Cormorant Island who had really featured in Esme's life over the years. She bridged the generation between Issy and Esme, perhaps she *knew* stuff, and could help . . .

Squaring her shoulders, Issy tiptoed back into the house and paused by her aunt's door, checking that Esme hadn't come to any harm. Pressing her ear to the door panel, Esme could be heard muttering: *Bastard. You Bastard.* That perplexed Issy; her aunt rarely used foul language or blasphemed. Thoroughly shaken, she went into the study, leaving the door open so that she would hear if Esme left her bedroom and crossed the hall. Taking up residence in the window seat, she looked across The Narrows to Jamestoun on the mainland. For once, she didn't see the beauty in the old white houses with their red tiled roofs, or admire the way the water sparkled in the sunshine and the clouds touched the hills beyond.

After half an hour, Esme's bedroom door opened and Issy heard the toilet flush. Steeling herself, Issy left the comfort of the window seat and walked through into the kitchen. Whatever her aunt's problem was, it looked as if Issy would be dealing with it on her own.

Chapter Twenty Nine
The Recycling Bin

S tanding by the kitchen sink, Issy strained her ears, in case Esme came into the kitchen. However, her aunt returned to her bedroom, slamming the door behind her. Issy let out a little huff of frustration, Esme was very good at keeping secrets, and if she chose not to share this bombshell – whatever it was, there was little she could do about it. On top of which, Esme had made it clear on more than one occasion that she wasn't ready to swap roles and allow Issy to become the designated adult in their relationship. She was fiercely independent and Issy knew that barging into her bedroom and demanding to know what was in those letters wouldn't work.

She tapped a fingernail against her teeth, a habit she adopted when thinking, and wondered if she should try to contact Brodie again. A mechanical, grinding noise drew her to the window. Glancing out, she saw the recycling lorry making its way towards Killantrae from The Narrows.

Damn. It was a Thursday and she'd forgotten to drag the recycling bins to the edge of the property. If she missed the collection, the lorry wouldn't return for another two weeks, by which time the bins would be overflowing. Annoyed that the mundane task of sorting out the rubbish would have to take priority, Issy walked out into the yard where three different coloured wheelie bins stood sentinel. One each for garden waste/compost/ food scraps, paper, card, tins etc; and one for any miscellaneous rubbish which didn't come under the previous headings.

There was no sound from Esme's room, but Izzy managed to glance in the side window as she dragged the green compost/garden waste bin to the edge of the drive. From what she could see, Esme had the letters spread out on the bed and was sitting with her hand on her chin, staring into space. This was her chance.

'Tea, Esme?' she called, tapping on the window.

Esme started, but turned her head to look at Issy and nodded. Shoulders slumped, she looked every day of her seventy odd years and fear gripped Issy's heart as she remembered how ill her aunt had been with pneumonia last winter. She watched as Esme gathered all the letters together and pushed herself off the bed, then went charging into the kitchen to put the kettle on before Esme changed her mind.

The water was just coming to a rolling boil when Esme entered the kitchen and sank down on the large pine carver at the head of the table.

Where to start? To break the silence Issy asked, 'Everything okay?' Patently it wasn't, but she could hardly ask outright what was in the letters. For a few seconds Esme didn't answer, then she took a deep breath and put the letters on the table, knocking the edges together to straighten them as one might a deck of cards. The action not only kept her hands busy, it delayed the moment when she would have to look at Issy and answer her question. When she spoke, her voice was surprisingly steady and she stopped her nervous fiddling with the envelopes.

'Issy . . . Back in the sixties I met someone. We had a summer fling.' She screwed her face up, at the apparent crassness of the expression, and then sighed. 'Long story short?'

'Please, if you can bear to tell me.'

'I can, darling. If you can bear to hear it.'

'Go on . . .'

'I say 'summer fling', but it was more than that. I'd found my soulmate, we fell in love and I thought, foolishly, that we'd spend the rest of our lives together.' She raised her head and Issy was dismayed to see her eyes were lambent with tears. 'We f -fell in love and wanted to get married. But, I was barely nineteen, and had just enrolled in Art School in Glasgow . . . staying on studying for a degree as a married woman simply wasn't an option. *He* had just started out on his career and was in receipt of his first commission. Issy, darling, you have to understand - things were so different back then. In many ways the legacy of the war was still with us and . . .' She gave a weak smile. 'Long story short, I said, so I'd better get my thoughts in order. *He* was exactly ten years older than me and was engaged to a girl back home.'

Issy was dying to ask her where *back home* was exactly, but didn't want to interrupt Esme's flow.

'He wasn't proud of the fact that he'd fallen for me while engaged to someone else. But love, and life, isn't neat - as you know. We arranged that, upon his return home, he would face the wrath of both sets of parents and break off his engagement to his fiancée, who – to make matters worse, he'd known since childhood. Then, he'd return and marry me, hoping that my father would grant his permission. But if he didn't, we would defy them all, and get married without their blessing.' As she remembered, her shoulders straightened and she had the light of battle in her eye. Then she turned her head away, as if she couldn't bear Issy's loving, sympathetic regard,

'Go on.'

'He never returned.' Her chin wobbled and a tearing sob escaped her. She stroked the letters as if they were the face of the man she'd loved. 'He said he'd write to me but I never received any letters. These letters . . . The letters he wrote – were kept from me.' Anger replaced sorrow and she threw them across the table. The kettle burst into shrill life and Issy got to her feet to silence it, desperate for Esme to continue. Although, now the genie was out of the bottle, Esme appeared keen to tell her everything. 'I'm guessing James intercepted the letters and hid them from me. Maybe Father had a hand in it, too. However, because of what came after, I somehow doubt that.' She gave a mirthless little laugh. 'It's funny when you think about it . . .'

'What is?' Issy reached out for Esme's hands which were freezing cold, and tried to rub some life into them.

'James – your father, has been on that window ledge in full view of those letters for over a month now. He must have known you'd find them when you started renovating the outhouses, that's why he'd been so against the idea in the first place. Not that he had any say in the matter, Issy, you stuck to your guns. You're braver than I was.'

Esme was beginning to ramble and it was hard to follow her train of thought.

What did Esme mean by *because of what came after?*

Would history repeat itself with her and Brodie? There had been plenty of passion the night they'd spent together but no indication where their relationship was headed. Maybe, her aunt's story would turn out to be a cautionary tale; one she could learn from. Her brow puckered as she walked over to the kitchen cabinet and took down a precious bottle of Twa Burns Single Malt. No, Brodie was better than that; she hadn't picked a 'laggard in love' a second time. She'd found her Lochinvar, she was sure of it. She poured two glasses of uisge beatha. If what Brodie had told her about the price of surviving bottles of single malts from lost distilleries was true, she calculated she and Esme were sipping almost five hundred pounds worth of whisky between them.

'To hell with it,' she said, more to herself than her aunt. 'Slainte.' She handed Esme her glass and they knocked back their drams with a deft flick of the wrist, in time-honoured fashion. Issy brought the bottle over onto the table and plonked it down in front of them. 'Don't stop now, Esme,' she urged, feeling that all the missing pieces of the family jigsaw were finally slotting into place.

'Three months passed, it was Christmas 1961 and I was persona non grata on the island because I'd been arrested for climbing up the anchor chains of the USS Proteus. Worse still, a group of us had taken it upon ourselves to stop the sailors from the Polaris Fleet coming here on furlough – spending their money in The Pickled Herring, attending the ceilidhs in the Village Hall, flirting with the local lassies, buying stuff from the Post Office and General Store to take home as souvenirs. We staged a sit in on the quay by The Narrows. We were arrested and taken over to Jamestoun to spend the night in the lock-up and then released. The powers that be didn't want to create any martyrs.'

'I bet my father was furious?'

'Incandescent. Looking back,' she shrugged her thin shoulders, 'I suspect we were nothing more than a bloody nuisance and, in the end, our placards, posters and posturing didn't alter the course of history. However, the islanders thought we were a bunch of commies – remember this was at the height of the cold war – and they wanted us off the island.'

'Tough call,' Issy said to fill in the silence, and poured Esme another dram. 'Is that why you didn't go back to Art School and finish your degree? You decided to dedicate your life to the Peace Movement?' Esme raised her head and sent Issy a strange look, as if wondering whether it was worth raking over the past to tell her the *whole* story.

'That came after . . .' *That phrase again.*

'After?' Issy prompted.

'After,' Esme bit her lip, as though answering Issy's questions came at a price. 'After I discovered I was pregnant.'

'Oh, Esme,' Issy whispered, unable to think of something suitable to say.

'As I said earlier, times were different; but you have no idea *how* different,' Esme rushed on, plainly anxious to explain. 'The contraceptive pill wasn't readily available – can you imagine my going to the local GP who'd nursed me through measles and chickenpox, and demanding the pill? I – an unmarried female with left wing sympathies, who'd made a thorough nuisance of herself and alienated most of the island. Anyway, father arranged for me to stay over in Tranent, near Edinburgh, with a distant cousin. The story put about was that the cousin had just given birth and needed a mother's help - and I needed to put as much distance between me and the Polaris fleet as possible.'

'And my father made it his business to intercept the letters in your absence?'

'Every single one. Thinking, no doubt, that once I'd had the baby and put it up for adoption, everything would be as it had been. So, my - my lover never knew I was pregnant or that I was waiting for him to return. If he had, he would have done the right thing by me and our child. To be pregnant and unmarried was a great disgrace in those days, Issy.'

'What happened to the child?' Issy probed, her voice catching at the thought of what her dear aunt had suffered.

'The baby was given to a childless couple and I left the island and went on my travels,' she said in a dispirited voice. 'I've often wondered . . .'

'Yes?' Issy sent her aunt a look of love and empathy.

'If he – if my child's father returned to Cormorant Island to look for me and . . .'

'My father had sent him away with a flea in his ear?'

'I guess I'll never know. Not now.' There was a hopelessness in her voice that wrung Issy's heart afresh. She tried to imagine how it must have felt for her aunt to lose the man she loved and to give away their baby. Then a thought struck her.

'Why don't you get in touch with *him?* Or, at least find out if his family still live at that address and could –'

'What would be the point? It all happened over fifty years ago, he's probably dead by now.' That thought seemed to cut her afresh and she dashed away a tear with the corner of her cardigan.

There was so much Issy wanted to ask, but she held her peace knowing Esme had been through the wringer. Maybe she'd press her for a few more details when she looked up to it. Maybe, given time, Esme'd volunteer the information herself.

Had she kept in touch with the couple who'd adopted her baby?

Did she give birth to a son or a daughter?

Why did she never attempt to get in touch with the child's father?

Now the stories Issy had grown up with made better sense . . . why her grandfather had left the house to Esme (guilt?), and why

James Stuart had quit the island for America (shame?). It even explained his donations to worthy causes, his connection with the church and his lay preaching – clearly, that was his way of salving his conscience, of righting the wrong he'd done to his sister. Had her grandfather been complicit in the deception? She'd never know . . .

'Come on, Issy, this will never do.' Esme collected the letters together and held them in her hands, uncertainly. 'I'll put these somewhere safe and then we'll finish dusting those beams.'

'If you're sure –'

'I'm sure.'

The recycling lorry arrived by the side of the house. There was a great clatter, much shouting and exchange of banter as the operatives collected the wheelie bin and trundled it to the lorry. The orange hazard lights bounced off the walls of the outhouse and found their way into the darkest corners of the cobbled yard. The light reflected off the brass corners of the sandalwood box containing James Stuart's ashes and drew Issy and Esme back to the sorry business of the letters and the lost child.

Esme was deep in thought for a few seconds, and then appeared to reach a decision. Patently, one she had to see through before she changed her mind, or lost her nerve. For a few moments, Issy thought she was about to throw her precious letters into the recycling bin and made as if to stop her. But, then . . . cool as you like, Esme left the letters on the kitchen table, walked over to the outhouse and removed her brother's ashes from the window ledge.

'You controlling bastard. You'll never see the top of that

Munro, James Alistair Stuart. You're going where you belong and getting the treatment you deserve.'

Then she walked over to the recycling lorry and threw sandalwood box, ashes and all into the giant maw of the mechanical beast where it was churned to mulch with the rest of the island's rubbish.

Chapter Thirty
Tea, Sympathy – and a History Lesson

An hour later, Issy took a break from the Herculean task of cleaning the outhouses and glanced towards the kitchen. Through the now empty window where her father's ashes had previously resided, Esme could be seen sitting at the kitchen table with Mary Tennant.

Issy let out a relieved sigh, Esme was safe and hadn't done anything else foolish.

After dumping the sandalwood box in the recycling lorry, Esme had brushed past her, put on stout walking boots and taken off along the beach. The set of her shoulders warned Issy not to follow, or to organise a search party if she didn't return. In fact, her whole demeanour suggested that anyone brave enough to intercept her on the beach would have their head bitten off in one satisfying chunk. She had to get her head round what was contained within the unopened letters, and she needed space to accomplish that. Issy didn't want to start speculating what Esme's next course of action would be. *She* was still recovering from the shock of her father's ashes being thrown into the lorry and Esme dusting off her hands, cartoon fashion, as if he was no more than a pile of potato peelings.

Entering the kitchen, Issy found Esme and Mary working their way down the bottle of Twa Burns as if it were supermarket whisky. At their elbow sat an ancient brown teapot sporting a lumpy, hand-knitted cosy and next to it, a plate of petticoat tail shortbread. Issy had never seen Mary touch alcohol before and was surprised to find her sharing a dram with Esme, particularly as the sun wasn't anywhere near the yard arm.

Desperate times called for desperate measures, seemingly.

'Here she is,' Esme said, acting as if the morning's dramatic events hadn't happened. Issy's entrance had halted Esme and Mary's head-to-head and she wondered what they'd been discussing. Her aunt was fond of Mary and she was a frequent visitor to the house. However, she'd be surprised if Esme had given Mary chapter and verse of what had unfolded this morning. Let alone acquainted her with the news that somewhere there was a grown up child bearing Esme's Stuart genes, if not her name.

'Come away in, Issy. We were just talking about Brodie and his grandfather . . . '

'Oh yes?' Issy addressed Mary Tennant sharper than intended.

Taking a deep breath, she got a handle on her emotions. As far as she was aware, no one knew about the plans for Twa Burns other than herself and the McIntosh men. And she had every intention of keeping it that way for as long as possible. Esme had enough to deal with, for now.

'Brodie was in the shop earlier, fetching a few *messages*, Wednesday being early closing day, ken? I gave him some homemade shortbread for his grandfather but he was so preoccupied asking about *you,* that he left without taking it. I wondered, would ye mind driving over to the eco-lodge and dropping it off, Issy?' Mary was all innocence, but Issy recognised matchmaking when she saw it. No matter how prettily it was dressed up.

'Oh yes?' This time, both women swivelled in their chairs to look at Issy directly. She took a deep breath and fixed a smile on her face, wondering if *I've had sex with Brodie McIntosh* was tattooed on her forehead because they were looking at her so speculatively. 'I could,' she shrugged, as though it was of no importance, 'if Esme can spare me.'

'And why would I not be able to spare you, child? Dinnae fash yourself over *me*, Ishabel Stuart. Throwing James' ashes in the recycling lorry was the best thing I've done in years; it was cathartic. There is a karmic truth, that how people treat you is their karma - but how you react to them is yours,' she said with some of her old fire. 'What goes around, comes around, isn't that how the saying goes?'

'Aye, it is that, Esme,' Mary said, slurring her words but nodding sagely.

'Yes, I know; but, Esme –'

'Never mind 'but, Esme.' The last thing I need is a nursemaid, Issy. Isn't that right, Mary?' Esme's jaw had the fixed, stubborn set to it which Issy recognised. Arguing with her aunt in this mood would only wear them out and change nothing.

'Aye, it is that,' Mary repeated, and sipped her neat whisky, more than a little tipsy. 'Esme disnae need, or wah-nt, molly – molly thingy . . .'

'Coddling,' Esme supplied.

Knowing Esme's history, Issy guessed she didn't, at that.

She'd always looked after herself – and that was how it would always be. Issy was relieved the letters had brought Esme some closure; after her initial angry outburst and propelling James' earthly remains into the dustbin lorry, she appeared to have accepted what couldn't be changed. She hadn't been abandoned by her lover, she'd been tricked by her family, people she'd looked to for love and support.

She knew the truth now and that was all that mattered.

The room had fallen silent and Issy became aware of Mary and Esme looking at her as if expecting something more.

'Shortbread,' Mary Tennant prompted, 'Brodie's grandfather?'

'Yes. Of course. Is Lindy over there?' Issy didn't want to get in a tussle of wills with Edith Cavell this morning.

'A very disappointed Lindy, as it happens,' Mary replied. 'She rang me to say she's on her way home. Turns out that Brodie's grandfather isn't infirm at all, quite the reverse. He's quite sprightly for an elderly gentleman, so - the wheelchair Lindy ordered from the Red Cross in Jamestoun will have to be returned, when I can spare the delivery van.' Mary and Esme rolled their eyes at the word *wheelchair*.

'Give Lindy her due, Mary, she does take her imaginary duties very seriously,' Esme quipped. However, Issy was too busy dwelling on Mary's description of Menzies McIntosh to smile.

Sprightly? That was the last thing they needed. She groaned, inwardly, betting her last penny that he was in command of all his faculties, too. That would make dealing with him all the harder. Right - time she found out . . .

'Do you want a lift back to the General Store, Mary? I'll have to shower and change first, though.' There was no way she was going into the enemy camp less than perfectly groomed for her first meeting with the head of the Kentucky branch of the McIntosh clan.

'No, you're aw'right, Ishabel, I'll make my own way home. It's been quite a while since Esme and I had a good old chinwag, and we have some catching up to do. *Tapadh leibh.'* Preoccupied with thoughts of Brodie, Issy only half-registered Mary's thank you, and completely missed the look which flashed between Mary and Esme as she left the two women alone in the kitchen.

On the drive over to Brodie's place, Issy thought less about Twa Burns' disputed inheritance and more about the last time she'd seen him. Only two days had passed, but it already felt like a lifetime since she'd lain in his arms; would he still feel the same about her? Had absence made his heart grow fonder, or once out of sight, had she faded from his mind? She'd have to keep her feelings hidden from Brodie's grandfather - in case he thought he could drive a hard bargain, with Brodie as a bargaining chip. The matter of the letters would pale into insignificance when Esme discovered Brodie and his grandfather's reason for being on the island.

A real double whammy.

She hoped her aunt was capable of dealing with the news when she was apprised of it. She swung into the driveway of the lodges and let the last thought fade from her mind. She needed to be razor sharp when she met the man she pictured as an octogenarian Lord Sugar; a man who'd let nothing slip past him. A man used to playing hard ball.

She'd hardly had a chance to park the car and switch off the engine before Brodie was out of the eco-lodge, vaulting over the balustrading as he had done on the previous occasion. Soon he was by her side and pulling her into his arms. He lifted a handful of her thick dark hair to his face and took in great lungfuls of her unique body scent.

'God, I've missed you, Issy. The sound and scent of you; the very idea of you – of us. The past two days have been the longest forty-eight hours of my life . . .' He turned his head sideways and spoke with quiet passion against her lips. Curling one arm round her waist, he raised the other to cradle her head. 'Ishabel Stuart - it turns oot, ah cannae live withoot ye, lassie,' he said in a very passable Scottish accent. Parting her legs with his right knee, he pressed closer, pushing her back against the Mini as their kisses deepened and grew more passionate. The paper bag containing the shortbread slipped from Issy's nerveless fingers and landed at their feet. The kiss would have gone on forever had not a gruff voice called out from the verandah.

'Brodie . . . Have you no manners? Let the young lady come up for air.' Brodie smiled against Issy's lips as he released her from the clinch – after one hard, long kiss.

'Guess not, Grandpa,' he laughed. Putting his arm round Issy, he pulled her into his side and guided her over to the steps of the lodge. 'Manners can go hang, sometimes.' He kissed Issy's neck and then let her walk up the few steps to the decking ahead of him.

'If I had a woman as beautiful as this young lady in my arms, I guess I'd forget my manners, too.' Menzies McIntosh stepped forward and held out his hand. He was tall and straight for his age with a head of thick, white hair and eyes as clear as the green sea-glass which washed up on the beach. No guessing where Brodie got his good looks from, Issy mused as her hand was held in a firm grasp. 'Menzies McIntosh,' he inclined his head slightly.

'Ishabel Stuart,' she answered, giving him a direct look. Friendly, but with just enough reserve to let him know that she was a pragmatic Scot and not easily swayed by gallantry and fine words. 'Pleased to meet you, Mingus.' She used the Scottish pronunciation of his name to further reinforce that they were on her territory, and that Twa Burns' ownership was as much about history and tradition as cold commerce. She experienced a pang of guilt when Menzies took a step closer and she saw regret and surprise in his eyes.

'No one, outside of my immediate family, has called me Mingus in many a long year, Miss Stoo-art – '

'Issy, please,' she said, inclining her head graciously.

'Very well - Issy. Now, come in and Brodie can rustle up some food and drink and you can tell me all about yourself.' He didn't let go of her hand; he slipped it into the crook of his arm and led her indoors.

My word, Issy thought, as Brodie sent her a helpless look - he really is the epitome of a cultured southern gentleman. Charm personified. Now she knew where Brodie had learned his people skills – at the feet of Grandpa Menzies. It was left for Brodie to pick up the bag of shortbread, carry it into the kitchen and make the coffee while Issy and Menzies sat side by side on the leather sofa. Issy caught Brodie's ardent look as he went through, and blushed as she recalled what had happened on the sofa, two nights previously.

Hiding a smile, she turned back to Menzies. 'Do you know the limerick regarding the pronunciation of your name?'

'I don't think I do. I hope it isn't too racy for an old man like me.' He put his hand over his heart, but there was a twinkle in his eye which made Issy suspect that, back in the day, he'd broken his fair share of them. She relaxed back on the sofa and recited the limerick as Brodie clattered around in the kitchen.

> *'A lively young damsel named Menzies,*
> *Inquired, "Do you know what this thenzies?"*
> *Her aunt, with a gasp,*
> *Replied, "It's a wasp,*
> *And you're holding the end where the stenzies"'*

Menzies laughed, delighted. 'Well that's a new one on me. Will you write it down so I can remember it when Brodie and I return home to the States?'

There was an awkward moment as an elephant lumbered into the room and stationed itself in front of the wood burning stove. 'Of course. How long do you plan on staying on *Eilean na Sgairbh*?'

Issy thought it was best to get right down to it, before she succumbed to the full force of his warmth and charisma.

'Let's wait until Brodie joins us?'

'Of course,' Issy replied.

Brodie came back into the sitting room with the shortbread on a plate and three mugs of coffee. He plonked the tray down on the wide coffee table and then sat at right angles to them on a leather rocking chair. He looked none too pleased at being relegated to the position of waiter while his grandfather flirted with Issy.

'You've met Lindy, then?' Issy asked, as Brodie passed a mug of coffee over to his grandfather. 'Her mother, Mary Tennant, made the petticoat tails – that's shortbread for the uninitiated,' she added, scoring another subtle point.

'Lindy, quite a determined little thing, isn't she?' Menzies laughed. 'I've never been so well looked after in my life. Are all the folk on *Eilean na Sgairbh*,' he had no trouble pronouncing the Gaelic name, 'as friendly as Lindy?'

'We're a friendly bunch,' Issy admitted, skirting over the bad history between the Stuarts and the islanders which centred on Twa Burns distillery. 'But we're clannish, too, if you get my meaning.'

'Meaning family comes first and you close ranks against outsiders?' he asked, raising his thick, white eyebrow a fraction.

'Exactly,' Issy said.

'Even if those outsiders could bring employment and prosperity back to the island?'

'Grandpa, you promised . . .' Brodie interrupted.

'Best we talk plain, Brodie. I can see that Ishabel,' he used her Sunday name, 'prefers it that way?'

'I do.' She put her mug back on the tray and turned to look at him directly. 'Fire away.'

'Brodie's told you why I'm here?'

'To claim what you regard as your own. Yes.'

'Twa Burns distillery and –' he paused. 'I'm getting ahead of myself. Let's start with Twa Burns, we could spend hundreds of thousands of dollars making attorneys rich while we dispute the McIntoshes claim to half of Twa Burns. Correct?'

'Correct.'

'And, forgive me, Ishabel – that's money you and your aunt don't have?'

'Correct again,' Issy said, her heart sinking. On the periphery of her vision she was aware of Brodie stirring restlessly as his grandfather's interrogation continued.

'I take it that you would like to see Twa Burns rebuilt?' Menzies persisted.

'And prosperity brought back to the island – of course I would. I don't dispute your claim but there are two obstacles, as I see it.' She got to her feet, walked over to Brodie's chair and perched on the arm of it. 'As I've explained to Brodie, I don't want my aunt spending the remaining years of her life in hock to the McIntoshes, no matter how generous the terms of the loan. '

'And the second obstacle?' Menzies probed.

Brodie found Issy's hand and twined his fingers in hers. It was plain that he deferred to his grandfather, however, his restless shifting in the chair made it obvious that he had plenty to say on the subject but was holding his peace.

'My aunt. She – she's had a bit of a shock this morning . . .'

'A shock?' Menzies sat bolt upright on the sofa. 'What kind of a shock. Is she unwell?'

'I can't go into the details, the story's not mine to tell. All I will say is that now is not the moment to broach the subject of Twa Burns' resurrection. I'm sorry, but that's how it is.' This time she got to her feet and extricated her fingers from Brodie's warm grasp. Menzies and Brodie stood up, too.

'Wait, don't go. Sit back down for a moment, Issy.' Menzies nodded to Brodie who led her back to her previous position on the wide chair arm. 'You know, this could be a match made in heaven.' Issy looked at him and tried to remain objective. Other than the size and terms of the loan, this was a great opportunity for the island and she didn't want it to slip through their fingers. The McIntoshes could rebuild Twa Burns on their own, but half a distillery was small fry and wouldn't be worth the time and effort required to clear the two burns and get the water wheels turning once more.

'A match made in heaven?' she queried. Was he referring to the distillery or to her relationship with Brodie? Or, in Menzies' eyes, were they inextricably linked – somehow, one and the same?

Brodie entered the discussion, as if sensing the track her mind was running along. 'What grandfather means, is that bourbon production and whisky distilling are two halves of the same whole.

Let me explain.'

'Please do.' The ice in Issy's tone made it plain that she was beginning to wonder if their relationship wasn't somehow linked to closing the deal. Brodie keeps her sweet, she talks her aunt round, contracts are signed; the job's done.

Brodie's fingers tightened around hers and he slowly circled his thumbnail along the centre of her downturned palm. His grandfather couldn't see it but Issy's body responded to his touch as though she'd been electrified. She swallowed hard and tried to remove her hand. She needed to stay centred, focused, and Brodie wasn't helping.

'Whisky needs to be stored in tempered barrels and most distillers prefer to store their uisge beatha in casks which have previously stored bourbon. It adds to the flavour of the whisky and that suits you canny Scots, because you can buy second-hand bourbon barrels cheaply from us.'

'Why don't you reuse the barrels yourselves?' Issy asked, refusing to be mollified, and bristling slightly at the reference to penny-pinching Scots.

Menzies took over the history lesson. 'Federal Law and the powerful Coopers Union have ensured that bourbon casks can be used only once. Imagine it, Issy, Twa Burns rebuilt and flourishing, and the whisky maturing in white oak casks which have previously stored *Mac's Kentucky Moonshine*.'

'History has turned full circle,' Brodie said, pulling her into his lap and kissing the top of her head.

'A match made in heaven,' Menzies agreed, getting to his feet and yawning. 'Jet lag Think I'll go and have my afternoon nap, as prescribed by Nurse Lindy . . .' To be honest, he did look suddenly very weary so Issy believed him. Although she also suspected that he didn't relish playing gooseberry and wanted to leave them alone. 'I'll leave Brodie to talk things through with you. Once your aunt's got over her – shock – we should meet. Discuss matters further, Ishabel?' He paused, and then held out his hand. 'A pleasure meeting you Miss Stoo-art.' He shook her hand and bowed over it with old-fashioned gallantry.

'You, too, Mingus.'

She and Brodie sat stock still until they heard his bedroom door close and then let out a long, relieved sigh.

'He likes you, Issy,' Brodie said as his hand found its way under her t-shirt and cupped her breast. 'Which is good, because I like you, too.' Now his thumb pushed past the thin lace of the bra and started circling her nipple, just as previously he'd circled the palm of her hand.

'You do?' Desire lanced through Issy and she took a deep, steadying breath.

'Can't you feel it?' He settled her more comfortably in his lap and she could feel his erection pushing against her bottom in a most suggestive fashion.

'I think I can,' she said, pretending confusion. 'But mostly I feel an overwhelming sense of jet lag.'

'You do?'

'Mm. I do. I had to cross several time zones travelling from Killantrae to here.'

'I think an afternoon nap is in order,' he said, straight-faced. 'I'm guessing you're too tired to journey home?'

'Exhausted,' she agreed as he pushed her off his lap and they got to their feet.

'In which case, if I might make a suggestion . . .'

'Yes?'

'I have a bed. Just over there – behind that thick, soundproof door. Would you like to make use of it, Ma'am?' He led her towards his bedroom by her hand, tiptoeing so as not to disturb his grandfather.

'It would be a pleasure,' Issy replied as they entered Brodie's huge double bedroom.

'The pleasure, Mizz Stoo-art,' Brodie responded, maintaining his solicitous air, 'will be all mine.'

Chapter Thirty One
Return to the Pickled Herring

'What'r'ye havin', ladies?' Irene inquired when Esme and Issy strolled into The Pickled Herring two nights later. A chilled out atmosphere - a mixture of laughter, clinking glasses and conversation was building nicely as the pub filled with locals and summer visitors. Despite Issy's reservations, it'd been arranged that Brodie and his grandfather would be in situ when she and Esme arrived at The Pickled Herring. Brodie would casually invite Esme and Issy to join them, they'd graciously accept and then he'd take it from there. No mention of Twa Burns or anything contentious, just a pleasant evening together, giving the old couple a chance to become acquainted.

Phase One of the master plan to break news of the McIntoshes' claim to Twa Burns to Esme.

'I'll have a Campari and soda and . . . Issy?' Esme's look suggested that Issy's mind was in another place and she wasn't listening. Her second, more telling look informed Issy that being away with the fairies was a common state these days.

'Make mine a double vodka, with soda water and lime,' said

Issy, pulling herself out of her dream.

'Nervous?' Irene pushed a glass under the optic and dispensed a double measure of vodka.

Issy's head jerked up. Irene was Cormorant Island's version of the Delphic oracle. She knew everything that was going down, even before it happened. Surely Brodie hadn't mentioned the business over Twa Burns with her, with anyone? That would be entirely out of character. What's more, she'd bet even money on Mary Tennant having said nothing about the letters Esme had found in the outhouses.

'Nervous?' she repeated, knocking back a large measure of her drink.

'Aye, there's a couple of mini buses bringing American tourists over from the cruise ship, and the hotel and Youth Hostel are full, too. The Herring's gonnae be packed the night, a'right.'

'Oh, that?' Issy laughed as she carried their drinks over to their table. 'No, not at all nervous. Put the drinks on the slate will you, Irene? I'll settle up later.'

'Sure, no worries, doll.' Irene turned to serve another customer. 'I'll gie ye a shout when you're up. Nice to see you, Esme, it's been a wee while, no?'

'Too long, Irene, too long. Cheers.' Esme clinked glasses with Issy as they sat down, nodding graciously to other islanders who looked surprised at finding Miss Esme Stuart of *Ailleag,* gracing the pub with her presence. 'I've stayed away too long, Issy.' She spoke with the air of someone who'd made a decision but wasn't ready to share it – just yet.

'From The Pickled Herring?'

'From the island. But, never mind all that, where's young Brodie?' Every time Esme mentioned Brodie's name, she looked at Issy as if expecting *her* to make an announcement concerning their relationship.

Issy glanced at her watch and neatly sidestepped the question. 'I thought he'd be here.'

'He'll be along; I've a feeling he's the dependable type?' Again, the questioning look, then Esme changed the subject. 'Issy – will you sing Wild Mountain Thyme, tonight - for me?' Issy reached over and squeezed her hand, suspecting the folk song was somehow linked with the letters.

'Of course. It always goes down well with the visitors. Esme, I think someone's trying to attract your attention . . .'

'Och, its Margot Munro, we were at primary school together; I thought she'd died last winter. Hey ho. I suppose if you're going to make Cormorant Island your home and build your business here, I'd better go over and talk to the old besom. You'll need the goodwill of the islanders behind you if you want to prosper, I've learned that to my cost over the years.' She put her glass down. 'If I'm not back in five, call me over on some pretext, before I lose the will to live. If I can stand five minutes in the company of her and the other old biddies, I'll be well on my way to becoming a regular at The Herring.' Fixing a smile on her face which would have done the Queen proud, she made her way over to Margot's table.

The pub reached capacity as the tourists from the cruise ship berthed in Ullapool arrived, their guide in tow, giving a running commentary on what to expect that evening. Soon there was standing room only as a contingent from the Youth Hostel came in, followed by Lindy and a couple of her girlfriends. For once, Lindy was dressed appropriately in skinny jeans and a bright red t-shirt; she waved over to Issy but didn't join her. Issy took her mobile out of her bag and checked for messages.

Where *was* Brodie?

Two minutes later he walked into The Pickled Herring - without his grandfather.

His forehead was puckered as he searched the room for Issy. When he saw her, the frown lifted and he gave one of his lopsided smiles before making his way over to the bar and ordering himself a drink. Experience had taught him that once the pub was packed, getting to the bar would be nigh on impossible. Issy sat back in her chair and allowed herself the luxury of studying him from a distance, as if this was her first glimpse of him. Would she still be attracted to him if he hadn't saved the day at her father's memorial service, sent Jack Innes-Kerr packing and made her feel alive for the first time in years?

Of course she would.

He glanced at her over his shoulder and smiled. Remembering their rendezvous on Mermaid Rock yesterday at low tide, Issy's heart stuttered and a warm flush of desire washed over her. If Esme had noticed her sudden enthusiasm for swimming, she was savvy enough to make no comment. The secrecy with which they'd met, added an extra frisson to their lovemaking and she wondered how she'd manage when Brodie's stay on the island came to an end, as end it must. Every time they made love, she expected the attraction they felt for each other to lose something of its sparkle; but it wasn't the case. Brodie was her new addiction – the more she had, the more she wanted. However, even as they climaxed and whispered the passionate, inconsequential things that lovers do, she sensed that, like her, Brodie was holding something of himself back.

Although neither of them openly expressed the thought, it was obvious they were unable to give full vent to the love they felt for each other until the business with Twa Burns was settled. The feelings they had for one another couldn't be allowed to cloud the issue. Issy watched The Pickled Herring's regulars make their way over to Brodie, slapping him on the back and engaging him in conversation. It was plain that he was accepted by the islanders in a way the Stuarts had never been.

That saddened her, but it also made her more determined to make things right between her, Esme and the community.

Brodie responded to the firm handshakes and joshing at the bar with good grace, but Issy could tell that he was impatient to join her. His attention kept sliding away from his bar room companions and towards her, his eyes filled with light and love. The smile never left his face, but Issy sensed he was on autopilot; charming and charismatic as ever, but anxious to leave the crush at the bar. Eventually, he extricated himself and joined her at her table, carrying a bottle of wine and some extra glasses. Issy's mouth went dry as he walked towards her, full of lean grace in his grandfather's kilt, leather jacket and biker boots. Beneath the jacket he wore a bright red t-shirt bearing a Gaelic logo: RUADH GU BRATH – *Redheads forever*.

Doubtless a present from Lindy.

Sitting down, Brodie put the wine and glasses on the table and leaned casually sideways towards her.

'Issy.' His knee pressed against hers.

'Brodie.' Looking straight ahead, she ran her fingers up the inside of his thigh beneath the table and felt the muscles tauten in response. 'Good evening, how are you?'

'G – good. I'm good,' he responded. 'Esme making new friends?' They glanced over at Esme who was listening politely to Margot Munro. They'd been joined by Esme's contemporaries who plainly could not believe that Miss Esme Stuart, left wing firebrand and black sheep of *Eilean na Sgairbh* was drinking in *their* pub.

'Where's Mingus?' Issy asked Brodie, removing her hand from his thigh.

'He was bushed after a trip over to the mainland today. He sends his apologies and wonders if he might call on you ladies tomorrow?' Brodie reached for Issy's hand under the table. 'What d'ya say?'

Issy liked the way his fingers encircled the delicate bones of her wrist and hand, but she was less sure about a home visit by Brodie and his grandfather. However, she knew that the meeting had to take place sooner rather than later - and decided that sooner was best.

Maybe, Esme would take the news better on home territory, surrounded by familiar things.

'Okay. Come over tomorrow afternoon; make it seem as if you were just driving by and wanted to pay your respects. I'm not sure how this is going to end – I only hope it's not in tears. Esme's tears.' Brodie's hand gripped hers tighter as if to reassure her that all would be well. As Issy looked into his moss-green eyes, seeking reassurance, then her gaze moved to his lips and her heart lurched. In that instant, she so wanted to kiss him - but knew she had to maintain her sangfroid in front of everyone. Reading her stiff expression and obviously aware of what she was thinking, Brodie began massaging her Mount of Venus with his thumb, drawing his nail across her palm in a manner guaranteed to elicit a response.

'I've checked the tide table, it's low tide at ten tomorrow morning. Wanna practice your silkie whispering on Mermaid Rock, Lorelei?'

'Stop it,' Issy hissed, 'I'm serious . . . '

'So am I,' Brodie replied in a husky voice.

'Issy – you're on,' Irene shouted over from the bar.

'Brodie McIntosh. You -' Issy wagged a finger at him as she broke free. But there was amusement in her voice and her eyes were the same soft, smoky blue as after lovemaking. Brodie's unrepentant grin made her stomach lurch in seismic fashion. It was obvious that he was loathe for her to leave him. But the band had set up and Issy walked over to discuss what she would be singing that evening. After a brief head-to-head, she raised her voice above the murmur of conversation.

'This is for the summer visitors to *Eilean na Sgairbh*, but especially for my aunt Esme.' She waved over to where Esme was trapped in the corner by the matrons of *Eilean na Sgairbh*. 'Wild Mountain Thyme.' There was a round of appreciative applause and some loud whistles because the song was a summer favourite.

Issy sang the old folk song; the melody and sentiments tugged at her heart in a way it'd never done before. It reinforced what couldn't be denied, her time with Brodie was running out – and she didn't know what she'd do when he left. Blinking away the tears, she poured all her longing into the words and was relieved when the regulars joined in with the chorus, taking the focus away from her.

When the song ended, Brodie got up from the table and made a beeline for Issy, holding his hand out. She took it and he pulled her into his arms and kissed her in front of everyone. This was followed by the delighted whoops of the revellers at The Pickled Herring and much handclapping. The tourists joined in, believing that the bonnie lassie kissing her kilted hero was part of the floor show.

'Thank God - ye've come oot o' the closet at last,' Irene observed, and the pub erupted with laughter. Smiling, Issy glanced over to her aunt to see how she'd taken Brodie's open declaration of love. But, Esme was on her feet, all colour draining from her face as she seemingly struggled for words. Issy rushed over. Surely the sight of her being kissed by Brodie wasn't enough to shock Esme? Shaking off Issy's hand, Esme pointed over to where Brodie was pushing his way through the crowd to reach them.

Soon he was at their side and Esme's ability to speak returned. 'That kilt. Where did you get it?'

'It's my grandfather's . . .'

'It's the Polaris Fleet tartan, isn't it?'

Now the whole pub was quiet, the drinkers' attention centred on the new drama.

'Yes,' Brodie replied. 'My grandfather was part of the Polaris Fleet in the sixties . . .'

'Which ship?' Esme struggled out.

'The USS Proteus, tending the submarines at Hunter's Quay on Holy Loch. Why?'

Grim-faced and ashen, Esme didn't reply. She half-walked, half-staggered over to where she'd been sitting earlier, and gathered up her coat and handbag. 'Issy, take me home. Now.'

'But, Esme – '

'Now.'

Alarmed at her aunt's tone, Issy did as commanded. Sending Brodie a helpless look, she guided her aunt out of the pub while he followed close on their heels. Earlier, Issy and her aunt had walked the short distance to The Pickled Herring, but Esme looked incapable of putting one foot in front of another. Her hands were shaking and her teeth chattered like castanets; when Issy touched her, she was icy cold.

Taking command, Brodie put his arm round Esme's waist and practically carried her to his Land Rover. 'She's in shock,' Brodie said. 'Let's get her home – you make her comfortable and I'll call the medics.'

Chapter Thirty Two
Just What the Doctor Ordered

'Esme, allow Doctor Brown to take your blood pressure or I'll call an ambulance and have you taken over to A and E in Jamestoun,' Issy threatened. 'Quicker than you can say 'fracking protest.'

Esme submitted with ill grace as young Doctor Brown fumbled with the blood pressure cuff.

'You'll have to wait until morning if you plan on that course of action,' the doctor observed above the whirring of the machine. 'The tide's turned and *Eilean na Sgairbh* is cut off for the night.' Issy sent him a *play-along-with-me-can't-you?* look. Esme, lying on the sofa, responded with a *don't-think-you-can-push-me-around, Ishabel Stuart* glacial stare. The blood pressure cuff buzzed as it inflated and they watched it in silence, as if talking would put it off its stroke, and the young GP would have to start all over again. He took the reading and unfastened the cuff and put the equipment back in its case. 'I expect you've been overdoing it, Miss Stuart, and nothing I can say will change that. But maybe you'll listen to your niece? At your age you might consider taking things a little more sedately.'

'Thank you, Doctor,' Issy interjected, before her aunt, even in her present condition, threw something at his head. 'I'll make sure she takes it easy for a few days.'

'I prescribe bed rest in that case, Miss Stuart.' He snapped the catches on his case and considered his next words, before finally addressing them to Issy, 'There are rumours circulating round the island that your aunt has been disposing of family heirlooms in the recycling lorry.'

'Really?' Issy said and gave her aunt a warning look.

'Yes; really. Having a clear-out is one thing, Miss Stuart, but the elder Miss Stuart lifting heavy, and possibly valuable antiques and disposing of them in an . . . an arbitrary and eccentric fashion is another. Quite worrying, I might add.' His demeanour made it plain he thought Esme was suffering from the onset of dementia. Throwing valuables in the back of a dustbin lorry being the first sign in his professional opinion.

'Don't be ridiculous, Doctor,' Esme responded, with some of her former spirit. 'I haven't been dispatching Georgian escritoires to the landfill in Jamestoun, despite what the old biddies in your waiting room might have told your receptionist. Apart from which, the opinion of the people on this island has never . . .' She looked as if she was about to explain *exactly* what she thought of the gossip mongers on the island, but Issy cut her off.

'Of course, Doctor,' Issy soothed, and Esme sent her another death stare.

But she didn't care – better the island thought Esme was having a senior moment, than to learn the truth about the disposal of her brother's ashes. That wouldn't go down well on an island - half of whose residents openly believed in the supernatural and the other half who followed the strict tenets of the Presbyterian Church.

'Her blood pressure is a bit low, bring her into the surgery in a couple of days when –' At least he had the good sense not to say – *when she's in a more receptive frame of mind.* That might well have proved a bridge too far. 'I'll check her over again.'

'I'll see you out, Doctor,' Issy said, hurrying him along. Now Esme appeared to be getting over whatever had caused her shock, Issy was worried that her aunt might have more forcible opinions to impart. 'Sorry to have called you out, but she really did look quite poorly when we got her back from The Pickled Herring.'

'The Pickled Herring?' He raised an eyebrow, implying that Esme had downed one too many port and lemons and was paying the price. Knowing they couldn't afford to upset the sensibilities of the priggish GP, Issy gave a tight smile and edged him towards the door.

'Let me, Issy,' Brodie interjected from the window, where he'd been waiting quietly, giving the doctor time and space to make his diagnosis. 'This way, Doc.'

'Thank you, Brodie.' Issy smiled, standing with her arms folded and a pensive look on her face. The front door closed and Brodie re-entered the room, the pleats of his kilt swinging against his knees in a fashion that made the phrase *the waggle o' the kilt* appear woefully inadequate. It was as if Issy was functioning on two levels – anxiety for her aunt and the outcome of her meeting Menzies McIntosh occupying her mind, while proximity to Brodie McIntosh was making the blood pump through her veins at warp speed. Just as well Doctor Brown hadn't fastened the blood pressure cuff over *her* arm. The potent cocktail of stress and wanton desire would have made the machine explode.

Brodie joined her, laying his arm across her shoulders and touching her neck in a proprietary fashion. Unconsciously mirroring his actions, Issy unfolded her arms and snaked one round his waist, pulling him close. United in their concern for Esme's welfare, they looked down at her aunt in the ensuing silence.

'Want to enlighten me as to what all *that* was about, Esme?' Issy asked.

'Want to tell, me what *that's* about?' Esme parried, waving her hand in the direction of Brodie's hand which had found its way through the thicket of Issy's dark hair and was now massaging the back of her neck.

'I asked first.' Issy's tone made it clear that she wasn't to about to let Esme off the hook.

Esme lay back on the cushions and closed her eyes, looking as if her customary fire had been extinguished, leaving her bone-weary and tired. When she eventually opened them again, they had a faraway look, as if she was remembering a past which seemed more relevant than the moment she was living in.

'I'll try. Brodie, give me your kilt pin.'

'Sure.' Puzzled, he unfastened the kilt pin and handed it over to her.

'Reading glasses, Issy. They're over by the newspaper, my dear

- thank you.' Issy handed over the glasses and Esme gave the kilt pin a thorough examination. Taking in shaky breaths, she held onto it momentarily before exhaling. 'This pin shows two dolphins flanking a hunter-killer submarine, the kilt Brodie's wearing was commissioned for the officers and men who manned submarine squadron 14, based in Holy Loch in the early sixties. The men who serviced the submarines were based on board the tender USS Proteus —'

'The Proteus whose anchor chain you climbed?' Issy immediately regretted her interruption as it earned her one of Esme's quelling looks.

'Issy, I won't be able to finish my tale if you keep up with the running commentary. Of course I'm referring to *that* Proteus.'

'Sorry, Esme. Go on.' Luckily, Esme was eager to tell her story and was prepared to forgive the interruption.

'Seeing Brodie in that kilt was quite a shock. It took me back to the days when I was young and foolish - a bit of a wannabe revolutionary. A time when I felt alive – and thought the world was mine to command. Turned out that it wasn't.' She shrugged and tailed off, as if remembering the letters stowed safely away in her bedroom. 'As for your pin, I have its neighbour,' she used the old-fashioned word. 'Its match. It was given to me in exchange for – for something else.' At that point her voice quavered, but she pressed her lips together - steeling herself for the tale she had to tell. 'I haven't looked at it in years . . . Issy, would you fetch down the long, thin box from on top of the bookcase, lovely?'

Issy reached up and groped around until her fingers locked on an old tin which had once held biscuits for cheese. She handed the tin to Esme who opened it and brought out a swatch of tartan which matched Brodie's plaid. Fastened to it was a submarine badge, twin to the one Brodie had handed to her earlier.

Puzzled, he knelt at Esme's feet, took the swatch out of her hands and compared the badge to his kilt pin. 'Identical,' he said to Issy over his shoulder. Then he turned his head and sent Esme a look of dawning comprehension.

'To be honest, I don't know why I kept this,' Esme said, holding Brodie's gaze. However, her expression made it plain that she knew *exactly* why she'd kept it, but wasn't ready to share it with them. At least - not yet. 'I thought – I *had* thought, that one day –' She pulled herself up short and left the sentence unfinished. 'I'd thought that one day I - we'd - return the keepsakes we'd exchanged, and . . . However, fate had other plans.'

The swatch of tartan and the pin, coupled with the letters discovered in the outhouses, marked a chapter in Esme's life of which Issy knew little. Esme barely mentioned the life she'd led before taking on the role of Issy's guardian in the mid-eighties when Isabella had left for Milan and James for Edinburgh. The edited version she'd shared a couple of days ago was the closest she'd come to opening up about her life. However, the past was catching up with her – with all of them, whether they liked it or not. Ancient secrets were being unearthed; old bones and sad memories revealed in the process.

The business of Twa Burns' ownership had just become more complicated.

Holding back the swatch of tartan and the badge, Esme handed the tin over to Issy – indicating that it should be put back on top of the bookcase. Issy sighed; just when she thought she'd made sense of everything, she was back to square one. What *wasn't* Esme telling them? There were gaps in this story – massive ones. How could she help Esme gain closure if she wouldn't even reveal the sex of the child she'd given birth to? Or what had happened to it? Using the moment to compose herself before turning round, Issy was beset with the need to go walking on the beach. That's where she did her best thinking. But, equally, she was loathe to leave Esme on her own in case she had a relapse.

Turning round, she wondered how to broach the subject. Demonstrating an uncanny ability to read her mind, Esme dismissed her concern.

'I'm not ready for a shawl over the legs and being put to bed before half past seven, Ishabel Stuart. I've merely had a wee *palpatooral* – a shock, brought on by finding the letters and seeing Brodie in that kilt. Pour me a glass of brandy and then off you go, back to The Pickled Herring. You're down to sing again this evening, Issy, and you can't let them down. I've got some thinking to do. And I need to be on my own for that. But, before you go – bring the letters through from my bedroom.'

Issy knew better than to argue with her aunt in this mood and did as she was told. Brodie raised a quizzical eyebrow, and Issy mouthed *I'll explain, later*. She hadn't shared the business of Esme's letters or the disposal of her father's ashes with Brodie. She needed Esme's permission for that. She'd tell him on the way to The Pickled Herring - before the island tom-toms beat her to it.

'We'll go back to the Herring, Esme,' Issy conceded, 'but on one condition. You let Brodie fetch Mary Tennant to keep an eye on you until we get back.'

'I don't need a babysitter!' Esme protested. 'Besides, Mary works too hard, I don't want to bother her.'

'Very well, in that case . . . good night, Brodie. Return to the Herring; tell Irene to scrub me off the running order . . .'

'God; when did you become so bossy, Issy? Okay, okay – ring Mary, if you must.'

'Resistance *is* futile,' Brodie agreed, pouring Esme out a small snifter of brandy and handing it over. 'Guess the apple didn't fall too far from the tree, huh, Esme?' He grinned as Issy spoke to Mary over the phone.

'Less of your cheek, young man. Don't think I haven't noticed the electricity sparking between you two. There's enough charge in the atmosphere to power a generator. We'll save *that* discussion for another time. Now away with you. I'm fine; the shock was simply an overreaction at seeing your kilt. It just dredged up old memories, nothing more.' *Memories best forgotten*, her expression suggested. Then she brightened, rationalising it all. 'There must be hundreds of the things kicking around in attics all over the world, keeping the moths happy.'

'You may be right about that,' Brodie conceded. 'The tartan is worn by the U.S. Naval Academy Pipes and Drums, nowadays, and I'm sure second-hand kilts make their way onto eBay all the time.'

'That's all sorted,' Issy said, ending her phone call. 'Once Mary arrives, we'll leave you in peace. It's been quite a night. I'm not really in the mood for singing, but *someone*,' she shot Brodie a suspicious look, 'has requested the *Ballad of Sule Skerry*.'

'Wonder who that could be?' Brodie adopted an innocent expression.

'So, Brodie, tell me about your t-shirt,' Esme asked, deftly moving them on.

'Lindy ordered the t-shirt on line; one for herself and one for me.' He pulled himself up to his full height so that the material lost its folds and creases and Esme could read the logo - *RUADH GU BRATH*. 'I took her word that it said nothing rude or offensive, or could get me in trouble. But you know Lindy . . . I like the folks round here, they've been really accepting of me - I wouldn't want to upset anyone, unnecessarily.'

I wouldn't want to upset anyone, unnecessarily.

He and Issy exchanged a significant look, sharing the same thought. The restoration of Twa Burns was nowhere near a done deal. They could hardly introduce his grandfather to Esme, let alone broach the subject of the disputed ownership until she'd recovered from her reaction to seeing the old kilt. What else might be dredged up in the process? Clearly, the closure they wished for would have to be delayed until Esme was well enough.

'*Redheads forever*,' Esme translated. 'Typical bit of Lindy self-promotion. Although, redheads – be they strawberry-blonde, Pre-Raphaelite or copper nobs, are nothing out of the ordinary on *Eilean na Sgairbh*. Red hair is a reminder of our Viking heritage – and years of inbreeding.' She laughed at Brodie's expression. 'But don't tell anyone I said that.'

'I'll go and fetch Mary,' he said, making a diplomatic withdrawal.

Issy waited until she heard his Land Rover roar off up the road, and then turned on her aunt.

'Okay, now we're alone, do you want to tell me what's really going on here?'

'No more questions, Issy. Not tonight. Okay?' She held out her hands and Issy took them. She knelt at Esme's feet and reluctantly agreed to her request, devoting attention instead to trying to rubbing warmth back into her aunt's ice cold hands.

Chapter Thirty Three
Beware of Islanders Bearing Gifts

T he first of the visitors arrived before Sunday Service at Mungo's wee church overlooking The Narrows. Much to Issy's embarrassment, she was still in her pyjamas when she opened the door to Margot Munro and three other churchgoers, dressed in best hats, matching handbags and shiny, wide-fitting shoes.

'Are you no well, Issy,' Margot asked, implying that was the only possible explanation for still being in pyjamas at nine thirty on a Sunday morning. Craning her neck, she looked past Issy and down the corridor which led into the square hall. It was difficult to judge if she was looking for Esme, or – which was more likely, trying to find out if Brodie had spent the night at *Ailleag*. Tongues had wagged and clacked down at the Post Office during his stay as a paying guest, but now he was renting the eco-lodge, such behaviour would be unacceptable. He could have only *one* reason for spending the night at Esme's house – and it had nothing to do with saving money. Much as islanders extolled that particular virtue!

Added to which, given Esme's history, few on *Eilean* na

Sgairbh would consider her a suitable chaperone. Bristling, Issy drew upon her inner resources and managed to find a charming smile. 'No well? I mean, not well?'

After more than a month on *Eilean na Sgairbh*, Edinburgh seemed a lifetime away. Issy found herself slipping into the easy ways of the island, and that included speaking like a native and reacquainting herself with the Gaelic she'd learned as a child. Not that *going native* presented a problem per se, Cormorant Island was to be her home for the foreseeable future. No; it was simply easier to hide behind a layer of Edinburgh sophistication and businesslike manner when dealing with anyone outside her circle of trust.

'And yer auntie?' Margo inquired, as Issy seemed disinclined to give too much away. On cue, the other three ladies shuffled forward and practically pushed Margot over the threshold. 'How is she today?'

'Much better. Wait . . .' But Issy's protest was in vain as Margot's gang shoulder-barged their way into the hall, closing the front door behind them. Despite having won million-pound contracts for Ecosse Designs, when it came to handling the matrons of Cormorant Island, Issy was a complete novice. Especially when those matrons had shoulders the Scottish Women's Rugby team would be proud of - and knew how to use them to good effect.

'That's rare, so it is. Lead the way, Issy, we have gifts . . .' As if by magic, jars of homemade marmalade, tablet, Dundee cake and a flask of soup were produced from handbags. 'Down here, is it? Esme will be glad to see us, I'm after thinking.'

416

I'm after thinking, she won't! For the sake of diplomacy, Issy kept her thoughts to herself as the Cormorant Island mafia pressed themselves against the walls and allowed her to pass between them. Powerless, she ushered them further into the house. 'This way, ladies.'

Esme was sitting at the kitchen table reading the paper and Pershing was on his perch by the window. When the deputation pushed through the door, she dropped her paper in surprise and frowned over her reading glasses. However, the ladies, for whom Mrs Doubtfire was a style icon, were not put off. For years, they'd longed to be invited inside *Ailleag*; now they'd made it as far as Esme Stuart's kitchen, they were in no hurry to leave. They stared around the room, openly taking mental notes, ready to report back to the other ladies in the kirk after morning service, that Esme Stuart was still in her nightie at nine thirty on the Sabbath. *And* kept a bottle of whisky on the table next to the milk and cornflakes.

'Margot?' Esme inquired, none too politely. 'You wanted something?'

'We were on our way to the kirk and thought we'd pop in to see how you were, after your wee 'turn' at The Pickled Herring the other night. See, we've brought food to build you up . . . in your convalescence. Ye ken?' She gestured to the other ladies who stopped staring at the surroundings and shuffled forward like the Magi, bearing gifts.

'I ken fine,' Esme replied shortly. 'It's very kind of you, but I am in no need of convalescence. As for my 'wee turn', as you put it, it was simply a combination of a long drive up from England, and overdoing things while I was down there.'

'Aye, England'll do that tae a body,' one of the other ladies commented, nodding darkly as they left their gifts on the kitchen table. 'I went there once. I never went back.' A chorus of *aye* . . . *aye*, greeted this, as though she'd been lucky to escape with her life.

'I really don't think . . .' Esme's impatience was beginning to show, so Issy stepped in.

'Oh look, Esme – tablet; you love that. Jam, Dundee cake and –' she shook the flask experimentally, like a cocktail shaker. 'Soup?'

'Cockaleekie. Just the thing for an invalid.' Esme reared up at the word and looked about to say something rude, so Issy intervened for a second time.

'Jewish penicillin,' she joked. However, judging by the churchgoers puzzled expressions, the reference went over their heads.

Whoosh – all the way across The Narrows.

'You need building up, Esme. You're unco thin,' Margot said. The other ladies smoothed down best wool coats over ample bosoms and nodded wisely. 'Living with those hippies, for years; a vegetarian diet, nae doot - tschk.' Tutting, she made the most of Esme's stunned silence at her effrontery, to seat herself at the table. Her three attendants did not have the nerve to join her, but stood to attention by the sink, like elderly bridesmaids.

'I'm overwhelmed.' Esme spoke with heavy irony.

'Och, wheesht, Esme. It's the least we can do. None of us is getting any younger; you were in Primary Three with me – which puts you at, what, seventy-three or four? You've fared better than most of us and don't look your age – but time, anno . . .' she struggled for the word.

'Domini,' Issy supplied, helpfully.

'Aye, *that*; it catches up with us all.' The other three ladies murmured their agreement. It was plain from Esme's thunderous expression that she didn't enjoy being bracketed with her contemporaries, or being consigned to the scrapheap of history. But Margot had moved onto other subjects. 'I see ye dinnae have *The Sunday Post* delivered by Mary Tennant, like the rest of us, then?' Margot held up Esme's copy of *The Observer* for the others to see, as if it was Exhibit A. The newspaper was evidence of Esme's left wing sentiments and informed them that it would take more than a palpatooral for her to start ordering *The Daily Mail*.

They took a collective step away from the table, as if Esme's newspaper was the equivalent of Salman Rushdie's *Satanic Verses.* Just as well they were unaware of the scorched first edition of Lady Chatterley in Esme's study!

'It simply wouldna be a Sunday for me, unless I'd read Our Wullie and The Broons,' one of the visitors commented, referring to characters in *The Sunday Post*'s comic section, which they'd all read since childhood. 'After – after church, naturally.'

Another chorus of *aye . . . aye.*

'Mr Brodie no around?' Margot asked, checking the draining board for three breakfast plates. 'He's a fine figure of a man,' she informed Issy, a prompt for her to reveal the nature of their relationship. 'Even if he's not Scottish,' she added.

'Brodie doesn't live here, he's taken up residence with his grandfather in the eco-lodge. I thought everyone knew that.' Issy smiled, but the smile was as false as her aunt's welcome. In the distance, the kirk's bell could be heard, summoning the faithful to church. 'I'd offer you all a cup of tea, but . . .' she shrugged.

Saved by the bell!

'Mungo can't be kept waiting,' Margot agreed. 'No, don't get up Esme, save your strength. We can come back and visit you another day when you're feeling better. Then you can tell us all about the antiques you threw away in the recycling lorry. What're you like, Esme Stuart?' she trilled, as if amused by the incident. 'You hav'nae changed since you were a wean.' The visiting party joined in with her laughter at Esme's latest eccentricity.

'I don't need to save my strength, but thank you for the thought.' Esme stood up, to demonstrate that she could still put one foot in front of another.

However, Margot's attention was now focused on Issy.

'I hear that yer not going back to Edinburgh, after that business with your fiancé, Issy. Just as well, as your auntie will need looking after . . . Is that no right, Esme?' Having no intention of answering either of Margot's questions, Issy opened her arms and ushered them towards the front door. Like wayward sheep who had lost their way.

'Now, ladies . . . I wouldn't want you to miss the service,' she said with a sweet smile.

'*Feck off,*' Pershing called out, loud and clear. '*Gei'us a drap o' the swally, doll,*' he added for good measure. Their shocked expressions said it all – the bird was the spawn of Satan, old age and a palpatooral hadn't robbed Esme Stuart of her prickly manner; and her niece had given herself to the tall American.

They'd pray for them; pray for them all at the kirk this morning. And give thanks to God for *their* simple lives . . . Then they'd return next week to pay another visit. When Issy returned to the kitchen, she found Esme with her head in her arms, half slumped over *The Observer*.

'Coffee, Esme?' she asked. More to get Esme to raise her head than for any other reason.

'Yes; please. And put a slug of Twa Burns in it. They obviously think the worst of us and it would be a shame to disappoint them,' she said, with grim humour. 'I wish their visit was motivated by kindness, but I know they're using my 'wee turn' as an excuse to pry into our lives and to hammer home the fact that I'm just like them. Anno domini, indeed,' she harrumphed.

'Esme,' Issy came round to her side of the table and enfolded her aunt in her arms. 'It'll take more than a stiff perm, a matronly bosom and the hide of a rhinoceros to make you *remotely* like them.' She kissed the top of her aunt's head and gave her another squeeze. 'Anyhow, I think we should have our coffee and then get dressed. Something tells me we'll be having more visitors before the day's over.'

'You're right. And I'll try hard to be more agreeable. You have plans to make your future here, I wouldn't want to jeopardise that.'

Issy walked over to the sink and slowly filled the kettle, using it as a ruse to hide her expression. Margot Munroe and her ladies she could cope with. Brodie and his grandfather were a different matter altogether. She had a gut feeling that the day of reckoning was at hand.

'And *you* didn't help matters any, Pershing,' she chided the parrot who glanced at her over his hunched up shoulder.

'*Silly tart,*' he said, pooping loudly and noisily onto the sand tray below his perch.

'Quite,' said Issy, putting the kettle back on the hob and lighting the gas.

At one point during that long Sunday, Issy thought of issuing timed tickets to admit those who wanted to pay their respects and inquire after Esme's health. They'd been 'popping in' all morning and the effort of keeping up the appearance of enjoying their company had proved exhausting. Under the pretext of her aunt needing to rest, Issy had finally been able to usher them out of the house, via the back door. She followed that by closing the shutters in the study and pulling down the blinds on all the side windows. Although *Ailleag* had a massive loft extension which ran the length of the house, it was in essence a bungalow. There was nowhere to hide, and anyone walking up the side of the house would see them sitting in the kitchen and demand entry.

Both Issy and Esme were beginning to regard Esme's

Wilderness Years - when she'd been estranged from the islanders, with a degree of nostalgia.

'Come on, Esme. Let's go into the sitting room - and if anyone else calls, we won't answer the door. You're a nine-day wonder - with your alleged disposal of antiques in the back of the recycling lorry, and your wee turn at the Herring. Once they see you shopping at the General Store, ask a few more impertinent questions and you bite their heads off, things'll return to normal.'

'You think?'

'I know.'

But Issy didn't know; and that was the point.

She had a niggling feeling that the proposed meeting with Brodie and his grandfather would make today's stream of visitors seem like a pleasant interlude. Earlier, she'd sent Brodie a text message explaining how they'd had enough visitors for one day. Maybe he and his grandfather could call by tomorrow? Or, better still, the day after – using the pretext of a visit to Jamestoun to call in and pay their respects? Brodie hadn't answered; however, Issy had put that down to the hit-and-miss nature of the signal on Cormorant Island. She'd probably achieve a better result if she tied a message to a cormorant's leg and sent it off in the direction of the eco-lodges. Her father's legacy to install phone masts on the far side of the island couldn't happen quickly enough, in her opinion.

'That's a fierce face you're pulling, Issy. Penny for them.'

'Och, you wouldn't want to know what's in my mind, Esme. My cerebral cortex – or whatever – must resemble tightly coiled strands of spaghetti; messages just aren't getting through. A bad case of brain fog.' She gave a rueful shrug of her shoulders.

'Must be a side effect of being in love with Young Brodie . . .'

'Esme!'

'Don't you *Esme* me in that indignant tone, Missy. I've got eyes, and I'm not so old that I've forgotten what *that* feeling is like.' Tellingly, she touched the airmail letters which were next to her on the coffee table.

Issy drew in a deep breath. 'Esme . . .'

'Yes?'

'When things have settled down, would you tell me more about the letters, the – the child; everything that happened back then?'

'Of course. When things have settled down and the house is less like Piccadilly Circus . . .' As if in direct response, there was a knock on the front door. 'Ignore it; they'll go away,' Esme suggested. Issy did just that, but the knocking continued, then they heard feet crunching over the gravel drive down the side of the house. They held their breath as the knocking started again, this time at the back door.

After a few moments it stopped and then Issy's iPhone quacked, signifying a text message.

IT'S BRODIE. CAN WE COME IN?

Issy sucked in a breath *–WE* could only mean one thing.

'Esme, it's Brodie. I – I'll be back in a minute. You stay put.' Nodding, Esme picked up her letters to re-read them for the umpteenth time and Issy rushed into the kitchen.

Brodie and his grandfather were visible through the glass panels on the kitchen door, flowers in hand. Issy's heart was beating fit to burst and she wasn't sure if that was down to apprehension at seeing Menzies on her step and all that implied, or the fact that she missed Brodie and wanted to rush into his arms.

The only place she felt safe these days.

'Cool and calm, Ishabel,' she counselled herself. 'One step at a time. You can't afford to get this wrong.'

Chapter Thirty Four
I Just Called to Say...

'Sorry,' Brodie mouthed at Issy as she opened the door to admit him and his grandfather.

Although feeling very much on the back foot by their sudden appearance, she managed a weak smile.

'Mingus, Brodie – welcome to *Ailleag*, I –'

'How's your aunt today?' Menzies cut to the chase, twisting the bouquet of flowers in his hands, as nervous as a boy on a Prom date. Now where had that thought come from, Issy wondered, reaching out for the flowers? 'They're for your aunt.' Menzies held the bouquet closer to his chest, reluctant to hand them over.

'She – she's resting. I – I'll put the flowers in water and make sure she gets them when she wakes up . . .'

'That's okay,' Menzies responded, 'I'll wait.' He pulled out the pine carver and took his place at the head of the table, as if it was his right. Just as Brodie had done that first morning when Issy had shared breakfast with him. What was it with the McIntoshes? Did they have an overdeveloped sense of entitlement – always expecting the best seat, choicest cut, finest wine?

'Would you like tea or coffee, Mingus?' Issy asked, ears straining in case Esme was moving around in the sitting room. She had to get to her first and explain how things stood – head Menzies and Brodie off at the pass.

'Know what? I'd love a glass of Twa Burns, if that's okay with you, Issy?' He nodded towards the bottle on the table. It'd virtually lived there since Esme and Mary Tennant had shared a glass the day they'd found the letters in the outhouse; the day Esme had thrown James' earthly remains in the recycling lorry.

'Of course,' she smiled, turning her back to pour out the scotch. *What's going on?* she mouthed at Brodie, hoping he was a gifted lip-reader. But he shrugged, as baffled as she was. Smiling sweetly, she turned, handed the whisky to Menzies and waited until he'd taken his first sip. 'Do you mind if I borrow Brodie?'

'Sure. Go ahead. I'll just savour this and hope that your aunt wakes up – real soon.' Judging by his tone it was plain he wasn't buying her delaying tactics. He bent his head to sniff the uisge beatha and Issy made the most of the opportunity to grab Brodie by the sleeve and drag him out of the room.

Once in the inner hall, she rounded on him. 'What the hell's going on? I thought we'd arranged to leave it a few more days before. . .'

'I know. I know.' Brodie raised his hand to ward off her anger. 'But Gramps can be very strong-minded. He's determined to bring the business with the ownership of Twa Burns to a satisfactory conclusion.'

'Satisfactory for whom?' Leaning against the wall, Issy folded her arms across her chest in a defensive pose. It was odd; for years she'd considered herself the sole heir to Twa Burns – albeit with insufficient funds to restore it to its former glory. Now, finding that she'd have share it with the McIntoshes . . . well, it didn't sit easily with her.

'Issy, I don't know. Since Gramps arrived in *Eilean na Sgairbh* he's been very much in the driving seat. He's the head of the family and used to getting his own way. Once his mind's made up, there's nothing I – or anyone else, can do to change it.' He touched Issy's folded arm, tentatively. Without thinking she shrugged off his touch. 'Issy – don't let this come between you and me. What we've got – what we could have . . .' Issy raised her head and looked into his face. His eyes were clouded with anxiety, his usual easygoing smile nowhere in evidence.

Unfolding her arms, she sighed and relaxed a little. 'You're right, Brodie. Trouble is, I feel like I'm losing not only my share of Twa Burns, but I'm losing you; *us*.'

'Issy . . .'

'*Us*,' she repeated, as if he hadn't spoken. 'Brodie and Ishabel of – of Mermaid Rock – lost; submerged beneath letters from the past, palpatoorals at the Herring and Mingus' arrival. Will we ever get 'us' back, do you think?'

With a groan, Brodie closed the gap between them and enfolded her in his arms. His body was warm and sweet smelling and Issy's reserve crumpled – reflexively, she raised her face for his kiss and sighed when it came. The kiss was deep and lingering and communicated his longing to have her in his arms; in his bed. Issy felt as if she'd just descended in a very fast lift – the last few feet in freefall. She relaxed, nothing had changed. The passion between them was just as strong – each kiss, touch and embrace only serving to make them want more.

'Nothing's gonna come between us, Issy. Not if we don't want it to. I don't give a damn about Twa Burns, bombed-out distilleries, or Gramps' pipe dream – not if it means I can't have you. And I want you, with every inch of my being. Never doubt that.'

The words were whispered against Issy's ear. She shivered, almost convulsively, as yearning for him, and for everything they'd shared swept over her.

'I don't doubt it, or you. But we have two very determined, not to say bloody-minded elders to bring together and a deal to broker. So . . . one more kiss and let's to it.' Although her tone was businesslike, the look she directed at Brodie was scorching. Linking hands behind his neck, she pulled him down to her level and steadied herself against the wall. Wrapping her right leg around his calf and slipping her hands down the back of his jeans, she drew him into her soft curves. Brodie groaned against her lips and when her tongue entered his mouth, he pressed his full weight on her, leaving her in no doubt that every inch of him desired her. For several minutes they were lost in each other and when they pulled apart, their breaths were ragged, uneven. Putting space between them, Issy adjusted her clothing and sent Brodie one last rueful, loving look.

Then they went their separate ways. Brodie to the kitchen and Issy to the sitting room.

Esme was standing by the fireplace and looking into the ornate overmantle mirror. When she turned, it was obvious that she'd reapplied her make-up, using blusher and lipstick to banish the pale, washed-out look which had dogged her since the night at The Pickled Herring. She'd also pulled up the blinds so the sun setting across The Narrows warmed the room and touched the threads of copper-gold in her hair.

She looked excited, wired. Issy frowned. What exactly was going on here? What was she not seeing?

'Esme, we have a visitor . . .'

'I know.'

'No, that's just it, you *don't* know. It's no one from the island – it's Br-'

'Issy, I *know.*' Her reply was so definite that Issy stalled. As she searched for the words to prepare Esme for the shock of learning that the McIntoshes were about to claim half of the Stuarts' inheritance, the door opened and Brodie walked in with Menzies. Issy shrugged helplessly and decided to let things unfold, but to be on hand if events proved too much for Esme. Brodie would do no less for his grandfather.

'Good evening, Esme,' Brodie began, 'You're looking better. May I introduce my – '

'Hello, Mingus; I've been expecting you.' Esme took a step away from the fireplace and walked towards him with her hands outstretched. 'You're late,' she chided, softly.

'Fifty years too late.' Menzies handed – almost tossed, the flowers to Issy as if they were of no importance. He took Esme's hands in his own, bent his head and kissed her on both cheeks.

'It's *never* too late.' Esme's face was filled with a tenderness and radiance Issy had never seen before, as though she'd been holding it back for this very moment.

'Esme . . .'

'I have your keepsake.' Esme reached into the pocket of her summer cardigan and retrieved the swatch of plaid and the kilt pin.

'And I've got yours.' Menzies pulled a silver quaich out of his jacket pocket. The same quaich Issy had knocked to the floor the morning she'd shared Brodie's bed. A quaich which she now recognised as the one in the silver framed photo on Esme's mantelpiece.

'You – you two know each other?' Issy asked, somewhat unnecessarily.

'Oh yes, we know each other,' Menzies confirmed, placing the swatch of plaid on the table and reaching for Esme's hands again.

'But . . .' It was Brodie's turn to look mystified. 'What the . . . How?' Issy remembered that he knew nothing about the letters, the child given up for adoption, her father's ashes. There had been no time to bring him up to speed because events had overtaken them.

Withdrawing her hands, Esme walked over to the sofa and sat down. She placed the quaich on a side table, patted the cushions and indicated that Menzies should come and sit next to her. Reaching for the faded airmail letters, she fanned them out on the empty cushion between them.

'My letters,' Menzies exclaimed. 'You kept them! But, I thought – '

'Not so much *kept* them as, *found* them.'

'I don't understand.' Menzies shook his head, uncomprehendingly.

'Issy, take my flowers and put them in water, and wait in the kitchen with Brodie until I ask you to join us.' Issy knew that tone, it brooked no refusal. She and Brodie exchanged a look. They'd thought they were in control of events, that they'd be the ones to decide how and when Esme would learn the truth about the distillery. Instead, they'd been outclassed and outgunned. Brodie held out his hand and Issy took it, feeling very much surplus to requirements; Esme's next words confirmed it. 'And, darling Issy – '

'Yes, Esme?'

'Close the door behind you on your way out.'

Chapter Thirty Five
The Truth is Out There

'Well, I'll be damned,' Brodie pronounced, rejecting tea in favour of a glass of Twa Burns. He knocked back a dram of the eighty-year-old single malt, like a man who'd reached the end of a gripping novel – only to discover that the last page had been ripped out. 'What just happened in there, Issy? Pershing? Anyone?'

Sensing that a response was required, Pershing obliged with: '*Ban the Bomb. Ban the Bomb.*' As if Menzies McIntosh's arrival in *Ailleag* had taken everyone back to the moment when the planet had stood poised on the brink of nuclear Armageddon.

'Not helping, Pershing,' Issy said, more sharply than intended. The parrot spat his nut onto the floor, shuffled along his perch and huddled in the corner in a huff.

'*Bad Boy, Pershing,*' he said, playing to the gallery. Then he looked over his shoulder in the hope that Issy would come over and pet him.

'Ban the bomb?' Brodie repeated. 'I'm guessing all *this* – the swatch of plaid, the badge, and the quaich goes back to when

Gramps was on the Proteus and docked in Holy Loch. But . . . how come he and Esme exchanged gifts in the first place? And . . . what were those letters Esme spread out on the couch between them?'

'I – I'm guessing they were written by your grandfather. I'm also wondering what else she has secreted away in the cracker tin.'

Uncomfortable that she couldn't reveal everything she knew, Issy hid her expression. It would all be explained, she told herself, when Esme and Menzies rejoined them. Besides, it would be better for him to learn the facts first hand, from Menzies. In the interim, he'd have to be patient. Pouring herself a dram of Twa Burns, Issy recalled Brodie telling her that the eighty-year-old single malt was worth a fortune – and here they were, drinking it like it was Irn Bru. Before Brodie had told her of his grandfather's claim to half of Twa Burns, she'd considered auctioning off the remaining bottles to raise money for her artists' studios. After tonight, however, she guessed that any money raised would be earmarked for paying her and Esme's share of rebuilding the distillery. Her plans for the workshops/studios had been kicked into touch. She sighed.

Twa Burns and everything connected with it was no longer, exclusively, *theirs*. Hers and Esme's. That would take some getting used to.

'*Slainte mhath*.' Brodie clinked his glass against hers, breaking her dream. 'You okay, Issy?'

'I'm fine,' she lied. 'How about you?'

'I'm good.' Although undoubtedly worried about what was unfolding in the sitting room, he was nevertheless doing his best to hide his anxiety. Replacing his glass on the table, he rubbed his face with his hands. '*Good?* Who am I kidding? I'm tying myself in knots here, trying to figure out what Gramps and Esme are discussing in there.' He jerked his thumb towards the sitting room.

Issy put down her glass. She'd grown up with stories of Esme's derring do; her peacenik days when she'd blockaded Holy Loch in a kayak alongside the *Glasgow Eskimos*, getting arrested outside the American Embassy during the Grosvenor Square riots, breaching the perimeter fence at Greenham Common, wire cutters in hand. She knew it all, chapter and verse – as did everyone else on the island. Esme made no secret of her politics, or the years she'd spent on the hippy trail.

The only secret she'd kept from them all was the child she'd given up for adoption.

Was this child the reason she always returned to Scotland at the end of her travels? Like a homing bird. Did she imagine that one day the child would come looking for her? Issy's heart squeezed in compassion for Esme's loss and for the cousin she would never know.

'Brodie, we'll have to be patient. Menzies and Esme have a lot of catching up to do. They'll bring us up to speed in their own time.' Moving closer, she wrapped her arms around him, bent her head and kissed the back of his neck, breathing in his pheromones. She wished all *this* – Menzies, Esme and Twa Burns would go away and leave her and Brodie free to return to his bedroom in the eco-lodge, where they'd close the shutters and . . .

Focus woman, she counselled herself, focus.

'Guess I'm not very good at being patient,' Brodie said, half-apologetically, grabbing her hands and manoeuvring her onto his knees.

Doubtless, Menzies McIntosh had kept the specifics of his time aboard the USS Proteus on a *need to know* basis with his family. As the tangled weave of the past unravelled, who's to say that Brodie might not come to view things differently? Maybe, even see *her* in a different light?

'Do you doubt me?' He tilted her chin so that he could see her expression.

'Not you. However, *family* is a powerful concept - and Scots are clannish by nature, even if they live thousands of miles away in Kentucky. It's in their DNA. There's only Esme and me . . . and I'm starting to feel outnumbered; the two of us up against the US branch of Clan McIntosh - who'll doubtless have an opinion about rebuilding Twa Burns. They'll be a force to be reckoned with, if your grandfather is anything to judge by.'

'They're bound to have an opinion – sure. But Gramps calls the shots – *and* holds the purse strings; that gives him leverage. I don't envisage my brothers and sister abandoning their careers and comfortable lives to come live and work on *Eilean na Sgairbh*, or get involved in the day-to-day running of the distillery.'

Unconvinced, Issy pulled a face. In her experience, money, or the promise of it, changed people. Jack Innes-Kerr was a prime example; once he'd discovered that James Stuart hadn't left his millions to Issy, he'd suddenly lost interest in her and supplanted her with Suzi the Intern.

'What about you, Brodie?'

'Me?'

'Yes. Could you give up everything and come and live amongst the cormorants?'

'Well, that would depend.'

'On what?' Issy held her breath.

'On the weather conditions on Mermaid Rock during the winter.'

'Weather conditions?' Puzzled, she leaned away from him. Was he serious?

'Yeah, I don't do cold.' Catching the banked-down humour in his eyes, Issy realised that she was over-thinking the whole issue. She was a complete stress-head, always wanting the i's dotted and t's stroked. Sometimes, she realised, that wasn't possible.

'I'm serious, Brodie.'

'And I'm not?'

'I – I'm not sure . . .' Looking down at the well-scrubbed table top, she traced along the grain in the pine with her fingernail. Brodie lowered his head until their eyes were level and she was forced to look up, into his face.

'I've never been more serious about anything in my life. I told you, the first time we made love on Mermaid Rock, that I wouldn't hurt you; nothing has changed. Look at me, Ishabel – I love you and nothing will alter that, except that you doubt me. Now may not be the time, or the place, for declarations of love, but let me spell it out. I fell in love with you that first morning over breakfast - at this very table, even though you made it clear that you wanted me out of *Ailleag* as soon as possible. No woman had even treated me like that . . .' He gave a self-deprecating shrug. 'First, I wanted you to like me. Then I wanted you to love me as much as I loved you. '

'You did?'

'Sure, I did. And, since your father's memorial service, only one thought's been in my mind.'

'Wh – what's that?'

'That in the not too distant future, we'll stand in front of Mungo and the good folk of *Eilean na Sgairbh* and . . .' He paused, and Issy joined up the dots.

'Brodie McIntosh . . .' Issy spoke softly, though her heart was leaping around in her chest like a wild salmon climbing up a waterfall. 'Is this a proposal of marriage?' She took in a shaky breath.

'Yes, Ma'am. Like I said - my timing's lousy. But I want you to know, whatever goes down tonight concerning Gramps, Esme and the McIntosh claim to half of Twa Burns, nothing matters to me other than we spend the rest of our lives together. *That*, Miss Stoo-art, is non-negotiable.'

Even though excitement was fizzing through her veins at his impassioned speech, Issy kept a level head. Brodie was right. They *had* to declare their love for each other before Esme and Menzies walked through the kitchen door. Unconditionally. Unreservedly.

Things would never be as simple as they were in that moment; they would never be as sure again that love, to paraphrase the movie, actually *was* all that really mattered.

'In that case . . .' signifying that she'd reached a decision, Issy lay back in Brodie's arms in a gesture of complete surrender. Unfastening the top three buttons of his shirt, she slid her hand inside and spread her fingers across his chest, starfish-like. His skin was warm and she drew comfort from touching him. Her stress levels dropped correspondingly and, echoing his earlier remark about the timing being lousy, she realised that she wanted nothing more than for Brodie to lay her over the kitchen table and make love to her.

Mad, passionate, impulsive love, the sort the poets write about and which required pyrotechnics, a fifty-piece orchestra and, for added effect, a full complement of cherubim and seraphim blowing trumpets and strumming harps.

Instead, she whispered softly in his ear, 'Brodie . . . D'ye not know that I'll love ye all my days, be they long or short?' Her words all the more powerful for being delivered in a soft, highland cadence. '*Bidh gaol agam ort fad mo bheatha, thusa's gun duine eile. I will love you my whole life, you and no other.* Remember?'

'Is that a yes?' Brodie stilled her questing fingers; like Issy, he had to be sure.

'The ayes have it,' she nodded.

Curving her free hand around his neck, Issy drew him down towards her in a passionate kiss. Brodie returned the kiss with interest, holding her so close that one of the spindles in the pine chair cracked under their weight. As the kiss deepened and their breathing became more rapid, Brodie's hand reached under Issy's t-shirt and cupped her breast.

They were so engrossed in each other that they didn't hear the kitchen door open.

'Get a room, you guys.' Menzies gruff, amused voice dragged them out of the world where only senses and feelings mattered. 'Kids, huh?'

'Gramps!' Brodie was the first to pull back, raising his head to look at the family elders in the doorway. Esme's skin was flushed and Menzies' clothes looked ruffled and untidy. Feeling caught out, he and Issy disentangled their limbs and adjusted their clothing.

'Don't,' Esme interjected. 'Stay just as you are.' Then she noticed Brodie's hand was inside her niece's t-shirt and pulled a comic face. 'Well, maybe not *just* as you are,' she laughed as Brodie removed his hand and then pulled Issy back onto his knee.

Seemingly, witnessing Issy and Brodie so wound up in each other evoked long-forgotten memories for Esme and Menzies. They exchanged a fond glance and joined them at the table. Menzies poured out two fresh glasses of Twa Burns while Esme placed the cracker tin on the table next to her airmail letters, swatch of plaid and the silver quaich.

'This whisky is potent,' Menzies observed, sipping it with great relish. 'And,' he cocked one of his thick white eyebrows in Esme's direction, 'has a lot to answer for.'

'Where to begin . . .' Reaching out, Esme stroked the back of Menzies' hand.

'I was on watch that day when Esme climbed the Proteus' anchor chain,' he said. 'She was some gal - full of piss and vinegar. Almost made it onto the deck, too, before she and other protesters had the hoses turned on them and fell back into Holy Loch. They were hauled out by the police, taken ashore and arrested. You kids have to remember, we're talking about a time when Cold War tension was at its height.'

'It all reads like ancient history now –' Esme put in, 'but –'

'Back then – it felt like the end of days. The world was on the brink of nuclear war. I saw it as my patriotic duty to protect democracy from the spread of communism . . . '

'Whereas, I regarded it as *my* duty to get the Yanks and their goddamn missiles out of *my* Holy Loch.' Esme reached out for Menzies' hand and gave it a squeeze. 'No offence.'

Menzies rushed on, apparently eager to get the story told.

'The image of Esme being fished out of the water by boat hook and thrown on the deck of a police launch haunted me long after they'd sailed away. She looked so small and defenceless.' He gave her a rueful, loving look and his green eyes twinkled. 'Boy, were appearances wrong!'

That raised a laugh, they'd all experienced Esme's determined spirit.

'I hadn't even noticed Mingus, I was too busy spewing water out of my lungs and trying not to drown.'

'I couldn't stop thinking about her. I made it my business to find out who she was, where she lived. I tracked her down to *Eilean na Sgairbh*.'

'He traced me through the newspaper article – the one hanging on my study wall.'

'I lucked out. I couldn't believe that Esme lived on the island where, my father, Archie McIntosh, had been born. It seemed like fate –'

'Karma,' Esme agreed. 'Helped by the fact there was little or no data protection in those days. So – he came to pay his respects, flowers in hand –'

'I took a risk and wore my best uniform to visit this fire cracker. No woman can resist a man in uniform. Right?'

'He did look sexy in his uniform; although,' Esme sent him a severe look, 'I was none too happy to have one of the *enemy*, an officer from the Proteus, standing on my doorstep with flowers in his hand. Like he'd come to court me . . .'

'Which I had.'

'Mingus nearly destroyed my street cred - I tried my best to get rid of him but he stood there, enquiring after my health, all chivalrous – and, did I mention sexy?'

'I think you did, Esme,' Menzies confirmed, sending her a crooked smile.

'With us so far?' Esme asked Issy.

'Ahead of you,' Brodie commented.

'Long story short?' Menzies touched the airmail letters as if they were a talisman. 'I called on Esme and discovered our joint histories. I checked out my father's stories about the Stuarts and the McIntoshes, the distillery, and our share in it. It all stacked up,' Menzies took a sip of his whisky and paused to gather his thoughts. 'But none of that mattered because we . . . '

'Became lovers,' Esme clarified, apparently anxious to keep the story on track. 'However, things were complicated. Mingus had . . .'

'I had a girl back home. A girl my parents wanted me to marry because *her* parents owned a bourbon distillery close to ours. A merger was proposed and our marriage would seal the deal. I was to return to Kentucky at the end of my tour of duty and we'd get married. But there was no way that was going to happen . . . Esme and I made a pact; I'd go home, tell our respective families how things stood.'

'In the meantime, I'd break the news to my family that, after all my anti-American posturing which had alienated half of the island, I wanted to marry an officer stationed – if that's the right word, on board a ship in Holy Loch.'

'Tell the kids what happened next,' Menzies urged, his expression grim.

'I know I keep saying it, but things *were* different in those days; parents expected to be obeyed, and my brother kept a very strict eye on me. I knew they'd never countenance my marrying Mingus, even if he was Archie McIntosh's son – *especially* if he was Archie's son'

'How's that?' Brodie interrupted.

'James suspected that Mingus was only feigning an interest in

443

me. That it was the distillery he had his eye on. He had the money, the lineage and the knowledge to restore the distillery and bring whisky production back to *Eilean na Sgairbh*. You know how strongly opposed James was to *that*.'

Issy shook her head to get all the facts in the right order. 'But wouldn't your father, my grandfather, have welcomed the distillery being rebuilt?'

'Ten or fifteen years earlier he might have, but by this time he was old and infirm. To all intents and purposes, James was the head of the family. He could be quite formidable when he chose, as you well know, Issy,' Esme explained. 'Father simply couldn't, or wouldn't, stand up to him.'

'What then?' Issy prompted.

'Esme didn't answer my letters . . .' said Mingus.

'And we know why.' Esme spoke softly, touching the wafer-thin airmails. 'They were intercepted by James, I'm guessing, and hidden in the roof of the outhouse, where they've remained, unopened, for fifty years. Issy and I stumbled upon them a couple of days ago when cleaning the outhouses.'

'Why didn't your brother just burn them?' Brodie frowned, obviously trying to understand James Stuart's motives.

'I'm guessing that James, being the god-fearing little prig he was, thought he was saving me from descending deeper into sin. However, his scruples wouldn't allow him to burn the letters - that would have been a step too far. Maybe he even thought to give them to me at some point in the future, once Mingus was off the scene and

I was safely married off to some nice laddie from the island. Who knows? Soon after that, James left *Eilean na Sgairbh* and found work on the Govan docks to pay for his passage to America; no doubt, in his mind, the matter was resolved.'

Her expression suggested this was far from the truth.

'Gramps, tell me you came back to look for Esme; to find out why she hadn't answered your letters?' Brodie's expression made it clear that's what he would have done in the circumstances.

'Sure I did, son; but I was refused admittance by James Stuart. Furthermore, he told me Esme had gotten married, moved off the island and had left them strict instructions *not* to tell me where she'd gone.'

'You didn't buy that, did you?'

'Not for a second. I returned several times when I was on leave, haunted The Pickled Herring and all the usual places on the island for information, but no one knew where Esme'd gone. They were pretty tee'd off with her at that point, because she and her friends had made things uncomfortable for the US servicemen who visited here on furlough.'

'I deprived them of their wee *bawbees*,' Esme said, scathingly referring to how trade had dropped off – thanks to her and the other peaceniks.

'Time passed, I was transferred back to the States, wrote more letters which were never answered and I figured . . . hell, maybe I *was* better off without her.'

He reached over and curled his hand round Esme's.

'Meanwhile, I thought he'd abandoned me and my – our -' Esme looked across the table at Menzies, as if unable to carry on with the story. She opened the tin and pulled out a faded piece of paper, cracking at the seams through being read many times over the years.

'Our child,' Menzies said in a quiet voice.

'Child?' Brodie echoed in a stricken voice.

'Yessir! Once those sons of bitches discovered Esme was pregnant, they sent her away, made her give up our child. But the name's on the birth certificate – Mary *Murran* Stuart, so there's no denying I'm the father.'

'I tried to trace Mingus,' Esme went on, her voice catching as she relived those awful times. 'However, the authorities were none too keen on giving out more than name, rank and serial number. Apparently, I wasn't the only lassie left holding a bairn at the end of the summer.' She sighed, refolded the precious birth certificate and placed it on the table between them.

'I don't know what to say.' Brodie looked at his grandfather with dawning realisation. 'I'm guessing that when you sent me over to suss out how things lay regarding the distillery, you were really sending me to find Esme?'

'It's never been about the distillery, it's always been about Esme. I –' He looked so forlorn, his age weighing heavily on him. 'It wasn't until your grandmother passed over, Brodie, that I felt I had the right to give connecting with Esme one last shot. Over the years, I've had . . . people, keep me up to date with what she's been doing.

But none of them picked up that she had a child.'

'I didn't know until a few days ago,' Issy explained to Brodie. 'No one knew.'

'It was nobody's business but mine,' said Esme. 'Mine and Mingus' – and he knows all the facts, now.'

'Which is more than I do,' Issy added, and then flushed, wishing she could call the words back. This wasn't about her and she had no right to feel hurt. She turned to Brodie. 'I'm sorry, I couldn't tell you about the letters or the child. I promised Esme.'

She sighed; this was turning out to be a pretty emotional day. Although, amazingly, Menzies and Esme seemed to be coping with it better than she'd imagined.

'One thing – the child – if I have a cousin somewhere, how do I set about tracking them down?' Brodie demanded to know.

'It's in hand.' Esme's voice was steady and she took command of the situation.

Now she had Menzies at her side, the after-effects of the wee palpatooral she'd experienced at the Herring had, seemingly, left her. *Full of piss and vinegar,* was how Menzies had described his first impression of her; it looked like nothing had changed! Getting to her feet, Esme glanced at her watch and started raising the kitchen blinds. It was late on a Sunday evening, no one would call now. She petted Pershing as she passed his perch and told him he was a good boy. Amazingly, the voluble parrot had remained quiet throughout this family conference. Perhaps he was more perceptive than they gave him credit for.

'Tea.' Breaking the silence, Issy slid off Brodie's knee, filled the kettle and placed it on the hob. 'And cake. Luckily, the good folk of *Eilean na Sgairbh* have overloaded us with cake. It'll help sop up the whisky.' She paused, listening to herself. 'I really am my father's daughter, aren't I?'

'Not at all, Issy, and you never will be.' Esme joined Issy at the stove and stroked Issy's thick, dark hair. Issy smiled and glanced over at Brodie, holding *their* secret close to her heart. There had been enough revelations for one day; they'd save their news until matters were resolved – Esme and Menzies, the future of Twa Burns, and how they could set about locating their child.

The tell-tale crunch of feet on gravel heralded an uninvited guest walking up the side of the house towards the back door. 'Whoever it is, will be getting a flea in their ear,' Issy said, annoyed. 'We've had enough visitors for one day.'

Chapter Thirty Six
The Great Reveal

The last person Issy expected to find when she opened the door was Mary Tennant. Sundays were sacrosanct in the Tennant household, it being the only day when the family did things together. Even if that meant dragging a reluctant Lindy with them to visit friends and relatives over on the mainland.

'Oh, Mary, hello.' Opening the door a crack wider, she allowed Mary a glimpse into the kitchen, hoping she'd pick up the vibe that something important was being discussed, take the hint and leave. Once she was over the threshold, *Eilean na Sgairbh*'s version of highland hospitality would kick in and Mary would be offered food, drink and treated like a welcome guest.

'Now isn't a good time, Mary . . .' Issy began, only to be interrupted by Esme.

'Au contraire, Issy, it's the best of times.' Her voice had an unfamiliar resonance – soft, sweet and mournful. Its sorrowful quaver caused Issy to stall with her hand on the doorknob and spin round. Taking full advantage of Issy's momentary lapse in concentration, Mary slipped into the kitchen and closed the door quietly, but pointedly, behind her.

'Mary . . .' Issy protested at the intrusion, only to be overruled by Esme.

'Come away in, lassie; you're always welcome here.'

Chastised, Issy stood to one side as Mary brushed past her in a silk tea dress and smelling of some delicious flowery scent. Mary Tennant was a handsome woman, tall and straight and with the tell-tale red gold hair of a typical islander. During the week she dressed as smartly as serving behind the counter at the General Store allowed, often hiding a fashionable outfit underneath a slightly-too-large-for-her, brown overall. Tonight, however, she had cast off her every day work clothes and looked especially attractive – hair freshly washed and styled, make-up immaculate, and sporting a pair of heels even Lindy would approve of.

'Sorry to intrude, Issy, but Esme sent me a text asking me to join you when we got back from visiting Tam's family in Jamestoun. I hope that's okay?' The way she spoke – so quiet and unassuming, made Issy feel a complete heel. Really, the business with Twa Burns and her desire to bring everything to a satisfactory conclusion was making her forget what was really important – friends and family, and Mary Tennant was a friend of longstanding.

'Of course it's alright.' Issy walked over to Mary and gave her a reassuring hug. 'Tea? Or, will you join us in a wee dram of Twa Burns? We're doing our best to finish it off tonight.' She pulled a wry face.

'That's awful kind of you, Issy.' Mary smiled, but her smile was strained – as if she knew Issy didn't want her there.

Sensing that, Issy went on with false brightness. 'Where are my manners? Let me introduce you to Brodie's grandfather . . . Mingus McIntosh.' He had, Issy realised, been standing quietly to one side watching the interchange between them. From the little she knew of Menzies, she guessed that such reticence was uncharacteristic.

'Mingus *Murran* McIntosh, to be accurate,' Menzies said, walking forward to greet Mary. He put a stress on his middle name and Issy wondered if she'd offended him by omitting it. In his eighties, he belonged to a different generation where such things mattered, especially if one was a second generation Scot trying to establish one's highland credentials. However, a second glance assured her that he seemed happy enough. Even if he was staring at Mary Tennant in a manner that was hard to fathom - almost as if he couldn't bear to drag his eyes away.

'Mary Murran Tennant,' she murmured, obviously taking no offence at his staring. Or the fact that he was in no apparent rush to free her hand. Issy observed the exchange, slightly bemused.

Murran, was an island name, but an uncommon one. Goodness knows she'd seen it countless times when dusting the Last Will and Testament glued to the back of the photograph of Archie and Young Johnny.

Menzies released Mary's hand, breaking the trance which had fallen on them. While Issy walked over to the sink, Esme joined Menzies and Mary at the kitchen table. Her face was inscrutable, her brow furrowed – as though she was making a supreme effort to keep her emotions in check. More puzzlingly, Brodie got to his feet, pushed his chair back from the table, and swore softly under his breath.

'Well, I'll be . . .'

The kettle whistled into life and Issy walked over to the stove to attend to it.

Feeling left out, Pershing started chanting, '*Polly put the kettle on,*' as Issy spooned Darjeeling tea into the pot. Pouring boiling water over the leaves, she was only half-aware of the scene playing out behind her.

'Hold your wheesht, Pershing,' she said abstractedly, trying to fathom why the intense atmosphere in the kitchen was making her feel twitchy, ill at ease – as if a storm was brewing. Something in Menzies' very formal greeting, his insistence on using his middle name felt *odd;* out of kilter. She stirred the leaves round in the pot, giving her brain a chance to catch up. When she turned round, Menzies, Brodie, Esme and Mary were looking at *her* curiously, as if waiting for a response.

'What?' She shivered, as though a whole gaggle of geese had just stepped over her grave.

She felt as if she'd fallen asleep during a blockbuster movie, and had woken to find that she'd missed a pivotal scene; the one where the hero gets the girl, or the murderer is revealed. The scene which explains what the movie is really about. 'Why are you all looking at me like that? Anyone want to tell me what's going on? Esme – Mary – Mingus?'

'Issy – haven't you worked it out?' Esme asked, tenderly. 'Mary is our daughter. Mine and Mingus'.'

The scales fell from Issy's eyes as she regarded the group assembled before her, seeing - as if for the first time, the same long straight noses, wide-spaced blue/green eyes, and thick hair in every shade from reddish-brown to strawberry-blond; or in Menzies' case, sandy turned white.

The penny dropped, tumblers clicked into place and she gasped: 'Oh my God, Esme. Are you sure?'

'Sure?'

'Sorry. Stupid question; it's the shock. Of course you're sure. But - Mary . . .?'

'Yes, Mary,' Esme affirmed. 'Our daughter. Your cousin.' She linked a hand though Mary's and Menzies' arms and held them close. Then she laughed as her niece's expression didn't alter. 'You look stunned my darling. Group hug?'

Speechless, Issy walked over, stiff-legged like an automaton. They formed a circle – heads touching, hearts beating, love emanating from every inch of them. After a few moments, astonishment gave way to elation and – in Issy's case – an awareness that the missing piece of the jigsaw had been found and put in place. The puzzle was completed.

She and Brodie were the first to break the circle, they had questions - lots of them, and wanted answers.

'Okay. Time out.' Brodie leaned against the sink with Issy in front of him, his arms around her waist and his chin resting on top of her head. 'Gramps, Esme – you have the floor.'

'I'd better do the talking,' said Esme. 'This turn of events is as new to Mingus as it is to you and Issy. Let's sit.'

They gathered round the table and as a glass of Twa Burns was poured for Mary, Issy suddenly realised that the distillery was Mary's inheritance, too. Tea forgotten, Issy started in with, 'How did Mary end up on *Eilean na Sgairbh* – and running the General Store, if she was given up for adoption?'

Spreading her hands onto the table, Esme studied her fingertips as she gathered her thoughts.

'The short version?'

'Please. The bare bones so I – we,' she looked over at Brodie, 'can make sense of all of this. You can colour in, later.' Before Esme could say a word, Mary spoke. From her expression, it was clear she'd never again be left standing at the back door, like an uninvited guest, waiting to be invited into her mother's house.

'Issy, you – *our* family, the Stuarts, had distant, childless cousins living on the east coast, near Tranent. That's where Esme was sent to give birth to me. Out of sight, out of mind and away from island tittle-tattle. When I was born, those childless cousins became my adoptive parents and they brought me up. When your father left to work in America and, after, your grandfather died, Esme bought the General Store.' She looked across at her mother who took up the story.

'It cost me every last penny the government paid out after the war as reparation for Twa Burns' destruction,' Esme explained. 'I moved my cousin, her husband and *our* child over from Tranent,' she reached out for Menzies' and Mary's hands, 'into the store. As far as everyone on the island was concerned, they were incomers from near Edinburgh; they didn't even know we were related. That was back in . . .' She looked at Mary to supply the dates.

'Nineteen sixty-five, when I was three years old. And I have lived here ever since, as close to Esme as possible, given the circumstances.' She smiled at Esme. 'When I about five years old, everything was explained to me - in simple terms, naturally.'

'Then . . . as she grew in maturity and understanding, she was told more. She was a bright child and quick to understand that everything we told her had to be a secret. Hers and ours.'

'Oh, Esme.' Issy touched her upper arm. 'To think you've kept this secret all these years; that all this time, my cousin lived just down the road.' Her throat thickened and her voice caught as a sudden realisation struck her. 'How awful it must have been when my parents pursued their own selfish interests and left my upbringing to you. When *your* daughter was being raised by other people. Mary – once you were old enough to know the truth, did you resent me?'

'Och, away with ye, Issy – what's past, is past. The truth was never kept from me, and – in fact, our shared secret bonded Esme and me closer together. What you grow up with, you accept, don't you?'

Issy thought about her own dysfunctional childhood and nodded in agreement. In many ways, Mary had experienced the love of three parents, while she . . . Getting to her feet, she fetched a piece of kitchen roll from near the sink and blew her nose, noisily.

'Please – go on,' she said, waving away their concern.

'When my adoptive parents died, Tam and I married and took over the running of the store. With Lindy's help.' Mary pulled a droll expression, and they laughed, lightening the atmosphere. Lindy wasn't meant to spend her life behind the counter of Cormorant Island's General Store and Post Office.

Her future lay elsewhere – Kentucky, maybe?

'I've just realised.' Issy looked at Esme and Menzies. 'Lindy is your –'

'Granddaughter. Yes.'

Now Issy understood why Esme excused Lindy's behaviour and had always been there to support her – and curb her wilder schemes.

'And *my* second cousin?' She clapped her hands over her mouth and gasped in awareness. 'Which makes Brodie my . . .'

'Second cousin by *marriage*.' Menzies joined in the conversation and gave Esme a purposeful look. One Issy had received many times from his grandson. 'At least he will be, as soon as it can be arranged.'

'Special licence; the works,' Esme agreed. 'We've got to make up for lost time.'

'So, let me get this straight – we're not blood relations?' Issy blushed, hating to raise the delicate subject at that particular moment. She'd heard of *kissing cousins* but what she and Brodie got up to in his bedroom back at the eco-lodge – and on Mermaid Rock, progressed wa-ay beyond kisses. 'Or should that be step-second-cousin-by-marriage?'

'Who gives a fu -,' Brodie stopped himself in time. 'Who cares? Forget about second cousins by marriage, Issy and I have a much simpler connection in mind.' The others grouped round the table looked at him uncomprehendingly, their minds still on the previous revelations. He was just about to elaborate when fresh footsteps crunched across the gravel and the back door was unceremoniously thrown back on its hinges.

Bristling with indignation, Lindy stood before them, hands on hips and giving out death stares. 'Well,' she huffed. 'Here's all youse having a party while *I've* had to give Daddy his supper and do a stocktake of the freezer. Typical. Bluddy typical.' Issy rose from the table and gave her new second cousin a great big hug, blinking away the tears misting her eyes and swallowing hard to dislodge the lump in her throat.

'I thought better of you, Brodie, I really did.' Lindy delivered her lines over Issy's shoulder with all the displeasure of a disappointed parent. 'And let go of me, Issy. Have you gone mad? It'll take more than a hug to put things right, let me tell you, *hen.*' At that, they all started to laugh: mother, grandparents, first cousins and second cousins - knowing that for once, they'd stolen the march on Lindy Tennant.

'Come and join us, Lindy – we've got something to tell you; much to explain. And we think you'd better sit down while you're hearing it.' Mary led her indignant daughter to a spare chair round the table. 'Over to you, Mother,' she said to Esme.

They all laughed again as Lindy mouthed *mother?* And then crashed heavily into the chair, her lips forming a perfect, round 'O' of surprise.

'*You silly tart,*' Pershing added, as though he'd known the truth all along.

Chapter Thirty Seven
Le Nozze di Esme e Menzies

C atching her mother's expression in the dressing table mirror, Issy knew that La Bella Scozzese was not best pleased.

'*Oddio, certo non me lo aspettavo,*' she seethed. 'I wasn't expecting *la tua vecchia zia* – your ancient aunt - to pull the rug from under us and marry a billionaire American. Esme has engineered this wedding on purpose, to upstage you. To upstage *me. Vergine santa*! How will I live with *l'umiliazone*?' Clasping her hands together, she gave an award-winning performance of a broken-hearted mother, who'd unknowingly nurtured a viper in her bosom. But her daughter, who'd stopped being impressed by such histrionics years ago, remained unmoved and squirted perfume on her décolletage and applied lipstick instead.

'You can drop the Italian, Mother, it's just you and me and - quite honestly, after your show-stopping performance at my father's memorial service, I'd prefer you to keep a lid on it. Just this once.'

'A lid on it?' Isabella spat out, as though the expression was alien to her.

Their eyes met in the mirror and their gazes locked, so alike -
yet so completely different. La Bella Scozzese was the first to look
away and Issy continued in a stern voice, the role of mother and
daughter reversed.

'A low profile,' Issy explained. 'If you can't behave, you'll be
confined to *Ailleag* and only allowed to join us at the wedding
breakfast, where – should you guarantee not to spoil Esme's day –
you will be allowed to sing your aria.'

'Allowed! I, La Bella Scozzese, *allowed* to sing at a wee heilan'
wedding? When opera lovers around the world would consider it an
honour - and pay me a king's ransom to sing at their nuptials.' Then,
reading the determination in Issy's face, she quietened down. 'Very
well,' she sighed, and drew on her silk gloves, ready to leave for the
church. 'I will be 'appy to sing an aria from the *Marriage of Figaro*
at Esme's wedding breakfast. The one, incidentally, I *was* saving for
your wedding day. But, no matter – opera is brimming with such
arias.' She reached for the tissue box, extracted a tissue and blew her
nose, noisily.

'When the day comes, Mamma, I will be very happy for you to
sing at my wedding.'

'Very well, Carissima.' Isabella fiddled half-heartedly with her
daughter's hair until Issy slapped her hand away. 'If it makes you
happy, I will behave myself.'

'You'd better,' Issy warned, although she did believe her mother
– this time. Last night, Isabella had arrived in *Eilean na Sgairbh* with
just two of her 'people' in tow and no hidden cameras. So far, so

good. Could it be that she'd learned her lesson?

'On the subject of weddings, I have something to tell you . . . now, don't pull a face, Ishabel; it's something *molto importante*.' She said the last in Italian and then continued in a broad Scottish accent. 'In one way, your father's death has done me a favour . . .'

'Mother!'

'Hear me out. His death has left me a widow, not a divorcee – which is much more acceptable in the circles I move in. Since we last spoke, I have had two offers of marriage – one from a *conte* and one from an Italian *principe* - of impeccable lineage, naturally.'

'The real McCoy or another Eurotrash royal to add to your collection?' Issy stopped applying blusher and turned to look directly at her mother. Isabella had a penchant for titles and now she was free to marry, Issy suspected that she'd soon be forced to air-kiss some wealthy *marchese* or *principe* and be expected to call him *patrigno*. Just to please her. She grimaced at the thought.

'The count – maybe; his title doesn't quite stack up. My people have researched his background.' Due to her fame and adoring public, La Bella Scozzese was a wealthy woman in her own right. With typical Scottish carefulness, she had no intention of squandering her hard-earned cash on any Tom, Jacques or Luigi who came her way.

'Very romantic,' Issy said.

'The *principe,* on the other hand,' Isabella ignored her daughter's sarcastic remark and continued in a dreamlike voice, 'can trace his family back to the sixteenth century. I quite fancy becoming a *principessa* for real – just like Turandot, a role I have sung many times.' She gave a little flourish with her hands and then regarded her reflection over Issy's shoulder, openly pleased that her daughter was listening to her at last.

Keeping her expression neutral, Issy couldn't resist teasing, 'Didn't Turandot chop off her suitors' heads? Hardly a promising start to a relationship. Let alone a marriage.'

'It pleases you to vex me, Ishabel, but you'll be the one with the *red neck,*' she used the old Scottish expression, 'when first your old auntie, and then your mammy, beat you to the altar. *Not,*' she shuddered theatrically, 'that I would honour that plain wee table in the kirk by describing it an altar. But, you get my meaning. I notice, by the way, that Brodie hasn't offered to make an honest woman of you. I warned you last time we met that you were punching above your weight. You'll have a job hanging onto *him*. He's a real stud muffin.'

'Mother, pul-eese, where *did* you pick up that phrase? It's gross.' Pulling away, Issy stood up from the dressing table. 'Excuse me, I have to check Esme, before Lindy puts so much foundation on her, she won't be able to smile without cracking her face.'

'Lindy – and Mary Tennant.' All traces of meekness disappeared as La Bella Scozzese grabbed Issy's arm. '*Dio mio* - yon Esme's fair *sleekit*, keeping *that* secret all these years. Did you know all about Mary Tennant – the shopkeeper, being her child? You and Esme have always been as thick as thieves.'

'No; not until recently. Besides, I don't know why you're being such a snob about Mary running the General Store. Correct me if I'm wrong, but didn't you live above Tartaruga's chip shop and ice cream parlour in Dumbarton before fame beckoned?' Turning, Issy took her mother's hands and clasped them in hers, a pleading look in her blue eyes. 'Mother, can't you just be happy that, in spite of the best efforts of our family, a right has been wronged and Mary has been reunited with her parents?'

That silenced her mother. Just as news of Menzies' and Esme's wedding had put paid to the whispers circulating round the island. The good folk of Cormorant Island might have been shocked to learn about Mary Tennant being Esme and Menzies child. However, when they discovered that Esme and Menzies were to be married in the wee kirk and Twa Burns restored to its previous glory, bringing much needed prosperity to *Eilean na Sgairbh*, all was forgotten– and forgiven.

'What does all of this matter to me in any case?' Isabella shrugged, removing her hands from Issy's grasp, as if the intimacy was too much for her. 'I will never return to *Eilean na Sgairbh* after today, there's nothing for me here. The only island I'm remotely interested in is Ischia, or Capri. If you miss your mother, Issy, you'll have to get on a plane and fly over to the prince's villa in the hope of catching her there.'

For a moment, La Bella Scozzese looked sad. Sad that she and her daughter weren't closer and that from now on their lives would take totally different directions. The summer sun streaming into the bedroom showed every line on her face and Issy was overwhelmed with love for her feckless, selfish mother and forgave her everything. Or, maybe it was simply the thought of seeing Brodie in church later that morning that made her heart swell and her eyes brim with tears. He loved her, of that she was one hundred and ten percent sure.

'Och, come on, Mammy,' she said, picking up her bridesmaid bouquet of ivory roses, thistle-like eryngium, tinus berry and eucalyptus leaves resting from a side table. 'Let's not fall out; today of all days. Let's knock 'em dead, it's what the Stuart girls do best, isn't it? Who knows, maybe the next wedding I attend will be yours and your Renaissance prince.'

That thought seemingly pleased Isabella Tartaruga. Linking arms, they went to check on the blushing bride – and to rescue her from the over-enthusiastic ministrations of her granddaughter, Lindy Tennant.

Issy found that standing in the porch of the wee kirk, as Lindy fussed round Esme calling her Grannie – channelling Jennifer Lopez in *The Wedding Planner,* naturally– highly emotional.

The last time she'd been in the kirk, her father's ashes had resided in a sandalwood box on the altar table, her mother had humiliated her in front of half the island, and Brodie had won universal approval by saving the day – *and* giving Jack Innes-Kerr his marching orders. Back then, Twa Burns was a blackened ruin, and her artists' studios a longed-for dream.

Now – everything had changed.

The McIntoshes and Stuarts were rebuilding Twa Burns

distillery, resurrecting their secret recipe for the single malt and rebranding it *An Dà Alli* – Gaelic for Twa Burns. Her artists' studios were to be accommodated in a building designated for the purpose as part of the *An Dà Alli* Visitors' Centre. The outhouses were to be revamped and given over to self-catering accommodation, leaving space for her to live and work in *Ailleag*. Thanks to a deal being thrashed out between Menzies and Esme over the rebuilding of the distillery, full employment would be returning to the island. And, surprise, surprise, it now seemed that the good people of Cormorant Island didn't hate the Stuarts, after all.

Who knew?

She actually believed that if Menzies McIntosh unveiled plans to erect a neon-lit replica of the Statue of Liberty half way across The Narrows, it would be rubber stamped by the planning committee during their next session.

Putting that cynical thought aside, Issy took a deep breath and allowed herself time to savour the moment before they crossed the threshold of the wee kirk. She watched her newly-found second cousin fuss round her Grannie, and the sight gladdened her heart. Ever since Menzies and Esme had openly acknowledged Mary and Lindy as blood of their blood, the general consensus among the islanders (once they'd recovered from the shock) was that it was a *good thing*.

It had taken almost fifty years for wrongs to be righted and Menzies and Esme to come full circle, but that didn't seem to matter. Happiness was the order of the day, and that's what counted.

Having just about ordered everything in her mind, Issy handed Esme's bouquet to Cormorant Island's newly appointed Wedding Planner and allowed her thoughts to stray towards Brodie Murran McIntosh. Recently, their relationship had, of necessity, taken second place to everything else. After today, all that would change; Menzies and Esme would depart on their honeymoon tour of the highlands and islands, thus enabling her and Brodie to drop the portcullis and raise the drawbridge at the eco-lodge.

Anyone who disturbed their peace would risk having boiling oil poured on their heads from the battlements – in true medieval style.

Inside the kirk, Mungo's wife Gillian stopped playing hymns on the electronic keyboard and struck up with the Beatles' *All You Need is Love*. Esme turned and looked at Issy quizzically. Holding up her hand, Issy grinned and confessed. 'Guilty as charged, m'lud. And if anyone in church objects to the choice of music, they can take it up with the Moderator of the Church of Scotland.'

'Bless you,' Esme responded. 'Bless both of you, my darlings.'

'Come on, Grannie,' Lindy said, handing Esme her bouquet. 'Best foot forward, no second thoughts. You've kept the groom waiting for over fifty years; this is it. Ready?'

'Never more so,' Esme replied, a catch in her voice as Issy and Lindy arranged themselves on either side, to walk her up the aisle. It being her express wish that no man should 'give her away'. After all, hadn't her father and brother given away what should have been the happiest years of her life?

The past and all recriminations faded when they crossed the threshold. For there, at the end of the blue carpet in front of the altar, were Menzies and Brodie. Issy only had eyes for *her* man, looking tall, dark and kilted in a McIntosh plaid, Argyll tweed jacket and waistcoat, white shirt and tie. No humongous badger pelt sporran or ridiculous frilled jabot; just a plain highland outfit, as befitted the occasion. Although he took his role as Menzies' best man seriously, it was plain that Brodie only had eyes for Issy as she walked up the aisle - as if she was the bride, not her aunt.

Their eyes met and, as Esme took the last few steps towards her long-postponed destiny, Issy concluded that love – true love – had nothing to do with weddings, distilleries, distant cousins or the a fifty-year-old love affair. But everything to do with the man standing at the front, the light in his moss-green eyes confirming what she felt deep inside, that they would love each other until the end of their days.

Then Mungo, resplendent in his Geneva gown and academic hood in the colours of Glasgow University, opened his prayer book and the service began.

Chapter Thirty Eight
Three in a Bed

S o many islanders wanted to attend the wedding breakfast that it was decided to hold it in Killantrae village hall. Constructed of corrugated tin, painted municipal green and mottled with rust from salt spray, the hall rattled and creaked whenever the wind was in the wrong direction – which was most of the time; and listed alarmingly on all other occasions. Scheduled to be rebuilt as part of James Stuart's legacy to the island, it was fitting that Esme and Menzies McIntosh's wedding breakfast should be held there.

Everything brought neatly full circle.

While Issy couldn't improve the hall's outward appearance, she'd given the interior a temporary makeover, courtesy of Menzies' cheque book. Now Cormorant Islanders had welcomed the Stuarts back into the fold, they happily worked flat out under Issy's supervision to get everything ready for the Big Day. Lindy, with her encyclopaedic knowledge of online shopping, had been commissioned to order bunting, flags, matching tartan table coverings and napkins. In short, all the paraphernalia necessary to transform the tin hut into the Great Hall of a medieval Scottish castle.

If the result was more *Brigadoon-with-knobs-on* than *Balmoral,* no one complained.

Catering for the wedding had been left in Mary and Irene's capable hands; and they'd hired the company which had organised James Stuart's wake a few months earlier. For the traditional 'bride's cake', Margo and the ladies from the kirk had baked and iced four square cakes depicting milestones in Menzies and Esme's story. A replica of the submarine badge Menzies had given Esme in 1961, a silhouette of Twa Burns Distillery at its height, and the combined flags of America and Scotland. And, just for sport, a cake showing two old folk walking hand in hand into the sunset.

Speeches over, toasts made and with the newlyweds off on a bespoke, tour of the highlands and islands, Brodie drove Issy through the gloaming to the eco-lodge. The rest of *Eilean na Sgairbh* seemingly happy to party on inside make-believe *Killantrae Castle,* under the supervision of Mary and Tam Tennant.

When Brodie and Issy arrived back at the lodge, Issy went straight indoors, returning with a bottle of champagne and two glasses - protesting that the night was too beautiful to shut out. Winter would arrive soon enough and then balmy evenings and beautiful sunsets would seem like a dream.

Brodie popped the champagne cork, sending it flying in the direction of the Wee Loch. Then he poured out two glasses.

'*Slainte.*'

'*Slainte mhath,*' Issy responded, walking over to lean against the wooden verandah rail. Glad of a breathing space, she sipped her champagne and gazed over the Wee Loch, enjoying the technicolour sunset while her mind processed the day's events.

Eventually, Brodie broke her thoughtful silence. Clearly, he had been marshalling his thoughts and now wanted to say his piece.

'It's never been about the distillery, you know that – don't you, Issy?' His words came out in a rush, as though he'd been rehearing them in his head all day and had to say them; to put the record straight.

Giving herself a mental shake, Issy took a deep breath before turning round to face him. 'I guessed as much when Mingus revealed that, while you'd been carrying out detective work on his behalf,' she sent him a mock-severe look, '*he'd* been more concerned with finding out if Esme was involved with anyone.'

'You're right - his priority was connecting with the woman he'd never stopped loving. Gramps is an honourable man and would never have done anything to hurt Grandma while she lived. However, once she'd passed over - and he discovered that Esme was unmarried and still living on the island, he knew he had to move quickly; neither of them was getting any younger.'

'Go on,' Issy prompted, sipping her champagne.

'With typical thoroughness, he had his lawyers prepare the necessary paperwork in advance - visas, proof of his being a widower, family birth and death certificates – Stuarts *and*

McIntoshes, some stretching way back beyond Archie and Young Johnny. All researched, documented and filed with the appropriate authorities.'

'Hoping that . . .'

'Hoping that once he explained to Esme, face-to-face, how he'd been tricked by her family all those years before –'

'She'd say '*yes*' to a second chance of love and happiness? That's quite a leap of faith. How did he know, after all this time that she still loved him?'

'It was a long shot, I'll give you that. But the way Gramps tells it – he took Esme's never having married as a sign. A sign that she'd never gotten over their love affair. Once he'd set his mind on getting back in touch, he went for it with typical Gramps-like efficiency.'

'So much hard work . . . and determination.'

'McIntoshes are nothing, if not determined.' Brodie sent her a burning, unwavering look which suggested he'd be just as thorough in bringing their relationship to a satisfactory conclusion, once the dust had settled. Then he grinned and topped up their glasses. 'Although, I gotta admit, having a team of attorneys and private investigators on the case made things easier for him.'

'So much lost time, though . . .' Issy's voice snagged at the thought of those wasted years; years when Menzies and Esme could have been together. Laying her head on Brodie's shoulder, she let out a heartfelt sigh which Brodie was quick to interpret.

'Issy,' he squeezed her hand reassuringly, 'Archie McIntosh lived well into his nineties and there's no reason why Gramps won't do the same. Determination, remember? Aren't you surprised how well he's taken on board that he now has a 'lost' daughter – and a whole other family?'

She nodded. 'If that didn't give him a palpatooral, nothing will!'

'He's a tough ol' buzzard,' Brodie said, his voice thick with love. 'Know what I can't figure out?'

'Go on.'

'How come his people didn't stumble across Mary during their investigations?'

'Maybe because Mingus didn't know of her existence and they weren't looking for her? The moral being - if you really want to conceal something, hide it in plain sight.'

'Hey – wanna know something else?' He grinned, chasing away the half-shadows of presentiment crowding in on them and their happiness.

'That depends,' she teased, eyes dancing.

'Who knew, when I set out on Gramps' quest that I would end up *sleeping with the enemy*?' He raised her hand and kissed the underside of her wrist, taking the sting out of his words. 'I sure as hell didn't.'

'The enemy? Really?' Issy shivered as the sun dipped below the horizon and the light started to fade.

'Let me finish.' He drew her closer and tucked her inside his Argyll jacket to protect her from the cool air coming off the Wee Loch. 'When I was blown in on the storm wind, I hadn't planned on meeting the woman I'd end up falling in love with. The bonnie heilan' lassie I'd marry.'

'Smooth-talker . . . Seriously, though, you'd be giving up a great deal if you came to live and work on *Eilean na Sgairbh*.'

'Such as?'

'The plankton. You're bound to miss the plankton.'

'You're kidding, right? I figure a silkie whisperer could come up with a few tricks to keep my mind off those little suckers.' His hand found the zip running down the side of her dress and he slowly unfastened it. Issy shivered as cool fingers worked under the cups of her wired bra and spanned her midriff.

'I could.' Issy pretended to give the idea serious thought. 'But there's another complication . . .'

'Complication?' His lips trailed along her collarbone and she leaned into the embrace. 'We've dealt with the plankton, what else is there?'

'I'm surprised you haven't worked it out for yourself. There's a third person we'll have to share our lives with . . . '

'God help me, *not* Cousin Lindy?' he asked, barely able to hide his dismay. Since discovering their family connection, Lindy had worn them out by prefacing each sentence with – Grannie, Gramps or Cousin Brodie/Issy. 'I'm seriously thinking of buying her that ticket to Las Vegas, just for the peace and quiet.'

'Worse than Lindy.' Issy struggled to keep the laughter out of her voice.

'What can be worse than Lindy?'

'Come with me . . .'

Zipping up her dress, Issy led him through the sitting room and into the kitchen. Where, in the corner by the fridge, was the unmistakeable bulk of . . .

'Jeez. Not that bluddy parrot!' He sounded so Scottish that Issy burst out laughing and threw her arms around his neck. 'How the hell did *it* get here?'

Issy had the grace to look guilty, she was pretty much handing him a fait accompli. She softened the blow with a passionate kiss before going on to explain.

'While we were at the wedding breakfast, Tam Tennant brought him up here in the grocery van. Pershing's bequeathed to me in Esme's will, along with shares in Twa Burns.' She turned and looked at Brodie, pleadingly. 'Oh, come on, Brodie. You *know* he likes you. It was love at first bite – remember?'

'Yeah, how could I forget? Still got the scars – and I'll probably spend the next twenty years in therapy. But - if that's the only way we can be together, then . . .'

Issy walked over to Pershing's cage and removed the cover. 'Hear that, my bonnie lad?' she crooned, hoping that Brodie would come to love the feathered fiend as much as she did.

'Bonnie lad? Evil beast, more like,' Brodie commented, but with a twinkle in his eye. 'And full of anti-American sentiment, too.'

'Och, all that Cold War stuff? Ancient history. He has no idea what he's saying and doesn't mean a word of it – do you my sweet?' She crossed her fingers behind her back, keeping them hidden in the full skirt of her dress.

Brodie sent her a sceptical look; however, he moved closer to the cage and Pershing sidled along the perch to meet him half way. The parrot looked annoyed at having had his beauty sleep disturbed and gave every appearance of blaming Brodie for it.

'*Love me; love my parrot* – is that it?' Brodie asked, resignedly.

'Something like that.' Slipping her arm round his waist, Issy rested her head on his shoulder. Left with no choice, Brodie caved and entered into negotiations with the parrot.

'Hi, big fellah; you and me are gonna be buddies. Right?'

'What do you say, Pershing?' Issy prompted. 'Friends?'

Giving a loud but resigned tut, the parrot fluffed up his neck feathers and appeared to give Brodie's proposal his full consideration.

Finally, he spoke. '*Go –oan, dahrlin – gei' Issy a wee kiss.*'

The words had a magical effect on Brodie.

'You're preaching to the choir, brother!' Laughing, he pulled Issy into his arms and did as commanded. Raising his head, he glanced over at the parrot and added, 'This could be the beginning of a beautiful friendship.'

A Note from the Author

If you have a dream - go for it. Life is not a rehearsal.

After working as a deputy head teacher in a large primary school, I decided it was time to leave the chalk face and pursue my first love, writing. In 2006 I joined the Romantic Novelists' Association's New Writers' Scheme, honed my craft and wrote Tall, Dark and Kilted(2012), quickly followed a year later by Boot Camp Bride (2013). I love the quick fire interchanges between the hero and heroine in the old black and white Hollywood movies, and I hope this love of dialogue comes across in my writing. Although much of my time is taken up publicising Tall, Dark and Kilted and Boot Camp Bride, I have finished SCOTCH ON THE ROCKS and look forward to writing number four. No rest for the wicked! I am a founding member of the indie publishing group: New Romantics Press. Our proudest moment was in November 2014 when we hosted an Author Event at Waterstones High Street, Kensington, London.

I hope you enjoy reading Scotch on the Rocks – I had enormous fun writing it.

More Books by the Author

TALL, DARK AND KILTED

A contemporary romance set in the highlands of Scotland

Fliss Bagshawe longs for a passport out of Pimlico where she works as a holistic therapist. After attending a party in Notting Hill she loses her job and with it the dream of being her own boss. She's offered the chance to take over a failing therapy centre, but there's a catch. The centre lies five hundred miles north in Wester Ross, Scotland.

Fliss' romantic view of the highlands populated by Men in Kilts is shattered when she has an upclose and personal encounter with the Laird of Kinloch Mara, Ruairi Urquhart. He's determined to pull the plug on the business, bring his eccentric family to heel and eject undesirables from his estate - starting with Fliss. Facing the dole queue once more Fliss resolves to make sexy, infuriating Ruairi revise his unflattering opinion of her, turn the therapy centre around and sort out his dysfunctional family. Can Fliss tame the Monarch of the Glen and find the happiness she deserves?

Some Reviews for Tall, Dark and Kilted

- This story is full of romantic Scottish themes; Kilts, bagpipes, scenery, Gaelic whisperings, Clan Urquhart tartans and Strathspey reels. Definitely an enjoyable read.
- I really couldn't put it down. Makes me want to buy my hubby a kilt.
- No complications just a relaxing story that drags you in to the end. Quite sad to finish it.
- You won't be disappointed ladies and men, you could learn a thing or two.
  - I truly enjoyed this book. I stumbled across it on Twitter. I was looking for a light read. However, I had trouble putting this one down.

BOOT CAMP BRIDE

Romance and Intrigue on the Norfolk marshes

Take an up-for-anything rookie reporter. Add a world-weary photo-journalist. Put them together . . . light the blue touch paper and stand well back! Posing as a bride-to-be, Charlee Montague goes undercover at a boot camp for brides in Norfolk to photograph supermodel Anastasia Markova looking less than perfect.

At Charlee's side and posing as her fiancé, is Rafael Ffinch, award winning photographer and survivor of a kidnap attempt in Colombia. He's in no mood to cut inexperienced Charlee any slack and has made it plain that once the investigation is over, their partnership - and fake engagement - will be terminated, too. Soon Charlee has more questions than answers. What's the real reason behind Ffinch's interest in the boot camp? How is it connected to his kidnap in Colombia? In setting out to uncover the truth, Charlee puts herself in danger ... As the investigation draws to a close, she wonders if she'll be able to hand back the engagement ring and walk away from Rafa without a backward glance.

Some Reviews for Boot Camp Bride

- Loved it.
- Another sparkling read, full of passion and laughter, but with a sinister undertone that keeps you turning the pages.
- A definitely great read, as was Lizzie's Debut book, Tall Dark & Kilted... roll on book 3!
- That good I read it twice!
- The dialogue between the two main characters, rookie journalist Charlee Montague, and world-weary photographer, Rafael Ffinch is brilliant and full of repartee.

Acknowledgements

First of all, thank **YOU** for purchasing my new novel. I had great fun writing *Scotch on the Rocks* and I hope you enjoy reading it.

Very few writers make this journey alone and I have a few people to thank.

Firstly, my beta readers who have kept me on track with helpful suggestions - Jane Little and Joan Davies-Bushby. A special big thanks to **Isabella Tartaruga** for helping me with *all* of the Italian in this novel. And how do I reward her? I create La Bella Scozzese and give her Isabella's name. If I say it's a flippin' cheek, quite a few of our Facebook friends will know *exactly* what I mean.

On the subject of Facebook, I must mention all the friends/readers/writers/ and followers who spur me on towards the finishing line - asking when the next Lizzie Lamb will be available. They know who they are and I am grateful for their friendship and encouragement.

Much thanks is owed to **Mrs Edna Walton** of South Uist who translated the Gaelic for me. The Scots' dialect, as spoken by Irenè and several other characters in the novel, comes courtesy of my family which has roots Motherwell and Whitburn.

I was really lucky to get permission from **Dr Nick Fiddes** at www.scotweb.co.uk to use one of the gorgeous photographs off their website for my front cover. The one I chose, ticked all the boxes and I think it looks great. Nick, a copy of Scotch on the Rocks will be winging its way to you, very soon.

In order to produce a typo-free manuscript, I had help from brilliant proofreader, eagle-eyed **Jan Brigden** (janbrigdenproof@gmail.com). My novel, both paperback and kindle version were formatted by **Sarah Houldcroft.** You'll find her at – www.vaforauthors.com. Check out her range of services for the time-strapped author.

As always, much love and grateful thanks to my co-conspirators and BFF's – Adrienne Vaughan, June Kearns and Mags Cullingford, aka **New Romantics Press**. I wouldn't have got this far without drawing upon their support, expertise and knowledge. Thanks also, to the **Romantic Novelists' Association,** in particular the talented writers of the **Leicester Chapter**, (*The Belmont Belles*).

Finally – a word about parrots. We have had our Hahn's Macaw **Jasper** for nineteen years and, in case anyone wonders, he can do and say all the things *Pershing* does – and more. Although, being a clean living parrot, he doesn't swear. He is funny, entertaining, good company, more demanding than La Bella Scozzese, and a lot of hard work – but we wouldn't be without him. If you read *Scotch on the Rocks* and decide you would like a parrot, think about it very carefully. Your parrot will be with you for a long time and could well outlive you. Read what the internet has to say on the subject; these gorgeous, voluble creatures need you more than you need them. If you do decide to have a parrot, buy a hand-reared one from a reputable dealer, then you and your parrot will be friends for life. Before I sign off, I have to say a big hello to Katie Phillip's parrot, **Bert,** who is Jasper's Facebook friend, although Katie and I know they'd probably have a *wee palpatooral* if ever they met each other.

Are Parrot owners totally mad? You bet we are.

Just as this novel was going to press my dear friend and former teaching colleague **Alison Lewin** slipped away from this world. Alison had been a supporter of mine from the get-go and was looking forward to reading Scotch on the Rocks. Sadly, that was not to be, but I hope her daughter Anna will read it in her stead, and think of all the happy times we shared.

I'd love to hear from you so do get in touch

lizzielambwriter@gmail.com

www.lizzielamb.co.uk

www.twitter.com/lizzie_lamb

www.facebook.com/LizzieLambwriter

www.newromanticspress.com

Before you go . . .

Please Tweet/ Share that you have finished *Scotch on the Rocks*

Rate this book ★★★★★

Novels Published by New Romantics Press

Lizzie Lamb

Tall, Dark and Kilted
Boot Camp Bride
Scotch on the Rocks

Adrienne Vaughan

A Hollow Heart
A Change of Heart
Secrets of the Heart

June Kearns

An English Woman's Guide to the Cowboy
The Twenties Girl, a Ghost and All That Jazz

Mags Cullingford

Last Bite of the Cherry
Twins of a Gazelle

If you've read and enjoyed our books, please leave a review
on Amazon or Goodreads.
Look out for new books from New Romantics Press
Autumn 2015/Spring 2016.

Made in the USA
Charleston, SC
25 June 2015